EDWARD TOVEY

THE FIVE HUNDRED YEAR WAR

AGINCOURT TO WORLD WAR I

In the land where his ancestors fought before him, an English
officer faces an agonising conflict between patriotism and love

MEREO
Cirencester

Mereo Books

1A The Wool Market Dyer Street Cirencester Gloucestershire GL7 2PR
An imprint of Memoirs Publishing www.mereobooks.com

The Five Hundred Year War: 978-1-86151-190-4

Printed and bound in Great Britain by
Marston Book Services Limited, Oxfordshire

Copyright ©2014

Edward Tovey has asserted his right under the Copyright Designs and Patents
Act 1988 to be identified as the author of this work.

Cover design - Ray Lipscombe

The address for Memoirs Publishing Group Limited can be found at
www.memoirspublishing.com

The Memoirs Publishing Group Ltd Reg. No. 7834348

The Memoirs Publishing Group supports both The Forest Stewardship Council® (FSC®) and
the PEFC® leading international forest-certification organisations. Our books carrying both the
FSC label and the PEFC® and are printed on FSC®-certified paper. FSC® is the only
forest-certification scheme supported by the leading environmental organisations including
Greenpeace. Our paper procurement policy can be found at
www.memoirspublishing.com/environment

Typeset in 11/16pt Goudy
by Wiltshire Associates Publisher Services Ltd. Printed and bound in Great Britain by
Printondemand-Worldwide, Peterborough PE2 6XD

Introduction

Auntie Alice with her husband and son

We called her 'Auntie Alice'. Except she wasn't an aunt at all -
just a little old lady called Mrs Hamilton. My mother used to drag
me along to see her on Sunday afternoons. She always wore black
and always sat in the same chair in the same corner of her room,
and it was only when she passed away that I had some inkling as
to why we used to visit her. But, of course, being a young boy who
was only interested in building model aeroplanes, I couldn't be
bothered at the time to ask my mother who this person was.

When she passed away, she left no real assets except her most treasured possession - a bag of medals. They belonged to her husband and her son. Inside this very ordinary bag was a note. It read: *If you could spare the time, I would like you to visit the grave of our son, Ralph, who was killed in the First World War. My husband died shortly after the war was over, so we never got to see where Ralph was buried. I would be grateful. Auntie Alice.*

Little did I realise what impact that bag of medals would have on my life. I put them away, but never forgot that message. Who was she, I asked my mother? She explained that she had been the mother of her brother's best friend. Which brother, I asked – you had three? She said it was Ted. They had joined up in 1914 in the Black Watch and saw the war through together, until Ralph was killed attacking a German machine gun position two months before the end of the hostilities. After the war, Ted left to go to America to find work and ended up as a journalist on the *Washington Post*, but he never forgot the mother of his best friend.

As I grew up, that bag kept nagging at me. I had finished at Eastbourne Grammar School and embarked on a career in advertising, which I enjoyed every day (well, most days!) of my life. I was lucky. I did well. I had a wonderful family. Life was hard, with long hours commuting every day. But that bag... it was always there, in the back of my mind.

Then I read Liddell Hart's *History of the First World War*. I couldn't put it down. The sheer horror of what had happened in that conflict deeply affected me. How could that happen, in the 20th Century? I got to near to the end, when the author was writing about the Allied advance in September 1918 and the attack on Mont-St Quentin, near Péronne. I thought, why does that name ring a bell? The bag! It was where Private Ralph Hamilton of The Black Watch regiment had been buried. I had to find out more.

My wife and I set off for the Somme in northern France. The piece of paper from the War Office with the medals said he had been buried two and a half miles north of Péronne, in the Communal Cemetery Extension. Strange name for a place of burial, I thought. We didn't know anything about the Commonwealth War Graves Commission at the time - it was well before the days when websites began to make research easy. So we went to Péronne, set the trip on the car odometer for 2.5 miles and headed north.

What greeted us was something I will never forget. Cemetery after cemetery, so many of them, rows upon rows of headstones, brilliant white in the sun, in regimented lines, like soldiers stranding on parade. Except these soldiers were dead. And most of them had those terrible words by Rudyard Kipling, who himself had lost his son: KNOWN UNTO GOD.

Two days later, we returned to Péronne exhausted, mentally and physically. No sign of Ralph Hamilton, just thousands and thousands of others. We drove down the main street and saw a familiar green Commonwealth War Graves sign pointing to a cemetery. And there we found him, in the middle of the town, not 2.5 miles north. Of course, we hadn't realised that Péronne had grown enormously since those terrible days.

The headstone read:

345760 PRIVATE R. HAMILTON, THE BLACK WATCH
2ND SEPTEMBER 1918. AGE 20
The Young. The Beautiful. The Brave.

The last six words had been chosen by his mother – Auntie Alice.

We go back, every couple of years, to say 'Hello' and 'Thank you'. He must have joined up when he was 16.

This book is to the everlasting memory of this one brave soldier, who gave his life almost one hundred years ago, so that I can sit here today, writing this story.

The Five Hundred Year War is fiction based on fact. The Holland and Waller families existed and were neighbours, and both had sons who fought with valour at Agincourt. The Hollands had a long and interesting history. Thomas Holland, The First Earl of Kent, married Joanna Plantagenet, The Fair Maid of Kent. After Thomas' death on active service in France, Joanna then married the Black Prince and one of their sons became Richard II. Thomas Holland's grandson, Sir John Holland, the Second Duke of Exeter, fought at Agincourt and was given the chance to redeem his family in the eyes of the Crown by Henry V. This he certainly did on the battlefield in 1415. John's father, the first Duke of Exeter, plotted, with others, to assassinate King Henry IV, and was subsequently executed. I had read much about the Waller family and noted that one of the earlier Wallers, by the name of Alured de Valer, is believed to have fought at The Battle of Hastings with William the Conqueror. He is mentioned on the Roll at Battle Abbey. With the blending of languages and the fact that there was no 'W' in either medieval Latin or Old French (William the Conqueror appears on the Bayeux Tapestry as Vvillelm) the name de Valer became, over the years, Waller.

As the history of WW1 is my main interest in life (apart from my family and classic cars!) I was reading an account of fighting around Péronne on the Somme in Northern France in September 1917, when up popped the name 'Second Lieutenant Richard Alured Waller, 5th Battalion, Royal Fusiliers'. I immediately remembered that very unusual name and thought there must be a connection between the Wallers of Agincourt and this young Englishman, the son of a canon from Warwickshire and the husband of Ethel from Crawley Down in Sussex.

From this, a story was born.

STILL THEY STAND

The headstones stand, row upon row
Like model soldiers made of lead
Proud, erect, ready to fight the foe
But <u>still</u> they stand, for they are dead.

Years ago, they were young, unsoiled
Where their feet had no fear to tread
But now, having trained, fought and toiled
<u>Still</u> they stand, for they are dead.

Now they are in a quieter place
No shells or bullets for them to be bled
Just a life filled with calm and peace
How <u>still</u> they stand, for they are dead.

Edward Tovey, winter 2013

This book was conceived through endless reading of historical and informative works about Agincourt and WW1. There are a few to single out for praise and thanks. Juliet Barker's wonderful work, *Agincourt*; *The Royal Fusiliers in the Great War* by H C O'Neil; *Douglas Haig - War Diaries and Letters*, edited by Gary Sheffield and John Bourne; and *Before Endeavours Fade*, by Rose Coombes.

The first days of World War 1 - August 1914

'Let go aft!' The docks at Southampton were a mass of shipping of every shape and size. Tugs rushed back and forth, shepherding the great lumps of metal into some sort of order. Some coming, some going. It was pandemonium. There were transport ships for troops, food supplies and ammunitions; at least half a dozen every day just carrying horses. The air over the harbour was thick with boiler smoke, choking everything that breathed. Convoys used to leave between ten o'clock and midnight, the slower boats first, then the faster turbine-driven boats carrying the troops known as the 'flyers'. Then there were the hospital ships bringing up the rear, some four hours later. Protection was given to the convoys by the Royal Navy – sailing out of neighbouring Portsmouth.

One of the troopships was *SS Martiban*. She had been on duty doing the round trip to Le Havre almost immediately after war had been declared. Although she was classified as a 'flyer', she had not been built for war work. She was one of hundreds of such cargo ships built to carry goods to and from Britain to the Empire and the Americas in the late Victorian days, and had been hurriedly commissioned for troop carrying.

The word 'flyer' was, in reality, a misnomer. The journey was a slow, tortuous affair. She rarely achieved more than five knots and each trip, there and back, including the loading and unloading, took days - meaning there was precious little time for the crew to take leave. One day off a fortnight was all that was allowed. The Ministry explained that there was a war going on and the ship owners were very content to receive the contract. Every trip to them was valuable.

The port of Le Havre came into view early one bright summer's day. It was August 13th. Even though it was only just after eight o'clock, there was a pleasant warmth in the air. The first to see the town were the high-flying seagulls which were following in the wake of the troopships. They were hoping to swoop on a tasty snack thrown overboard, but sadly for them, discarded cigarette butts were not really what they were looking for. The SS *Martiban* had left Southampton harbour in convoy in the middle of the night and arrived a day and a half later on the French Channel coast, after a quiet and uneventful voyage. The only sounds to be heard were the droning of the ship's engines, the slapping of the waves against the hull, the screaming of the gulls and the excited chatter of the troops walking the deck. They were the lucky ones, as the majority were down in the bowels of this old and smelly former cargo ship. It was a singularly unpleasant experience, as many of the soldiers, even though the crossing had been calm, were suffering from mal-de-mer. The air was rank.

Corporal Richard Waller of the 4th Battalion the Royal Fusiliers was one of the first ashore after the old tub had moored alongside the quay. He was a regular soldier and part of the British Expeditionary Force sent to France when war had been declared with Germany. He wondered as he walked down the gangway what his father would be thinking about at this momentous time in their country's history. Richard had joined his father's old regiment the previous year as a private soldier, even though Colonel Hubert Waller (Retd) had tried long and hard to persuade his son to take a commission. Richard had never felt entirely comfortable at the expensive fee-paying school his parents had sent him to and it was a form of rebellion on his part that had prompted him to join up as a lowly ranker. The other option was to go to Sandhurst to train as an officer - something he had long since rejected in his mind. If he was to do well in life, he thought, it would be by his own efforts and not because his father, who had spent a lifetime in the officers' mess, wanted him to follow suit.

After assembling on the quayside, Richard had orders to take his section, with the rest of the battalion, to the town of Harfleur. It was a two-hour march away and he remembered his father telling him that this was where one of his ancestors had landed in 1415, that's five hundred years ago he thought, with Henry V and had ended up fighting against the French at Agincourt. This time however, the French were their allies.

The weather was hot, so hot in fact that when the Fusiliers marched up the hill from the town to the rest camp outside Harfleur, almost a hundred of the 650-plus men that made up the battalion had fallen out with heat exhaustion. The battalion's medical team was hard-pressed to attend to the casualties - and the fighting had not even begun.

The cool air of evening, when it came, was very welcome, but with it came the most terrible thunderstorm, which completely drenched everything in sight. To many of the men, this was the first time they had been away from home, and hardly any of them had been abroad before. In fact many, particularly those who worked on the land, had rarely, if ever, been out of their local communities. To them, a visit once a year to a travelling fair in the nearest town was the farthest they ventured away from home. It was different for the officers, some of whom, along with a few of the senior NCOs, had been posted overseas with the regiment, serving in India and Egypt.

After spending a couple of days under canvas, having had time to get their clothes and belongings dried out following the storm, they were ordered back to Le Havre to prepare for their onward journey. When they marched through the streets, they were greeted like heroes by the local residents and it made them wonder what they had been missing all these years. The townsfolk were very keen to sell the 'Tommies' as many items, such as oranges and cigarettes, as they could. The Fusiliers did wonder where the English cigarettes had come from – probably 'acquired' from the army stores in the town.

At the same time as troops were arriving in their thousands at the French port, vast quantities of food supplies had started to come ashore at harbours up and down this stretch of the Channel coast. The British Army was, in reality, ill-prepared for a continental land war, having been accustomed to fighting small colonial campaigns, and GHQ had to learn the hard way how to organise and support a large new citizen army. In addition to the staple diet of the British soldier of bacon, bully beef, butter and cheese, there were luxuries like dates, jam, pickled walnuts and chutney coming ashore. These tended to make their way to the officers' mess rather than to the squaddies' mess tins, but at this stage of the war, the troops had not a lot to complain about. And if they were still short of home comforts, there were places like the YMCA and the Salvation and Church Armies to visit. They had set up branches in the French and Belgium ports selling all sorts of goods, food and cigarettes - often at lower prices than the troops would pay in England.

Just as the Fusiliers were becoming accustomed to the tastes of home, the call came to entrain at Le Havre Station for Amiens, for the journey onwards to the Belgium border.

After spending what seemed an eternity in cramped conditions on the train, the early enthusiasm of the men following their arrival on the shores of France was beginning to wear a bit thin. Arguments started about petty things such as who had pinched someone's Woodbine cigarettes. No one owned up, of course. Rattling through the flat countryside of Northern France could have been a pleasure, but in reality it was anything but. The only things that brightened up their journey were the advertisements emblazoned around the carriage.

'Look Corp,' said Private Harris. 'This one says we can go to Le Touquet, wherever that is, for a day at the seaside. Can I get off at the next station and buy a ticket?'

'Very funny, Harris,' said Richard. 'I tell you what though -

see that advertisement for Gauloises cigarettes? I had one of those once and I nearly coughed myself to death. Don't go anywhere near them - worse than a German bullet!'

The trains were extremely sparse and uncomfortable compared to the carriages they had travelled in from Charing Cross to Folkestone. These French trains were the longest they had ever seen in their lives, some 36 carriages in length, with men and horses sharing the space. Each carriage had painted on the outside 'Hommes 40, Chevaux 8'. The reality was that these numbers were often well exceeded.

Richard was aware that they had been travelling without much sleep for the best part of two days and whenever the train pulled up at a station en route, he tried to make sure that the men could get out and stretch their legs and get a bit of fresh air. Inside the carriages, the smell of body odour caused by the extremely hot conditions and the smoke from the continual puffing of cigarettes was very hard to live with. He also tried to make sure that the battalion kitchen provided hot drinks and food of some description for his men. There were times when he bartered with some of the French peasants, who had positioned themselves with hastily-prepared stalls on the platforms, for fruit, bread and tobacco to supplement their rations. It was fairly obvious that someone had thought a lot harder about provisions for Les Chevaux than for *les soldats*.

After arriving at the small town of Taisnaires, they left the train and marched on as part of an advance battalion to La Longueville, where they were billeted for the night in a collection of old barns. Here they spent a comfortable night, bedded down among the warm bales of straw. The farmyard smells were comforting, particularly to those who came from rural communities. The chickens gave them an early morning wake-up call at first light and after a breakfast of porridge, bacon and a mug of 'char', they set off to march east, passing through Mons on the way.

They were cheered at the roadsides by the Belgium people, while some of the young girls - and some not so young - took the opportunity to throw their arms around the Fusiliers and kiss them heavily on the lips. This brought a frown from the Sergeant-Major, but he realised he was powerless to prevent it.

'Come on now', he said, 'keep your eyes to the front.'

They took up positions close to the Conde Canal just north of the town of Nimy. After such a long, gruelling march in full kit, all they wanted to do was to lie down and go to sleep – however the army had other ideas. The entire British Expeditionary Force was holding the line of the canal, ready to meet the advancing German Army, and as well as the Fusiliers, there were many fine regiments present, including the Scots, Irish, Northumberlands, West Kents, Middlesex, East Surreys and the Duke of Cornwall's Light Infantry.

It was just getting dark. The evening was close and balmy and Richard's platoon was one of two positioned at the Nimy Bridge under the command of Captain Finlay. The sound of the water running through the canal was audible. The men were unusually quiet, not knowing exactly what to expect. The eerie stillness in the air contributed to the nervous anticipation. The training they had been subjected to back in England was one thing, but they had the feeling that everything they had been taught was about to be put to the test. These Fusiliers were a regular army, even if half of them were reservists who, until three weeks before, had been either working in a day job in 'civvy street' or tilling the land, mainly in the south east of England. Having put behind them so many miles in the last two days, they were pleased to be in a fighting position, instead of slogging it out mile after mile on the hot dusty roads.

Captain Finlay gathered his officers and NCOs around him. 'I know you are all tired,' he said, 'but we must get dug in before the night is out. We have been told that at least one Jaeger Division is not far away, in the woods to the north of the canal. Corporal Waller, get your men to use the high ground on the right to cover the approach to the bridge. Make sure your machine gun section is dug in deep and has the widest field of fire possible, just in case the Hun manages to cross the river higher up. If they succeed, they may well try and come down the road on our side of the canal, as well as directly across the bridge. The same order applies to the light mortars.'

'Yes sir,' said Richard. He was dismissed and went back to his section. 'Right men, as soon as we get dug in we can grab some hot grub and char and get some well-earned kip. Tomorrow could be interesting.'

Even though they put their backs into digging their positions, it was not until about two in the morning on August 23rd that they were well enough dug in to get some shut-eye. It was an extremely tired but mentally very alert bunch of men who hurriedly prepared themselves at 6.30 am when they heard the news that a German cavalry section of six riders was approaching the bridge. Richard went round to make sure that each of the men had their ten pouches full of ammunition for their Lee-Enfield rifles and that there were crates of spare ammo - just in case.

'Come on you dozy lot!' shouted Richard. 'Jerry's about to come knocking on our door.'

This was the start, they thought, each wondering how they would react when the bullets started flying. It was a beautiful morning, bright and clear, and the birds were going about their business without a care in the world. But their peaceful lives were about to be shattered.

'Johnson, Harris and Field, aim your rifles at those troopers, but hold your fire until I tell you,' ordered Richard.

The three men were the best shots in the battalion and Richard was confident that they could bring down all six with two volleys. Harris had won the Battalion shooting cup at Bisley the year before and had a reputation for rarely missing a shot. Before he had joined up, poaching on farmland around his village had been his speciality.

'Wait for it - when they have reached the centre of the bridge we'll let them have it.' A few seconds passed and Richard said, 'Fire!'

At the volley, three of the Germans fell out of their saddles immediately, and one of whom started to crawl away, dragging a leg behind. Their mounts had bolted and the two on the ground didn't move. The remaining three men hesitated, presenting easy targets. They were dead before they had hit the ground.

'Harris, get that one who's crawling away,' said Richard.

Harris took aim without panicking and at about 300 yards, put a bullet in the man's back.

'Right, number one section,' said Richard, 'go out and bring in the bodies. Some may still be alive. Intelligence will find them useful. We will cover you.'

This was the first action that Richard, or anyone from his battalion, had been engaged in since landing in France - apart from fighting off the women on the streets of Havre - and his heart was thumping like mad. The adrenalin was making him feel quite light-headed. Then, all of a sudden, all hell broke loose. Heavy and light artillery shells, along with mortar bombs, started screaming through the air above their heads. The Germans had found their range and they began taking casualties.

'Stretcher bearers!' the shout went up.

Captain Finlay stood up and was instantly hit by shrapnel in the head, but he managed, with help, to walk unsteadily back to get the wound dressed. In the meantime, the men just had to take the incoming fire until the British artillery could respond. It wasn't long before hordes of the enemy appeared, wearing field grey uniforms, jackboots and black helmets with spikes. They started to move forward in numbers from the far side of the bridge.

Richard's platoon opened up with their Lee Enfield rifles, firing with deadly accuracy at the phenomenal rate of around 15 rounds a minute. Such was the energy of the bullets even at 700 yards that they passed through two or three of the enemy before their force was spent. Wave upon wave of German soldiers pushed forward and the artillery fire grew hotter and hotter, with the British guns of The Royal Field Artillery now joining in. The Fusiliers' Maxim machine guns and mortars combined with great effect, and the advancing Germans were brought to an abrupt and costly halt.

After only a few minutes, piles of grey-clad corpses were piled up on the bridge, alongside the canal and in the adjacent fields. Those left standing retreated over the bridge and dug in on the banks on the other side of the canal.

'Cease fire!' shouted Richard. He went from man to man to check they were OK and sent those who had been wounded back to the first-aid tent, either as walking-wounded or by stretcher.

After the deafening noise of the past hour or so, the world seemed to have gone into reverse, with hardly a sound except for the groans of the wounded pervading the air. Suddenly the Fusiliers realised what they had done. They started to stand and cheer. 'Look at them run!' one shouted. But as soon as they stood up, the enemy started to fire again from their new positions, bringing the celebrations to an abrupt halt.

'Get your bloody heads down!' Richard shouted.

They saw Captain Finlay return, his head swathed in bandages. Just as he was stooping down to enter a dugout, he collapsed lifeless on the ground. He had been hit by a sniper's bullet. Four other officers had now been killed or wounded in the space of half an hour, and the situation was starting to get critical. Richard had nine dead and twelve wounded, which was about a quarter of the platoon, and both machine guns had been knocked out. He shouted to the radio operator to get a message to Battalion HQ to report on their casualties, and ask for further orders.

Shortly after noon, the battalion was forced to retreat to Mons. They had taken over 150 casualties, and the French Fifth

Army had retired. The odd thing was that while the fighting was going on, the church bells had been ringing, calling local people to Mass. Nothing, it seemed, not even a war, would stop prayers to the Almighty. Maybe now though, they were praying for peace of a different kind.

The 4th Battalion had fought a courageous rear-guard action and were responsible for seriously delaying the German advance at a decisive time. Two Victoria Crosses were won that day by the battalion, the first of the Great War.

After the action, there was considerable pride among the Fusiliers, as not one German had successfully crossed any of the bridges held by them up to the point when they were called on to retreat. While the 4th Battalion rested in the grounds of Mons Hospital, Richard was told that at two the next morning, they would be on the move again. He decided not to mention it to them that night.

The French had suffered badly during the month of August and had not only lost 200,000 men but much of their confidence. In contrast, the British had fought well and had given the Germans a bloody nose, which was all the more remarkable considering that the British were heavily outnumbered, with only two divisions against the Germans' six. This apparent success by the British bred a huge mistrust between the two Allies and severely marred future relations between them for the rest of the war.

Richard Waller's ability to use his initiative and earn the respect of his men brought him promotion later that year to the rank of Sergeant, and he was seconded to another Fusilier battalion, the 3rd Londons, who were heavily involved in the fighting at Neuve Chappelle. In May 1915, he received a commission in the field to Second Lieutenant. This had been a very difficult time for the Regiment; they had been exposed to gas attacks for the first time and their casualties had been unsustainable. They were subsequently withdrawn to rest and re-equip.

Shortly afterwards Richard was summoned by his CO and told that he was being posted to GHQ in St Omer, to work on General Haig's staff. When Richard protested that he didn't want to leave his unit and asked why he was being transferred, he was simply told that it was an order 'from above'. He wondered if the move had anything to do with his father.

Northern France – October 1415

'NOW STRIKE!'

Five thousand archers, who minutes before had knelt down, kissed the ground, prayed to the Almighty and placed small pieces of the earth in their mouths in a solemn ritual, raised their longbows to the sky and fired off a volley of arrows. It was so frightening to the Frenchmen in the field before them that all they could do before the metal arrowheads tore into their flesh was stand frozen in fear of the impending carnage. The order to strike had been given by Sir Thomas Erpingham on the Somme – a region in Northern France where 500 years later, English and French forces, who had become allies, experienced death on a different but no less awful scale. It was a cold, wet morning. It was Agincourt. The date was October 25, 1415.

An army led by Henry V had left the southern shores of England on board some 1500 ships in August of that year.

Many had gathered in the Solent, with the King resting the night before at Portchester Castle. Henry had long planned this invasion in order to strengthen his position at home. Fighting a war on foreign soil was always popular, but he also wanted to improve his financial position by gaining lands in France. The invasion fleet was unusual. It was formed not of the normal men o' war, but from an assortment of private merchant vessels of all shapes and sizes which were more than capable of crossing that dangerous but important stretch of water, the English Channel, which had for so long protected the shores of Henry's beloved country.

The King's fleet was led by the magnificent *Trinity Royal'*. At over 500 tons, she was at that time one of the biggest ships afloat and proudly carried on her mainsail the royal coat of arms. There was no mistaking the powerful message this sent out to friend and foe alike.

Some two days after leaving England, the mouth of the Seine opened up to the armada. Henry's first mission was to take the port of Harfleur on the northern bank of the estuary, but he decided to land his troops in the bay of Sainte-Adresse, which was a few miles away from Harfleur, a place where an invasion force would not be expected. He had given strict instructions that no one was to set foot on French soil before him and the ultimate punishment awaited anyone who disobeyed, regardless of status.

At a meeting of all the ship's Captains on board the *Trinity Royal*, Henry entrusted the mission of surveying the land and looking for living quarters for his men to Sir John Holland, his 20-year-old cousin. The decision to entrust this very important mission to Sir John surprised many. It was not simply on account of his age, but the fact that his father, the First Duke of Exeter, had been executed by Henry's father, Henry IV, for treason.

Taking Harfleur did not go according to plan, and the siege lasted for almost six weeks before the town surrendered. The guns from Henry's fleet had fired almost non-stop for days on end and had reduced just about every building within the walls of the town to rubble. At one stage, the French attempted to break out through the main gate, but were pushed back by the high-spirited Sir John Holland, supported by his father-in-law, Sir John Corwaille. Aside from the fact that it was crucial to secure the harbour before Henry moved on with his army, Harfleur had always been seen as the port from which any invasion of England from France would take place, so its capture gave Henry peace of mind as well as a valuable piece of real estate.

The English army, numbering around 12,000 at this time, was in a pretty poor state. Many of the soldiers involved with the siege around Harfleur had contracted dysentery and were in no condition to fight. The length of the campaign had also taken its toll and disease had decimated the numbers, so much so that Henry decided to move his soldiers on foot to Calais. This was the only English stronghold in Northern France and it was here that they could rest, recover and re-equip over the winter months. It was during the march north towards Calais that Henry's columns were intercepted by French forces far superior in number to those of his own. Although Sir John Holland had successfully surveyed the land while the siege at Harfleur was taking place, what no one realised at the time was that Charles d'Albret, Commander of the French Army, had been able to deploy a large, very experienced, well-armed and armoured body of troops between Harfleur and Calais, thus making it inevitable that the two armies would meet somewhere on the Somme. Given the state of Henry's army, this was a confrontation he would happily have avoided at this moment.

The battle was fought by the wood close to the village of Agincourt, near the hamlet of Tramecourt. The French forces, which numbered some 20,000 to 30,000, including some 7,000 to 10,000 mounted knights, were positioned to the north of the village in order to prevent Henry's army from reaching Calais. The night of October 24 saw both armies at the mercy of the torrential rain and the next morning was cold and damp. Henry deployed his army of around 6,000 tired and hungry men - a number seriously reduced through sickness on the march from Harfleur– across a 700-yard wide section of the battlefield. Henry's army had no mounted cavalry, but he had 5,000 longbowmen and 900 men-at-arms. Unlike the French, who had obviously not learned the lesson of what happened to their noble horsemen in the mud at Crécy, Henry's forces were all foot soldiers and once again, the ground conditions and the fearsome English longbow would prove decisive.

The tactics used by the English and Welsh commanders were to place the longbowmen on either flank, with the men-at-arms and knights in the centre and a small number – around 200 longbowmen - at the very centre. The archers on the flanks drove long pointed stakes at an angle into the ground in front of them to make the cavalry veer away from their course. A galloping knight weighed in the region of half a ton and when travelling at 20 miles per hour, it could be a fearful sight, so it was crucial that the archers did as much damage as possible at a distance of between one and two hundred yards.

The French facing them were stationed in three lines, each one numbering around 6,000 men with the mounted men-at-arms and French noblemen numbering some 2,400 in total on each wing of the lines. At the centre were the dismounted men-at-arms, who included the most important individuals, some of whom were members of the French royal family. At the rear were 6,000 to 9,000 soldiers and armed servants, who had arrived late.

As at Crécy, one of the most important features of the battle was the terrain. The recent heavy rains had turned the battlefield into a quagmire and once the heavily-armoured French knights had fallen to the ground, it was virtually impossible for them to get back up. This meant they were in no position to carry on as an effective fighting force. The winners in this engagement would be the archers. Lightly armoured or even without armour, they were mobile and could fire the longbow at a phenomenal rate of ten to twelve arrows a minute.

On the morning of the battle, three of the French Dukes with their armies had not arrived, so for three hours nothing happened. Then, unknown to those on the battlefield, some sections of the French wings charged the English archers and they were decimated and driven back in confusion. The dismounted French men-at-arms then moved forward, but being heavily weighed down by armour, they began sinking deeper and deeper into the mud. As a consequence, they became easy targets for the longbowmen, who rained down arrows on their stationary targets. Those who did eventually reach the English line were so closely packed together that it became impossible to raise their weapons to fight.

After some serious fighting, by sheer weight of numbers, the French started to push back the English line. Any gaps that appeared were soon plugged by the archers, who took up axes, swords and anything they could lay their hands on to savage their opponents. The French could not deal with these fast, lightly-armoured warriors and many were slain or captured. At the same time, the French second line attacked, only to be caught up in the carnage and confusion from the first line. their commanders were killed or captured just as the first line had been. The third line then attacked, with the leaders being decimated, causing their men to turn and ride off to safety.

While the battle was still raging, Henry was advised that his brother, the Duke of Gloucester, had been wounded, and he summoned his household guard to cut a path through the French lines, in order to go to his aid. Henry stood over his brother's body, beating back waves of Frenchmen, until he could be rescued. Historians say that nobody on the battlefield fought more bravely on the day than Henry.

This was a miserable day for France. As at Crécy, where they had lost around a third of their nobility, the number of casualties was staggering. Three dukes, five counts, ninety barons and the constable were among the dead, as well as notable captives such as the Marshall of France, Jean Le Maingre, and the Duc d'Orléans, a French General, famous poet and second in line to the French throne. The latter was found under a pile of dead bodies leaning against a walnut tree, and was taken prisoner by Sir Richard Waller, who had fought with distinction during the battle. He held him prisoner at Groombridge Place in Kent for 24 years, until a huge ransom had been paid.

The only success for the French on the day was the capture of the King's baggage with 1,000 peasants. Thinking that the English rear was under attack, Henry ordered that all prisoners should be executed, but because the English nobles and senior officers were keen to get as much ransom money as possible, they refused and it was left to the ordinary soldiers to carry out this order. This massacre of prisoners counted heavily towards the French losses.

GHQ British Army, Montreuil-sur-Mer, winter 1916

It was early in the year and unbelievably cold. The snow lay deep on the ground, and with Montreuil so high up and exposed, the biting wind blew in from the English Channel with a vengeance. Anyone foolish enough to venture out was well and truly hatted, coated and booted to keep out the cold and prevent slipping on the icy cobbles. It was no big secret among those in the know at GHQ that at some stage soon there would be a need for a major offensive on the Somme, to relieve pressures elsewhere on the Western front.

'Waiter - another whiskey, if you please.'

Lieutenant Richard Waller was a member of the advance party of staff officers from GHQ who had been relocated from their headquarters in St Omer to Montreuil. On this particular evening, he was dining out in the town with his

CO, Colonel Jeremy Scott. Montreuil, once a seaport not far from the fashionable resort of Le Touquet, was an attractive old walled town, standing proudly high up on a hill and encircled by ramparts.

'I'll have the same please, but make mine a large one!' Colonel Scott said.

They normally dined at the officers' mess, but occasionally it made for a pleasant change to eat out, away from the suffocating influences of army life. After all, there were some six hundred staff officers at GHQ, based in the old Ecole Militaire building in Montreuil, and conversation about private matters became somewhat difficult in such a close working environment.

'Well, how are you finding things at GHQ? I know you've been here for a few months now, but it must be very different from serving in the front line', the Colonel asked.

'To be honest sir, while I find the job I am doing interesting, I do have this enormous guilt complex about sitting in the relative safety of a place like this when the rest of my regiment is having such a rough time,' Richard replied. 'I have also just heard that they are being moved to the Somme, which knowing what I know, makes me feel even more uncomfortable. I remember being told when I agreed to take up a staff position at GHQ that it was 'monkish in its denial of some pleasures, rigid in discipline, exacting in work, but neither austere nor anxious'. In other words, it was a safe office job, away from the front line.'

'I really don't know what you're worrying about,' said the Colonel. 'You've got a pleasant little number here, with a plentiful supply of ladies, enough to eat and drink and you're relatively safe. Most people would die – ha ha! – for a situation such as yours. And you've already had a long spell in the front line, whereas many of the officers here have had no physical front-line experience at all. So why does it worry you so?'

'It just does, I'm afraid', said Richard. 'You see the huge lists of dead and missing and the thousands upon thousands of casualties going to and from the hospitals on the coast, and I feel I should be suffering along with the others. I didn't join up to become a staff officer. Coming up through the ranks made me well aware of what privations the lower echelons of the British Army suffer, and reading the communications reports about what my regiment has been involved with just makes it worse. There is also the family thing. My father, and my ancestors going back for centuries, served king and country on the battlefield, so I suppose I feel I should be there as well.'

'If I was you, I would stop worrying about it,' said the Colonel. 'Your father probably used his influence to get you the position here, and although you seem to resent it, you are doing a very worthwhile job – and, after all, someone has to do it. You have the added benefit of being able to bring some practical experience of this war to the table – something appreciated by me and your fellow officers. The rest of the staff will be coming over very soon from St Omer, and you're seeing that lovely girl who works at the hospital. Try and get it out of your system.'

Still troubled by his thoughts, in particular one fact that everybody now seemed to know - that his father had secured him his 'cushy little number' - he left the restaurant and headed off to meet his girlfriend. One of the advantages of being billeted away from the officers' accommodation, although only temporarily, was that he could meet her in parts of the town that were not generally frequented by the military. It was nothing to do with being ashamed at being seen out with her, far from it, but it would save a lot a hassle from the other officers if he kept the relationship under wraps. Since GHQ had started to be moved to the town, it had become something of a fortress again and passes had been issued to all the local residents, so movement within the town was somewhat restricted.

He first met Simone after he had been in Montreuil for only a couple of weeks. There had been a dance at the officers' mess and Simone had been invited, along with several other nurses from the local hospital and some British nurses from the Queen Mary's Army Auxiliary Corps who were based in Le Touquet. Richard hadn't gone to the dance with the intention of finding 'a young lady'; he had gone because he had been told by his Commanding Officer that his presence was required. But he rather liked the look of this very attractive young French girl and had asked her if she wanted to dance. As he was not particularly well trained in the art of guiding a young lady around the floor, they had many awkward moments, but laughed them off as part of the learning process.

Despite Richard's limited French, they seemed to get on well enough and when the dance was over, he asked if he could walk her home. As they meandered through the cobbled streets of the town, he asked her about her family and her job. She told him how much she missed her father, who was away at the front, and there were days when her mother was so depressed that she stayed in bed all day. Letters from him had been very few and far between.

It was very cold as they walked along, but they were so deeply engrossed in conversation that they hardly noticed. It only took about ten minutes to walk to her house, and when they bid each other goodnight, Richard took the opportunity to ask her if she would like to go out for a meal one evening. Without wishing to show how excited she was by the prospect, she just said that would be very nice.

'How can I get in touch with you, and by the way, I don't know your surname?' Richard asked.

'It's Deberney, Simone Deberney, and if you would like to leave me a message at the hospital reception, I can then reply to you at the Ecole Militaire. That is where you are based?' she asked.

'Yes, it is. Well goodnight, Simone,' he said slightly awkwardly, taking her hand in his and giving it a gentle squeeze. She went into her house to be greeted by her mother, who said, 'Are you all right? You look very flushed.'

'I'm fine thank you.' She skipped up stairs with her head in the clouds.

Over the next month they met a few times, but the opportunities to enjoy recreational pursuits together in the town were few and far between. They either went for a walk through the town or down by the River Canche, or for a drink in one of the bars in the town. One evening they went to the local theatre, to see a black and white film featuring Charlie Chaplin, which they both found extremely funny. Humour was universal when portrayed in that slapstick kind of way. On the evening when he had arranged to take her out for dinner, he called round at her house. Her mother answered the door.

'Ah, you must be Richard' she said. 'Welcome, I am Simone's mother, Cécile, and I am very pleased to meet you. You seem to have made quite an impression on my daughter!' she said smiling.

'Thank you Madame. I think your daughter is utterly charming and very good company.'

As he said that, Simone came down the stairs wearing a simple yet stunning purple dress, and he thought she looked absolutely beautiful. She quite took his breath away. There was that moment of slight embarrassment before Simone said, 'We won't be too late.'

'Oh, it doesn't matter at all, just have a good time,' her mother replied, slightly envious and wishing that her husband could be home to be able to take her out to dinner.

They spent the whole evening talking about this and that, enjoying each other's company. The language barrier did not appear to be a problem. Richard had learned French at school and Simone had likewise learned English, and while occasionally they had their difficulties, they got round them somehow – generally with a smile. The food wasn't brilliant and the choices strictly limited, but it didn't seem to dull their appetites and, after all, there was a war going on.

The time seemed to fly by, and before they knew it they were finishing their desserts and asking for the bill. They both realised they were falling in love with one another. When he walked her home, he kissed her for the first time and the softness of her lips when she opened them slightly made him dizzy with desire.

'Perhaps you would like to come round to my house one evening after work?' she asked looking up at him. 'If it is on a Tuesday, my mother will be out at her classes.'

A few days later, Richard dropped a note at the hospital reception to say that he was free on the following Tuesday and would come over at around seven, if that was still OK. He was excited by the prospect of seeing Simone again, and he left GHQ in a rush to make sure he was not late arriving. He knocked gently on the door and saw the net curtain move before hearing footsteps coming towards the door.

'Hello Richard,' she said, kissing him on both cheeks. 'Come in. You see, I like your name because it is the same in French as it is in English, even though it is pronounced differently!'

'Enchanté, Mademoiselle', said Richard with a soft smile on his face. 'Is that the only reason you like me?'

'Not at all! My mother is out until about nine o'clock, so we have a little time to ourselves before she returns.'

Simone looked beautiful, and he realised how lucky he was to have met her. She wore no make-up apart from a little lipstick and always looked so happy and content, even though she worried constantly about her father away at the front. Looking at the photograph of her parents in the lounge, he could see that in many respects she was the image of her mother, who, at the age of thirty nine, was still a strikingly good-looking woman.

Her father, Gilles Deberney, had been called up to the army

in 1914, and had only been home on leave three times since he left. He was an officer in the 8th Regiment of Infantry, which was part of the 2nd Infantry Division. He was involved with the retreat to the Marne and in 1915 he was moved to the Champagne sector, where the regiment suffered huge casualties with over 3300 killed, missing or wounded. So far he had been lucky to survive intact, given the terrible mortality rate, particularly among officers. He had suffered nothing more than a shell splinter in his forearm, but his family had not heard from him for over three months. They knew from a letter they had received in the previous year that he was going to Verdun and even though the French government had tried to cover up details of the losses. They knew from the newspapers that the casualties were terrible, with neither side gaining any significant ground.

Richard sat down on the settee next to her, a little nervous and unsure where this might lead. She was so unbelievably attractive and he knew that he wanted to make love to her, but he was relatively inexperienced and it was still very early days in their relationship. He certainly didn't want to spoil things between them. From what she had said so far, she seemed keen to invite him round when her mother wasn't there, but it was Simone who solved the problem by saying,

'I am very fond of you, Richard, but I want us to get to know one another before we get too serious, if you know what I mean. But that doesn't stop us enjoying a little aperitif, does it?'

He reached out and stroked her hair, which was wonderfully soft. Running his finger down to her chin, he brought her lips up to meet his, which were full of expectation and desire. Her lips parted as he kissed her deeply, and he began to explore her with his tongue to which she responded with an urgency which took him a little by surprise. 'I have a feeling Mademoiselle Deberney, that we had better leave it there or I might not be responsible for my actions!' he said with a smile on his face.

She kissed him on the cheek, stood up and said, 'As aperitifs go, that was very nice. I shall eagerly wait for the main course, at the right time.' Swinging her hips, she went into the kitchen, re-emerging with a bottle of wine and two glasses. 'Perhaps you would like to do the honours. I am sure my father wouldn't mind if we opened one of his bottles of burgundy. I'm sure that we could both do with a drink - before mother gets back.'

Suddenly, Richard was miles away, thinking about the conversation he had had with his CO a couple of weeks before. Why now? He wasn't sure.

'Sorry Simone, I was just thinking about my being here with you and how wonderful it is. And at the same time not far from here, there are men from my regiment dying in their thousands in terrible conditions and sometimes it makes me feel very uncomfortable. It just hits me from time to time, for no apparent reason. No matter which way I look at it, I know that at some stage, I will feel the need to go back to active service.'

'No Richard,' she exclaimed, 'I need you here with me! Let the others do the fighting – you've done your bit. I don't want to lose you as well as my father. Oh!' She suddenly realised what she had said.

'I didn't mean that – about my father I mean. It's just that we haven't heard from him for so long that sometimes you assume the worst. And I really do miss him so.' The tears started to roll down her cheeks.

Richard had suddenly lost his sense of calmness and had retreated deep into himself.

'Promise me you won't make any hasty decisions, Richard, about going to the fighting, without talking to me first?' asked Simone.

He leaned towards her and kissed her very gently on the lips, using his handkerchief to wipe away the tears. He did not answer her question.

A logistics meeting of GHQ staff had been planned for first thing on the Wednesday morning at L'Ecole Militaire to discuss the issues with moving supplies for the forthcoming offensive up the line to the front. This former military school for French officers was the perfect building. It could accommodate all the senior officers covering operations and intelligence; finance and discipline, transport and supplies, all under one roof. There was also plenty of available accommodation for billets in the neighbouring houses in the town. With the prospect of a huge push on the Somme, getting general supplies, ammunition and troops in vast numbers was going to be a massive logistical problem. An additional 650,000 recruits had joined the British Expeditionary Force in the previous year alone – many of them arriving in northern France.

'Right everyone, please sit down and let's get on with it.'

Colonel Scott of the Procurement Directorate was chairing the meeting, and he called upon Lieutenant Richard Waller to outline the problems facing them. Richard had been briefed by Colonel Scott some months before to come up with proposals, and he had spent the time wisely, assessing an area which was completely new to him. He had spent many hours with the Royal Flying Corps going over reconnaissance photographs of the ground proposed for the offensive, as well as talking to artillery, transport – mechanical and horse, signals, medical, infantry, pioneers, engineers – anyone, in fact, who might have some involvement in the 'big push'.

'Before I pass you over to Richard,' he said, 'you don't need me to tell you how important it is to keep this absolutely secret. It must not be discussed with anyone else outside this team without my prior permission. Is that understood? Right then, Richard.'

Richard stood up from the giant circular table around which all those who had been invited to attend were seated. Most seemed to be smoking either pipes or cigarettes and there was a thick haze permeating the room. He had been given the job of addressing his peers, and he was a little nervous at being given the presentation to do, and at the size of the task he had been asked to talk about.

'Good morning gentlemen' started Richard, his voice a little shaky. 'As many of you are no doubt aware, the location for the proposed attack is the Somme, which is far from ideal for launching an offensive. From what we know from existing maps and aerial photography taken by the Royal Flying Corps, it is almost exclusively an agricultural province, almost devoid of any transport infrastructure. But it is here that the British and French sectors join one another, so it is considered that an attack could be mounted jointly from this part of Northern France. To supply an army of the size anticipated, it is essential that work is carried out urgently on both the road and railway systems.'

Standing in front of a blackboard which contained a rough hand-drawn map of the area, Richard pointed to the town of Albert.

'Let's take the railway first. At present the railway line which links the Somme at Albert to the rest of the French rail network is totally inadequate. We estimate that we are going to need thirty trains a day, just to service the requirements of the Fourth Army, and once the offensive is under way, the number of trains needed could rise to 70 a day. Currently there is only a two-line system, one of which is a non-standard gauge. The importance of this offensive dictates that we have to construct two new standard gauge lines, in addition to the extra sidings, elongated platforms and supply depots. To help with this task, we have initially arranged for up to 18,000 British railway workers to be seconded to the war effort here in northern France. This is necessary because many of the French railway workers have been called up to fight at the front, and they are well understaffed.'

This was the first time Richard had ever had to stand up and present to a room full of people, or at least the first time since his days at Worth School in Crawley, and once he had got over his initial nervousness, he felt that it was going rather well.

'With regard to the roads, this is another major problem, for several reasons. Firstly, 95 per cent of the roads in the area are nothing more than farm tracks, wide enough for a horse and cart and nothing more than lanes of mud. Secondly, those roads that have been widened are already falling apart under the thousands of marching feet, the hooves of the horses and the wheels of trucks and gun limbers. Thirdly, the only hardcore of any substance in the area is chalk – which, as you know, is hardly suitable, and there is no local supply of stone in any quantity. So supporting, repairing and maintaining these roads, which are so important to the success of this mission, is crucial.' Clipping some enlarged photos to the blackboard, he continued, 'If you look at some of these photographs, you can see what an awful state the roads are in, with the constant movement of troops and traffic. And please bear in mind that the use they are getting at the moment is a very small percentage of what it is going to be like in the next few months. In addition to the 800,000 tons of supplies arriving at the ports every month, we have to move three million artillery shells to the forward positions. Transporting quantities of this size has never been achieved before on the battlefield and is a major logistical operation. One last thing to mention at this stage - we are talking about an army of 400,000 men, 100,000 horses and over 1,000 guns. Where are we going to put them all? The villages in the area could probably billet a thousand men at the most. I have been to many of them – they are often no more than hamlets. We are talking about 400,000 men. Tents and huts, farms and barns are going to have to be the answer, but keeping the scale of this operation hidden from the German spotter planes is going to be very difficult. That gentlemen, is the size of the task that faces us. I will now pass you back to Colonel Scott.'

'Thank you, Lieutenant. I think you have outlined the immensity of the problem before us very well. I have got to produce a report for the Quartermaster General, General Sir Travers Clarke, to discuss with Field Marshall Haig by the end of next week at the latest, with our proposals on how we are going to plan this operation. They will not want to hear why it cannot be done, but how it can be done. There is enormous political pressure from the French to get this offensive under way, so we need to agree on working parties today, based on our collective experiences.

'John, you will head up the Light Railways Directorate and take charge of the whole railways issue. I want a full appraisal of the number of men you will need to construct this new rail system and working plans as to how it will all link to the existing network. Richard has mentioned the manpower that can be made available. Arthur, you will deal with the roads. This will include any new roads that may be required and the routes from and to the embarkation points on the coast to the larger towns such as Amiens, Albert and hopefully on to Bapaume and Péronne. Cecil, you're in charge of accommodation for the men and animals. Pay careful attention to areas of woodland for cover. As you know the Somme is known to be very flat, so the natural terrain will not offer many opportunities for shelter. Frank, artillery and munitions is your baby. You did a fantastic job at Neuve Chapelle last year, although this is on a slightly larger scale!

'One point you did not cover, Richard, was food and water. In your initial report to me you highlighted the issues, so I would like you to draw up your proposals for dealing with these two very important subjects. If you bear in mind that the water supply here is probably just enough for the local population, there is going to be a need for new wells and miles of pipes carrying water from high points to as near to the front line as possible. This is going to be a summer campaign, so the need for water in huge quantities is going to be critical. Not just for drinking but for washing, for the horses and for vehicles. Well done, Richard – an excellent presentation. Short, sharp and to the point. Exactly how the General will want to hear it.'

After a short pause, Colonel Scott said, 'Lastly, gentlemen, I am sure that you would like to know where we intend to launch the attack. Having mentioned earlier that it is where the British and French sectors join, you will probably already have got a rough idea. The intention is to launch the offensive to the east of Albert in a line from the River Somme in the south close to Curlu, and to the north just north of the River Ancre around Beaumont Hamel and Gommecourt.'

Turning to the wall behind him, he said, 'As you can see from the map, it will give us a front of around twelve miles. That gives you an idea of the scale of this operation, with the obvious objective of pushing the German line back towards Bapaume.

'Right gentlemen, I will see you individually to answer any of your questions. Help yourself to tea and biscuits. Richard, you come in first please for a moment.'

When they arrived back at Colonel Scott's office, the Colonel sat down and said, 'That was an excellent piece of work, Richard. Now I hope you will appreciate rather more how valuable your input into this operation is and you'll put behind you any thoughts of wanting to get to the front line.'

'I really do understand the importance of this job, Sir, it's just a case of whether it is me doing it or someone else,' Richard replied.

'I want total commitment from you to this,' said the Colonel firmly. 'I have given you an important role. So far you have done very well and I don't want you to let me down by confusing your innermost thoughts with what I consider to be those crucial to the war effort. Bear that in mind.'

'Yes sir, I certainly will.'

And with that, Richard turned and left the room to go and get a breath of fresh air.

On the way down the stairs, he bumped into Captain Frank Skinner, who had been given the task of organising the munitions.

'Hello, Richard. I thought you did very well today. Do you fancy a bite to eat at Maison Canche?'

'Yes, that would be good. I could use a drink as well!'

Richard had got on well with Frank since he had joined the GHQ staff in 1915. They came from very similar backgrounds and although Frank was quite a few years older, they found they had a lot of things in common - one of which was that they both came from Kent.

'This sounds like a really big show coming up' said Frank as they were walking towards the restaurant in the square.

'No question about that, but I suppose we mustn't talk about it. Doctor's orders and all that!' said Richard.

Frank smiled and said, 'I suppose you're right. Come on - let's see what they have on the menu today.'

They pushed open the door to find there were only a few locals sitting at the bar. As reasonably regular customers, Madame had kept a quiet table at the back of the restaurant for them, and always gave them an effusive welcome.

Throwing out her arms to greet them, she said, 'Bonjour Monsieur Richard et Monsieur Frank. Ca va?'

'We are very well, thank you, et vous?'

'Très bien, merci - although I am missing my husband very much. You wouldn't like a little distraction upstairs as a starter?' she said with a naughty smile.

She had a massive bosom, which both men were convinced had attracted a lot of attention while her husband, who she 'missed so much' was away.

'Merci, we love you dearly, but we have got a war to fight you know!' said Frank smiling.

That comment hit home with Richard, who said to Frank when they sat down, 'Don't you ever feel that we could do so much more if we were actually on the front line, rather than sitting on our backsides at GHQ?'

'I have often thought about that,' said Frank. 'But I was persuaded to take up this job because of my supposed ability in administration. Organising a railway timetable was my job in civilian life, which makes it odd that the Colonel didn't give me the railways to sort out. So in a way, I am following my chosen career path. But I know why you are asking me that. My advice to you is just to get on with the job you have been given and make the most of it. Before we get too deeply into this discussion, let's find out what Madam can offer us today.'

'Madame!' called Frank, 'what have you on the menu today?'

'To start with, I can offer you some vegetable soup – from my own garden, you understand. Then I have some very nice beefsteak.'

'Are you sure it is not horsemeat?' said Richard.

'Of course it is, but it sounds better somehow as beefsteak to you British. The French eat horsemeat all the time you know,' she said.

'Can you find us a nice little red in the cellar?' said Frank.

'They're in very short supply now you know, but I will find you a nice petit Bordeaux – will that do?'

'That will do very nicely, thank you, but we'll be watching what you charge us!'

She walked away giggling and swinging her derrière.

'Now about your little difficulty,' said Frank. 'Is this playing on your mind just because of your parents, or is there another reason?'

'I'm not really sure,' said Richard, 'You see, I first rebelled against my father by joining up as a private and not taking the commission he wanted me to. I didn't like the idea of sons of fathers getting on in the army through the old boys' network. I wanted to prove myself, and he was horrified when I joined the regiment as a lowly ranker. When I was in Belgium, I had no such thoughts. I was there doing my duty for king and country, regardless of the casualties or the conditions we were fighting in. Now while others are suffering so much, we are sitting here in a nice restaurant, drinking wine and eating passable food. There's also this thing that keeps haunting me about one of my ancestors. He fought at Agincourt you know, and captured a French General. I suppose that is in my genes – daft, isn't it?'

'Not at all,' said Frank. 'You probably grew up at home with stories of military life and of family heroism. Your father, I believe, fought in the Boer War and was a career officer. Given the fact that you are an only child, it's not entirely unreasonable of them to want you to survive and carry on the blood line. After all, you had a couple of close calls in Belgium and you are doing an important job here. It's not as though you are a conscientious objector or something.'

'I hadn't really thought of my responsibility to keep the family going,' said Richard. 'Anyway thanks for your thoughts on that. I've just got to get it out of my system somehow.'

A wonderful aroma reached their noses, and Frank said, 'Good, here comes the soup.'

After a little while Frank said to Richard, 'You never talk about your family seat.'

'Not a lot to tell really. The family has been around for quite a while. My father took a great interest in discovering his roots some years back. Apparently it goes back to Norman times when one Alured de Valer arrived in England in 1066. He was granted lands by William and over the years, the name gradually evolved into Waller. The family bought Groombridge Place, near Tunbridge Wells, in around 1400. And as far as I know, Sir Richard Waller, my namesake, captured Prince Charles, the Duke of Orléans, at Agincourt. He was second in line to the throne of France at the time and was held captive for over 24 years at Groombridge until France paid the ransom for his release. Can you imagine having a prisoner in your home for all that time?'

'They probably became quite good friends,' said Frank jokingly.

'As a matter of fact, from what my father told me, I think

they did,' said Richard. 'I believe he was held in 'honourable restraint' as they called it, rather than locked up in a cell. And I found out that whilst he was a 'prisoner', and even after he returned to France, he was a generous benefactor to the village.'

'Now I can see what having a family with a history like that can mean to someone. Presumably you have a family crest somewhere. I'm really quite envious.'

A couple of days later, Richard called at the main hospital in Montreuil to see if Simone was finished for the day. The reception area was packed with people both civilian and military, some waiting for visitor time, some waiting to be seen. She had been working there since the war started, initially as a nurse when it was purely a civilian hospital. Now, because the whole coast near Montreuil had been turned into a major centre for dealing with casualties from the front line, it was seeing more and more British soldiers who could not be treated by the Royal Army Medical Corps. It was just gone seven, the time when her shift ended, so she was very pleased to see him.

'This is really a lovely surprise. I didn't expect to see you until the weekend.' She threw her arms around him and kissed him fully on the lips.

'Let's walk a little. Apart from a break for lunch, I have been sitting at a desk all day and I could do with some fresh air. I'll make sure you're home before it's too late,' said Richard.

They strolled arm in arm through the narrow cobbled streets, following the line of the ramparts. It was possible to walk all round the town on the rampart walls, but in the dark, it was too dangerous. Although it was a real winter's evening, with the occasional flurry of snow, it was beautifully clear with a full moon, and they were just happy to be away from the pressures of work and content to be in each other's company.

'The last time I saw you, you were deep in thought about wanting to go and fight. I hope you have changed your mind,' said Simone. 'I see some terrible wounds in the hospital and I don't want you ending up there, or worse.'

'Well, I had lunch with Frank today' Richard replied, 'and he pointed out that it was my duty to protect the blood line of my family, as I have no brothers or sisters. This is something my father was obviously thinking about when he used his influence to get me a staff job.'

They stopped walking and, standing under a gas light, Simone asked, 'What do you mean, protect your blood line?'

Richard realised that he had not told her about his ancestors. 'Well, my family comes from a long line of descendants with the name of de Valer, who arrived in England with the Norman invasion. And several of them became Knights of the English Realm.'

He thought it unwise to mention that one of them captured the second in line to the King of France.

'So, you are quite famous then, and you come from a French family!' said Simone. He could see a mischievous smile appearing on her face.

'Well, sort of,' he said, a little embarrassed.

'Oh, you are my very special prince and I shall bow to your every wish!' she exclaimed teasingly.

'Come on, it's time to be getting you back,' he said.

As they started walking back to her house, she asked, 'Can I see you on Sunday? I don't have to work and mother often goes out with her friends. Do come round – please!'

'All right, I shall come over at around eleven o'clock and if the weather is not too cold, we can get a boat on the River Canche and take a picnic. I can ask Madam in the restaurant to make us something if you like.'

'No,' she said emphatically, 'I will prepare a picnic for us. It will be a surprise!'

CHAPTER FOUR

South East England, autumn 2012

'Here is the news at 6.30 from BBC South East. Good evening. This is our top story tonight. It has just been revealed that a treasure hunter in Kent has uncovered a truly remarkable hoard of gold. Using a metal detector in a field near the Kent/Sussex border, the man, who has been identified only as John, found the coin in a leather purse, which was in a very poor condition. It contained seventeen gold coins, believed to date from the early 15th century. A spokesperson for the local museum in Tunbridge Wells said that the coins could well be regarded as treasure trove. They've now been sent to the British Museum for analysis. It is believed that they are of significant value, not just for the weight of the gold, but from an historical point of view. It is known that the part of Kent where the coins were found has strong historical links with two important local families who lived in the area around the time of the battle of Agincourt. As soon as we hear more on this story, we will let you know. And now to our other main story this evening…'

Montreuil, early 1916

Richard was desperate to see Simone again. With the build-up to the forthcoming offensive taking over his entire life, day and night, it had been nearly two weeks since they last met. All he was doing was working, eating and sleeping, with no time for anything else. He did manage to leave his office for a short while to deliver a message to her at the hospital, suggesting that they meet for a couple of hours on the coming Sunday, having first cleared it with his CO. They had originally arranged to go for a picnic, but he had to tell her that time would sadly not allow it, this time. A note had arrived back at GHQ to say that she was very much looking forward to seeing him again - picnic or no picnic.

It came round very quickly. Richard had been up since 6 am to finish off a section the report which had been troubling him. He rushed out of the door, so as not to be late to meet her. She was waiting for him dressed in her warm woollen coat, and looked tired. It was fairly obvious that they were both exhausted – Richard from the endless paperwork, meetings and statistics going round in his head and Simone from the long hours and never-ending intake of patients, both civilian and military, at the hospital.

He had thought about hiring a boat and going for a row upriver, but he knew that there would be better days, both weather-wise and work-wise, in the future, so a walk would have to suffice for now. Both rather preoccupied, they walked mostly in silence, but that did not seem to matter. It was still very cold, but at least it was dry. There were other couples out walking, some of the men showing obvious signs of injury from the war, which got Richard thinking again. Still, Simone seemed unaware of what was going on around her. She was just happy to be with her man, walking arm-in-arm, even for a short while, a million miles away from the stresses of everyday life.

'I have to be back at GHQ at midday,' he said when they arrived back at the Bastion de la Portelette, the main entrance through the walled ramparts. 'I am very sorry. Perhaps I can see you one evening during the week, when things have quietened down a bit?'

She kissed him gently on the cheek and said with a big smile, 'That would be really nice, and I do understand. Just let me know when you might be free and, hopefully, we can have some time together - like the last time?'

He blushed a little at the memory and squeezed her arm in response. They walked together back up towards the Place Gambetta, where they said their goodbyes. He was still thinking about how much work he still had to do, to complete the report for his CO to present to Lieutenant General Sir Travers Clarke, the Quartermaster General of the BEF. Clarke had been summoned by Field Marshall Sir Douglas Haig, Commander in Chief of the five BEF armies, to get his ideas on how the offensive could be supplied, and time was of the essence. As Richard had been told by Colonel Scott, the proposed offensive on the Somme took priority over everything, even on a Sunday. So, it was back to the office, head down and just get on with it. There was no option.

He had managed to hurriedly put a note through Simone's door at home almost a week later to say that once his part of the report was finished, he should be able to get a day off to meet up. He apologised for being so tied up with work, but sadly there was a war on, as the people of Montreuil knew only too well.

When Richard arrived for work at GHQ the following Saturday, feeling close to completing the project, he asked about the possibility of having some time off. He was told in no uncertain terms that it was out of the question, but if his part of the report was completed by close of play on the Tuesday, he could leave the office at 7pm. Work came first. If he was honest with himself, he wasn't really surprised, but thought he must get a message to Simone to let her know.

He buckled down and worked solidly for the next three days and when Tuesday came round, he telephoned Colonel Scott to report on his progress. He was asked to bring the report to his room straight away.

'Well done, Lieutenant. If you just sit there for a while, I'll run my eyes over it and cover any questions I have while you are here' said the Colonel. While he was waiting, Richard stood up and looked at the large map of Northern France on the wall. Geographically it seemed enormous, but the proposed battle area was, in fact, quite small for such a huge operation.

'Thank you, Richard. I have no questions and you seem to have covered all the topics well. Let's hope the General is impressed. Now, you can have the evening off. Go and enjoy yourself,' he said with a twinkle in his eye.

After supper in the officers' mess, Richard put on his greatcoat, as it was still bitterly cold outside, and walked the short distance to her house. Cécile opened the door.

'Ah, bonjour Richard. Ca va?'

'Très bien merci, madame. I hope Simone has arrived from work?'

'Yes she has, and I am sure that she will be delighted to see you. Please come in. I am just going out to see the friend I play cards with every Tuesday. Simone, Richard is here to see you,' she called up the stairs. They heard the sound of rushing feet and Simone came down the stairs two at a time, then slowed, not wanting to embarrass herself in front of her mother by embracing Richard as she would have liked.

'I will leave you two lovebirds to it' said Cécile. 'And be good!'

When Cécile had closed the door, Simone threw her arms around Richard's neck and they kissed each other without pausing for breath.

'Oh, Richard!' she said at last. 'I know it is only just over a week, but it seems such a long time since we last met. Did you manage to get all your work completed on time? Come into the sitting room.'

'Yes, fortunately I did. I'm really sorry we can't meet as often as we would like, but I am here now, so let's make the most of it. The CO is driving us very hard at the moment and there is precious little time for anything other than work. It is probably the same for you.'

'Come and sit down with me. I want you to kiss me like the last time you were here. Remember, the little aperitif we had?'

She raised her head towards him and he gratefully accepted the fullness of her lips, which yielded to his touch and parted to receive his exploring tongue.

Breathing hard, she said, 'I love your kisses Richard. They make my whole body tingle.' Whilst he was gently caressing her lips with his finger, he saw that she was unbuttoning the white silk blouse she was wearing.

'Richard, I have seen you looking at me here, maybe wondering what is inside. It excited me so much to watch you. Now you can feel me and tell me if it excites you.'

As she opened her blouse, he placed his hand rather clumsily on her breast. He felt her nipple harden under his touch. She was not wearing a brassière, just a flimsy petticoat, and he could see the firm shape of her through the material. It just took his breath away. 'You are too beautiful for words, Simone,' he whispered in her ear.

Like her mother, Simone was very well developed. As he saw her respond to his touch, his excitement grew. He knelt on the floor in front of her and pushed her blouse from her shoulders so that it fell back, allowing him to slide the straps of the petticoat down her arms. As the material fell away, Richard was mesmerised by what he saw. Her nipples were reaching up to him, as if to say, 'they are yours, do what you want.' Simone let out a sigh and held a breast up to him saying, 'suck me gently Richard, until I can't stand it any more.'

He stayed kneeling in front of her, soaking up her beauty before saying, 'That was the most sensuous moment of my life.' He moved his hand under her skirt, but she gently pushed him away, saying, 'Not yet Richard. There will be a time, but not now.' Noticing the bulge in his trousers she said, 'I can tell that you need some looking after. Undo your belt.'

Preparing for the offensive at GHQ, February 1916

It was a grey and overcast morning when Colonel Jeremy Scott, along with other senior officers, arrived to see Lieutenant General Sir Travers Clarke. The meeting had been arranged in order for them to present their proposals ahead of the meeting with Field Marshall Haig later that week. It was to be held at the Château de Beaurepaire, just outside Montreuil. They had all worked extremely hard to get the documentation to the stage where the first draft could go to the senior general for his comments, but they knew there would be many revisions before it went before the Field Marshall.

Clarke had a brilliant mind and supplies were his forte, but like the other officers on his staff, an exercise of this size and nature was new to him. They also knew well that Haig had a reputation for detail and that his analytical abilities were much prized, so they feared that when the documentation reached 'the big man', they would be in for some tough questioning. There was also a rumour that General Sir Henry Rawlinson was about to be appointed to command the Fourth Army for the attack, so there was a chance that they would have to go through all this again once his appointment had been confirmed.

Another complication was that it appeared that the French General Joffre was dictating what strategy should be adopted and Haig was under orders from the Minister of War to go along with it. After two horrendous years during which the French had suffered 1.4 million casualties, Joffre was insisting that the British should 'pull their weight' as he put it, and he wanted an attack by the summer at the latest.

As usual, they had not been given enough time to plan fully for such a massive offensive. Everyone on the staff was aware of the enormous pressure being exerted from above to get the offensive under way in order to relieve the problems elsewhere on the Western Front. Colonel Scott had called his team to the meeting in his office, so that they could individually present their proposals to him before he saw the Quartermaster General.

'Right gentlemen, we have not had the time for a full, formal review of your proposals, so I just hope to God there's nothing totally daft in there' he began. 'I trust that you have borne in mind the fact that both Haig and Clarke are not ones for new-fangled ideas. They are both traditionalists at heart. Perhaps we can start with you, John. Can we realistically get the railways we need built in time?'

'Well, sir, I don't know whether a date has been set for the launch of the offensive, but in addition to the time needed for the construction of the new lines, there is also the time needed to bring everything up to the front line area, to be in a state of readiness for the preparatory artillery barrage. That will take the best part of four weeks. Arthur will fill you in on that in a moment. Here we are in early February and I can't see the physical work on the railways being completed until August, even if we got the go ahead now.'

'Well, you know what I am going to say, because you can guarantee that I shall be *told* what the timing is later in the week, when Clarke meets Haig. Just do it – that's what he will say,' said the Colonel. Looking at his watch, he said, 'I'm sorry gentlemen but we will not have time to go through all the reports, for which I apologise. We must just look at artillery and munitions. Haig will have a particular interest in this, because I know that he and the other generals feel this will be the key to the success or failure of the offensive. Frank, can you cover this in some detail please?'

'Thank you, sir. Having been involved at Neuve Chapelle last year, I agree that, particularly if General Rawlinson is leading this attack, artillery will be on top of the list of priorities. This will be a gunner's battle from the start. From a tactical point of view, the generals realise how important artillery is, but they haven't yet worked out how to use if to its best advantage. However, that's for later. First, we obviously need vast numbers of both heavy and medium field guns and howitzers. But we also need to train up many more gunners, and that takes time. Depending on the range needed, I estimate that we will need on average one gun for every 35 to 40 yards. So on a front that we have been talking about, that's about 1,400 guns. And that excludes any artillery that the French may have. We will need 18 pounders and 4.5 inch howitzers in volume – both of these have a range of about 6500 yards. Heavy guns from the Royal Garrison Artillery – 60 pounders, 6 inch, 8 inch and 9.2 inch will also be needed. These have a range of up to 10,500 yards.'

'Do we have quantities to call on in these kind of numbers?' asked Colonel Scott.

'No, but the factories are going full steam at the moment, so I think it's feasible,' said Frank. 'With regard to the ammunition, both shrapnel and high-explosive shells should be available in the quantities which we will need - 200 per gun per day should be the requirement. That's around two million shells for the seven day bombardment. And it won't stop there.'

'Thank you Frank, that at least is encouraging. If I'm going to get quizzed today, those are the sorts of figures he will want to hear and want to know that we can supply them – dependant on timing!

'Sorry, gentlemen, we'll have to leave it there for now, the General doesn't like to be kept waiting. I hope he'll approve the principle of what we are suggesting, but no doubt there will be some changes to make before he meets up with Haig. Thank you for your considerable efforts.'

With that, he turned and hastily left the room. Frank turned to Richard, who was sitting next to him, and said, 'Are you OK? You've been very quiet of late.'

'Yes, I'm fine. Just a bit tired and pre-occupied that's all.'

'It's not the old issue is it?' asked Frank.

'No, I've only just realised that working all the hours God made is starting to catch up with me,' said Richard. 'And trying to have a meaningful relationship with Simone at the same time is proving to be very difficult – especially as I think I am falling head over heels in love with her.'

The meeting between Clarke, Haig and his most senior officers was held in his main office at the Château de Beaurepaire which oddly was still partly occupied by the family who owned it. It was not unusual for there to be the sound of children running up and down the corridors while Haig's staff were busy planning the war. He was fortunate to be surrounded at the château by a group of the finest military experts in the Empire, most importantly people whose judgement he could trust and rely on.

Everyone was gathered in the large room at the rear of the château facing the garden when the Field Marshall walked in. The room was dominated by a huge map of the Western Front and an enormous Louis XIV table with twenty matching chairs. General Haig was a lithe and alert man with dashing blue eyes and a very distinguished presence. He was also a man of considerable intelligence and a disciplined personality - his daily routines rarely varied. He left his bedroom at precisely 8.25 each morning to walk down the staircase. He checked the barometer in the hall, took a four-minute walk around the garden and arrived promptly at 8.30 am for breakfast. Back in his study by nine o'clock, he then worked until 11 am and then met his army commanders and heads of departments at GHQ before having lunch at one o'clock.

In the afternoon he would visit the headquarters of some Corps or Division by car, then ride a few miles back on horse, accompanied by an escort of the 17th Lancers. To complete his routine, he would walk the last three miles back to GHQ on foot. He would then work till eight o'clock, have dinner for an hour and then work until 11 pm. His responsibility at the time was enormous. He had nearly a million men under his command in 38 divisions, bolstered in recent months by a huge recruitment drive at home and throughout the Empire.

'Good morning, gentlemen, and thank you for attending this meeting,' said Haig. 'I am aware that the time scale I set you was tough, but I hope that you have come up with some answers. Perhaps you would all like to stay for lunch afterwards and Travers, would you accompany me in the car this afternoon so that we can discuss your proposals in greater depth?'

'Of course, sir,' Travers replied.

'Right, the floor is yours,' he said nodding to the General, who at this point got to his feet and proceeded to go through the main elements of the offensive from a supplies point of view. What surprised the General was the fact that Haig did not write down a single note during the whole presentation. At the end he said, 'So, if we were to launch the offensive in midsummer, it would be perfectly feasible to have enough troops, artillery, ammunition, food, water and transport to carry it out?'

'If a plan of action was agreed with regard to the exact location for the launch and the date was in July or August, I believe, providing the go-ahead is virtually immediate, then, yes, I believe it can be done,' said the General.

'That's excellent news then. All I have to do now is inform General Joffre,' said Haig with a wry smile on his face. 'Thank you, gentlemen, for your hard work and please convey my thanks to your teams as well. Let's adjourn for lunch.'

Travers Clarke waited outside for the Field Marshall to appear. His car and driver were already waiting and within a minute he came striding out. The driver opened the door and once Haig and the General were seated, he pulled up the leg cover over both passengers, as it still felt like midwinter, even though spring was just around the corner. The driver had been briefed by Haig's ADC as to where they were going.

'We've got about half an hour before we get to Divisional Headquarters, so I just want to talk through what you presented this morning' said Haig. 'Obviously what we talk about here is strictly between us. I know I can trust you, Travers.'

'That goes without saying, sir.'

'What do you think of the location for the offensive?' said Haig.

'May I speak frankly, sir?' asked the General.

'Of course, that's why I asked you here out of earshot of the others' said Haig.

'Well, I understand the thinking of Joffre behind the need for a combined attack by both British and French forces, but this attack will live or die by the effectiveness of the artillery barrage. The Germans have had two years to build their fortifications and we know their trenches and dugouts are really well constructed and deep. So it will take a lot of high explosive to destroy the entrenchments and force them out into the open.

Their barbed wire is plentiful and the barrage must destroy the best part of it or we will not reach the set objectives.'

'I agree so far, please go on. What about the terrain itself?'

'Like most of Picardy, the Somme is a very pleasant agricultural area made up of villages, small hamlets, farms and woods. The river running through it has created a mile-wide flat valley which is well below the level of the surrounding countryside. Chalk ridges and smaller valleys appear out of the flat landscape and it is along these features that the enemy has built his front line. This formidable trench system runs from south of Fay in the French sector to Gommecourt in the north, a distance of around twenty miles. As I understand it from air reconnaissance, the trench system is in three lines about two hundred yards apart, linked by communication trenches, and most of the villages in the area have been strengthened to provide mini fortresses. To be fully effective, the artillery barrage must creep from one trench line to the next without dropping on our own troops. The Observer Corps and the Royal Flying Corps must really be up to the task or it could be a disaster.'

'You sound as though you wish this attack were somewhere else,' said Haig.

'I wish it could be. Because for the reasons I have explained, we have not launched an attack against the enemy so far in this war where he has had so long to prepare and dig in. If you want my honest opinion, I fear the worst.'

'Well, to a degree I go along with what you say. General Joffre wants an attack and he wants it to be where our respective sectors meet. For that reason and probably that reason only, the Somme is the right choice. I have heard him say that he doesn't care where the attack is as long as there is one! What we must do is plan this assault so as to leave as little as possible to chance and to avoid as many casualties as possible.'

'Just between ourselves,' said Haig, 'General Sir Henry Rawlinson will be appointed on March 1st to command the Fourth Army, whose job it will be to conduct the initial stages of the offensive. His headquarters will be based at Querrieu, just outside of Amiens. General Gough will command the Reserve Fifth Army to exploit the breakthrough. Rawlinson will be talking to you after he arrives.'

Turning to look out of the car window for a moment, Haig said 'This really is very pleasant countryside you know. It's such a terrible shame that so much of it is being destroyed by a war that no one really wants.'

He looked back at his companion and said, 'Thank you for this talk, Travers, I value your opinion.'

They pulled up outside the Divisional Headquarters in Hesdin, where Haig was paying a flying visit. 'You can take the car back to Montreuil' he said to his companion. 'I know life is difficult at the moment, but once the plan has been signed off, the implementation should be easier. Well, let's hope so anyway. I'll ride back a little later.'

Sitting in a quiet corner of the officers' mess later that day, Richard was drowning his sorrows in a bottle of claret. The fug in the room from the cigarettes and pipes made seeing from one side to the other, almost impossible. The weather outside did little to cheer him either, as it was pouring with rain and everyone who came in was cold and soaking wet, although the GHQ building where they were based was only a couple of minutes away. Richard had felt acutely the pressure that he had been under over the past few weeks to prepare his part of the presentation to Haig. It was so different to being a soldier at the front and it was the first time he had been asked to work on something so detailed and complex. Being the worrier that he was, it had given him many sleepless nights. He had already consumed at least half the bottle and realised that if he drank any more, he would be in no fit state to meet Simone after work. He signed for the bottle to go on his mess bill and staggered slightly as he made for the door.

He knew that if Simone wasn't too busy, she would leave the hospital at about 6.30, so he waited just across the road sheltering in a doorway. Simone saw him as soon as she came out of the entrance and wearing a huge smile, she ran across the road and threw herself into his arms.

'Richard, I've missed you so much. I have been so worried about you… and about us. It's seems like ages, I was beginning to think that you didn't want to see me any more, but here you are! Come on, you can buy me a drink before you take me home. With any luck Maman won't be in.'

Before he could respond, she had taken him by the arm and was pulling him across to a bar in a very narrow side street off La Grande Place, somewhere not often frequented by the military. They shook the rain from their coats and sat down at a small table close to a roaring log fire.

She looked at him with concern. 'What's the matter

Richard, why are you looking so serious?'

'Sorry,' he said, 'I am really tired. We've been working so hard for the past two weeks that I haven't had time to think about anything else, except you of course.'

'Oh Richard, you are so sweet. I knew you had a lot on your mind. The message you put through the door was very welcome and it was a shame that I couldn't see you, if only just for a minute.'

'I don't think you not have appreciated me waking you up at two o'clock in the morning.'

'But my bed would have been so warm,' she said teasingly.

'Don't! Just being with you has cheered me up no end. I've missed you dreadfully – come on, let's get that drink.'

The bar was warm and cosy and the heat was making Richard drowsy. After they had had a couple of drinks, he stood up. 'Let's get out of here, or I shall fall asleep' he said. 'And that doesn't mean I am bored with our conversation!'

'I know what you need,' she said, whispering in his ear.

'Let's walk you home,' he said. 'You are just too naughty for words!'

They strolled through the streets holding hands until they reached the house. He asked her if she had heard any news from her father, but all he got was a shake of the head and a sad look on her face. They arrived at the house to find it empty.

'Mother will not be back until after nine, so take me upstairs now, Richard. I need you and I want you to make love to me' she said.

He was a little surprised by her directness, but he knew now that it was what she wanted too.

'Are you sure you want to do this?' he asked.

'I've never been more certain in my life,' she replied quietly. 'Have you got something to make sure we don't have a baby?'

He reached into his pocket, having been given some friendly advice from the Medical Officer at GHQ. Simone knew they didn't have too much time before Cécile would be back. They walked up the stairs and entered her bedroom, which was at the rear of the house. Simone walked over to the window to draw the curtains and Richard remembered the wonderfully sensuous moment when he had undressed her the last time they met. With her back to him, he went up and put his arms around her, kissing her on the neck. She turned and said to him,

'I want you now, Richard.'

She removed her uniform and let it fall to the floor. With just her petticoat, drawers and stockings on, she lay back on the bed.

'Here Richard, come into me, now!' She quickly slipped off her drawers. He raised himself above her and she gently guided him in. Richard moved slowly at first and then managed to hold back until he sensed that Simone was almost there. Then, with a scream of unbridled joy and passion, she climaxed. He rolled off her and lay there panting. It had all happened so quickly.

'That was beautiful, Richard,' she said, cuddling up to him. 'It was every bit as beautiful as I hoped it would be. When I stopped you last time, I realised just how much I needed you. I expect you noticed! I don't want to, but we had better get up before Maman returns.'

She raised herself from the bed, removed her petticoat and went to the wash basin in the corner to remove any signs of their love making. Watching her movements, Richard felt a huge wave of love for her as she stood there. She had such a striking figure and in the half-light she looked statuesque, her skin like alabaster. She raised her left leg, resting it on the stool beside the basin and leaning forward slightly, she slowly washed herself between her legs. Looking back towards the bed in the mirror, she could see what effect this was having on her lover. He knew she was taunting him. He got up and put his arms around her from behind. He put his hands on her breasts and gently rubbed both her nipples which grew hard to his touch.

'Richard, we mustn't,' she said, unconvincingly.

By this time however, Richard was gently moving himself against her and she could feel how much he wanted her. She was ready for him again, putting her arm around his bottom and pushing him against her. She moved from the wash basin back to the bed, which was still warm, and lay face down on the corner wearing just her stockings and pushing her body up in an arch.

'Richard, take me again now, please!'

He thrust deep inside her and she once again screamed out. But this time it was a cry of animal pleasure, the kind she had not known before and her climax was immediate.

'Oh, my God, Richard, where did that come from?' she said. 'I've never had a feeling like that before!'

Richard was still on his knees behind her with his swollen manhood standing out in front of him.

'Was I too quick for you?' she asked. She turned to him and took him in her hand, gently caressing him up and down.

What neither of them had realised was that Cécile had come quietly into the house and had been watching from the doorway.

CHAPTER SEVEN

South east England, late autumn 2012

'…and before we go across to the weather forecast, we have some further news about the hoard of gold coins found recently in a field near Tunbridge Wells. It's been confirmed by the British Museum that the coins date from the fifteenth century and there could be an interesting story behind them. Our reporter Mike Holben caught up with local historian Clive King, who emailed in to us after hearing our earlier report about the coins on this programme a few weeks ago. We have Mike in the studio. Mike, what did you find out by talking to Clive?'

'Thanks. Well, I started by asking him what his thoughts were on the find and he has an interesting hypothesis on how these coins could have got there. Clive has recently written a book about the Waller family, who lived at Groombridge Place near Tunbridge Wells. Now Sir Richard Waller fought with King Henry V at Agincourt, which, as most schoolboys will know, was in 1415. During the battle he captured a very important French General, the Duke of Orleans. He held the Duke captive for twenty-four years while waiting for the French to pay a considerable ransom for his release.'

'So Mike, could these coins have anything to do with the ransom?'

'Almost certainly not. Clive has the view that during the Duke's imprisonment, he was allowed to visit the nearest church to pray, and that was in Speldhurst. He may have been taking the coins there, as apparently he became a very generous benefactor to the church and paid for many alterations and repairs during his time at Groombridge.'

'So how could they have got into the field?'

'Well, they could simply have fallen from the Duke's waistband while he was riding his horse going to church. The find was apparently very close to the old turnpike road that ran from Groombridge to Speldhurst.'

'Thank you for that, Mike. I am sure that that story will run and run. And now over to Sarah for the weather.'

Montreuil -
the tension increases

The day after the presentation to Field Marshall Haig, Colonel Scott summoned a meeting of his fellow officers to review the overall strategy and to update them on the comments he had received from General Clarke as to how the plans for the offensive had been received. After a good night's sleep, they all seemed re-invigorated and probably aware that, at least for the next few days, there would be a period of respite from the endless pressures, until it all wound up again.

'Firstly, gentlemen, I just want to pass on to you the grateful thanks of the Field Marshall and General Clarke for the considerable efforts you all put in to the presentation' began the Colonel. 'I understand he was visibly impressed and asked very few questions. It enabled him to be able to go to General Joffre and report that such an offensive is possible – even if they will argue about the date of commencement. We cannot do much more at this stage. There will be some senior appointments made in the run up to the start of this offensive, and no doubt there will be different views as to how it should be managed. Our orders are to be ready to meet the new team when the appointments are announced and be ready to put the requisition programme in place. We also need to review whether we need to staff up internally. The rest of GHQ will arrive from St Omer in the next few days and I will talk to you about that separately if I may, tomorrow. That's all for now – go and get some well-deserved rest!'

Richard decided to walk to his office by a long circuitous route round the old town ramparts, to give himself time to think. Although it was still cold, it was bright and sunny and very clear. He looked north towards England, and suddenly felt very homesick. The French coast was only eight miles from the Montreuil and over the English Channel was Sussex, where his parents lived. The previous day's visit to the house had left him yearning for Simone even more. He just couldn't get her out of his mind.

He turned to a problem that had been troubling him for some time. He had heard that his regiment, The Royal Fusiliers, were to be posted to the Somme from Flanders, which would be right in the front line should the summer offensive take place. Should he resign his staff position in order to rejoin his regiment, or stay put in the relative safety of Montreuil? With his mind in a state of uncertainty, once again he walked in through the main entrance of GHQ.

When he reached his office, there was an envelope on his desk addressed to him in what was very obviously a lady's hand.

'Who's got a letter that smells of perfume then?' asked Frank with a big smile on his face. 'If that's not from Simone, then I want to know who it is from and how you manage to attract so many women to your nest!'

'Well, I won't know until I open it, will I?' he replied, and with that he wandered down the corridor to get away from prying eyes. It was not a hand that he recognised but on opening it, he quickly realised that it was Simone's mother, Cécile.

The rumours circulating about the appointment of General Sir Henry Rawlinson to lead the Fourth Army on the Somme offensive were confirmed on March 1. He was quite young by most standards for his senior rank, but was none the less highly respected, with a distinguished military career behind him. His reputation had been enhanced at Neuve Chapelle in 1915, when he had used the revolutionary tactics of massed artillery to smash the German lines. He held the belief that if the artillery couldn't crush the enemy's guns and demoralise the enemy infantry by their firepower, the attack would not succeed. This policy was adopted as best practice for the rest of the war. The concentration of guns at Neuve Chapelle was so tight that there was one gun for every six yards of line. The fact that Rawlinson was about to attack a German line that had been in place since 1914 reinforced the belief that artillery would again play a major part.

After taking up his new appointment, Rawlinson called a meeting at his Fourth Army's headquarters with, among others, Lieutenant General Sir Travers Clarke, an old friend, and

Colonel Jeremy Scott and his team to review the supply situation. He then changed his mind and decided that he was happy to drive over to Montreuil and hold the meeting there. It would give him the opportunity to meet the other officers involved with the planning. He was aware that Haig had already started the ball rolling to pacify the French General Joffre and inform him that an attack was possible in the summer. What had changed in the meantime was the disastrous losses the French had suffered at Verdun, where they had used up most of their reserves and therefore would be relying on the British more than ever before to take the initiative.

'Morning Travers,' said Rawlinson, 'it's wonderful to see you again.'

'Good morning Henry, and congratulations on your appointment. May I introduce the team that has been working on the supply side for this offensive since the start of the year?'

He introduced them one by one, starting with Colonel Scott. Travers then introduced Major Frank Skinner.

'I'm very glad to see you again Frank' said Rawlinson.' I was delighted to hear about your DSO for your work at Neuve Chapelle. Your contribution was invaluable. More of the same please. What is your area of responsibility?'

'I'm on artillery and munitions sir, just like before.'

'That's really good. If you hadn't been, I would have got you moved onto it!' He smiled. 'With your permission, of course, Scott!'

The rest of the team were all unknown to the General, until he came to Richard.

'May I present Lieutenant Richard Waller, sir. He is new to

the team, but he's already impressed us with his grasp of the strategic planning requirements.'

'Ah,' said the General. 'If you are a Fusilier, I bet I know your father. He served with me in India.'

'Yes, sir, that will be him. He retired four years ago, but he has re-enlisted with the Royal Sussex in Crawley, where he is I/C recruitment.'

'Splendid. Please give him my kind regards when you next write to him. I hope he was not responsible for getting you transferred to staff from your battalion.'

Richard blushed. 'Well, sir, I suppose he thought I could use some administrative experience. I'm sure he would like me to be an adjutant, just like he was in his latter years with the regiment.'

'There's nothing wrong with that, but don't get the urge to go and knock Jerry about again until you've finished doing the excellent job you are doing here.'

'No General, I won't.'

Richard had arranged to have a meal with Frank that evening at Maison Canche, but he did not want to get into a question and answer session over his love-life, even though he knew it was inevitable. Frank put his head round the door and said, 'Are you OK for this evening?'

'Yes fine,' said Richard, 'shall I meet you there? I just want to pop in and see Simone for a minute at the hospital – that's if the matron doesn't throw me out!'

'See you there at 7.30 then.'

Richard wandered down towards the hospital, which was not far from the main square in Montreuil. They knew him at the reception, so he just gave the concierge a wink and ran up two flights of stairs to the ward where Simone worked. The first person he saw was Brigitte, who worked on the same ward as Simone.

'Richard, ça va?' she asked with a huge, beaming smile.

'Very well thank you.' He kissed her on both cheeks - just as Matron appeared from behind a screen.

'You know you are not allowed up here! You must wait until the staff have finished for the day,' she said with a look of contempt on her face.

'Please, can I just see Simone for one minute or leave a message for her?' asked Richard.

'The answer is no – you know the rules. Just because you are in uniform, you think you can walk in here whenever you like.'

It was obvious that her 14 stone of starched linen were going to be an immovable object, so with that he retreated, managing only to whisper to Brigitte that he would meet Simone after work the following day.

Frank was already sitting at a table in the restaurant, with Madame on his lap and her arm round his neck, when Richard walked in. There was always a good atmosphere in the place, helped along enormously by the warmth from the fire and the patron's huge personality. Given the size of Madame, he quickly realised that it was her weight which was responsible for Frank being so red in the face. Or was it the alcohol? Or both?

'Monsieur Richard, it is good to see you!' she said. 'I hear you have got the ladies' hearts fluttering in the town. What is it you have got that gets them all so excited?'

He wasn't sure exactly what it was that she was referring to, but she raised herself up to greet Richard in typical French fashion and embraced him with a bear hug which left him momentarily breathless.

'Take no notice' said Frank, 'she is just trying to get all the latest gossip from me. Can we have two glasses of whiskey please? We have had a very long, hard day meeting our new boss.' He stopped, suddenly realising he shouldn't be talking shop in front of people in the restaurant.

'Can we have our usual table please? Somewhere quiet where we can have a talk?' asked Frank.

With that they were directed to their table in the corner.

'Did you get to see Simone?' asked Frank.

'No, the dragon was on duty, but I did manage to leave a message with one of her friends. I'm going to meet her after work tomorrow. Tell me, have you ever had a situation where you are being desired by both a mother and her daughter?' asked Richard.

'What do you mean? I don't understand,' said Frank.

'Well, I have received a very private letter.'

'Saying what? From whom? I don't follow.'

'Can I tell you something in complete confidence? The letter you saw on my desk, the one you said smelled of perfume, didn't come from Simone, but from her mother. She has written the most intimate letter to me, which, if Simone knew about it, would end the relationship, even though I have done nothing to encourage it. She says she wants me to go round and talk to her. I don't know whether you have seen her or not, but she is every bit as beautiful as her daughter. I don't know what to do.'

'Yes, you do,' said Frank seriously. 'Firstly, I assume the good lady is married and therefore she is out of bounds, even if she is desperate for your body because, like many other French ladies, her husband is away at the war. Secondly, I have seen the way Simone looks at you and it would break her heart if she found out.'

'I know you're right,' said Richard, 'but I wonder what you would do in the same situation?'

After the battle, Agincourt 1415

The sky over Agincourt on the evening of the day of battle was blood red. It was almost as though some heavenly being had observed from on high the piles of bodies lying on the ground and lifted them up in honour of their valour on the field of conflict. Henry had fought an inspirational battle, in the belief that God would help him overcome his enemies. Courage, determination and professionalism had won through, from the skill of the archers who were prepared to engage the enemy at close quarters to the men-at-arms, who had stood firm when placed under severe pressure.

For the French, the scale of the defeat was unbelievable. Not only had they lost a battle in which they outnumbered the enemy by around four or five to one, but the decimation of their nobility was truly terrible. So many fathers, sons and brothers from single families were killed that it would take many generations for the French nobility to recover. What put the losses in perspective was that the English only lost one senior figure in the battle – Edward, the Duke of York.

After the battle, Henry returned to the bloody fields and ordered the killing of any wounded Frenchmen left on the ground. Only those of any perceived value were saved. It was distressing to see the great number of bodies, stripped naked by this time and probably unidentifiable, lying pile upon pile on the ground. 6,000 French dead, who were unable to be identified, were buried in a mass communal grave. These were not the only warriors to be buried en masse on the Somme. Many hundreds of thousands more would follow some 500 years later.

Views on the losses vary, but it is generally held that the English and Welsh lost between 250 to 450 men, whereas the French lost between 6,000 – 8,000, of which 1200 to 1800 were slaughtered prisoners. For his services to the King, Richard Waller was knighted and was allowed to include on the family crest a shield bearing the arms of France suspended from a walnut tree along with the motto *Azincourt, Hic Fructus Virtitis*. The neighbouring estate to Groombridge Place, where Waller lived, was owned by the Holland family. Sir John Holland also fought with great honour at Agincourt. So from a small corner of Kent, two 20-year-old sons of England gave valiant service to King and Country on a foreign battlefield. And both, eventually, became very rich as a result.

It was too late after the battle to set off for Calais and the men were desperately tired, so they camped for the night, Henry receiving the most important prisoners in his quarters during the evening. Although many of them were wounded, Henry treated them with courtesy, respectful of their endeavours for France.

Richard Waller and John Holland sat in council with the King and his advisors while they discussed their move north. It was John Holland who spoke first.

'The men are absolutely exhausted, sire. Might I suggest that we rest them for two or three days, to enable them time to recover their strength. The dysentery, as well as the battle, has taken much out of them. Men are still dying of this dreadful ailment, including two of your most trusted knights, the Earl of Arundel and Sir John Daubridgecourt. There is no French army to defeat, lands have been won and there is no particular urgency to return to England, other than to pass on to the nation the news of a great victory.'

'You speak with a wise voice on such a young body, Holland" replied the King. 'Yes, we will rest awhile here. Make sure the prisoners are well guarded and well fed. The ransom money will come in very useful for all of us. Men such as you, Sir Richard, and you young John, who raised your own armies of archers, need to be recompensed, and not with just a fancy title!'

Richard and John retired to talk about their endeavours on the battlefield and to drink some of the fine plundered burgundy which had come their way. They had been neighbours for ten years and had grown up together, sharing hunts, fishing in the River Eden, chasing local wenches and generally behaving as normal young members of the gentry do. It had been a good battle; now should come the rewards.

The march began to Calais, which although only 45 miles away, took the best part of three days to complete. On arriving close to their destination, Henry stayed for the night with his prisoners in the walled town of Guines, while the rest carried on to Calais. To avoid any problems with the local citizens, the main army camped outside the town with only the senior commanders allowed within Calais itself. They wanted to prepare the population for the arrival of the King.

Henry and his entourage arrived the next day to an enthusiastic reception. 'Welcome to the King – our sovereign Lord!' they cried. Henry was due to stay in Calais until November 11 (a date which would have a very different significance 503 years later) and on this day all those who had surrendered or had been taken prisoner at Harfleur and Agincourt were under oath to give themselves up to him. This they did without compulsion. It would have been easy for them to disappear back into a corner of their homeland, for there were no English in France apart from in Calais, but they chose the honourable path and presented themselves to Henry.

Obtaining ransom money was a complicated procedure. Putting a value on each prisoner was difficult enough, but each individual who had taken one or more prisoners had to enter into a bond with the King, which could be, and often was, a costly affair. In monetary terms today, a prisoner might be worth as much as £15,000 to £60,000 to the King. If, however, he came from noble stock the price could be much, much higher. Sir John Holland, who had fought with great distinction at the battle and had served his king exceptionally well during the campaign, found that at the end of it all there was a chance that he would be out of pocket. Some years later, Sir John was still owed considerable sums for ransoms from the campaign. And by some standards, the size of his band of fighting men was not large. Sixty archers and twenty men-at-arms were contracted to serve with Sir John, two of whom were lost at Harfleur during the siege, four in battle and one died at Calais on the way home. Many other noblemen who took larger groups of men to battle had to mortgage their estates to fund the cost of the campaign, so the need to obtain ransom money was crucial.

The following year, Sir John, along with four others who had fought at Agincourt, were made Knights of the Garter, which, although an award of high honour, was a 'cheap' way for the King to reward his most loyal subjects. In the year he was appointed a Knight of the Garter, Sir John had the title of Earl of Huntingdon restored after it had been confiscated by the King when his father was executed in 1400.

All the brave warriors returned with their prisoners via the Cinque Ports to England to a quiet reception – except for the King who, on his return to the capital, stopped first at Canterbury Cathedral. The grand fleet that had set sail from Southampton some four months earlier had been disbanded, and although the King had promised to pay for the return crossing, funds were not forthcoming, so individuals had to find a way to pay for their own fare. This they achieved either by selling goods or, in some cases, by releasing prisoners in return for a promissory note or hard cash.

The King arrived at Canterbury to give thanks to God for the success of the campaign. At the great shrine where he was to pay his devotions and make his offerings, the significance of the fact that the tombs of his father, Henry IV and Edward, The Black Prince were both there, was not lost on him. His victory at Agincourt had won him the right to take his place alongside the victor of Crécy.

Sir John Holland went on to an illustrious career as a soldier and as a representative of the King. Six years after Agincourt, he was captured by the French at the battle of Bauge after having held various important commands with the English forces in France. The ransom for his release after four years in a French prison was negotiated to include the release of some French captives from Agincourt who had been held in England. In 1435 he was appointed Admiral of England, Ireland and Aquitaine and four years later, the King's Lieutenant in Aquitaine and later Governor of the province.

On his return from Agincourt to Groombridge Place in Kent, Sir Richard Waller awaited the arrival of his prisoner – the French General, Prince Charles, the Duke of Orleans. The Duke was brought over with other captives from both Harfleur and Agincourt to England, where the business of sorting out the ransom payments was taking place. The Waller family hailed from the days of the Norman invasion and by the early part of the twelfth century, the family title had become Alured de Valer of Newark in Nottingham. Grants of land were received by the de Valers after the invasion and they had settled comfortably in middle England. Richard Valer, now Waller, was born in 1395 and lived at Groombridge Place from 1405 following the purchase by his family of the estate from Lord Clinton.

As he returned from the battlefield late in 1415, so did many an archer, and they celebrated their famous victory in the local hostelry at nearby Speldhurst. Richard took the title of 'Sir Richard Waller of Speldhurst, Sheriff of Kent', which was bestowed upon him after the battle by Henry V.

The Duke of Orleans was a deeply religious man and a well-known poet. He was also second in line to the French throne, so the ransom demanded from the French government was considerable. The Duke realised that his imprisonment was likely to be a long affair – as did Sir Richard - so they agreed that he would be held in 'honourable restraint'. This meant that he could have relative freedom to come and go as he wished, on the understanding that he made no attempt to return to France.

Being a poet, the Duke used this time to pen many great works and he also became involved with the family chapel in Groombridge and the church in Speldhurst. It was to be twenty-four years before the ransom was fully paid and the Duke returned to his native country. Through the kind treatment he had received from the Waller family, when he returned to France the Duke contributed greatly to the rebuilding of the now somewhat decaying Waller mansion at Groombridge. He also became a very generous benefactor to the two churches which had given him so much comfort during his time in Kent. He requested that the Waller family crest include some remembrance of him – a tree in full leaf with one of the branches displaying the Fleur-de-lis, the Arms of France. The Duke went on to become the King of France.

CHAPTER TEN

BBC News, spring 2013

And to end on a happier note after a gloomy day for the financial markets, at Christies' auction house today a treasure trove of coins found recently in a Kentish field were sold for a record sum of £145,000. The coins, which date from the early 1400s, the time of the Battle of Agincourt, were found by a local man from Tunbridge Wells and are believed to have been lost by a French general who had been taken prisoner by an English knight at the battle. It is believed that he was on his way to pray at a local church and that the coins were to have been his gesture of thanks to the community for their kindness towards him during his captivity. More information on this story can be found on the BBC web site at www.bbcnews/goldcoins.

France at war, 1914-1916

The house Cécile and Simone lived in was one of those charming three-storey houses you see in many French towns. The architecture was not unlike some of the Dutch-style properties which had become popular in the nineteenth century and were predominantly the domain of the working middle classes. Cécile's husband had been employed as an Under Manager in a bank before war broke out, and, as a family, they were reasonably well off. They had great hopes for Simone, their only child. Sending her to a good school with some private tuition had improved her chances of finding a worthwhile career, but everything was thrown into turmoil when hostilities began. In response to the call for mobilisation throughout the country at the end of July 1914, tens of thousands poured into the recruitment centres. France was enthusiastic, despite the preaching of the socialists for a Franco-German pact against the war. Gilles, Simone's father, had joined the call to arms almost immediately and Simone decided to train to become a nurse. Fiercely patriotic and a soldier in the Active Army Reserve, Gilles prepared himself to leave everything behind in order to help protect the country he loved so dearly.

Mobilisation was ordered on August 1st. Planning had been in progress for some time and over 4,000 trains transported 1,500,000 men to their appointed rail heads, all within the space of two weeks. These included the front-line troops as well as those designated for the defence of Paris. Gilles was an officer in the reserves and his battalion, the 8th Regiment of Infantry, was based in Boulogne, about thirty miles from Montreuil. He joined the packed trains heading for the coast after saying an emotional farewell to his family, firmly believing that he would help push the enemy back over the border and be home for Christmas.

The 8th Regiment first went into action at Dinant in Belgium, where the grim realities of fighting an enemy quickly became apparent to most of the men. They took serious casualties but were determined to do their bit in repelling the Germans. They were up against a formidable force however – four corps strong, who within days had crossed the River Meuse. Gilles and his fellow soldiers had been sent on a forced march in the August heat to Namur. Their mission was to try to stop the 2nd army of General Bulow from breaking out of Belgium around Maubeuge. The harshness of war hit home to him early on when he lost one of his best friends to a German bayonet in a brave, but unsuccessful counter attack on August 23rd.

There followed a series of desperate defensive actions, counter attacks and retreats, all the way back to The Marne, and then on to the Champagne sector in March the following year. It was eight months since Gilles had seen his family and Christmas had come and gone, by which time he had hoped for it all to be over. Because of the horrendous casualties his regiment had suffered, they were withdrawn from the line to be re-formed and he was given home leave.

Gilles was full of anticipation at seeing Cécile and Simone again. He had missed them terribly, particularly during the long, dark winter months when they had endured terrible hardships, and the conditions in the trenches were simply appalling. There had been awful shortages of food and warm clothing and in all the time he had been away, he had only received four letters from home and one parcel. He couldn't help but feel on occasion that he had been forgotten. This was no fault of his family, who regularly wrote to him, but of course he was not to know that. Letters were known to regularly 'disappear' into the chasm of war.

The journey home seemed to take forever. First he had to report to barracks in Boulogne - which meant going via St. Quentin and Arras before heading home to Montreuil. He was grateful for the company of Henri Chardin, who had travelled back from the front with him. They had left together on the journey to Boulogne from Montreuil in August the previous year and were the only ones to return of the twenty of the 8th Regiment who reported on that day. Seven had been killed, eight were missing believed dead or had been taken prisoner, and five others had been hospitalised. Gilles had been hit by a shell splinter in the arm in January of that year, but it wasn't enough to get him sent home - even though he had lost the use of two of the fingers on his left hand.

On leaving the station on a bright, sunny spring-like day in March, he headed for home. He had to walk through the main square, so he decided to stop at the bar where he used to spend many a happy hour putting the world to rights with his colleagues before the war. The patron hadn't changed, but the clientele had. Now only the more elderly men from the town frequented the bar.

'Ah, Gilles, it's great to see you again,' said Marcel, grasping him by the hand and kissing him on both cheeks. 'We had heard nothing other than what we had read in the papers, and that we didn't believe anyway. Have a glass on the house. Has it been as bad as we thought?'

'Well, I'm not sure how bad you thought it was but yes, it was bad. The only good thing is that the war has not reached here yet.'

After a brief catch-up on what had been happening in the town, Gilles said, 'Thank you for the drink, I must go and see my family. I will be in to see you again in a couple of days.' And with that he picked up his kit bag and set off for home.

The spring flowers were out in the garden, and as he knocked on the door he heard the running of feet from inside. The door sprung open and Simone stood there, unable to take in the sight in front of her.

'Papa,' she cried, not knowing what to say, as the person she had been expecting was her friend Isobelle, not her father. 'We did not know you were coming. We have had no letter or anything. Come in, come in!' She put her arms around him and gave him an enormous hug. 'Oh, I've missed you so much!' she said. On hearing all the commotion, Cécile came rushing out from the kitchen.

'Gilles!' she exclaimed holding her hands up to her face. 'My God! What a shock. Are you on leave? Why didn't you write? And look at me. I haven't brushed my hair or put on my make-up. You must give me a minute.'

'Come here woman, do you think I am worried about that when I haven't seen you for such a long time?'

With that he lifted her off the floor and kissed her greedily on the lips. Simone had burst into tears of joy and the three of them went into the lounge, where there was a fire roaring away in the hearth.

'Simone, go and get your father a glass of wine and his slippers. Sit down Gilles, you must be tired.'

'Yes, I am. We have been travelling for three days to get here. The trains just run when they can these days. It was a nightmare,' he said.

'How long have you got?' she asked. 'We have had no letter from you. The last one was about three months ago. We have been so worried. Simone has been having bad dreams about it all.'

'I have a fourteen-day pass, but as it has taken a while to get home and I have to report back to barracks on the 22nd, I only have nine days here.'

Cécile went behind him as he sat on the settee and put her arms around him, kissing him on the head, saying, 'Oh, my Gilles. I have missed you so much. In my life, in my arms. To talk to. It's been awful. But you are here. And you have not been hurt?'

'I have been very lucky. Charles was killed at Namur, along with so many others. I had a wound in my arm from a shell which damaged some nerves, so I have lost the use of two fingers, but maybe when all this is over, I can get someone to see if I can get the use of them back.'

'You sit by the fire and have your glass of wine. I'll see what we can find for supper.'

When Simone went back into the lounge, she found her father fast asleep in front of the fire, absolutely exhausted and dead to the world. She went up to him and gently stroked his head. It was then that she noticed for the first time a twitch on the side of his face. And it wouldn't stop.

That was in the spring of 1915. Gilles went back to his regiment and all three battalions of the 8th Infantry Regiment were involved in heavy fighting for the rest of the year. Casualties had been terrible – since the start of the war, the 8th had lost over 5000 men. Gilles was granted a 28-day leave late in November that year and had been promoted to the rank of Capitaine. At least his family had started to receive more letters from him, as he had stayed in one theatre of operations for a few months now.

And then came Verdun. It was February 1916 and the slaughter on both sides was catastrophic. It was a battle won by no one, but lost by many. They say that the life-blood of France drained away in the mud at that horrible place.

Spring in Montreuil and the South Downs, 1916

Richard knocked on the door of the house in Montreuil with some trepidation. He knew that Simone was at work and since he had received the letter from Cécile at his headquarters, asking him to come round and see her privately, he had been worrying about what it was she wanted to talk to him about. He had his thoughts on the subject, but dismissed them as fantasy.

'Come in Richard,' she said with her head to one side, taking his hand in hers and kissing him on both cheeks. 'I've been waiting for you to come and see me. Let's go into the kitchen, it is nice and warm in there.'

'Would you like a cup of coffee?' she asked.

'Yes please. That would be nice. What is it you wanted to talk to me about?'

She put the kettle on the stove to bring it to the boil. 'Well, this is a little embarrassing. You remember when you came round to see Simone a few days ago?'

He sat there thinking. Surely she didn't know what had happened between him and Simone?

'Well, you didn't realise it at the time, but when you and Simone were in her bedroom, I was standing at the top of the stairs watching you. I just happened to get back early and you were obviously so involved with one another that you didn't hear me come in. At first I wanted to creep back down the stairs, but I have not had anyone in my bed for so long that watching the two of you excited me beyond words. And all I wanted was for you to come into my bedroom and do the same things to me. There, that has shocked you, *n'est ce pas?*'

Richard blushed profusely. The first thing he thought of was that she had seen every private thing they had done together. Simone would be totally mortified if she found out.

'Well, I don't know what to say. That was a very private moment for us both and I think it was wrong of you to stand there watching, even though this is your house. I am certainly embarrassed that you happened to see what was going on, but what you are saying is just ridiculous. I am your daughter's boyfriend and we are very close, as you know. You are a very beautiful woman and if you cannot wait until your husband comes home on leave, then you must find another way of overcoming your difficulty. But I will not be involved.'

'You don't understand, do you? It's you I want. Ever since you came into our lives, I have yearned to have you all to myself. It has been a fantasy for me, but seeing you two together the other night just turned the tap on, if you understand. There are many men I could have gone to bed with, but it's you I want. The more I think about what you and

Simone are doing, the more I want you. Will you do it for me?'

'No, Cécile, I won't. Absolutely not. What on earth would Simone think if she could hear of this conversation, let alone what you are suggesting?'

Richard got up out of the chair, ready to walk out of the door when she shouted after him, 'I could always tell Simone that you and I have been to bed with one another. What do you think about that?'

'I am going now and by the end of the week, I shall be on leave for fourteen days to see my family in England. By the time I come back, I hope that your wicked thoughts have gone away and Simone and I will continue our relationship as a normal young couple in love with one another.'

'Not in my house you won't!' she shouted as he walked out of the door.

Colonel Scott had left a message on Richard's desk, asking him to pop in and see him before he went on leave. Richard knocked on his door and entered after hearing a loud 'Come in!'

'Hello, Richard. Thanks for popping by. I have signed off your request for leave, which is a good idea. I was going to suggest it anyway - even if you hadn't asked. There are a few reasons why you should get away at this time. Firstly you deserve it. Secondly, we are going to be very busy round here very soon, what with the war as well as the rest of GHQ arriving in the next couple of weeks, so I'd rather you got away now rather than later. Thirdly, I've noticed that your mind is not always on the job as much as it should be. A little birdie tells me that a lady is involved and the one thing I cannot have is an officer who can't keep his mind on his job - particularly at this incredibly important time. So a couple of weeks away might put things into perspective a bit. Do you follow?'

'Yes sir,' said Richard. 'She is rather beautiful though.'

The Colonel smiled. 'And say hello to your parents from me. Tell them from me that you are doing an excellent job. I know your father would be pleased to hear that. There is also the possibility of promotion to Captain soon.'

Richard left a message at the hospital for Simone saying that he needed to meet up with her and asking if she could make it that evening after work. He said he would call round at lunchtime and collect her reply from reception. The one thing he didn't want to do was bump into the matron, who was more frightening than the whole German army.

As soon as his morning duties were complete and he had started to brief Frank on things that needed to be progressed while he was away, he left his office at GHQ, telling Frank he was just popping round to the hospital for a couple of minutes and asking if he wanted a quick drink in the bar at about 1.15pm.

'Yes, that would be good. I could use getting out of here for a short while,' he replied.

Richard was well known at the hospital reception, and as soon as he put in an appearance, the cheery concierge passed him a note from Simone saying that she couldn't wait and why hadn't he been in touch for over a week? There were lots of kisses on the end of the message. With the note stuffed in his pocket, he walked across the cobbled square to the café where he was meeting Frank.

'I'll have a beer today, I think,' said Richard, 'what would you like Frank?'

'I'll have the same, thanks.' Richard ordered the drinks and they sat down at a table right by the window.

'I suppose you can't wait to get away?' said Frank once they had settled.

'Mixed feelings really, if I am honest,' said Richard. 'I will be nice to see the old country again and my parents. Although as my father has re-joined to help the recruitment drive, I am sure he'll be giving me all sorts of friendly advice! You know he is a soldier through and through?'

'Yes, I had heard,' said Frank, a wry smile on his face. 'We all know what these old soldiers are like.'

'Then there's Simone – I shall miss her a lot,' said Richard thoughtfully. 'Even though there's a war on, and she worries constantly about her father who she adores, she always manages to stay cheerful. She really is a lovely person. I told you about that letter that came for me at GHQ? It was from Simone's mother asking me if I was interested in looking after her as well as her daughter. Can you believe that?'

'Yes, I remember you mentioning it, but are you serious that she wanted to have a sexual relationship?' asked Frank.

'Yes, I went round to see her and I obviously told her where to go. She wasn't pleased. I hope to God that Simone doesn't get to hear about what she was suggesting. That could make life very difficult. It's all because, like so many other women, she is desperately missing her husband.'

'You couldn't introduce me to her I suppose?' Frank said jokingly.

'That may be one way of solving the problem, but it would only raise another. Remember what you said to me about her being a married woman.' Richard said. He took a long swig of his beer. 'That's another reason why I shall be pleased to get away for a bit - to have time to think and let things cool down a bit. Don't press me any further about it, Frank.'

Sensing that this was becoming an awkward conversation, Frank changed the subject. 'Have you got much more to hand over? I have to go to Rawlinson's headquarters this afternoon and I won't be back until Friday. By then you will be gone.'

'No, there's only one or two small things and I can leave a note on your desk. Thanks for looking after things while I am away. I guess it's going to be hell when I get back.'

'I've got a funny feeling that's the understatement of the century' said Frank.

That evening it was dry and a bit chilly as Simone came out of the hospital. Richard had made a decision not to say anything about Cécile in the hope that by the time he came back from leave, it would all have been forgotten. Simone was always so pleased to see him and it made him realise how lucky he was as she wrapped her arms, and some of her body, around him.

'It seems so long, Richard, since I last saw you. But then, I always seem to be saying that. I hope you are not running away anywhere tonight, but are going to spend some time with me.'

'Of course I am, you have me for the whole evening,' he said kissing her with great passion.'

'Richard,' she exclaimed, 'you really have missed me, I can tell!'

The last time they had met of an evening, Colonel Scott had sent his clerk over to the bar to call Richard back to an emergency meeting, and Simone had been left to make her own way home.

'I would like to buy you dinner at Maison Canche. Is that OK?' asked Richard.

'Oh, Richard, I am not really dressed for the occasion. As long as you are happy for me to sit with you in my uniform, then that will be lovely.'

'I'm sure the people in the restaurant understand that there is a war going on and I think you look beautiful in your uniform anyway. So is that a yes?'

She kissed him gently on the lips, took him by the arm and walked with him towards the restaurant. It was a lovely evening and although the menu was getting ever more limited, it was an occasion for them both to savour.

It was a shame that Richard then had to spoil it with the news about his forthcoming leave. The news came as a bolt out from the blue to Simone. 'Oh no, Richard. When are you going and how long will you be away?' she asked, looking very tearful.

'I only knew about it yesterday,' he said, 'and there is a big job I have to do which will take a long time, so they thought I should take some leave now rather than later. I am leaving on Friday morning to go home to my parents.'

'Oh, that is terrible, that's the day after tomorrow. How long will you be gone?'

'I have a 14-day pass, so I will be gone for two weeks,' he said.

Looking forlorn, she said, 'Well, at least it is not a 28-day pass like my father had last year. And I need you to make long, passionate love to me before you go. We can't go back to the house tonight because my mother has some friends round, so I need to make sure we can meet there tomorrow. We must make love or I shall be very upset.'

With that, she took his hand under the tablecloth and rested it on her upper thigh, looking longingly into his eyes. Richard was thinking about what her mother had said about never coming back to the house.

The South Downs in England were always at their best at the beginning of spring. The sheep had produced their annual flocks of lambs and the fields were full of wild flowers. Birds were everywhere, singing happily as if to welcome the warmer weather and the longer days. When Richard had visited the Somme on a reconnoitre with some of Rawlinson's staff, he had noticed how similar the rolling hills, fields and woods were to those in the flatter parts of southern England. Richard's parents lived in Crawley Down and his father had recently bought a Humber car. His pride and joy, it was the first quality small car Britain had produced and he was delighted with it. He thought driving down towards the coast would give them both time to have a good chat away from his wife, who got too emotional in these situations to be able to discuss things logically.

They pulled in at Alfriston on the way, and stopped for a drink at the Star. This quaint old coaching inn had been there for centuries, and it was the perfect place to talk about everything that was dear to both of them.

'I am aware that you are probably not pleased that I used my friendship with Harry Bishop to get you seconded to a staff position after your time with the Royal Fusiliers in Flanders,' said his father. 'But I hope you can understand how your mother and I felt. You are so precious to us and your mother went through a very bad time when you were born – both medically and psychologically. It was so bad that she was advised never to have any more children.'

'I do understand father, I really do,' said Richard. 'But that argument could apply to half the soldiers serving in the armed forces. You must see it from my perspective as well. You were a soldier, and you are once again. Your job is to get as many young men as possible to sign up to fight for King and Country. And yet you fail to understand that there are times when you just can't sit on your backside watching everyone else going off to the front while you are sitting behind a desk. I know someone has to do the job I am doing, but why does it have to be me? There are plenty of capable officers who have been wounded and can still do a desk job but can't go back to the front. They would welcome the chance to do something worthwhile. While I am able-bodied, I feel it is something I must do.'

'You say I don't understand,' said his father, 'but of course I do. I didn't spend thirty years as a soldier without understanding exactly what you are saying. But you are my son and I am being selfish. I don't want to lose you.'

Tears started to glisten in the old soldier's eyes, which embarrassed both of them.

'Come on, dad, let's leave it there' said Richard. 'You have said what you wanted to say and I respect that. I have said my bit and I hope that you respect that too.'

His voice choked with emotion, Hubert Waller took his son's hand and gripped it tight. 'Do what your heart tells you to do son, but never lose sight of how much you mean to us.' With that, he gave him his old battered silver cigarette case, which he had carried around in his military tunic for as long as he could remember. 'A keepsake from home,' he said and they both walked back to the car.

They carried on down towards the coast, where Cuckmere Haven joined the English Channel at the Seven Sisters cliffs.

'We can leave the car here,' said Richard's father, 'and follow the river down to the sea, and then climb up to Seaford Head. The views from the top are breathtaking.'

As they were walking along the river's edge, Richard turned to his father. 'I told you I had been introduced to General Sir Henry Rawlinson and he sent you his warmest regards? As did Jeremy Scott, come to that.'

'You're in very good company there. Rawlinson is an outstanding soldier, as he has proved time and time again. I assume his appointment means there is going to be another big push again soon? Is that what you have been working on?'

'The answer to that is yes,' said Richard, 'but more than that I cannot say. The fact that he has his headquarters just outside Amiens might give you some idea as to where it might be.'

They had reached the point where the River Cuck flowed out into the sea. It opened up the most astonishing vista between the Seven Sisters on one side and the cliffs stretching towards Beachy Head on the other. The horizon in front of them was as wide as could be, looking directly across to France.

'That's very odd,' said Richard, 'If I look directly across the Channel towards the coast of France from here, that's where I'm based. Montreuil is really called Montreuil-sur-Mer. Centuries ago it used to be a port and it's now quite a way inland. On a clear day, I wonder if you could see France from the top of the cliffs?'

'I don't know about that,' said his father, 'but I do know that on occasion last year you could hear the guns from northern France and Belgium. And that's a long way away.'

Richard picked up a couple of flat skimmer stones from the beach and sent them bouncing out across the water, as he used to do as a young boy. As he hurled the last one in the direction of France, he imagined that it carried a message to Simone, a message of love telling her how much he missed her. The skimmer bounced seven times before sinking; a good sign.

They started to climb up the coastal path up to the top of Seaford Head. It was a beautiful day and Richard realised how much his country was worth fighting for.

'This was a good idea, coming here,' he said. 'It makes you understand how special England is and why we need to protect it.'

He started thinking about returning to France, about the big offensive coming up and for a time, they walked along in absolute silence. After a while, his father said, 'Penny for your thoughts?'

'Oh, you know - going back in a couple of days. It's been lovely being at home with you and Mum. It's given me time to think without being under the pressure of staff headquarters.'

'You don't talk about it, but do you have a girlfriend somewhere?' asked his father.

'Yes, there is someone very special. She is beautiful, understanding and very French! Her father is a captain in the infantry and he has had a bad time. They don't see him very often. She is one reason I shall look forward to going back.'

Now that you too must shortly go the way
Which in these bloodshot years uncounted men
Have gone in vanishing armies day by day,
And in their numbers will not come again:
I must not strain the moments of our meeting
Striving each look, each accent, not to miss,
Or question of our parting and our greeting,
Is this the last of all? Is this – or this?

Last sight of all it may be with these eyes,
Last touch, last hearing, since eyes, hands, and ears,
Even serving love, are our moralities,
And cling to what they own in mortal fears:-
But oh, let end what will, I hold you fast
By immortal love, which has no first or last.

Eleanor Farjeon

Northern France – April/May 1916

While Richard had been away, the transfer of the remaining staff from GHQ at St Omer to Montreuil had been completed. It had been the right thing to do, to move in stages. It avoided the possibility of a breakdown in communications when the offensive was at a critical stage of planning. The officers' club, which had become busier than ever, was one of the few places where those commissioned in the British Army or from Allied armies based in the town could rest and relax.

There was a theatre in the town, which was also used as a cinema, but was mainly frequented by junior officers, NCOs and other ranks. The club had a few advantages over the bars and restaurants in the town - the first being that a decent bottle of wine was only five francs, with champagne at 15 francs. Dinners were laid on once a week by the Entertainments Officer, with a band in attendance and occasionally ladies – mainly nursing staff who were 'bussed in' for the evening. It was at one of these functions that Richard had first met Simone. The food at these dinners was good and there was plenty of fish from the nearby ports along the coast. All in all, it was a very pleasant way to spend some spare time and it was only a three-minute walk from their offices.

One other advantage was that the Commander-in-Chief rarely entered the premises. Apart from dances with the nurses and the occasional friendships which developed with local girls, most of the officers led a fairly monastic existence. Richard appeared to be one of the rare exceptions.

By and large, the people of Montreuil – commonly known as Montreuillons - had a reputation for being very respectable, but prim and quite dull. Both Simone and her mother would be described as respectable, but under no circumstance were they prim or dull. Quite the opposite in fact. Richard would love to have taken Simone to the officers club, but that was strictly against orders. Some of his peers even found the fact he had a friendship with a French girl rather distasteful.

On his return from leave, Simone greeted Richard with unbounded joy and he quickly realised just how much he had missed her. At present he was working six days a week, from 8.30 in the morning until after ten at night, with only half-hour breaks for meals, and he was desperate to make up for lost time. But he wanted to do something special with her and very much liked the idea of taking her to the seaside. The officers' cars from the pool were not available for 'joy riding', but it was relatively easy to get the train to Le Touquet, so he suggested to her that if she could get the following Sunday off work, they would catch the first available train and have almost a full day there.

'I will have to speak to the dragon, but I will say that I have to visit a sick relative' said Simone. 'She will surely let me have the time off. After all, while you were away, I worked every day. She owes it to me.'

'That's fixed then,' said Richard, 'I will call for you at 7.30 am. And bring your costume!'

Montreuil was chosen as the new headquarters for GHQ rather than St Omer because it was considered a much more suitable centre for the vast operations that were pending. It was also selected because it was on the main road from London to Paris; it was in a central position to serve the needs of the forces based in Dunkirk, Calais, Boulogne, Dieppe and Havre; and it was not an industrial town, so was relatively quiet.

It was also very attractive, being an old walled town situated high up on a hill. The Ecole Militaire had been easily converted into staff offices and there was plenty of billeting accommodation in the town and in the nearby châteaux, one of which housed the Field Marshall.

General Rawlinson soon got to work on the master plan for the summer offensive. The big questions were: Where to attack? For how long should the bombardment be? Should the troops attempt to push forward in the first phase of the operation? He had realised that one advantage the British had was that most of the German first line system was under observation from the British lines, lying as it did on the forward-facing slopes of the Somme ridge.

So, on April 3rd, Rawlinson and his Chief of Staff, Archie Montgomery, took their long-considered proposal for the Somme offensive to Haig at Château Beaurepaire. Haig was looking for something that was going to impress General Joffre, and, after going through the document in some detail, he considered that Rawlinson's plan lacked strategic purpose and was not bold enough. The nature of the ground appeared not to have been taken into account either. These were fairly damning criticisms and by and large, unfair. If there was a lack of strategic planning, it could be laid at Haig's door, as he had given Rawlinson no clear aim or task. The adverse comments about the ground were also unfounded, as they had been included in the document that Jeremy Scott had put together.

Haig proposed to Rawlinson that the first phase should include the first and second German lines, not just the first, and being well aware that the artillery would not reach the second line at the outset, there should be a short Hurricane bombardment of the second line when the artillery had been brought up. Then the infantry could rush forward while, at the same time, the French would attack from Maurepas to Hem and there would be a diversionary thrust by the British at Gommecourt.

This method of attack did not sit comfortably with Rawlinson. He had been used to the 'Bite and Hold' principle, where you bit off a piece of the enemy's line and held it against a counter attack. Then move forward later when you had secured your position. This was to be an outright breakthrough, and although there was no shortage of artillery and ammunition with which to hit the German lines, Rawlinson felt there were considerable risks. However, there was a weakness in Rawlinson's generalship and he agreed to go along with Haig's plan, saying 'It may be necessary to incur risks in order to achieve the objectives. No doubt the Commander-in-Chief will decide and instruct me accordingly.' A classic example of covering one's proverbial backside.

CHAPTER FOURTEEN

A day at the seaside

The journey from Montreuil to Le Touquet took no time at all. The train followed the River Canche in a westerly direction before it was due to head north to Boulogne, and Richard and Simone left the train in Le Touquet full of eager anticipation. Fortunately the day was beautiful and although a little chilly first thing, it soon warmed up. For mid-April it was just perfect. They stopped first in the town to buy hot chocolate and croissants in one of those typical French boulevard cafés where everyone seemed to just sit and spend time contentedly watching the world go by – even in wartime.

'This is heaven, Richard,' said Simone, eating every little crumb left on her plate. 'Why do simple foods like croissants taste so much better when you eat them in cafés, rather than at home?'

She was wearing a long, flowing elegant dress underneath a tight-fitting jacket and carrying a floral umbrella. She looked so pretty that he was really proud to be out in her company.

'I can't remember the last time I went out for the day to the seaside. I was probably only ten years old!' she said. Richard, absolutely delighted to be out of the office and away from his brother officers, was just as content.

'I have a little secret to tell you,' he said. 'You remember when I was on leave?'

'Of course, it was one of the saddest periods in my life!'

'Well, I went to the coast in England with my father and we went for a long walk along the beach and up onto the cliffs. When we were by the water, which was directly opposite across the Channel from here, I picked up one of those stones that I call skimmers - do you know what I mean? They bounce over the waves. And I threw it as far as I could with a message for you. It bounced seven times. That's a sign of good fortune.'

'Are you going to tell me what the message was?' she asked, looking at him with those large adoring eyes.

'Do you really want to know?'

'Stop teasing me, Richard! Of course I want to know!'

'Well, I was trying to get a message to you over those sixty-odd miles to say how much I missed you and loved you. There, I'm all embarrassed now,' he said quietly.

She stood up from the table, threw her arms around his neck and with tears in her eyes, she whispered in his ear, '*Je t'aime aussi, Richard.*'

It was the most beautiful thing he had ever heard.

They stayed at the café for a while longer, just soaking up the sun and their love for one another. There seemed to be a growing number of officers and NCOs walking along and Richard was keen to be away from them, even though he would have been very proud to be seen with his very attractive French companion.

'Let's go and find somewhere where we can just be on our own. How about going onto the beach?' he said.

They walked through the town and Simone was excited to see the shops, which were far more numerous and of better quality than in Montreuil. Le Touquet was a very fashionable town and many of the French and English aristocracy had holiday homes here. It's true to say, however, that the English probably deserted the place when war broke out.

'Oh, Richard, just look at these dresses – aren't they beautiful! My mother would love it here. Maybe when my father comes home, we can all come here. That would be good, would it not?'

He thought it wise to change the subject and said, 'Come on, I can see the sea. Let's head to the Paris-Plage and take off our shoes and go for a paddle. And then, if we are brave, we can hire a changing hut and go for a swim. I bet the water is absolutely freezing!'

As they walked down towards the beach, Richard noticed that many of the smart hotels on the seafront had been converted into hospitals. They saw nurses pushing wheelchairs along the promenade, with patients who had lost limbs or been blinded by gas.

'Look at those poor men,' said Simone. 'It makes me think of all the patients we have at the hospital, and how futile this terrible war is. England and France are going to be left nations of wounded heroes with not a lot of hope for the future. I wonder when it will all end?'

Richard did not want to let those depressing thoughts ruin the day. 'Here, let's sit on the wall and take off our shoes' he said. 'Then we can walk along the sea shore and dip our toes in the water.'

She looked at him. 'I'll just have to be discreet and take off my stockings' she said. 'Gentlemen are supposed to turn their heads away.'

'Not on your life' said Richard, 'I'll help you if you like.'

She gave him a brief, teasing look when she had reached the tops of her thighs.

'Last one in the sea is a sissy,' he said. They ran towards the vast expanse of water, all but alone on the beach. 'Christ, it's cold,' Richard said.

'I thought you were a big, brave soldier,' Simone said, 'It's not too bad, it just takes a while to get used to it.'

They walked along hand in hand until they came to some rocks.

'When I was a young boy, we used to go to the seaside and hunt for crabs. I wonder if there are any under the rocks?' He bent down and lifted up a couple of rocks and saw bubbles coming to the surface.

'Ah, there's one' he said. He dug into the sand and brought out a small crab which wiggled its claws. He walked towards Simone. 'Get that away from me, I don't like crabs!' she screamed. That was an invitation for Richard to chase her squealing and giggling along the sand. They both fell down, laughing. There was nobody about, so it didn't matter that they were behaving like a pair of young children.

'I hope you have got rid of that crab,' she said.

'Look, there is nothing in my hands!'

Looking at him in that seductive way, she said, 'Well, there should be.' She took his hand and put it up under her skirt. He felt the softness of her petticoats as he moved up her leg to the top of her thigh. She lay back as his touch moved over her loose suspenders and she opened her legs for him. He went under her drawers and touched her opening. Her breathing started to quicken.

'Feel me there,' she gasped.

He moved his fingers slowly and deliberately. She brought her knees up and her dress fell back.

'Take my drawers off,' she said softly, 'I want you to see me.'

He knelt in front of her, looking at her eyes as he slowly pulled them away. He then lowered his glance to the dark patch between her legs where his hand had been.

'There. Can't you see that I'm ready for you, my darling handsome soldier.'

The weeks leading up to the 'off' – Somme 1916

At the Fourth Army Headquarters in Querrieu, there was frantic activity as General Rawlinson and his senior officers put the final touches to the master plan for the offensive. They, of course, had to liaise with GHQ, whose role it was to decide the strategy of any campaign in the British sector. They also had to arrange the supply, from home or from their own workshops, of all the equipment needed to mount a successful operation. This was a massive undertaking, with over 800,000 tons of supplies arriving at the French ports every month. They also managed the transport system, including the railways, and apart from moving half a million men to the correct railheads, there were 450,000 horses to transport, 20,000 lorries to organise and maintain and 250 broad gauge trains and light railways to operate. No wonder the staff officers were working around ninety hours a week with only a short leave allowed every three months – if they were lucky.

It was about a month later, in the middle of May, that Field Marshall Haig finally agreed to the proposals. The only question mark was over the date. Haig and Rawlinson wanted August 15, but Haig knew this would not be acceptable to General Joffre. When they had last met, Joffre had said to Haig that for three months the French alone had been taking the weight of the German attacks at Verdun and had paid a huge price in both men and equipment. If they continued at this rate, he said, they would be ruined.

Four dates in July and August were mentioned to Joffre as dates when an assessment of the readiness of British forces could be reviewed. At the mention of August 15 as one of the four, Joffre went into a rage, protesting that the French Army would cease to exist if it were left that long. Haig then said he was prepared to commence operations on or about July 1st. However, he had a major concern over the quality of his troops.

'I have not got an army in France but a collection of territorial divisions untrained for the field' he said. 'The actual fighting army will evolve from them, but we are not yet ready.'

He had hoped to achieve victory in 1916, but came to realise that this was highly unlikely. His policy for the Somme offensive was to ensure that his divisions were trained to the best of their capabilities in the time that was available to them, to secure as much artillery and ammunition as possible to provide the most effective bombardment to shatter the German trenches and wire and to support the French by taking the pressure off Verdun. This, he hoped, would leave them in a position to finish the war the following year.

So, just as Agincourt on the Somme in 1415 had seen the

modern military concept of firepower in the shape of the English and Welsh archers, the Somme in 1916 was where the British were about to fight their first real Continental battle in modern warfare on a decisive front. The scene was set for one of the biggest disasters in British military history.

The build–up continues apace

It was June 1916 and the roads leading up to the front were crowded with artillery, infantry, trucks and carts of every size and description, all delivering their loads. Once at the front they unloaded, then turned around and made the return journey back to reload before returning to the front, thereby creating a never-ending stream of traffic. There were gun limbers pulled by horses or mules, endless columns of ammunition trucks, field guns, howitzers, ambulances, despatch riders, cavalry and rank upon rank of infantrymen.

The dust they kicked up was indescribable, except when it was occasionally damped down by the rain, but it did not seem to affect many of the soldiers, who were singing their favourite marching songs as they went. There were, however, many who were inwardly extremely nervous, and for whom laughing and talking was merely a way to stop them thinking about what lay ahead.

From the ridges where their lines were situated, the Germans were watching the movement of this massive army below them. They had heard for weeks on end the constant noise from the trains in the Ancre valley bringing up men and supplies, so it was no great secret that the Allies were on the move. The only thing they didn't know was when the attack was going to take place. The Germans had a well-trained and formidable army. Their efficient conscript system meant that half the young men between 20 and 22 had at least two years' military training and the serving army units could be constantly supplemented with trained reservists. They were ready, and had been for months, but the size of this military movement still put fear into their hearts.

While all this was going on, the British artillery continued to pound away at the German lines. The planes of the Royal Flying Corps were constantly spotting the enemy positions and helping to direct the guns. They were well dug in and camouflaged, but they needed to be. The German artillery was giving out as good as it got.

Most of the British guns were 18 pounders and 4.5 inch field artillery pieces, but as the days wore on, larger pieces such as the 8 inch howitzers from the Royal Garrison Artillery started to appear. These were monstrous weapons and difficult to position, but were very simple in design and very accurate. The infantry that were marching up or digging in were pleased, apart from the noise, to see all these guns in action, as they were aware that their chances of survival over the next few weeks depended on the artillery cutting the wire and destroying the German front line.

The Roman road from Albert to Bapaume is as straight a road as you will ever see, interrupted only by the occasional undulations. If you stand at one of its highest points on a clear day, you can see for literally miles. The order had come for the Royal Fusiliers to move up to the front line. There were 21 battalions of this famous regiment in France at this time and twenty of them would be engaged in the battle of the Somme.

The 2nd battalion set out from just outside of Albert, having been billeted in the area for several weeks. They headed in a north-easterly direction before turning due north to cross the River Ancre, close to the small hamlet of Hamel. When they left their billet, there was a sense of excitement in the air, but after a few miles a hush descended among the men, brought about by fears of the unknown, the heat of the day and the tiresome marching.

On reaching their destination, the men were happy to drop where they stood and wait for further orders. They were in full marching order and the day was hot, but the area was extremely pleasant with gentle rolling hills and valleys and with the river running through the wooded areas back towards Albert, from where they had departed some hours earlier. There was minor artillery activity but not enough to trouble them - yet.

The Company commanded by Lieutenant Thomas Holland was about 240 in number with four platoons of 60 men in each. They had been together for a while now, but had suffered heavily at Gallipoli during 1915, having been stationed in India when war broke out in 1914. Thomas Holland had been commissioned into the regiment as a subaltern just in time for the third battle of Krithia. Oddly enough, in the fighting there he expected to face the Turks, but found himself fighting Germans who had been seconded from the cruiser *Breslau* and were being used as land troops. So almost a year to the day since he joined the regiment, he was about to face the Germans again – 1200 miles from his first encounter. The contrast between the two places could hardly have been greater. He also had it in his mind that his father had told him on several occasions that the Holland family had fought in northern France, some five hundred years before.

Sergeant Ron Lewis was a tireless, professional soldier. A regular of some 17 years standing, he was adored by his men and was one of Thomas Holland's platoon commanders. The men liked him because he was fair. It didn't mean that on occasion they didn't hate his guts – they did, because it is in the make-up of a soldier to hate authority most of the time. Now was about to be one of those times.

'Right you lot,' he shouted, 'you know what you've got to do now. The job you love the most, digging a bloody great big trench. Three of the buggers in fact, about 150 yards apart and for as far as your eyes can see. And we are going to do it by the book, because it is going to save your miserable bloody lives. Now get moving! Machine gun sections – come with me!'

The new trenches had been mapped out towards the end of May and for this offensive, almost 3,000 yards were required. There were also 1,500 yards of communication trenches to be dug. Most of the digging was done at night in an attempt to minimise the effect of the German artillery. On the first day, having arrived just after midday, the men made a start in the hope that Jerry was having his afternoon siesta. For the first four hours all was quiet. They had made quite good progress, and even Sergeant Lewis appeared to be impressed.

'Cor blimey, boys, that's what I like to see. Put your bloody backs into it, without me shoutin' and hollerin' at you all the time. Break off now for a cuppa and a wad. Corporal, take them back to the encampment for a little rest before we start all over again.'

Serious groans broke out from the men, but they knew they had only just started.

Back at camp, they queued up for their tea before lying down in the sun for a well-earned rest.

'Right, before you all fall asleep,' shouted the Corporal, 'we shall start digging again at ten o'clock tonight. And why are we doing that? Because that nasty little man called Jerry likes to use us as target practice, so the less he sees of us the better. Got it?'

'Yes, Corporal,' shouted Private Wilkens, 'but there's one small problem with that.'

'And what's that then, Wilkens? Don't tell me you're afraid of the dark.'

'Oh, sod it, you guessed.'

'The trouble with you Wilkens, is you're too predictable.'

'What does that mean, Corporal?'

'It means I can read your fuckin' mind, you 'orrible little soldier!' said Corporal White, smiling.

At that moment, Lieutenant Holland walked over to his men. Corporal White shouted, 'Men, attention!'

'Stand at ease, men!' said the Lieutenant. 'I just wanted to say well done for today's work. Sergeant Lewis said you did really well. As we are going back at ten tonight, you're free to have some rest until 8.30 when you will be called for a hot meal. Make sure you take some warm clothing with you, because it still gets a bit cold at night. Although we've found a way for you to keep the cold out!' He said this with a smile on his face. 'We shall return here just before dawn. There'll be light duties during the day, but you need to get at least six hours' sleep. As you may or may not know, there is a river nearby, the Ancre. Organised parties will take it in turns to go down there so you can have a swim, starting tomorrow. While you're in the water, your clothes will be put into boiling tubs and washed to get rid of the lice – well some of them anyway! Tell the Corporal if you want to go. I'm sure Sergeant Lewis will tell you later, but there will be strict orders tonight to make sure Jerry doesn't know what we are doing. No talking unless you are spoken to and no smoking. I repeat, no smoking! That's all for now, go and get some shut-eye. This routine of sleeping during the day and working at night will continue until we have completed digging the trenches.'

They moved forward stealthily with their entrenching tools to the same ground they had left earlier that day. The night was very quiet and humid. It was very close, with thunder in the air, and the men sweated as they walked up to the front. The enemy was less than a mile away, so there was no smoking and no singing as they marched. It was so eerie and oppressive. They started digging.

It was about ten minutes later that the shelling began.

'Take cover!' shouted Corporal White, as the sky was filled with flashes of high explosive cracking all around them. Their trenches had not yet reached any significant depth, so the amount of cover was limited.

'Christ almighty, where did that lot come from?' screamed Wilkens as the German machine guns opened up.

Lieutenant Holland sent a message back to instruct the British guns to respond, giving them the map reference. The noise was horrendous and several of the men in the shallow trenches were buried as the shells landed all around them. Fortunately, no serious casualties were suffered and the digging was resumed as soon as the bombardment ceased.

It was some twenty minutes later when the British guns sent their shells hurtling over with tremendous effect towards the German artillery positions. 'Better late than never,' thought Thomas. The Germans were obviously positioned on the edge of a wood, because the high explosive from The Royal Field Artillery seemed to set the whole wood on fire. The Fusiliers could see frantic activity around the German guns from the light of the fires.

After a short while, it all went quiet again and Sergeant Lewis led his platoon back the three quarters of a mile to their encampment. Some of the men had not experienced shell fire before and for them it was a scary experience. The older hands appeared to take it in their stride, but once they were back at camp, they smoked a few more cigarettes than usual.

After breakfast, fatigue duties were posted on the temporary notice board. Stan Wilkens and his best mate Tom Adams were on latrines. Wilkens got the impression that he was being picked upon for the worst of the duties, because he was seen as the platoon comedian and therefore a troublemaker.

'Come on, let's get this shitty job over with' said Stan. 'We've put our names down for a swim in the river and the party's leaving at 10.30 am prompt.'

The Ancre was a small, attractive stretch of water, which rose halfway between Albert and Bapaume and ran in a south-westerly direction, joining up with the River Somme at Corbie, not far from Amiens. Before the war, the river had been a favourite haunt for fishermen, small pleasure boats, weekend walkers and swimmers, mainly boys and men showing off their prowess to young maidens. On fine summer Sundays, the people of Amiens used to leave the town in droves and head for the station to get the train to Corbie, Albert, Aveluy or Authuille. In 1916, the river was mainly used by the army, but fishermen still used their nets to catch eels, the local delicacy, which they skinned and smoked on the banks of the river.

Stan and Tom were two of the first to negotiate the thick reeds on the water's edge before diving into the fast flowing river.

'God, this is freezing!' exclaimed Tom. 'Just like swimming in the Tyne back home. Only this is a bit cleaner!'

'Get away, man,' said Stan. 'How can you call this clean? Half the British army have been swimming in here. Most of 'em haven't washed for months and they're covered in lice.'

'Yes, well for all that, I'd rather be here than in all that muck from the factories back home.'

They both tried to duck each other under the water before grabbing some soap to give their hair a good wash to get rid of the dreaded lice. They were swimming in groups of twenty and while they were doing so, their clothes were put in the wash house to be fumigated. But within days, the men were itching again.

On the march back to camp, Stan asked Tom if he had received any post from home lately.

'Yes, I got a parcel a couple of weeks ago. There were some fags and cake in it. Remember? I gave you a bit. Me mum put a letter in and me sister made me some socks. Very good they were too! Me dad's not too well. He's had a bad dose of the bronchitis from working down the mine. God, I wouldn't do that job for all the tea in China. I'd rather be here!' he said. 'What about you?'

'I got a letter a few months back, but I ain't really got no-one to send me one. As you know, I didn't know me dad, and me mum died in the workhouse when I was three. Me foster family were good to me, but I was one of seven in the house and I think they were pleased to see me go when I joined up. I used to send them a bit of me pay, but I never heard from 'em so I thought, sod it – why should I bother? So I don't any more. Doesn't bother me. When I'm done with the army, I'll go back home, get a job, marry some gorgeous girl, so I won't need help from anyone ever again.'

With that, he changed the subject. 'Need to get some good shut-eye this afternoon. We're going to be digging all night again.'

When they arrived back at the trench system, it was pitch dark and they had a bit of a surprise. Expecting to be digging up the countryside for the rest of the night, they were told by Corporal

White that their platoon was to act as a covering party in No Man's Land. The Royal Engineers were going out in front of the trench lines to lay barbed wire and they needed some support. Their job was to protect the engineers in the event of an attack by a German fighting patrol. Leaving their backpacks and entrenching tools behind, they crept forward towards the German trenches with rifles at the ready. Lieutenant Holland was in charge of the party, with Sergeant Lewis as his number two.

They moved forward some one hundred yards at the crawl or on their stomachs, not daring to make a sound. They had passed by the barbed wire party some while back and felt completely vulnerable out in the open, not knowing what was ahead. They were one line abreast, about three yards apart when a star shell shot into the night sky, lighting up everything around them.

As quietly as he could, Sergeant Lewis whispered, 'Lie perfectly still, don't move, and don't look at the star shell. Pass it on.'

For what seemed like an eternity, they lay like rows of felled tree trunks waiting to be taken to the timber yard. Suddenly, a second star shell went up and the German artillery started a colossal barrage, which had the men quaking in their boots. But they suddenly realised that the shells were going over their heads and dropping on the barbed wire party and their comrades digging the trenches.

'Cor, I bet they've copped it,' shouted Stan above all the noise of the artillery.

'Shut up Wilkens, or I'll put you on a charge,' said Sergeant Lewis.

They lay there for another ten minutes after the barrage had finished and then, under orders from Lieutenant Holland, they turned slowly and ran stooping back towards their lines. They had reached about half way when the shells came over again. This time shrapnel was flying everywhere, bursting right above them. Someone screamed out and there was a call for stretcher-bearers. It was a difficult night for the Fusiliers, but there was much worse to come.

Montreuil, June 1916

Richard was exhausted. He had been working day and night for weeks in preparation for his duties as part of the summer offensive, and he was concerned that he was letting his relationship with Simone slip. Since they had enjoyed that wonderful day at Le Touquet, he had seen her only for brief moments. When she was free, he was working and when he was off, she was on duty at the hospital.

Cécile had tried on several occasions to invite him to the house when Simone was at work, but he always found a good reason not to take up the offer. One morning when he was walking to the officer's mess for lunch, he saw her crossing the cobbled square and realised what a stunning beauty she was, elegant, sophisticated, sensual and extremely attractive. And she had a walk that turned the head of every man that she passed. For a moment he thought about asking her out for lunch, but he knew what a mistake that would be.

Simone did manage to get a message to him, inviting him to the house for tea the following Sunday. It was the first day they had been off together for some while, so although he was apprehensive about how to deal with Cécile, he accepted the invitation and suggested they go for a walk beforehand, just so that he could spend a little time alone with her.

As they strolled along the river bank, she held him close. There were several rowing boats making their way upriver, with young couples enjoying the early summer sunshine. 'I know you've been working hard, but I have been so very lonely without you' she said. 'They are all talking in the hospital about something big about to happen, because all the bars and restaurants have been empty of soldiers for weeks.'

'You know I can't talk about it,' said Richard, 'but the French Government are very keen that we do something to help the situation at Verdun. If we can prevent some of the German army from reinforcing the Verdun front, it will help them win the battle there. So in a funny sort of way, I hope I am helping your father.'

'But you are not fighting…' she stopped, realising that she had said the wrong thing. 'I'm sorry, Richard, I didn't mean to say that. Of course you are doing your bit and I know that you feel you should be where the fighting is. All the papers ever talk about is the men at the front. They never talk about all the work that goes on behind the scenes. I love you for what you are, Richard, not where you are. From a selfish point of view, I would rather that you were here with me and I certainly do not love you any less. Promise me that believe me?'

'Of course I do,' he said. But it raised that old worry in his mind again.

They arrived at the house, Richard deep in thought about

what Simone had inadvertently said. She could sense that he had become moody. It was the first time in their relationship that they had had any sort of upset, and it troubled them both.

'Before we go in, Richard,' said Simone, 'tell me that you still adore me and that I am a silly woman for saying what I did.'

He smiled at her honesty and reassured her with a kiss. 'Yes, you're a silly woman,' he said, 'but I love you so much.'

Cécile had been busy baking for their guest; she obviously wanted to impress. The table was laid with some very neat sandwiches and a delicious-looking sponge cake. Richard was very much on edge in her presence, but was determined to act as normally as possible, for all their sakes.

'Gosh, I feel like a king!' he said. 'I haven't seen a tea like this since before the war. For some reason, my mother doesn't like afternoon tea, but I always thought it was the perfect way to break up the day. You've gone to a lot of trouble on my behalf.'

'Nonsense,' Cécile said. 'From what I hear from Simone, you are as close to being a king as we are ever likely to have in this house. Your ancestors came from Normandy and fought at Agincourt, she told me. I am not sure that I should welcome you,' she said teasingly, 'as the English caused so much misery to our nation. So many noblemen died that day. It was a disaster for France.'

'Mother, it was 500 years ago,' said Simone. 'It's all in the past.'

'Yes, I know. I was only, how do you say, pulling the leg! Simone tells me that a member of your family captured the

Duc d'Orléans. You see, as families we are closer than you think!'

The rest of the afternoon passed without too much awkwardness. Cécile kept subjecting Richard to long hard stares, but he did his best to ignore them.

'Have you heard from you husband lately?' he asked her, trying to deflect her thoughts back to Gilles.

'We had a letter about a month ago saying that his regiment was being withdrawn from Verdun after suffering terrible casualties, but he did not say where he was being sent to next. He was hoping to get some leave, as he hasn't been home since last November. He has been promoted to Colonel – he says it's because very few officers have survived. Did you know that he was injured in the arm? Well, it has got worse and he has almost no use of the fingers of his left hand now. But sadly, that is not considered bad enough to get him sent home. He also got a slight head wound from shrapnel at Fort Vaux, but after a couple of days in the field hospital, he was back in the line. From what we hear, he has been very lucky. We worry so for him. They say that the life expectancy for an officer is only four to six weeks. That is terrible, n'est ce pas?' She shook her head. 'Did you know that Simone hasn't been well? She cut her leg and it became infected. She was at home from the hospital for a few days.'

'Oh, Simone, that just goes to show how little I have seen of you lately. I didn't know. Is it better now?' he asked.

'Yes, it has almost entirely healed. In a couple of days, it will be back to normal.'

Richard suddenly realised that he was expected in the

officer's mess at 6.30 pm for a special concert that had been laid on for the top brass.

'I am afraid that I must go, because I am on duty tonight in the mess,' said Richard.

'I hope there are no women there,' said Simone, 'you only belong to me. We met at one of those dances, remember'?

'Now then, Simone, you must not be possessive of your man. If he loves you, he will always come back to you,' said Cécile, looking at Richard as she said it.

'I wish you both good night, and it's a concert, Simone, not a dance!' said Richard. 'Thank you, Cécile, for the very special tea and perhaps Simone you will walk with me just to the end of the road?'

'Of course, just let me get my cape,' she said.

When she had gone upstairs, Cécile whispered to Richard, 'Don't forget, Richard. I have something waiting for you.'

At that moment, Simone came down the stairs before Richard could reply. Cécile's comment had caused him to blush, and Richard was grateful for the darkness in the hallway.

A few days after the Sunday tea, a letter arrived from Gilles, the first they had received for months, dated January. Cécile couldn't wait to open it.

My dearest Cécile

Well, we are still at Verdun and the killing goes on and on. Everyone, including me, seems to have lost sight as to what we are fighting for. This is just an awful war of attrition with two armies trying to murder one another in the most horrific way. I am just amazed that I am still alive to be able to write to you. The only good thing is that I have adopted a little furry friend, a black dog who found his way somehow onto the battlefield and has not left my side for the past two months. You can't believe what a comfort it is to have someone warm and cuddly to stroke and to talk to who is not in uniform! I hope we both last the course. My batman does a wonderful job in finding him scraps of food, so he doesn't go without. He even seems to have got used to the shelling.

Anyway, how are you both? I can't wait to get away from all of this and come home on leave. November seems so long ago now. I know we are being moved soon, so hopefully I will get some leave then. Our soldiers are truly wonderful, considering the tons of iron and steel that are being thrown at them every day. They put up with so much, yet are still full of hope and courage.

Please give Simone lots of kisses from me, I miss her warmth and vitality so. And thank her for the package, which amazingly did arrive in one piece. The scarf and socks came in particularly useful. And to you my darling, I am missing you so much. Pray that this can't go on for ever, so that I can be home in your arms so very soon.

Your ever loving husband, Gilles.

CHAPTER EIGHTEEN

BBC local news – summer 2013

You may remember a story we ran earlier in the year about a treasure trove find of gold coins in a field just outside Tunbridge Wells. Apart from the fact that this was very good news for the lucky finder when the coins sold at auction for a record amount of money, the find has stimulated tremendous excitement among local historians. It has been confirmed by the British Museum that there is a strong possibility that the coins could have belonged to the Duke of Orleans, who was being held prisoner at Groombridge Place after being captured by Sir Richard Waller at Agincourt in 1415. This indeed seems to refute the story which some historians believe, that he was imprisoned at The Tower of London, and not at Groombridge. There is also evidence from the church in Speldhurst that the Duke was a major benefactor during this period, and that is where he was reported to go to prayers daily. We should soon be able to piece together the whole story about his capture and his twenty-five year 'stay in honourable restraint' in Kent until the ransom demanded for his release was paid.

A time for reflection

The evening following Richard's visit to Simone and her mother, there was a letter waiting for him in the post box at GHQ after he had finished work. It was from his father telling him that his mother was very ill with a tumour, and they were not sure how long she had to live. The doctor had said it was a malignant growth and thought that she might have about nine months to a year.

This news completely knocked Richard for six. When he had seen her in the early part of the year, she had looked a picture of health. The letter said she had known about the illness when he had visited home, but had not wanted to worry him. Could he get compassionate leave, his father asked?

Richard went back to his room to consider the ramifications of this news. Under normal circumstances, there was no way that he would be allowed leave in England just two months after the last one. Leave was supposed to be taken every three months and this was normally only for a short break, usually taken in Paris, Amiens or one of the coastal towns in France. At the moment you got leave every six months if you were lucky, but with the big offensive coming up, it would be out of the question. What should he do? He was torn between devotion to his parents and loyalty to his colleagues.

He decided he should talk to Frank. He was one of those guys you could talk to about anything and he always seemed to give a balanced perspective on things.

'Are you going to the mess tonight?' asked Richard when he saw Frank in the corridor.

'Yes, I was. Why?' he asked.

'Well, there is something I'd like to talk to you privately about.'

'I know,' said Frank, 'it's about Simone and her mother.'

'No it's not, it's something a bit more serious. Do you mind if we go the Maison Canche?'

'No, of course not. I'll meet you there at about nine. OK?' said Frank.

Madame was delighted to see them.

'It's been so long!' she exclaimed, 'where have you been? I don't know what all you English are doing, but you are either very busy or my restaurant is not your favourite place any more.'

'I'm afraid we have been very busy, Madam' said Richard. 'We have been working so late every night that the mess has been the only place we've seen outside our office. Still, we are here now. Can we have our usual table?'

'Of course,' said Madam. 'As you can see, we are not busy!'

They sat quietly in the corner of the restaurant and ordered two brandies. Richard explained his dilemma to Frank.

'I am really sorry to hear that about your mother, Richard.

I can't really help you decide what to do, that's for your own conscience. I suggest you go and talk to Colonel Scott first and see what his reaction to a request for leave would be. You are not committed to take it. But his response may provide you with the answer.'

Richard thought for a moment and then said, 'Yes, that's a good idea. He knows my father and will have a view himself. But I don't expect him to do me any favours – particularly just now.'

Richard realised he was not the most exciting company that evening, so after a very average meal he suggested to Frank that a bottle of wine in the mess might be a better way to cheer themselves up, and it would certainly be a lot cheaper than the restaurant. In the end, they had a bottle each and went to bed slightly the worse for wear, but feeling rather more relaxed.

When he got back to his quarters, Richard took out some paper from his desk and started composing a very difficult letter to his father. It read:

Dear Dad

I was so sorry to hear about mother. I hope she is not in too much pain. While I understand her thinking of me, I only wish she had said something when I was home. I am in a very difficult situation at the moment. Something very important is about to happen, in which I am playing an important role. It would be impossible for me to get away in the immediate future, but I promise that as soon as I can, I will apply for compassionate leave and come home. Give mother my absolute love and tell her that I am thinking of her all the time. Give her courage, dad, to help her through. My thoughts are with you too, and I hope you understand. Your ever-loving son Richard.

As he sealed the envelope, a strange feeling came over him that he was saying goodbye to an important part of his life.

The artillery barrage preceding the offensive started in earnest on June 24th, the guns having been moved forward to their battle positions. The great bombardment that was intended to tear the heart out of the German Empire began with a mighty roar on a twelve-mile front. Thousands of shells took to the sky over the Somme, just as 500 years earlier arrows had rained down on the enemy at Agincourt. With more than 1,500 guns and howitzers opening up, the impact on the morale of both the attackers and defenders was considerable, but for different reasons. During brief pauses in the bombardment, parties went out into No Man's Land to assess what damage had been caused to the German trenches and wire. The initial reports were not encouraging. The enemy were relatively safe deep underground.

On the other side of the English Channel, the roar of the guns was heard as far inland as South London.

One week before the attack

On Sunday, June 25th Sir Douglas Haig stepped out into his garden at the Château Beaurepaire for his usual morning constitutional. Being a man of habit, he walked around the grounds for four minutes before he was due to set off on horseback to Montreuil. That morning the sound of the guns, which had begun firing in earnest the day before, was so clear that they could have been ten miles away, not 60. The sound made Haig conscious of his extraordinary responsibility towards the safety of the troops under his command, and the enormous pressure for this engagement to succeed.

Normally Haig enjoyed this time of the day, particularly when riding his mount along the country road towards the ancient fortress town set high up on the hill. It was so different from St Omer, and so much more pleasant. But today he was on edge. In some respects he would be sad at the thought of leaving Montreuil; he wouldn't mind living here when the war is over, he thought. He was moving in a couple of days with his Chiefs of Intelligence to Beauquesne, some fifteen miles behind the lines, for the duration of the battle. From there, the sound of the guns would be much, much louder.

When the entire headquarters staff had moved to Montreuil in the spring, it had completely transformed the town. The military now outnumbered civilians by two to one and passes were required for everyone, including the civilians, to enter or leave the walled town. In many ways however, the townsfolk were not too displeased at the presence of the military, as it was very good for the local businesses and the Mayor had agreed with GHQ a local tax for every soldier based in the town which amounted to around 5000 francs a year - a not inconsiderable amount of money in 1916.

The Ecole Militaire had become the nerve centre of GHQ and Haig and his ADCs passed it by as they made their way to church. Most people in the town went to the Abbey in the Place Gambetta on Sundays. They also went there in these difficult times to take mass on many other days during the week. There was a lot to pray for. By June 1916, the French were mourning the loss of far greater numbers than the people of the British Empire. The Commander-in-Chief was also in need of some spiritual comfort.

He arrived exactly two minutes before the service began, which gave him time to reach his seat for the start of the service. The minister was well aware of Haig's need for punctuality, so he made sure he started on time. It was not the Abbey that he attended but a small wooden building which represented the Church of Scotland. Being a devout Christian from north of the border, Haig's need for prayer at this place today was as strong as it had ever been in his life. He was worrying about the forthcoming battle and needed the comfort and reassurance the church had always given him. It would be his last visit here on a Sunday for some while.

A short distance away, in the Place Gambetta, two residents of the town were praying every bit as hard as the Commander-in-Chief. Although Cécile had received a letter from Gilles recently, it was dated January, so she had no way of knowing what had happened over the past two months. All she knew was that his regiment had been withdrawn from the slaughter at Verdun, which in itself was a relief, but after that, nothing.

Simone was also praying for her father's safe return, but she had another reason for some searching answers from God. She had not heard from Richard for two weeks now; not a call, a letter, and nothing had been left at the hospital reception. At first, she assumed his work was preventing him from getting in touch. She had noticed the increased activity in the town in the past month with staff officers hurrying around everywhere, but now she was worrying that it was something else. She had heard the increasing sound of the guns yesterday and had a dreadful feeling in her stomach. Surely he couldn't have gone without saying goodbye, not her Richard? She had something very important to tell him.

The General's visit, Monday June 26th

'Come in Holland,' said the Lieutenant's CO, Jimmy Strudwick. 'I have just had a communication from GHQ to say that General Rawlinson and a party of senior officers and their staff are coming to visit us tomorrow. Apparently they want to see some of our front line trenches and some of the artillery positions and have a gander at the German lines while they are here. I will obviously be in the escort party, but I want you and Martin to accompany me, as you've both been out into No Man's Land at night. They're arriving at about eleven o'clock. As this is a daytime visit, we must obviously not put any of our party in danger. These are the 'red hat brigade', not used to mud and scary bangs and the like! Any questions?'

'Has anyone worked out exactly where they are going to go, sir?' asked Thomas Holland. 'There are still one or two areas where it's relatively safe from German artillery and from where you can get a good view of the enemy front line. The extreme right of our front line is a good place, very close to the banks of the Ancre.'

'Thank you, Holland. The answer to your question is no, not yet, because we only knew about this visit this morning. Typical, eh? But I'll take your observation on board. We'll meet again tomorrow morning at ten to run through it all. I suggest both of you let your senior NCOs take the night patrols tonight, so you're fresh in the morning. That's all!'

The entourage from GHQ, complete with escort, arrived on time almost to the minute, which was surprising considering the number of hold-ups there had been on the way. There was a complete army on the move, with vast stockpiles of supplies and ammunition and vehicles being transported everywhere. Although outriders made sure their passage was as clear as possible, broken-down lorries blocking the road and gun limbers which had come adrift from artillery pieces to be dealt with, not forgetting the occasional shells, which were coming over with an increasing regularity the closer they got to the front line.

'Good morning, General' said the Colonel. 'Welcome to the Royal Fusiliers. A good journey, I trust?'

'Yes, fine thank you. Dodging all the soldiers and vehicles on the road was a bigger hazard than the German shells,' he said jokingly.

In addition to the General, the party was made up of his ADC and members of his personal staff. There were also about a dozen staff officers, who were responsible for some of the planning side of the operation. Jeremy Scott, Frank Skinner and Richard Waller had all travelled in the same car, which, it had to be said, was not the most comfortable ride. They were stiff and tired by the time they arrived, and were pleased to get out of the car and be offered a refreshing mug of tea.

The General's aide called everyone together for the briefing session.

'The reason for our visit, as I am sure you already know, is to get a real feel for how the land lies here,' he said. 'We have our maps and aerial photos, but it is important that we see for ourselves the terrain and the conditions the men will be faced with. Without taking anything away from the infantry, the artillery will be playing a major part in this offensive, and it's important that we hear from you how the coordination is working between you and the gunners, because if there are any issues, now is the time to address them. It's fairly obvious from the amount of activity around here that we have not got long to overcome any potential difficulties. We also want to hear from those who have been out in the front line and have taken patrols into No Man's Land what the conditions are like and how they feel about the quality of the German soldier we will be facing.'

While his aide was briefing the officers on the reasons for his visit, Rawlinson was going round talking to as many men as he could. He was very much liked by his fellow officers and the men for the way he appeared to care for their welfare and was prepared to visit the operational areas for himself instead of relying solely on reports submitted via the normal channels to GHQ. He was an infantry man who had learned his trade fighting small colonial wars in India, Burma, Sudan and South Africa. This offensive, however, was his first major battle as a Commander.

He spoke to as many officers and NCOs as he could before moving forward, under escort, to take a look at the German lines. The shells were coming over and there was some concern for the safety of the party, but he was insistent on seeing the lines for himself.

'Which of you officers has been out into No Man's Land?' he asked.

Holland came to attention and said, 'I was out the night before last sir, covering a party of Engineers who were laying wire.'

'Did you have any brushes with Fritz?' the General asked.

'Only with their artillery, sir. As we were lying 150 yards forward from our trenches, star shells went up and they plastered the area behind us. They hit some of the Engineers and our Fusiliers who were digging communication trenches.'

'The fact that they hit your lines meant they could see what was going on – even in the dark. How was that?' he asked.

'Maybe just luck, sir, or a German patrol heard the sound of our digging or the wire being cut,' said Holland. 'Their shooting was very accurate though. They'll have been watching our front line being constructed for some time, and they'll have worked out the yardage to a fine margin. We did call for return fire as soon as the shells came over, but it was some while before the Royal Artillery replied.'

He turned to Frank Skinner. 'Find out why the response was so slow, Frank' he said. 'We can't afford to let that happen. We have plenty of guns and ammunition, so there's no excuse. Let's take a look at the German lines.'

Richard went up to Thomas Holland and introduced

himself. 'Hello, I couldn't help noticing you're a fellow Fusilier' he said. 'I'm seconded to staff at GHQ from the 4th Battalion. I was very interested to hear of your foray into No Man's Land. Perhaps you could tell me a bit more about it.'

'Sure, be pleased to. What do you want to know?' asked Holland.

'Well, just between me and you, I started the war in a front line battalion and got transferred to GHQ last year. If the truth be known, I am itching to get back.'

'You must be crazy,' said Holland, smiling. 'Have you asked for a transfer?'

'No, we've been so busy on the planning side for this little show that I know they would never have agreed to it. But now that most of the work is done, it might be a different story.'

'I'll tell you what,' said Holland, 'why don't you ask your Colonel if you could come on a night patrol with us and say that it's for intelligence purposes? We're due to go out tonight to try and assess the strength of the Germans in front of our line, and if possible to capture a Jerry. That might sort out your problem one way or the other. What do you think?'

'Thank you for that. I'll talk to him on the way back to your camp,' said Richard.

General Rawlinson was heading back to Fourth Army headquarters at Querrieu, while the rest of the party were staying overnight at a nearby artillery headquarters. Jeremy Scott was happy to agree to Richard's request to go out on a night patrol, provided he did not put himself at unnecessary risk. Richard was over the moon. He went to find Thomas Holland to thank him and to get kitted out.

'I'd better let my CO know,' said Thomas. 'I'll tell him it's so you can get a clear picture of how a patrol works and report back to the General. Anything for the big man is bound to be OK! Have you done any night stuff before?'

'No' said Richard, 'except when we were in Belgium in 1914. We arrived late at our positions and were still digging in at two in the morning.'

'Come on, I'll take you down to the quartermaster to get some proper kit, not stuff with red flashes on it. That would soon make you a target for Jerry!' said Holland.

At precisely eleven o'clock, they crawled through the mud towards the enemy lines. There had been quite a lot of rain in the last week and everywhere was very wet and slippery. They got as far as the first row of German barbed wire and crept alongside it without being spotted.

Suddenly, they heard the sound of voices and realised that there were German patrols right in front of them, on their side of the wire. Holland was quite fluent in German and as the purpose of the patrol was to pick up as much information as possible, they lay very still trying to hear what was being said.

All of a sudden, the Germans started shouting to one another and almost instantly they disappeared, presumably into a trench or a dugout. It was fairly obvious that Thomas' party had been spotted. Richard tugged Holland's sleeve as if to indicate that they should retire, and then a star shell went up and the whole field was lit up like daylight. Immediately Jerry opened fire on them with rifles and machine guns.

The noise was horrendous. Richard, Thomas and the rest of the platoon pressed themselves as low to the ground as possible with their rifles at the ready, all waiting for the bullet with their number on it. After about ten minutes, the firing stopped and Holland tried to assess whether anyone had been injured. There was no groaning, so he assumed that all was well and indicated that they should stay still for a few more minutes in the hope that they could carry on.

While they were still lying there they heard voices again, but this time the Germans were on the British side of the wire. Thomas signalled to his men to draw their knives and clubs as the Hun started to make their way towards them. Within a couple of seconds they realised that there were only five Germans in the party, so Thomas motioned to Corporal Johnson and Privates Wilkens, Adams and Munro to get ready to use their rifles to shoot four of them, making sure that they left the German wearing the officer's hat alive.

On a signal from Thomas, the Fusiliers opened fire and Thomas and Corporal White rushed forward to disable the officer, who quickly raised his hands in surrender. They dragged the prisoner behind them, and with the other members of the platoon they ran as fast as their legs would carry them back to their lines. Their comrades gave covering fire as they fell headlong into the trench.

'Everyone OK?' asked Thomas Holland.

'Everyone present and correct sir, no injuries,' gasped an exhausted Corporal White.

'We'd better get this prisoner back smartish,' said Holland. 'Well done everyone. That was a perfect grab. Double tots all round, Corporal. Take responsibility for the prisoner and march the men back.'

'Yes, sir,' said the Corporal. 'Come along now, look lively. That was a good effort, Wilkens. And you managed to keep your mouth shut while we were out there, a superb achievement!'

'Thank you, Corporal, I must say I enjoyed putting a bullet right between that Hun's eyes.'

Thomas and Richard made their way back, smoking cigarettes to help calm their nerves. It was a pitch black night and it had just started to rain again.

'Well, that was your first taste of action for quite a while. I can assure you it's not always as exciting as that. They must have known you were coming,' said Thomas with a wry smile on his face.

'I'm still trying to get my breath back,' Richard replied. 'I was very impressed with the way everyone knew what to do and carried out their orders to perfection. White was such a calming influence over the men, they trusted both him and you without question.'

'Soldiers like White and Sergeant Lewis are the backbone of the army. Never underestimate their importance at a time like this,' said Thomas. 'How did you feel out there, Richard? Has it made you want to transfer back to the thick of things or will you be happy going back to a desk?'

'There's no doubt in my mind. It's not just the action I miss, it's the comradeship among the men. The friendships are so much more important when you're depending on the guy beside you. I realised that for the first time in Belgium when we were guarding the canal at Nimy. We were taking bad casualties and yet everyone fought for one another. That feeling is irreplaceable.'

When Thomas reported back to his CO, Jimmy Strudwick shook him warmly by the hand and said, 'That was a fantastic job, Thomas. I can't tell you how delighted divisional headquarters are, especially when the General is in the area. That prisoner is from the 99th Infantry Regiment. Intelligence didn't even know they were in the vicinity. I will talk to Corporal White and the others later. How did the staff officer get on?'

'Oh, I think I can safely say that he found it a little more exhilarating than sitting behind a desk, sir!'

'Well, if he wants a posting to an active Fusilier battalion, we're a bit short of experienced officers at the moment. Just mention it in passing. We don't want to upset the general staff.'

The same day, an advance party from the 2nd Battalion of the Royal Fusiliers went up to the forward trenches. It had been decided at divisional headquarters that because the Battalion had such a wide expanse and depth of ground to cross on the day of the attack, that they should dig trenches going out into No Man's Land to cut down the distance of exposure from enemy fire when the time came to attack. The shells were flying over as they went, with the German counter battery fire seeming to be just as heavy travelling in the other direction. The British gun positions had been well dug in and were skilfully camouflaged to avoid the attention of the enemy spotters. The advance party went past one battery which had been dug into a bank which was about 10 foot deep and so well hidden that they could easily have passed it without realising it was there, had it not been for the noise.

It was a tense, nervous time for everyone. Standing in a

trench with water well over your ankles was no fun, especially as thousands of shells screamed over towards the enemy with thousands coming back in return. And it was these shells you had to worry about. Where the next one was going to land? Would you receive a direct hit? Were you going to be hit by one of the millions of red hot pieces of shrapnel flying through the air, or were you going to be buried under the mass of earth that rained down when a heavy shell landed nearby? It was a terrifying time. The noise was deafening, and trying to get some sleep was almost impossible. Some of the men looked as though they were about to go mad. The calming influence of the NCOs was enormously important.

Then night came and it was out into No Man's Land to dig new trenches. Casualties were high and this was before the main attack had even begun.

The following day was miserable, with a great deal of low cloud and drizzle. Richard had had his transfer to the 2nd Battalion confirmed, but he was worrying about Simone and the fact that he had left without saying goodbye. What would she be thinking? One thing was certain – he couldn't write to her from the front line just a few days before a major offensive was about to start.

He was deep underground in a dugout with Thomas. The room was big enough for around twenty-five men and was about as safe a place as you could get in a front line position. It wouldn't count for much if the dugout took a direct hit at the entrance or a mighty shell landed right on top, but apart from that it was relatively safe, and certainly drier than the trenches.

'Come on,' said Richard. 'Let's go up to the trench for a while and watch the barrage. With any luck, we won't see the likes of it again.'

They stood there in awe at the noise. There seemed to be more guns than ever, more even than on the first day. Picking up his binoculars, Thomas saw that the hills around them were covered in a white smoky mist. Puffs of differently-coloured smoke were bursting all around, with huge explosions shooting into the sky.

At that moment the German artillery decided to respond again and shells started raining down thick and fast. Richard and Thomas decided it would be safer to retreat into the dugout, and it wasn't long before a shell landed on the parapet close by, causing the ground to shake alarmingly. The shout went up for stretcher bearers, and the entrance to the dugout was showered with debris. Thomas picked up the field phone and put in a call to the battery behind their lines, requesting information on where the German artillery appeared to be coming from.

Excerpt from Haig's diary – June 27th: 'I visited Rawlinson at Querrieu. He has ordered his troops to halt for half an hour after the 'off' and consolidate on the enemy's last line… I said that this must depend on whether the enemy has reserves available and ready for a counter attack. I directed him to prepare for a rapid advance and as soon as the last line had been gained, to push on advanced guards of all arms as 'a system of security' to cover his front. I told him to impress on his Corps Commanders the use of their Corps Cavalry and mounted troops and, if necessary supplement them with regular cavalry units. In my opinion, it is better to prepare to advance beyond the enemy's last line of trenches, because we are then in a position to take advantage of any breakdown in the enemy's defences. Whereas if there is a stubborn resistance put up, the matter settles itself! On the other hand, if no preparations for an advance are made till the next morning after the commencement of the attack, we may lose a golden opportunity.'

The Hollands' estate, Kent 1417

'Good morning, sire,' said the doorman. 'Is Sir John expecting you?'

Richard dismounted and replied, 'No, I thought I would call by in the hope he was in. I have a proposition for him.'

'Very well sire, please come in. I will announce your arrival straight away.'

With that, he closed the door and rang for the manservant. In a couple of minutes, Sir John came leaping down the wide marble staircase.

'I say, Richard, it's good to see you. Come into the drawing room. There's a good fire roaring away in there.'

'May I take your cloak and whip sire?' asked the manservant. He bowed and took them away.

'Can I offer you some form of refreshment?' asked Sir John.

'No, thank you kindly. I have come to talk to you about another little escapade. As you know, it's been two years since

Agincourt and whilst I still have the Duke of Orleans prisoner in my house, I am getting bored and need another challenge. John of Lancaster, the Duke of Bedford, has asked whether I want to put together a small army to go with Henry to France once again. Apparently, now that we have regained Harfleur, Henry wants to recover the French possessions that belonged to the English crown. He has set his sights on Normandy and Rouen before heading to Paris. There should be some rich pickings, what do you think?'

'Well, there is just the small question of paying for it. Are you going to be able to fund it?' Sir John asked. 'You still haven't been paid the largest ransom from Agincourt yet.'

'I was rather hoping we might combine forces and that you could help with the finances until the Duke's ransom is paid. An emissary has been sent again to negotiate with the King of France's advisors, so hopefully we may hear something soon. What do you think? You can rest assured that the King will be looking to us to support the campaign again.'

'I need to give it some thought. I am still owed money, maybe not as much as you, but at least when the title of Earl of Huntingdon was restored to my family last year, the lands that came with it yielded a handsome sum - although I haven't seen much of it yet. Are you going to be at Groombridge for a few days? If so, I will visit shortly to let you know. Now, let's have a drink.'

A week later, Sir John visited Sir Richard at Groombridge Place, having decided that they should be putting a force together.

'I suggest that we attempt to take around a hundred men

with us,' said Sir John. 'At Agincourt, we took some fine Kentish archers, and although some are still waiting for their bonus from the ransom, I think the prospect of another good pay day will sway them. Will you send a message to John of Lancaster to inform him of our decision?'

'Without delay,' said Sir Richard. 'I will ask how long the campaign is envisaged to last, as we need to budget our costs. I will prepare a list of our requirements including pay for the men, victuals, weapons, carts and the like. We could be away for some while.' He paused for a moment, and then asked, 'How are your funds at present? I can raise a mortgage on Groombridge on the basis of expected income and hopefully that will be enough to see us through.'

'Fortunately, I am able to raise my share without putting the family home at risk. I can mortgage some of the agricultural lands if need be,' said Sir John. 'Shall we shake on it?'

CHAPTER TWENTY THREE

Gilles comes home on leave, June 1916

Three days after Simone and Cécile prayed in the church, Gilles walked back into their lives. The Almighty had listened to their pleas and returned him to them safe.

'Oh, my God, Gilles, just look at you!' Cécile exclaimed, holding her hands up to her face. He was looking thin and gaunt with deep sunken eyes. There was a vacant look on his face.

'What sort of welcome is that after all this time?' he said.

'I'm so sorry' she said. 'It's such a shock. We didn't know you were coming. We were in church only last Sunday praying for your safe return and here you are. Come here and give me a big hug.'

Even through his uniform, she could feel that he had lost a lot of weight. It was almost eight months since he had been home. But it was the gaunt look on his face that concerned her the most.

'Come and sit down, take off your boots and I'll get you a cup of coffee. I expect you are exhausted.'

She didn't want to say anything about how ill he looked. Maybe he just needed rest and feeding up. She hoped so.

'Do you want anything to eat?' she asked.

'Not yet. Have you got any of that brandy left? I could use that more than food at the moment.'

She poured him a generous glass, which disappeared in a single gulp. This concerned her because although Gilles liked a drink, he had never knocked it back like that before.

'Just leave the bottle,' he said. 'I'll sit here for a while'.

He didn't even ask about Simone, which was not like him at all. Within fifteen minutes he was out for the count. He had not even undone his uniform. Cécile decided to leave him for a while. It gave her time to adjust to him being there, and to walk up to the shops to buy something special to cook for him when he woke up. He always loved her coq au vin, so a visit to the butchers was first on her list.

Simone came home at seven o'clock and her mother just managed to stop her from making a lot of noise when she entered the house for fear of waking her father. In the hallway, she put her fingers up to her mouth as a sign to be quiet and whispered in her ear that her father was home and asleep in his chair.

'Oh my goodness, that is wonderful news,' she said quietly, 'I must just go and kiss him. I won't wake him up, I promise.'

As she crept towards him in the half-light of the room, she could see how thin he looked.

'Oh, what have they done to you, my darling papa?'

She kissed him, noticing that the twitch on the side of his face that she had noticed on his previous visit had got much, much worse.

He had been asleep for about six hours when Cécile decided to wake him. She touched him gently on the shoulder and he nearly jumped out of his skin. He stared up at them with wide misty bloodshot eyes and said, 'Oh, I'm sorry. I was so deeply asleep.'

He turned his head to one side and saw his daughter.

'Simone! Come here and let me look at you. You look more beautiful than ever. I've missed you both so much. It has been a very hard time.'

And with that he started to sob freely. The pent-up emotion of all those months away suddenly hit him; seeing his family, thinking about his friends both dead and alive that he had left behind; the futility of war. It all became too much for him to deal with. Simone had not seen her father cry before, except at the funeral of his mother. It made her start to weep as well.

'Everyone I left with to go to Boulogne has gone' he sobbed. 'All killed or missing. None left. Only me. And for what? I hope that some day someone will be able to explain what it's all been for. Coming back home means so much to me - to see the two most important people in my life. I am so sorry for the tears,' he said, looking embarrassed.

He was obviously very emotionally disturbed. Simone went and sat on the floor by her father's chair and he stroked her hair, something she had enjoyed ever since she was a little girl.

'How long have you got, my love?' Cécile asked.

'I have a twenty-eight day pass. I have to report back to headquarters on July 20th. The rumour is that we will be joining Fayolles 6th Army on the Somme. Anything will be better than Verdun. It was hell on earth.'

'Come on, now, let's eat. I have made your favourite, coq au vin.' She moved closer to him. 'It's so good to have you back,' she said tearfully, giving him a big hug. 'Simone, open a nice bottle of wine so we can celebrate your father's return. How is your hand? Have you got any feeling back in your fingers?'

'A little,' he said. 'I thought I would see if I could get something done about it while I am here. Perhaps someone at your hospital could see me, Simone?'

'I can ask tomorrow, if you would like me to?'

'Thank you, that would be kind,' he said in a very tired voice.

'We got a letter from you a couple of weeks ago,' said Cécile. 'It was dated January. It took for ever to get here. You talked about a dog you had adopted. Who is looking after it while you are away?'

He pushed his plate of food to one side, having eaten only half of it. 'Oh, he went away one day and didn't come back. I hate to think about what might have happened to him. I really missed him. There I am, worrying about one mangy old dog when there were thousands dying every day. What strange times we are living in.'

Halfway through the meal, during which Gilles had drunk more than he had eaten, he said to Simone, 'You're looking a little sad this evening, what's wrong?'

'Well it's lovely to have you home father, but my boyfriend, the English officer I wrote to you about in my letters – I hope you got them by the way?'

With that he nodded.

'Well, he has been working here at the British headquarters on the plans for a big battle, but some part of him was desperate to get back to his regiment at the front line. I thought I had persuaded him that what he was doing here was worthwhile, but I haven't seen him for two weeks now and I am worried that he may have decided to go back. When mother and I heard the guns a few days ago, I feared the worst. But what I don't understand is why he didn't talk to me about it. We mean so much to one another, it's breaking my heart.'

She burst into tears. Her father held her hands.

'Have you been to his headquarters to try to find out where he is?'

'Oh Father, there are so many British soldiers there, thousands of them. I wouldn't know where to start.'

'Well, tomorrow, ask your matron if you can take an hour off work. I will come and meet you and we will go together to see what we can find out.'

'Thank you, Father, I just need to know, that's all.'

It was grey and misty when they arrived at the Ecole Militaire. Her father pointed her in the right direction and she went to the reception desk, where a Corporal was sitting.

'Yes, Mademoiselle, how may I help you?'

'I am looking for Lieutenant Richard Waller, please. Do you know if he is here?'

'Can I ask what it is about?'

'It's a personal matter. He is my boyfriend and I haven't heard from him for a while. I just wanted to know whether he had been posted away or not.'

The Corporal gave a wry smile. 'I'm sorry Mademoiselle, we get quite a few ladies in here saying the same thing. I'm afraid that I am not allowed to divulge information about people here without authorisation.'

He could see that she was in a very distraught state and was of a mind to help her if he could. 'Tell you what' he said. 'There is a gentleman who knows Lieutenant Waller very well. He is Major Frank Skinner. He always goes to lunch when he's here at about 12.30 pm – which is about now. If you would like to take a seat and wait for a little while, he should come past. I will tell him that you are here and ask him if he could have a word. That way, I won't get into trouble and you may get the answer to your question.'

'Thank you very much. That's very kind of you,' she said.

Although it was overcast outside, it was very hot in the reception area and Simone had to take off her coat. 'Are you all right?' asked the Corporal. 'You look a little pale.'

'I'm feeling a little dizzy. You couldn't get me a glass of water, I suppose?'

'Hang on. John, could you please get this young lady a glass of water? I can't leave the desk. Won't be a moment, Mam'selle.'

About five minutes later, there was an exodus of people from the building with those officers who could spare the time, going off to the mess just around the corner. They were only allowed half an hour for lunch at the moment, so it was a visit to the mess or nothing. Lunches in one of several restaurants in La Grande Place were out of the question.

'Excuse me, sir,' said the Corporal as Frank Skinner went past. 'There is a young lady here who would like a word with you.'

Simone got a little unsteadily to her feet, and said, 'I am Simone, Richard's friend. He spoke a lot about you and I just wanted to ask if you could tell me what has happened to him.'

He held out his hand and with a welcoming smile he said, 'I'm very pleased to meet you. I never had a conversation with Richard without your name coming up. And I can see why. You are very beautiful.'

'You are very kind, Monsieur,' she said blushing.

'Come with me,' he said.

They walked down the corridor to a small meeting room, which contained a desk and two chairs and not much else. Once they had both sat down, Simone took a long drink from the glass of water, which made her feel a little better.

'Did Richard ever talk to you about his unhappiness at sitting behind a desk while his Regiment was fighting at the front?' asked Frank.

Simone's heart was in her mouth. She had a feeling she knew what was coming.

'Yes,' she replied, 'he did talk about it. But I thought that I had convinced him, looking after my own interests if I am honest, that what he was doing here was very worthwhile and that he had already done his bit.'

'Well,' said Frank, 'he talked to me often and I know he talked to his commanding officer. It really played on his mind. When he went home in April, he had long discussions with his father about it. They had a bit of a disagreement, but it would appear that they both in truth saw each other's point of view. After all, Richard's father was an officer in the army, so he should have understood better than anyone what Richard was going through. It was his father pulling strings, as we say, that got Richard the 'safe' job here. And that was what Richard resented.'

He could see she was very upset and didn't want to prolong her agony. 'Did you know that a few weeks ago he had a letter from his father to say that his mother was very ill and asked if he come home on compassionate leave?'

'No, I didn't know that!' she exclaimed. 'Oh! Poor Richard. He is so fond of his mother.'

'He wrote back saying it would be impossible to get away at the moment and he would apply for leave when the pressure at work had died down a bit. Being an only child, he was feeling that he had let them both down by not going home.'

After a short pause he said, 'I shouldn't tell you this, but I know how much you meant to him. He went with a group of brother officers from GHQ on a reconnaissance mission and the battalion they went to was the Royal Fusiliers. He went out on a night patrol…'

She gasped, 'Don't tell me he was…'

'No, he wasn't hurt. But he came back from the patrol convinced that his place was with them. They were short of officers and he asked his CO for a transfer while he was there, and he didn't return to GHQ. The orderly clerk was asked to send his kit and belongings to his unit.'

'But I just don't understand. We are so much in love with one another. How could he go off like that without saying goodbye or even writing to me to explain?'

Frank sat in uncomfortable silence, not knowing what to say. Tears were streaming down her face and she was unable to take it all in.

'He's been gone for quite a while now and I have heard nothing' she said.

'I am sure you know that getting letters from the front is not easy. Your father has been away hasn't he. How many letters have you had from him?' Frank asked.

Even as he spoke she could hear the sound of the guns from the front.

'Is that where Richard is? Where those guns are?'

'I can't tell you that, I'm afraid. I wish I could do more to help. You know where I am if you need anything. I mean that,' he said.

With that, he stood up and escorted her to the door.

'If you hear anything, would you please let me know at the hospital where I work? You see, I think I am carrying Richard's baby.'

She left GHQ in a daze. She could not believe Richard would have left without saying goodbye, no matter what was playing on his mind. But for one reason or another, he had. She was convinced that he loved her and in that there was some measure of comfort. But all the while that she could hear the guns in the distance, she knew that he was in a position of some danger, something she had not experienced with him since they had met.

She had arranged to meet her father at his favourite bar just off the square, once she had finished at GHQ. She walked in and saw him sitting on a stool at the far end of the bar. He looked as though he had already had quite a lot to drink, but after all he had been through in the last two years, who could really blame him?

He turned and rose a little unsteadily to his feet, but there was something about his smile that worried her. It looked empty and without warmth. This damn war, she thought. In the space of 24 hours, one of the two men in her life had returned a shadow of his former self, and the other had just walked out of her life.

She took him by the arm and led him out of the door.

'Did you find out anything about your Richard?' her father asked with a slurred voice.

'Yes, but let's talk about it when I get home tonight. I have to go back to work and I am already late. Matron will kill me. Is it all right if I leave you on the corner?'

'Yes, my darling. Off you go.' He kissed her gently on the cheeks, but she could see that twitch again and she wondered whether he was aware of it.

Excerpt from Haig's diary, June 29: 'General Hunter Weston came to see to me and stayed for lunch. He seems quite satisfied and confident (about the forthcoming offensive). I gave him a kind message for his Divisional Commanders. I told him that I realised all the difficulties and hard work they had had in training their divisions and in preparing their trenches for attack, also that I had full confidence in their abilities to reap success in the coming fighting.

After lunch, I motored to HQ X Corps at Senlis and saw General Moreland. He is quietly confident of success. Then I went on to HQ III Corps at Montigny and General Pulteney. He also is quite satisfied with the artillery and wire cutting… After dinner, my adjutant Birch came to report on his visit to VIII Corps today. The conclusion I came to is that the majority are amateurs, and some thought that they knew more than they did of this kind of warfare, because they had been at Gallipoli. Adversity, shortage of ammunition and fighting under difficulties against a superior enemy, has taught us much!'

The waiting is almost over - June 30/July 1 1916

The time leading up to zero hour was long and painful. For those who had been part of the advance party of Fusiliers, it had been even worse. Although they had been occupied digging trenches out into No Man's Land, they had been under constant artillery fire for almost a week and had suffered serious casualties as a result.

In the days before the 'off', they had written letters to their nearest and dearest, which they had passed to the Chaplain. Richard had been thinking about the two letters he had to write, both difficult, but for different reasons. The one to his parents he decided to write first:

Dear Mother and Father, I have re-joined the regiment in the front line and I am writing this short note, which you will receive only if something happens to me during the next few weeks. I am sorry that I could not stay at GHQ, but Dad knows the reasons why. If I do not come out of this, I want you to know how much I love you both and that I am so grateful to you for all you did for me as your son. Mother, I hope your illness is not causing you too much pain and that with your iron will and the help of the doctors, you will come through it. Father, you understand why I am here, because being a soldier has been your life as well as mine. I am absolutely certain that I will come through it OK, but in case the unexpected happens I shall rest content knowing that I have done my duty. I just hope that it is enough. Till we meet again.

Your loving son, Richard.

P.S. Please find enclosed a photo that was taken of me in the square at Montreuil. I never look very good in pictures, but this one is not bad.

The letter to Simone took a lot of thinking about. He wanted to make sure that he said what was in his heart and he asked for this one to be sent whether he survived the attack or not.

My dearest Simone. I hope that you do not hate me for leaving you, albeit temporarily I hope. I had talked to you about what I felt I should be doing for the Regiment and the opportunity came along, so I took it. It was not the way I should have left, but in some ways maybe it was better this way. I haven't stopped loving you for a moment since I left, and never will. You have given me such happiness and I hope you will give me much more in the future. Our day at Le Touquet will stay with me for the rest of my days.

Tomorrow is the big day. The guns that you can hear in Montreuil are where I am. I have made a good friend in Thomas Holland, and we have spent time talking about our lives and our loves. I hope you don't mind but I told him all about us. I hope to come through this with honour and without pain, having done my duty so that I can see you again soon, with my conscience clear. Then, who knows what the future will bring for us? Please take great care of yourself.

Yours for always, Richard.

It was the afternoon of June 30 and the rest of the 2nd battalion were due to leave the village where they had been billeted, to make their way up to join the advance party at the front line. The significance of the forthcoming battle had suddenly dawned on them and there was an enormous amount of emotion being released which had been bottled up over the past few weeks. Senior Divisional and Corps commanders from the 29th Division, of which the 2nd Battalion were attached, turned out to watch their battalions march past and even among the elderly officers, there were many standing there with tears streaming down their faces.

As the men marched along, they were generally very quiet, each deep in their own thoughts. There were a few who sang as they went, probably to give themselves something to do rather than dwell on the next 24 hours. There were some men travelling in the other direction – signallers who had been making sure that the telephone wires between the front and the artillery positions were functioning after being hit by shells. There were 7,000 miles of underground cables to maintain. There were also a few soldiers being escorted back by military police after inflicting themselves with wounds. There were staff officers and police everywhere, directing the flow of human and mechanised traffic.

Feelings of comradeship were very high. The older troops were trying to reassure the younger ones, saying, 'You'll be fine. Just remember all you've learnt and what the Sergeant has told you.'

The afternoon was beautiful – even a little hot - which was a pleasant change from the rest of the week leading up to the attack, when it had rained almost every day. The battalion passed through lines of artillery, where the guns had been firing almost continuously for six days. Gunners were stripped to the waist working the guns either as loaders, shooters or carriers. It was appallingly hard work. Many had burst and bleeding eardrums, and they all looked grey and dark-eyed with exhaustion. They also knew that their job was far from over. They had the good grace to cheer the men as they went past. A little further on, the battalion passed a whole series of wide trenches, which had been prepared for burials - not a great comfort to those who witnessed them.

They reached the assembly trenches in the early evening. There was considerable confusion, as there were two lines of trenches – the front line provided with dugouts, the rear line stepped and traversed with no accommodation in the nature of dugouts or shelters. Finding their way to their allocated positions was difficult, as there were so many troops trying to do the same thing. Even though there were staff officers attempting to direct the lines of troops, they still often took a wrong turning. Huge complications then occurred when they tried to turn round and move back along the narrow trenches. Cursing and shouting was the order of the day. The trenches were deep in mud after all the rain and the constant tramping of feet was making it worse. Little did they realise at the time that there were around 8,000 soldiers for every mile of front line trench. They were packed in like sardines.

Eventually, arriving where they were supposed to be, they joined up with their advance party, which for the past few days had been digging trenches out across No Man's Land. They had taken many casualties from the German artillery and were pleased to see their comrades join them. They settled down to get what rest they could, but the trenches were so crowded and narrow that sleep was almost impossible. There was no room to lie down. All you could do was sit sideways or stand up leaning against the parapet and hope that passing troops didn't wake you with their packs or rifles as they went past. Smoking was strictly forbidden in case Fritz spotted the glow, but of course, everyone did it. Most just stood there thinking of home. Some were seen kissing photographs of loved ones they kept in their top tunic pocket. Others were crossing themselves in prayer.

Excerpt from Haig's diary, letter to his wife Lady Haig, June 30:
'The attack is to go in tomorrow at 7.30... I feel that everything possible for us to do to achieve success has been done. But whether or not we are successful, lies in the Power above. But I do feel that in my plans I have been helped by a Power that is not my own. So I am easy in my mind and ready to do my best whatever happens tomorrow.

At four o'clock on the morning of July 1st, it was just light enough to see the German lines. It was a little damp and some drizzle came, but it did not last long. The day was fairly clear, apart from some mist hanging about in the low-lying areas near the rivers and streams.

The Chaplain was holding a communion service for those who needed some comfort and wanted to say their final prayers before they went over the top. A few ammunition boxes had been stacked to create a temporary altar with two lit candles on the top, which were shielded from the enemy.

'The Lord be with you,' he intoned.

'And also with you,' they replied. A few prayers were said and a hymn was sung very quietly, almost in a whisper. The Chaplain went along the line of men giving communion and blessings to those assembled in front of him.

'Go in peace,' he said. 'And by the way, if you get back quickly you will find a tot of rum being dished out with breakfast!' With this news they hurried back. They were greeted by Sergeant Lewis.

'Right,' he said, 'I want two volunteers to go and get breakfast and two to get the urn of tea. We shall not be dispensing the rum until it arrives!'

This was a big enough incentive to inspire Wilkens to say to the Sergeant, 'Do I get an extra tot if I go Sergeant?'

'Well, the answer to that Wilkens is yes!'

Suddenly, Lewis was surrounded by volunteers. The four selected left their kit behind and set off. A faint smile came onto Lewis' face. They were a good bunch of lads, he thought to himself. He thought back to the Dardanelles, where he had walked around steadying the nerves before the attacks by the 2nd at Gallipoli and Suvla. The fighting there had been bloody and they had left many a good friend behind on the barren cliff tops. His conduct in both of those engagements had earned him a recommendation for promotion, but he preferred being close to his men, so he had politely turned it down.

Born and bred in Bradford, Lewis had joined the regiment, a regular battalion, at the age of 16 and seen service in South Africa. He was stationed with the Fusiliers in India when war broke out and they came home by troopship in October of that year. Some months later, they were heading back east, this time to the Dardanelles. Following the disasters there, they went to Egypt before being sent to the Western Front. Now, at 32, he was a seasoned campaigner. Many of the officers in his regiment were much younger and lacking in front-line experience, so it was left to NCOs like Lewis to reassure the men as best they could.

After breakfast, Sergeant Lewis and Corporal White went round talking to the men and giving out the tots of rum. The artillery was still going over and some was coming back, but there was an eerie silence among the men. None of the usual banter was being exchanged. Lewis went up to Wilkens.

'I know we haven't got parade this morning, Wilkens, but there's no excuse for having your tunic undone.'

'I thought it was a bit hot, Sergeant,' he said tongue in cheek.

'Don't get funny with me boy. It's cold, damp and miserable, just like you, so get it done up.'

'Yes, Sergeant.'

When he had gone, Wilkens turned to Adams and said, 'How could he see my tunic was undone from over there? He must have eyes in the back of his head.'

At 5.30 am, the 2nd Battalion of Fusiliers took up their final positions. 'A', 'B' and 'E' Companies moved into the Sunken Lane, which offered some cover before the off, with 'D' Company, who were to attack and occupy the site of one of the biggest mine explosions on the Somme, at Hawthorn Ridge. 'C' Company was being held in reserve. It was a nervous time. They had been told that several mines were due to explode a few minutes before zero hour.

As the morning drew on, the German artillery seemed to increase, as did the casualties. A huge shell had landed in a trench to their left and had killed or wounded 24 in one platoon. Everyone was keen to get going. As on the previous six days, the British artillery had opened up at 6.25 am, and this day would be no different except that it would lift from the German front line at 7.30 am rather than the usual 7.45. Those who were stood to in the trenches could see the shells landing on the enemy lines just 200 yards away. Some sat on the parapets and cheered.

They were as ready now as they were ever going to be, bayonets fixed, rifles loaded, the last adjustments made to their kit. Wilkens and Adams shook hands. 'Good luck mate' said Wilkens. 'If I don't make it, look my missus up and tell her I did me bit and that she was the only one for me.'

Officers, many still in their teens, kept checking their watches. Their pulses were starting to race. 'Only a minute left to go!' With whistles in mouths which were dry from the nerves, the last few seconds ticked by.

Richard and Thomas were in command of 'D' and 'E' Companies respectively, which were stationed some 200 yards apart. They had been talking for part of the night together in the dugout and had become really good friends. It was this kind of friendship Richard had experienced in Belgium early in the war with the BEF, and one he had missed during his time at GHQ. He had made good friends there, like Frank, but this kind of comradeship was different and special.

During the night they had talked about all manner of things, mainly to keep their minds occupied with thoughts other than what was coming in the next 24 hours.

'How did you come to find out about your connection with the Waller family of old?' Thomas had asked.

'Well, it was one of those strange coincidences really. I never realised I had a middle name until one day a teacher in the junior school said, 'Here comes little Raw'. I didn't know what he was talking about, so I said, 'Pardon, sir. What did you say?'

'I called you Raw because those are your initials. RAW.' So when I got home, I asked my mother what my middle name was and why it had never been mentioned before. She was a bit embarrassed. She told me it was Alured. 'What sort of name is that?' I asked. 'You probably don't know anything about your past,' she said, 'but the Waller family is very old and your father thinks it started with a Norman family arriving at the time of the Battle of Hastings called de Valer, and over the years it has become Waller. And Alured was the Christian name of the first de Valer he could find from the records.'

Thomas was looking a little puzzled. 'So what was the coincidence?'

'Well, some years later in history we were discussing the Battle of Agincourt and guess what, the name of Sir Richard Alured Waller came up. He was a famous man living on the Kent/Sussex border who was knighted for his services to King Henry V on the battlefield. So my father, being a proud military man, wanted to keep the family name alive. He saddled me with a name I've been trying to hide ever since!'

'Now I understand. And talking of coincidences, I believe my family also dates back generations to the same part of the world and I have heard mention of Crécy and Agincourt. There could be more to this than meets the eye. God willing, we will get through this and we can talk about it some more.'

They both stood up, somewhat embarrassed, and embraced, wishing each other God speed.

'Take good care of yourself, Richard,' said Thomas.

'I will, and you too.' No more needed to be said.

They went around from man to man, offering what help and encouragement they could and sensing the nervous anticipation - or was it fear? They said their goodbyes to each other, shaking hands and wishing each other the best of luck.

'See you in the Hun trenches!'

Richard had only been with his platoon for a short while, so he only knew a few of his men by name. But that did not seem to matter. He was there with them and would be leading them over the top. He was every bit as nervous as they were.

Messages had been flying back and forth reporting that they were all ready. And still there came the sound of the artillery, escalating to a massive, deafening crescendo with earth-shattering bangs, swishes and crumps.

'Corporal White!' Richard shouted, 'I'll be going over first. Make sure everyone follows as soon as possible, a prod with the bayonet in the bum if necessary!'

'Don't worry about that, sir, they know me well enough by now!'

Smoke and gas started to drift towards the enemy lines.

'Good luck, Sergeant, see you in the German front line.'

At 7.20 am, ten minutes before they were due to climb up the three rung scaling ladders with rifles at the ready and advance toward the German lines, a massive explosion occurred. The Hawthorn mine had exploded prematurely, under the trenches held by the Infanterie-Regiment 119, warning the enemy that an attack was imminent. Eight minutes later, on time, a further seventeen mines detonated. At 7.30 am the Royal Field and Garrison Artillery held their fire while the first waves of troops started walking towards the enemy.

Gilles visits the hospital

Emotionally drained, Simone made her way home from work. In addition to the news about Richard, the dragon of a matron had made her life very difficult for the rest of the day for getting back late from visiting GHQ at lunchtime. Having left the hospital at about eight o'clock, she walked home slowly, thinking about Richard, her father and the baby. She had missed two periods, but it was still early days, so she decided not to say anything to her parents yet, as it might all go wrong. There were too many other things to worry about at the moment.

When she got home, her father was fast asleep in the chair. Cécile came out to meet her. 'How was your father when you left him at lunchtime?' she asked her daughter.

'What do you mean?' asked Simone.

'Well, he got home at four o'clock, totally drunk,' she said.

Simone was taken aback by this. 'We parted company at the corner of the square at just after one thirty as I had to rush back to work' she said. 'He must have had a few drinks while I was at GHQ. I assumed he was going back home after I left him.' She sat down. 'Mother, I am really worried about him. He's mentally worn out. He has a terrible twitch and he doesn't seem to be able to concentrate on anything. I was thinking at work today that I would ask a doctor to take a look at his hand and see if we can get a view on his mental condition while he is there.'

'That's a good idea,' said Cécile. 'I am just as worried about him as you are. He has shown no real interest in me yet, which is most unlike your father. He is such a loving man.' She was reminiscing about happier days with Gilles.

Thinking more about her husband than her daughter, Cécile had forgotten to ask what happened at Richard's headquarters.

'How did you get on at lunchtime?' she asked.

With that, Simone burst into tears, partly because of the situation with Richard, but also because she was so tired. 'Oh, Maman, he has gone. He has left to go and fight at the front with his regiment.'

'Why didn't he let you know?' her mother asked.

'I just don't know. He often talked about going back to his men. If I'm honest, I thought that one day he would go. But why he chose now, I am not sure. I saw one of Richard's brother officers, a really nice man called Frank, who was probably his best friend at GHQ. Richard had told him the reason why he wanted a transfer to the front, but Frank said he felt there was another reason for Richard going, but couldn't say what it was.'

That comment made Cécile wonder whether what she had said to Richard had had anything to do with his decision.

'The last time Richard and I spent any time of consequence together was when we went to Le Touquet,' Simone went on. 'He told me that day how much he loved me. Oh, Maman, I have to tell you that I am pregnant with Richard's baby.'

Cécile was visibly shaken by the news. She had to steady herself by holding onto the table.

'Ah, that's why he has gone' she said bitterly. 'Men, you can't trust them!'

'How can you say that?' said Simone. 'Richard would have had no idea I was expecting his child, and anyway, he would definitely not have gone away if he had known. He loved me too much.'

'That's what you say. Men are all the same. They have their fun and then run away from their responsibilities.'

Simone was upset and puzzled at her mother's reaction.

'You know Richard well, you were close to him' she said. 'How can you say that about him? There were times when I was a bit jealous of your friendship. Do you really think he would behave like that?'

Cécile rushed up the stairs and slammed the bedroom door. Simone walked slowly upstairs and fell on her bed weeping. Everything was going wrong. Richard had left her. Her father was at the end of his tether with the war and her mother had turned against her at a time when she needed her most.

She went off to the hospital the next morning, her mother and father still in bed. She didn't want to face either of them, but she had arranged for her father to go to the hospital at 11 am. She hoped he wouldn't forget.

She met Dr Froget on his rounds.

'Did you arrange for your father to come in today?' he asked her.

'Yes I did. I have said that I will meet him in reception.'

'Bring him up as soon as he arrives and we'll take a look at him.'

Her father did arrive, albeit a little late. He looked washed out.

'Papa, come along with me. Dr Froget is waiting.'

They walked along the cold, austere marble corridor until they reached the consulting rooms at the end. Simone knocked on the door and there was a shout of 'Entrez!' from inside. On entering the room, Dr Froget got up out of his chair and shook Gilles by his good hand.

'Please take a seat, monsieur. Simone tells me that you have a problem with your left hand. Before I examine you, would you like to tell me how it happened, what was done and what your symptoms are?'

'Of course. Last year I took a shell splinter in my forearm – there, you can see the scar.' He extended the arm to show the doctor. 'They took out several small pieces of shrapnel at the dressing station, but at the time I was left without the use of the finger nearest my thumb. Since then, the next two have become useless as well.'

'Are you sure that all the bits of splinter were removed?'

After a few seconds Gilles said, 'Sorry, what was that?'

'I said are you sure they took out all the shrapnel?'

He looked vacant for a moment and then said, 'Yes, I think so. They didn't say at the dressing station that there might be some left behind.'

'Please monsieur, lay your arm on the table and lift your fingers one by one.' Gilles' coordination was poor and his ability to raise his fingers even worse.

'I think we will take an X-ray, but we'll probably find we will need to reopen the wound,' said the doctor. 'I think we will find some more pieces inside, and it is they that are causing the problem. Can you come in for a couple of days – say from tomorrow?'

Gilles did not reply.

Simone said, 'Papa, did you hear the doctor? Can you come in tomorrow?'

'What for?' Gilles asked.

'To have your arm looked at.'

'Oh yes, I am on leave at present,' Gilles said.

'Don't worry about that,' said Dr Froget. 'I can sign you off until such a time as I consider you fit enough to go back. Please be here at 8.30 tomorrow morning.'

'Thank you Doctor for seeing him' said Simone. 'I shall bring him in in the morning.'

Gilles stayed in the chair and gazed straight ahead. After a couple of seconds, aware that the doctor needed to get on, Simone took her father by the arm and said, 'I will take you down to the entrance.'

'Come back and see me in a moment, Simone, when you have seen your father off,' said the doctor.

When she had said goodbye to her father, she went back to the consulting room and knocked on Dr Froget's door.

'Ah, come in Simone' he said. 'I am fairly certain that we shall find some more shrapnel pieces. They tend to move around a bit, so not to remove them will cause further damage. What I am more concerned about is your father's mental state. I am not a qualified psychiatrist, but I would say that he is almost certainly suffering from some form of breakdown or battle fatigue. I can introduce him to a colleague of mine, Dr Maurent, who can give an opinion. What I would suggest is that he looks at your father when he comes in for his operation. That way, he will not realise his mental state is being assessed, which, certainly for the moment, would be better. Then he can decide what needs to be done to help him.'

'Thank you Doctor, I really appreciate your kindness, knowing how busy you are,' she said.

'Well, we have to help those who are doing their utmost to help us, don't we?'

When Simone got home from work that evening, her father had obviously been drinking heavily again. The whole house smelled of alcohol. She wanted to wake him up and tell him that he was behaving very badly, but how could she when she knew what he had been through lately and how much he was suffering inside? But she also knew that if he didn't sober up, there would be no operation tomorrow. She gently shook his shoulder.

'Father, wake up, you must not have any more to drink or they will not carry out the operation tomorrow. Dr Froget is only doing this as a favour to me. He is a very busy man.'

'OK, I know. You don't need to tell me. Get me a coffee,' he said grumpily.

'Mother will be home any minute. Try and sort yourself out before then – for all our sakes.'

Simone wasn't sure whether to tell her father about the baby yet. She had not discussed with her mother who was going to tell him. In fact, she had not spoken to her mother at all since last night. One thing was certain, now she knew her father was going to be assessed by a psychiatrist, there was no way it was going to be mentioned until after his operation - at the earliest.

That evening after Cécile had come home, Gilles was very quiet. He knew that his drinking had upset the family equilibrium and there was an uneasiness in the family relationship which they had rarely, if ever, experienced before. The fact that he was also showing very little interest in his wife was not helping the situation. She had gone without a man for a long time and her frustration was starting to show.

'Go on upstairs to bed' she snapped at him. 'You're not much use down here and you're probably even less use up there.'

Simone was surprised by this attitude from her mother and wondered what had brought it on.

To Simone's surprise, her father did turn up at the hospital at the appointed hour. With Matron's permission, she met her father in the reception area and took him to the ward where he would be prepared for his operation. Simone loved her father deeply and despite all the trouble he had given them lately, she was pleased that she had been able to do something to help him through this difficult time. After all, this war was not of his making.

Dr Froget performed the operation on Gilles' arm and, as

he suspected, found some small pieces of shrapnel that had lodged very close to the nerves. With his arm heavily bandaged, Gilles went back to the ward to recover. Just after lunch, Simone went up to see him. Although he was only partially awake, he did smile and showed her that he could wiggle his fingers. Well, at least that might make him feel a little better, she thought. She said she would come back and see him just before she went off duty.

Cécile went to see him in the afternoon and was pleased to see that at least he looked a little better, with a bit more colour in his face. The rest he was having in hospital and the fact that he had not had a drink had obviously helped.

'The doctor has said I can come home the day after tomorrow,' he said.

'That would be really good,' Cécile said. 'It will give you a chance to relax and perhaps you might even be able to make love to me, if only with one arm! I have missed you so much.'

She stroked his good arm and kissed him on the lips.

'Perhaps, if I am not too tired,' he said.

'I shall keep you awake with the power of my love, I promise you' she whispered.

She kissed him on both cheeks and left full of hope that in the next few days things might improve between them. She walked away wondering if Richard was all right and thinking about what they might have done together had he returned to the house. The thought still caused a flutter of excitement inside her, and she hoped he would return one day soon. She realised that having such thoughts was quite wrong considering what her husband had been through recently, but she couldn't help herself.

As it was only a short distance to the house from the hospital, Cécile collected Gilles after the doctor had completed his rounds and declared him fit to go home. They walked slowly together, enjoying the summer sun and the fact that they could walk arm-in-arm for the first time in ages. With his arm heavily bandaged, they attracted a lot of sympathetic looks from passers-by. The doctor had told Simone that as far as his colleague was concerned, he was convinced that Gilles was simply suffering from complete exhaustion and two weeks' complete rest in the bosom of his family would do him a power of good. He agreed that after three days in hospital, Gilles looked a different man from the one who had come in a few days earlier. Simone was so pleased that she skipped all the way home. All she had to worry about now was Richard, and the baby.

Simone took her mother to one side while Gilles was asleep in his chair.

'I have been thinking about the best time to tell father about the baby' she said. 'Now we know it's just rest he needs and not something worse, I'd like to tell him very soon. It would be awful if he found out before I could tell him.'

'If that's what you want, then go ahead,' Cécile said in a matter-of-fact way. 'But leave it until tomorrow, let him rest today.' She did not want any distractions for Gilles that evening, because she was determined to get him to perform in the bedroom.

'Shall we wake him now?' said Simone. 'So we can have supper together?'

'Leave it for fifteen minutes, then I can serve the meal.'

When he woke up, Simone asked him how his hand was.

'Oh, much better! Look, I can move all my fingers a little and with time, perhaps I'll be able to use them properly again. Thank you for arranging the hospital visit for me. I probably wouldn't have done it by myself. I was too tired, you see.'

She got up and gave him a big hug and kissed him on both cheeks. The fire was close to burning out, so she went to the scullery to get some more wood.

'Let's eat, perhaps we can have a glass of wine?' she said. But she quickly realised that it was a foolish thing to have said, as they were trying to get Gilles to cut down on his drinking.

'No thank you,' he said. 'A glass of water will be fine.'

A short while later, Cécile went up to bed. 'See you in a few minutes?' she said to her husband.

'Yes, I'll be up in a little while.'

She had been preparing herself mentally for this evening all day, like a bride on her wedding night. When he came into the room, she was waiting for him dressed in the most alluring attire. She had chosen a sensuous black nightgown, which left very little to the imagination. She had also splashed out on an expensive new perfume just for the occasion. Gilles didn't appear to show much interest and Cécile cuddled up to him on his good side.

'I am ready for you, Gilles, please make love to me, now,' she whispered in his ear.

He looked at her, not saying anything. 'I am not sure that I can do what you want. It's been so long and I've had so much on my mind.'

'Why don't I try and help you?' she said. She slipped off the top of her nightgown, exposing her breasts, which in the past had been guaranteed to have the desired effect. She took him in her hand, rubbing him gently, but to no avail.

'Here,' she said, 'feel me here. Does that do anything for you?'

'You know how much I adore you, Cécile, but I can't make it happen. I am so sorry.'

She was too upset for words. She had never failed to arouse him before. And that spoilt daughter of hers…

She got out of bed and put her nightgown back on.

'By the way, our daughter is expecting a child' she snapped. 'There, perhaps that will give you something else to think about.'

When she found out that her mother had spoken to her father about the baby, Simone was furious.

'Why did you do it? Why? We only talked about it last night and agreed that we would tell him today. Father will be so upset with me. I must go and talk to him before I leave for work.'

She went upstairs to the bedroom and sat on the edge of the bed.

'I am really sorry Papa that mother has told you about the baby before I had a chance to. I wanted to wait until you were back from the hospital and had rested a bit. Please don't be too cross with me.'

He looked up at her and said, 'My little one, there is so much sadness in the world at the moment. The last thing you need from me is a lecture about the rights and wrongs of what you have done. I have been lying awake most of the night thinking about it since I heard the news. We are living in very strange times. France is dying on its feet. We will need a new generation of young people who will learn from the mistakes of others, so that what we are experiencing now will not happen again. Your mother will worry about what the neighbours will say, but she will have to deal with that herself. I assume your English officer is the man responsible and that you must love him for it to have happened. So I hope for both of your sakes that it is what you want. I will not love you any the less because of it. If anything, even more.'

On hearing such sympathetic words, Simone burst into tears and gave her father a huge hug.

'Thank you father, for being so kind and understanding. Richard does not know about the baby yet, but I know that he will be pleased. He is such a fine young man. I hope that you can meet him one day soon.'

She kissed him on both cheeks and left the house without talking to her mother.

CHAPTER TWENTY SIX

At home in Crawley, June 1916

Richard's mother had deteriorated in the last few days and she felt that she needed to see her son. 'I wish Richard could be here,' she said to her husband. 'It would give me such a lift, give me something to fight for. I do miss him so.'

Hubert Waller was at a loss to offer her any words of comfort, because he knew from past experience that the way the military worked, in the situation that Richard found himself in at the moment, there would be no likelihood of any leave. Trying to put a brave face on it, he said, 'I will get a letter off to him today, or better still - to his Commanding Officer, Jimmy Strudwick. I know him. I'll see what can be done.'

The house, which in reality was too big for their needs, had been very quiet of late. Hubert had arranged for a servant to help keep it clean and to keep his wife company whilst he carried out his recruitment duties at the local Town Hall, which had become the recruitment centre in the area for the war effort. They had five bedrooms and Mollie, the servant was happy to live in for £2 a month including her board. The arrangement was working out well.

Even so, it was becoming impossible to get his wife out of the house, even just for a short drive in the car. The month before, he had taken her down to the coast at Cuckmere Haven where he and Richard had gone the last time he was home on leave, but she was exhausted by the time they had got back home. Whilst by the coast, they had parked on the top of the cliffs and they could hear the 'crump, 'crump' of artillery fire from across the other side of the Channel. The southerly wind was bringing the death and destruction from the battlefield much closer to home.

If I should die, think only this of me:
That there's some corner of a foreign field
That is forever England. There shall be
In that rich earth a richer dust concealed;
A dust whom England bore, shaped, made aware,
Gave, once, her flowers to love, her ways to roam,
A body of England's, breathing English air,
Washed by the rivers, blest by suns of home.

And think, this heart, all evil shed away,
A pulse in the eternal mind, no less
Gives somewhere back the thoughts by England given;
Her sights and sounds; dreams happy as her day;
And laughter, learnt of friends; and gentleness,
In hearts at peace, under an English heaven.

Rupert Brooke

The front line – July 1st 1916

The trenches, which had been dug out into No Man's Land by the Fusiliers in the week leading up to the attack, stopped just short of the Sunken Lane. At four in the morning on July 1st, they had punched through the last remaining few feet of earth to open up a field of fire for the supporting machine guns and to create an access for 'A', 'B' and 'E' Companies to crawl through into the relative cover of the lane. They were only 200 yards from the German wire and they could clearly see the German trench snaking its way through a shattered orchard. They noticed that the wire was still basically intact, with only a very few small gaps for the infantry to penetrate. They quickly camouflaged the new holes in the bank and waited for the order to pull back along the tunnel, so that they and the machine guns would not be put out of action when the mine went up.

Just before 7.20 am the troops were warned that the giant mine up on Hawthorn Ridge would be detonated in ten minutes' time and that they should be ready for the impact. However, a few minutes later, it detonated prematurely, sending a column of flame, earth and debris a hundred feet into the air. The ground rumbled for a couple of seconds before the huge mushroom appeared, setting off alarm bells deep down in the German dugouts. No. 252 Tunnelling Company had built an underground gallery 300 metres long, 25 metres down under the German lines to pack in 40,000 lbs of explosive. The ground shook uncontrollably. This was the signal for the Germans to increase their artillery fire on the British lines, causing the troops to lie as low as they possibly could in the trenches. Shells were raining down by the thousand. 'I thought they weren't supposed to have any guns left,' shouted some comedian.

At 7.28 am the other mines went up. The tremors through the ground were so great that they caused casualties on both the British and the German sides. Arms, legs and ankles were broken, mainly caused by collapsing trenches. These were the lucky ones. They were quickly recovered and taken back to the first aid stations.

The explosion of the Hawthorn Redoubt mine was the signal for Richard's 'D' Company to advance toward the crater in order to take it while the Hun was still in a state of shock following the explosion. There was considerable confusion as to why it had exploded ten minutes early, but Richard took the initiative and blew his whistle to signal the advance. The British artillery had been ordered to lift the barrage in their sector at 7.20 am and to concentrate their fire on the second and third lines of defences. The 160 men of 'D' Company rose out of their trenches and started up towards the ridge where the crater had formed. All hell had broken loose. Shells were crashing down everywhere; machine guns were spraying interlocking fire across the open ground and smoke of many different colours drifted across towards the German line.

The explosion had caused minimal casualties in relation to its size, so after recovering from the initial blast, the enemy were out in force ready for the oncoming Fusiliers. Richard was aware of others running alongside him and the ground was a mass of shell craters, some small, some huge. There was about 100 yards to go to the wire and he could hear and see soldiers falling in great numbers. He kept ducking and side-stepping, holding his pistol in one hand and keeping his other hand on his helmet, angled forward so any bullets would hopefully glance off. Private Stephens, who was next to him, suddenly stopped and slumped to the ground, hit in the throat.

Richard looked across to his right to try to see what progress Thomas was making with his Company, but it was impossible to see anything that far away. All he knew was that they had come out of the Sunken Lane into the open ground and he could see men moving forward. But who they were, he couldn't determine. He had other things on his mind at the moment, like staying alive and keeping the men going forward.

He could see Sergeant Lewis pushing on hard, so far dodging everything that the Hun could throw at him. He saw two more men hit on his right by the same burst of machine gun fire, one riddled with bullets right across his chest, the other hit in the arm so badly that it almost came off at the elbow. His scream was drowned out by the constant sound of artillery fire, which was sending murderous red-hot shrapnel flying everywhere.

With about fifty yards to go, Richard realised that he could not see any gaps in the wire in front of him. He leapt into a shallow shell hole and called across to Sergeant Lewis, who was still keeping up with him, despite all the equipment he was carrying.

'Can you see any openings in the wire, Sergeant?'

'None to speak of sir.' He got out his binoculars and scoured the ground ahead.

In the meantime, the rest of the Company had hit the ground to take what cover there was. The numbers remaining seemed frighteningly small. There were twenty or thirty German bodies lying about, presumably caught up in the explosion from when the mine went off. Some of them were beyond recognition.

'Sergeant, there is one small gap about ten yards to the left of the remains of that broken tree. But there are at least two machine guns on the far side of the crater covering the gap and the rest of the rim. Can you get the two mortars to direct their fire on those guns – it's the only way that we have any chance of moving forward?'

'Right away, sir.'

Richard called to the signalman who had stayed in close touch from the off. 'Parker, can you get a message to HQ to tell them we are held up on the western side of the crater and that we're calling for artillery to lay a barrage back down on the first line?'

'Yes, sir. Shall be done.'

'Well done, Parker.'

Meanwhile, Sergeant Lewis was trying to locate his light trench mortars.

'Collins, Sharp, Brown – get that mortar over here, but keep your bloody heads down. There are snipers over there on the ridge behind the crater.'

'Jones, Patrick – where's Patrick?' he shouted.

'Got hit Sergeant,' said Private Jones.

'Right, Simmonds, go with Jones and Cruxton and get that second mortar into action. Fire the rounds alternately with no.1 mortar to keep the bloody Hun's heads down.'

'Messages sent to HQ and the artillery battery sir,' said Parker, 'but we have just had a message to say that the battalion commander has been killed.'

Richard was shaken by the news and he shouted across to Sergeant Lewis to try and assess how many were left able to fight in front of the wire.

'We've lost about half the men sir. There are a lot wounded out in No Man's Land unable to move.'

'Thank you, Sergeant, you've done a splendid job,' Richard said.

Just as he said that, Richard saw two of his men crawling along fully exposed trying to find a shell hole to shelter in. Within seconds one had been raked with machine gun fire and the other had had his head taken off. Richard gripped his pistol so hard with anger that he wanted to stand up and empty his gun in the direction of the enemy. Sergeant Lewis saw what was going on and slid alongside Richard to calm him down.

'Keep your head down, sir. We don't want to lose you as well,' said Lewis in a calm, measured way.

The machine-gun fire from the other side of the crater and the never-ending German artillery bombardment were causing terrible casualties, and unless the mortars and the artillery could put them out of action fast, Richard would have some very difficult decisions to make. Everywhere there were piles of bodies and Richard had no idea whether they were alive or dead. Many were hanging on the wire with terrible injuries, pleading to be put out of their misery. They had started off with 160 men and it looked as though only a third of them were left.

Lower down the slope towards Hamel and the River Ancre, Lieutenant Thomas Holland was having just as difficult a time. Even though he had received a commendation from Divisional HQ just before the off for his capture of the German prisoner on the raiding party, it counted for nothing at this moment. The early excitement and enthusiasm had quickly worn off when they realised that not only was the wire not cut, but that the German dugouts, although badly battered, were still intact, and when they realised that the attack was under way the enemy came pouring out. In a costly mistake, the artillery that had been ordered to stop the bombardment in front of the Hawthorn Ridge at 7.20 am to coincide with the mine going off also stopped the bombardment on the whole 8th Corps front ten minutes before the men went over the top. This gave the Germans ample time to prepare for the attack. They had time to get out of the dugouts, set up their machine guns, accurately range their guns on the gaps in the wire and be ready to fire on the lanes the British soldiers would be using to approach No Man's Land. As a result, the casualty rate was worse than Richard had experienced in his sector. And that had been bad enough.

Those who had mustered and had been standing waiting against the banks of Sunken Lane were caught by deadly accurate machine gun fire the second they came out into the open ground. And if the bullets didn't get them, then the German artillery, which had that precious ten minutes' warning of the impending strike, fired with deadly accuracy at the approaching men in khaki.

Thomas was leading 'E' Company waiting in the lane. They had already taken 30 casualties from shell fire before the advance started, but by the time they had crossed No Man's Land, they were down to 61 fighting fit and were cut off from supplies of ammunition and reinforcements. Thomas had been wounded slightly in the leg, which was giving him difficulty with walking, but with the number of casualties they had taken, he was in no mood to go back to the dressing station even if he could have done so. Like Richard away on his left, he would have some serious thinking to do once he knew exactly what had happened elsewhere. For now, unable to move backward or forward, he awaited orders from above.

The mortars had done their job and silenced two of the machine guns which had given them so much trouble. With HQ demanding that they go forward, not only to take the crater but also to relieve pressure on the neighbouring battalion which had taken the village of Serre and was in danger of being isolated, Richard passed word to Sergeant Lewis to get ready to resume the attack.

'Wilkens!' exclaimed Sergeant Lewis, 'I'm glad to see you continue to lead a charmed life. Did you see what happened to Corporal White?'

'Yes, Sarge, he got a direct hit from a shell. The last time I saw him, he was flying through the air, well what was left of him anyway.'

'You haven't seen Tom Adams have you?' Wilkens asked.

'No, sorry lad, all I know is he's not here with what's left of us.'

Snipers, rifle fire and shells were still reducing their numbers, but with the machine guns out of the way, Richard felt they stood a chance of making it. With the mortars continuing to fire smoke and high explosive rounds, two pioneers from the battalion crept forward with wire cutters to enlarge three of the openings created by the early artillery fire. Leaving the mortars to continue firing and bringing the only operational Vickers machine gun into action, a rifle platoon gave covering fire while the rest of the Company advanced. Richard led one group through the middle gap, while Sergeant Lewis and Corporal Wooley went through the other two gaps.

On reaching the rim of the crater with two more wounded in the charge, they quickly realised that holding the crater would be virtually impossible with the numbers they had left. The village of Beaumont Hamel was still held by the Germans, and if they launched a counter-attack the odds of holding it were very slim. Still, Richard called Private Parker to send a message back that most of the crater was in their hands and that they would continue to hold it until receiving further orders. He did report that the artillery had not bombarded the first trench as requested.

As the day wore on, Thomas Holland and his Sergeant, John Richards, stood to in a forward trench taking cover from the enemy fire, surveying the carnage in front of them. Piles of bodies lay there in the heat, attracting swarms of flies. There were also movements from some of the wounded who were obviously in a bad way, desperate for medical attention and water.

Then something really surprising happened. A Red Cross flag was being waved by the Germans in the trench some hundred yards or so in front of them. At first, they were not sure what it meant, but Thomas realised that they were offering a cease fire so that the wounded out in No Man's Land could be collected. He told Sergeant Richards to raise a rifle in the air with a white handkerchief on it and instructed his men not to fire while the Germans and the British collected the wounded.

'Send a message to the artillery to cease fire until further instructed,' Thomas said.

Sergeant Richards went and collected as many stretcher-bearers as he could find and along with anyone who could walk, they went out to do what they could. There were far more wounded British than there were Germans, so Thomas kept an eye on the enemy trench just in case they finished their work first and decided to end the truce. He did notice one German stretcher going back loaded with a Vickers machine gun and some carrying wounded British soldiers who would become prisoners of war. Still, this gesture had undoubtedly saved many a life and as such, Thomas raised his hand as a gesture of thanks when it was obvious that the collection was complete.

They had brought out over seventy wounded men, some of whom wouldn't make it, but many more would live to fight another day. Thomas had sent a message to 'D' Company to find out if Richard was OK and was delighted to hear that he was. Apart from the temporary truce, this was the only good news on a miserable day for his regiment. Not one member of Thomas' Company had reached the German wire, let alone the trench.

The expected counter-attack at Hawthorn Ridge took place just after four o'clock in the afternoon. The German artillery zeroed in on the crater and within minutes both mortars were out of action. That left one machine gun and about forty rifles. Richard called for an immediate response from the British artillery, but it was slow in coming. Then they saw the hordes of grey uniforms charging round the rim towards them and he knew that there was no way they could be stopped. He had called for reinforcements, but knew it was a pointless exercise. The Lee Enfield was a great rifle and in the right hands it could produce rapid, accurate fire, but the Hun just kept coming. There was no more ammunition for the Vickers, so Richard shouted to Sergeant Lewis to fall back to the other side of the crater.

'Right, I want covering fire from number one platoon. The rest of you fall back to the far rim of the crater' he shouted, 'Number one platoon, fall back when the rest are in position. Right, go!'

It was a long way round the lip of the crater, and by the time they had reached the other side, they had lost four more men.

'Right, covering fire so number one platoon can get back. Give it all you've got!' shouted Sergeant Lewis. *I don't know what I'd have done without him*, thought Richard. *I hope to God he survives.*

Once they had all retreated to the edge of the crater, it was obvious that the enemy would slowly creep round, and by Richard's estimation, they were outnumbered at least six to one.

'Sergeant, fall back to the Sunken Lane. We've got to find some cover, or we'll be wiped out.'

'You heard what the officer said, run like hell and weave from side to side. Last one there buys the drinks tonight!'

Richard lay gasping against the bank, watching what was left of his Company fall into the lane. 'Sergeant, get the men on the top of the bank just in case Jerry decides to follow up his attack.'

Oddly, about twenty infantry from another battalion had come across when they saw Richard and his men falling back and had joined them in the relative cover of the lane provided.

'Which lot are you?' Richard asked.

'We're from the Bradford Pals. We were attacking towards Serre when we got separated and completely lost our way. Is it OK if we join you?'

'You're the most welcome sight today, lads. Stand to upon the bank for now,' said Sergeant Lewis. He was from Bradford and suddenly felt very much at home with the newcomers.

'Is there an NCO among you?' shouted Lewis.

'Yes, Sergeant, I'm Corporal Barnes.'

'Right, we need to know who we've got left between us, can you do a roll call? Can you get on with that, laddie?'

'Yes, of course Sergeant.'

The news from 'D' Company was grim. Out of the 160 that

had started out at 7.20 am that morning, there were just 45 in the trench, and some of those were carrying injuries.

'It's enough to make a grown man cry,' Sergeant Lewis said quietly to himself. And he did.

As evening came, men started drifting back under cover of darkness. Those who had been caught in No Man's Land and had taken cover in any shell hole they could find walked or crawled slowly back towards the lines they had left only twelve hours earlier. It seemed like days. Many were in no position to walk and were reliant on stretcher bearers going out time and time again to bring them in. Flares shot up frequently into the sky, every time forcing the men to flatten themselves against the ground. The Germans were not going to let this wholesale removal of wounded take place without trying to add them to the growing number of dead.

After a long, hot day, the evening was balmy, with dust and fumes from the battle clogging the air. Out there on the battlefield were 150,000 British, French and German soldiers - dead, alive, wounded or driven insane by the horror and noise of this wholesale destruction of part of the human race. It had been the most awful day.

Observers were trying to make sense of what had happened. Battalion reports were conflicting, signals were confusing – the only thing of any certainty was that the day had been a disaster. Very little ground had been taken and no matter how the Generals or the politicians tried to dress it up, the line had barely moved at all by the evening, with nearly 60,000 British and Commonwealth casualties, almost 20,000 of them dead.

The 29th Division of which Richard and Thomas were part had had a terrible time, suffering over 5000 casualties. The enemy still held both Thiepval and Beaumont Hamel, making it impossible to forward reinforcements and supplies, so in spite of the utmost gallantry and the huge loss of life, those that had made some progress had to withdraw during the night back to their own lines.

Wilkens sat down with his head in his hands. Normally the joker in the pack, he was shattered both emotionally and physically. Of his best mate, Adams, there was no news. Soldiers had been coming in all evening – some in groups, some individually. Military police were directing them back to their battalions. He just had to wait and hope. The remnants of 'D' and 'E' Companies returned at around midnight, having been ordered to withdraw. Hundreds of men with every wound imaginable were walking as best they could, helped by others when they couldn't. Some had gone totally mad. It was a pitiful sight. These proud, brave men, every one a volunteer, had been reduced to an ambling column, not really knowing where they were going. They were just glad to be going away from the carnage. A few ambulances went past, but with many more carts and wagons loaded up, the numbers seemed to go on and on. The 29th had suffered the worst casualties of the day, with the possible exception of the Newfoundland Regiment. Not something to be proud of.

Thomas and Richard greeted one another with tears welling up in their eyes. Comradeship was the most important part of the day and with so many officers becoming casualties, for both of them to have survived was something of a miracle. Thomas was limping from his leg wound, which needed dressing before it turned septic, so he hobbled off, promising to return at the earliest opportunity to share a drink with his friend. While he was away, Richard thought he would write to Simone, just to tell her that he had survived the first day and how much he loved and missed her. He had hoped to get a letter from her, but sending and receiving post was difficult in the current circumstances. Many a letter from the front in the next few weeks would be the last a soldier's loved ones would ever receive.

With the CO killed in action and many other officers killed or wounded, there needed to be a dramatic restructuring of the battalion. They had lost 538 men, including 23 officers, with a further eight officers lost during the week before July 1st. The casualties were far worse than they had suffered at Gallipoli. For the next 24 hours, the salvage of the dead, wounded and equipment from No Man's Land on both sides continued under heavy artillery fire.

The body of Private Tom Adams was brought in; he had been shot with a single bullet through the eye. Wilkens burst into tears when he heard the news.

We found the little captain at the head;
His men well aligned.
We touched his hand – stone cold – and he was dead,
And they, all dead behind,
Had never reached their goal, but they had died well;
They charged in line, and in line they fell.

The well-known rosy colours of his face
Were almost lost in grey.
We saw that, dying and in hopeless case,
For others' sake that day
He'd smothered all rebellious groans: in death
His fingers were tight clenched between his teeth.

For those who live uprightly and die true
Heaven has no bars or locks,
And serves all taste… or what's for him to do
Up there, but hunt the fox?
Angelic choirs? No, justice must provide
For one who rode straight and in hunting died.

So if Heaven had no Hunt before he came,
Why, it must find one now:
If any shirk and doubt they know the game,
There's one to teach them how:
And the whole host of Seraphim complete
Must jog in scarlet to his opening Meet.

Robert Graves

Excerpt from Haig's diary, July 1: 'Glass rose slightly in the night. A fine sunny morning with gentle breeze from the west and southwest. Some mist at first in the hollows. This was very favourable because it concealed the concentration of our troops. The bombardment was carried out as usual and there was no increase in artillery fire, but at 7.30 am (the hour fixed for the infantry to *advance) the artillery increased their range and the infantry followed the barrage. Reports up to 8 am most satisfactory. Our troops had everywhere crossed the enemy's trenches. By 9 am I heard that our troops had in many places reached the 1.20 line (i.e. the line fixed to be reached 1 hour and twenty minutes after the start). They were held up just south of Hawthorn Ridge but 31st Division is moving into Serre village. The Gommecourt attack was progressing well. 46th Division had the northern corner of Gommecourt Wood. 56th Division by 8 am were in the enemy's third line trench. At 9 am it was reported that out troops were held up north of Authuille Wood but on their left were entering Thiepval village. Hard fighting continued all day on front of Fourth Army. On a 16 mile front of attack varying fortune must be expected. It is difficult to summarise all that was reported.*

Many of these comments proved to be inaccurate or incorrect. The First Day of the Battle of the Somme was the worst day in the proud annals of the British Army. 57,000 casualties, 19,000 of them fatalities. Some gains were made in the southern sector and by the French; elsewhere, the British attacks had failed. This was just the first day – the Battle of the Somme was to continue for several more months. The following day, Sunday, July 2nd, Haig went to church.

CHAPTER TWENTY EIGHT

Counting the cost after the first few days

The newly appointed Commanding Officer of the 2nd Battalion, Lieutenant-Colonel William Ashurst, called his fellow officers together on July 4th. General Sir Henry Rawlinson had moved swiftly to appoint a replacement for Jimmy Strudwick, as there was a desperate need to restructure the Battalion. Such was the devastation on July 1st among the Fusiliers that in the short term they were to be withdrawn from the battlefield and moved to a quieter area to recover. This left Richard with a dilemma. He had left his staff job at GHQ to be with the front line troops and certainly did not want to be away from the men with whom he had been through so much, even though their numbers had been greatly reduced. He was also very keen to stay in the same battalion as Thomas.

'Good morning, gentlemen. I am sorry to be meeting you in such sad circumstances, but this proud regiment demands that we get ourselves back to an effective fighting unit as soon as possible. To that end we will need to move to a quieter sector and reorganise for a while. The combined experience of the officers who have served with the 2nd Battalion, along with their NCOs, will be crucial to the rebuilding that needs to be done. Captain Johnson, you will be promoted to Major and Waller and Holland, your promotions to the rank of Captain have been confirmed at long last. Sorry, it has taken so long to come through officially. Well done to you all. Seventeen new Second Lieutenants will be joining straight from training in England, so they will need all the help they can get from you experienced men who have been well and truly tested over the past two weeks. We will also have four Lieutenants transferred to us from other battalions. Any questions before I go into details of the revised Company personnel structure?'

Richard Waller stood up. 'Sir, I appreciate the confidence that has been shown in me with my promotion, but I would prefer to stay with an active battalion. I left a staff job at GHQ to be in the front line and would like to continue with a fighting unit.'

'I feel the same, sir,' said Thomas. 'All I want to do is get back fighting the Hun and the sooner the better. We have got a big job to do to make sure that the friends we lost on July 1st did not die in vain.'

'I sympathise with your predicament gentleman. I felt the same after losing so many colleagues at Ypres. I shall speak to Divisional HQ. As you know, there are 21 battalions of Fusiliers in France at present. Many of them have been in action on the Somme, and many have also suffered grievously. So there is a great shortage of experienced officers. Whilst I personally need you with me, I will ask about a transfer, probably to the 10th. I will get back to you.'

'Thank you, sir.'

Out of the gloom comes a ray of hope

My Dearest Richard, I was so, so pleased to get your letter. I thought that perhaps I had lost you forever, and then it arrived, talking about your love for me and I suddenly felt on top of the world. You mentioned our day at Le Touquet and it meant so much to me too because I have to tell you that we are having a baby after we made love on the sand dunes on that very day. So you must come home safely, because we have so much to look forward to. I have told Cécile and my father. Mother didn't take it very well, but father was so sweet and he can't wait to meet you. He is off again after three weeks' leave, so I doubt whether he will be home again before Christmas, unless the war is over by then. Who knows? Are you coming to see me soon? I need and love you so much. Cécile keeps asking after you. Please, please write to me again soon. Je t'adore. Your Simone.

Richard had to read the letter again and then again to take in what it said. He and Simone were having a baby. He was going to be a father! He couldn't believe it. They had worried from time to time about taking precautions, but it had seemed so unimportant when it came to it – almost as though it was something they both wanted but without saying so. That special day in Le Touquet had been in April, so the baby would be due around Christmas time. He wondered what his parents would say. They were both fairly strait-laced, so it would probably come as a complete shock. His mother, being ill, might be excited about the birth. It might give her something else to fight for. He decided that he would write at the first opportunity and tell them all about Simone.

The CO called Richard and Thomas to his HQ to tell them that their transfer had been agreed and they would join the 8th Battalion with immediate effect. They were delighted to hear that Sergeant Lewis had requested a similar transfer and was joining them in a couple of days. They were to proceed to Albert without delay, in order to get to know the other officers and key NCOs before they were sent back to the front line.

They were both delighted to be together and spent the evening at a cheap café in Albert, eating fried eggs and potatoes and drinking *vin blanc*. The wine was awful, but it didn't matter.

On the evening before they were due to move up, the town of Albert was heavily shelled and an ammunition dump containing 50,000 grenades detonated, causing some casualties in the Battalion. It was not what they wanted on the eve of the advance from Albert.

Excerpt from Haig's diary, July 4; 'I visited Sir H. Rawlinson soon after noon. I impressed upon him the importance of getting Trones Wood to cover the right flank, and Mametz Wood and Contalmaison to cover the left flank of attack against the Longueval front. I told him that Joffre would not attack Guillemont when we attacked Longueval, so it might be necessary for us to cover our own right flank. Concern had been raised about the shortage of heavy ammunition (especially 9.2) as so much had been used due to two extra days of bombardment. I visited two casualty clearing stations at Montigny, one under Major Thomas, the other under Colonel Macpherson. They were very pleased with my visit. The wounded were in wonderful good spirits.

The next challenge –
the Somme, second week
of July 1916

Richard and Thomas joined up with the 8th Battalion on July 6th and were immediately committed to two Companies which had lost many of their senior officers. Thomas took over 'A' Company and Richard 'D' Company. The 8th had been given the task of attacking Ovillers the following day, a village that had been heavily fortified and had become a German stronghold. Over the past week, it had become a difficult and costly nut to crack. But in order for the British to push forward, the village had to be taken so that the 8th Division could link up with the 32nd Division at Mouquet Farm behind Thiepval. They could then move on to the final objective, Pozières, a ridge-top village a kilometre away on the Albert-Bapaume Road. It was odd how these small French villages – sometimes no more than just a few houses - were taking on such a huge significance.

Two Fusilier Battalions, the 8th and the 9th, along with the 7th Royal Sussex, were given the task. Richard thought it strange how fate often played an important part in one's life. The Royal Sussex was his father's current Regiment. They were to launch their attack in the dark from assembly trenches in the middle of No Man's Land. Their objective was 250 yards away and they had been informed that an aggressive artillery barrage would start at 4.15 am and go on for four hours.

As soon as the British guns opened up, the Germans replied and rained shells of every description down on their trenches. Before they had even got out of the trench, the British had lost about twenty per cent of their men to shellfire. Richard began to wonder whether he had made the right decision to change Battalions, considering the news on casualties that he had just been given. He called Sergeant Lewis over and said, 'I know the men have got very heavy packs to carry, but it is imperative that they get across No Man's Land with all speed, because the German trench is the only place where there is any shelter.'

Above the noise of the artillery bombardment, Lewis shouted, 'Some of the men have been issued with twenty Mills bombs each, sir. That's in addition to everything else they have got to carry. Could we have every other man leave his bombs behind, and let those without get to the trench as quick as they can in the hope that we can take it and the others can follow up in the next wave.'

'I think that's a risk worth taking Sergeant, considering the distance. Organise it please, and well done. Let's hope the men will be grateful!'

At 8.26 am 'A' and 'D' Companies crawled over the parapet

and lay in the open, ready to advance. The two Russian saps which had been driven out into No Man's Land by the Tunnelling Company were manned with Stokes mortars, ready to give covering fire. So far, it was believed that they had not been spotted. The weather had not been good, but at least it was dry. The biggest danger as they lay there, apart from the high explosive shells, were the fumes from the gas shells which lay in hollows in the ground, a veritable death trap for anyone wounded falling into the hole.

Four minutes later, the first wave went forward and in a further five minutes, Richard blew his whistle and shouted, 'Advance!'

Their first obstacle was to get through their own wire, but they immediately got caught up in the first wave of Fusiliers, who were fully exposed to the enfilading German machine-gun fire which had begun its deadly chatter. After a matter of seconds, there were corpses lying everywhere. 'D' Company used the bodies of their comrades from the first wave as a springboard to leap forward over the wire and rush towards the enemy trench. It looked as though everyone from the first wave had been wiped out. There was not a single person left standing. With Richard in the lead, they got halfway across before the machine guns of the Prussian Guards located them. They traversed their fire, spraying them as if from a garden hose. Many went down and Richard saw Sergeant Lewis leap into a large shell hole where there were quite a few men sheltering behind the lip. The mortars were firing, but as yet had not hit either of the machine guns.

'Sergeant!' shouted Richard after hitting the deck, 'Get

those men to give some covering fire. Pour as much lead as you can at those machine guns.'

They opened up with everything they could and immediately silenced one of the guns. Private Roberts, who was the best shot in the Company, dropped two Prussian Guards who were about 100 yards away, standing on the parapet. 'Arrogant bastards,' he thought.

As soon as the second machine gun turned its attention to 'D' Company on their left, Richard indicated to Sergeant Lewis to get the men up and charge the last eighty yards to the first line of German trenches. The men rushed forward like madmen with something to prove. They had taken severe punishment from the Hun since July 1st and now it was time to dish some of their own out. Those who were carrying Mills bombs threw them as they ran and leapt into the trench. At the point of the bayonet, they drove the Prussians out.

Sergeant Lewis was seen taking on two or three men at a time in the confined space. He was an inspiration and Richard resolved to put him in for a gong. As the Prussians turned and ran towards their second line, the Fusiliers poured as much fire into them as they could. They had no compunction about shooting them in the back as they ran.

Two Vickers machine guns had followed up the advance and were now giving the Hun a taste of their own medicine. They were being cut to pieces, even at a range of about 150 yards. The Fusiliers sat up on the German first line parapet and cheered as they would at a Saturday afternoon football match. This was the first time in days that they had had something to cheer about.

Richard could hear serious fighting going on their left flank and he wondered how 'A' Company were getting on. He had heard that the Royal Sussex had made it to the first line and were following it up, but as yet there was no news of Thomas.

Just like Richard, Thomas was on the receiving end of a tremendous pasting from both the artillery and the German infantry. 'A' Company had been in the third wave of the attack on Richard's left, the remains of Ovillers church being their marker on the horizon. There was a sunken road running at a slight angle to their line of attack, and anyone who tried to cross the road was mown down by a machine gun positioned at the brow of the hill, which had an uninterrupted field of fire down the road.

'We must either go round the hill or get that bloody gun put out of action,' said Thomas. He yelled across to a young subaltern to get a message back to the mortar section to lay down a blanket barrage on the gun that was causing so much death and destruction. Taking with him Lieutenant Blair, the bombing officer and Lieutenant Walton, the signals officer, they went at a run until they came to the German wire. From here, unseen by the enemy, they could call down artillery fire on the first line trenches and also direct the mortars. As the wire was waist high, intact and about twenty feet in depth, Thomas ordered Walton to put down the fire on the wire first and then creep it towards the trenches. They would just have to keep their heads down for the next fifteen minutes or so until the artillery responded.

The German trench was only about 25 yards from where they were hidden and they could plainly see troops in grey uniforms throwing the potato-masher bombs at their men out in the middle of No Man's Land. To have fired at them with their pistols would have given their position away, so Thomas slid back to the first group of men that he could see and ordered three of them to follow him. They spread themselves out about 20 yards from where Thomas and the other two officers lay and opened fire at the grenade throwers.

The effect was immediate. The bombers disappeared, but the machine gunner spotted them and all hell broke loose. One of the riflemen was hit in the head and shoulder and Lieutenant Blair took a bullet through the neck from a sniper. Then the barrage started and thanks to Walton's accurate map references, the wire was blown apart in four places.

Careful not to charge too soon in case the barrage hadn't crept forward, Thomas waited to give the order until he saw the shells hitting the first line of trenches. He blew his whistle and yelled for those trapped in No Man's Land to run for all they were worth.

Excerpt from Haig's diary, July 7: 'After lunch, I visited HQ Fourth Army and saw General Rawlinson. I directed him to get Mametz Wood and push on towards Pozieres. At the same time Gough would connect between Ovillers and Baliff Wood and between Leipzig Redoubt and Ovillers; reconnaissance would be pushed forward towards Pozières with a view to attacking it in co-operation with III Corps. I then went to HQ Fifth Army and saw General Gough. I learnt that his troops had not yet captured the whole of Ovillers. His first objective is therefore to get that place and connect with III Corps. Lord Esher arrived from Paris. He says they are all very pleased with the work of the British Army. Our success has just made the difference of the French continuing the war, for another winter.'

Returning to the front

The time had come for Gilles to go back to his regiment. Although he was feeling so much better in himself - the fact that his hand was almost back to normal helped - he was apprehensive about returning. His visit home had not been an outstanding success. Cécile was disappointed in him, and it showed. Simone, on the other hand, had showered him with love and affection, and for that he was very grateful. He loved his daughter so much that there was no way he was going to be at crossed swords with her over the pregnancy. He hoped it would bring her nothing but happiness.

Cécile was another matter. He loved her with a passion, but that passion wouldn't manifest itself in the way she wanted, and she wasn't prepared to accept that it was something to do with the war. While he understood that she needed a man, he felt that she might have appreciated what he had been through in the past two years and shown some kind of sympathy towards his predicament. After all, his need for her was just as much as her need for him.

The 8th Regiment of Infantry had, by and large, ceased to exist as a fighting unit. Now a Colonel, Gilles had been transferred to Marshall Fayolle's 6th Army, which was scheduled to take part in the September offensive on the Somme alongside the British 5th Army. He just hoped that things would be better than they were during the retreat to the Marne and at Verdun. First, he had to report to barracks in Boulogne before heading down to Amiens.

His goodbye was a stilted affair. Simone was full of tears and had given her father a good luck charm – a very small toy bear that he had bought for her on her third birthday and had been with her ever since. He was deeply touched and promised to take good care of 'Tedi' as he was affectionately known. Cécile wished him well with a kiss on each cheek and a hug, but it lacked the warmth he would normally have expected, and this saddened him greatly. He walked to the railway station, wondering why the physical side of being in love was so important to his wife. He had shown her and told her how much she meant to him, but that was obviously not enough. He decided that a couple of drinks in his favourite bar before he caught the train might help the sadness he felt.

Back home, a nation waits

The papers were printing the grim news of the casualties and page upon page of men's names appeared. The county regimental system of the British Army meant that battalions were made up of men from individual cities or large towns, so the impact of a disaster such as what had just occurred on the Somme was catastrophic. Whole communities went into mourning, with everyone rushing out to buy a paper to see if there were any names they knew. Women were seen wailing in the streets when they realised the extent of the tragedy. Husbands, fathers, sons, brothers, cousins, schoolfriends, workmates, all gone – nobody was left untouched. All the women wore black and the men wore dark suits or black armbands. Cities, towns and villages up and down the country were in a state of shock. A terrible event had happened, and it would take a long, long time for them to recover.

Who knows the thoughts of mothers who wait,
Whether in grandeur, or lowly state;

Who knows the sacrifice of those who give,
Their all, their sons, that we might live.

Rhymes from a Lost Battalion Doughboy
L.C. McCollum

In the town of Crawley, there was concern over the fate of the 7th Battalion Royal Sussex Regiment. As part of the 74th Brigade, their job was to attack in a line towards Pozières and on the day, it was one of the few success stories. They had carried the German front line and with the 8th and 9th Fusiliers, had consolidated the position.

But it was at a heavy price. Richard's father read the newspaper with dread. They knew from his letter that he had gone to the front and that the 2nd Battalion Royal Fusiliers were engaged in the battle somewhere, although where exactly he knew not. He was unaware that Richard was now with the 8th Battalion. He studied the lists assiduously but could find no mention of his son, although there were many names listed from the Fusiliers. He breathed a sigh of relief and went to tell his wife the news.

CHAPTER THIRTY THREE

At Haig's headquarters, a few days after July 1st

Haig received a visit from the French Generals Joffre and Foch. They wanted to discuss 'future arrangements' between the Allies and in particular, to point out how important it was in their view that Thiepval was taken at the earliest opportunity. Haig explained that it might help the progress of the battle if the French could attack Guillemont at the same time, and at this point General Joffre lost control of himself. He shouted that it was not something that he could approve of and that the British should attack Thiepval, Pozières and Ovillers without delay. Relations were anything but harmonious.

South of England and France, 1417-1419

The two Knights of the Realm met at The Hollands to discuss the forthcoming campaign. Henry V's brother, John of Lancaster, had replied to their letter to say that they would be warmly welcomed on the adventure and that Henry had sent a personal message to thank them for their support. At the end of the message, he stated that 'every Lord, Knight, Esquire and valet and all others must provide themselves with victuals for three months.'

'Well, that makes it perfectly clear who is funding this, as if we didn't know!' said Sir John. 'Have you worked out what this is likely to cost?'

'I estimated that we would be away for six months and Henry states that we have to pay for the first three months,' replied Sir Richard Waller. 'I would think that we may as well work on the basis that we will be funding the whole campaign. The mounted scouts, archers – some of which will need to be mounted - and men-at-arms will cost six pence a day. Farriers and cooks are five pence a day. Boy runners are three pence a day. Ten thousand arrows cost 100 nobles and we will probably need at least thirty thousand, even taking into account ones that can be reused. Both long-range and armour piercing arrows will be needed. Wine, salted beef, pork, herrings, corn, peas and beans and the horses and carts to carry the victuals will cost around fifteen hundred nobles. We can obtain supplies in France as we travel along. So for six months, I estimate that this adventure is going to cost around three and a half thousand nobles.'

Slightly shocked by the figure, Sir John said, 'The ransoms from my thirteen prisoners at Agincourt came to two thousand seven hundred nobles, some of which is still owed to me, and I had to pay the King a bond of two hundred nobles. So unless we can claim some additional booty, we will not make a fortune out of it. Although it has to be said that the King was generous with the grants of lands after the battle.'

'I too am still out of pocket from Agincourt,' said Sir Richard, 'and the King wanted his bond even though the ransom for the Duke has not yet been paid. So as you say, we must get what we can out of this campaign, or I could end up losing the manor house!'

They had agreed to gather at Lengthington Green one autumn morning in 1417. There was an air of considerable excitement on the village green. A couple of fires were burning, with huge urns suspended over the flames, offering warming food to those men-at-arms who were about to set off. Heraldic banners from the Waller and Holland families were blowing in the breeze, giving the gathering the feel of a country fair. Horses tethered to carts were grazing on the lush grass and children were running around playing with sticks and hoops.

There were around 120 men and boys in the party. Wives and mothers were standing anxiously ready to wish their loved ones a safe return, hoping that pouches full of silver and gold would accompany them home. It was going to be tough for them whilst the men were away.

'Men, listen up!' shouted Sir John. 'Fill your bellies while you can, as we have a three-day march to Southampton from where we will depart for France. The King has ordered that village bakers and brewers on our journey are to provide us with refreshments as we pass. Ladies, we will ensure that your men are looked after whilst they are fighting for the honour of the King. Now say your goodbyes, as we shall shortly be on our way. God bless you all!'

The long column wound its way from Kent across the border into Sussex and across the great Forest of Anderida. Much of the wood and iron for the archers' bows and arrows came from this forest, so the archers themselves felt at home walking through it. There was much chatter and laughter. Let the men enjoy these moments, Richard thought. The journey will not always be as happy as this.

The Solent came into view on the third day as they approached from the South Downs. Henry had supplied a fleet of 30 ships and there were many seconded merchantmen lying sedately at anchor in the inlet - an impressive sight indeed. The Sheriffs of Hampshire, Kent, Wiltshire and Oxfordshire had been ordered to purchase, at the expense of the King, 200 cattle from within their counties and bring them to the harbourside. When Richard saw these creatures, he wished he had been told in advance, as this could have saved them purchasing their own. Still, it virtually guaranteed that the men would be well fed for their troubles.

Sailing across the English Channel to Harfleur, Thomas was reminded of the time when he had accompanied Henry on his first voyage. It had turned out well and he was hopeful of a repeat performance. Richard came up and stood by the rail, watching the coastline of France hove into view. They had said Normandy was a beautiful and very rich part of France – he hoped it was true.

Henry's conquest of Normandy was rapid, mainly due to the fact that France had lost so many of its professional military officers at Agincourt. So far, John and Richard had not taken any prisoners but had ransacked a huge château near Lillebonne and collected some fine gold and silverware. It was a good start. Loading their cart with the booty, they were heading next to Rouen, which Henry considered a crucial city to capture, given that it had a population of over 70,000 and a wealth of valuable assets contained within its walls. It was also strategically placed on the route to Paris.

After Agincourt, Rouen had been significantly fortified and reinforced, and capturing it would, without doubt, be a very different proposition to the open land battle that had been fought in 1415. Given the lack of manpower on the English side, it was going to be impossible to breach the walls and storm this great city, so Henry and his military advisors decided on a policy of 'surround and starve'.

Whilst this was arguably a very sensible tactic, John and Richard realised that their budget for the campaign would very soon be exceeded if this policy endured for many more months. They talked it through and decided to approach John of Lancaster to explain their difficulty, in the hope of a extracting a promise of some financial help.

'Good day, your Grace,' said Richard. 'We are pleased that the campaign is proceeding well, but we have the difficulty that we will soon run out of money for our army. We budgeted on the expectation, following your guidance, of a six-month campaign which has cost us over £1000 so far. We are now in our ninth month. With the decision to encircle Rouen and starve the population into submission, we envisage this going on for many more months. May we request some assistance from the King in order that we can continue our support? So far, we have accrued nothing more than a few gold and silver trinkets.'

'Oh, come now my dear fellows,' John of Lancaster said, 'I happen to know that your haul was considerable, but I accept that soldiers have to be paid and you can't pay them in gold and silver. May I suggest that we value what you have and that the King buys the trinkets, as you call them, from you? That way, you can keep your army intact, still be here when the city falls and you will be guaranteed vast wealth. How does that sound?'

They looked at one another, slightly suspicious that the valuation might fall well below the real worth of their haul.

'I can tell what you're thinking,' John of Lancaster said. 'As you both have been great supporters of the King's endeavours to claim back what is rightfully ours in France, we will draw up an agreement whereby the King will give you £1000 now against any goods that you may acquire on the campaign, and the valuation can be carried out when we return to England. And I won't tell the King that you had doubts about the accuracy of his valuation!'

They both realised the significance of this last statement, but they also thought it was a fair offer. 'We are very pleased to accept and thank you for your kind consideration' said Richard. With that, they bowed and retreated from the royal tent.

The siege carried on for seven months. By December of 1418, the people of Rouen were eating cats, dogs, horsemeat and even rats. 12,000 of the poor were kicked out of the city in an effort to save food, but Henry would not allow them past the siege line. They were forced to live in the ditch under the walls which had been dug to protect the city, where they died in their thousands.

A month later the city finally surrendered. The rich pickings promised by John of Lancaster materialised and both Sir John Holland and Sir Richard Waller, and their army, became wealthy – again. They did well to keep the faith with John of Lancaster, as he would later become Regent of France in the name of Henry V's son Henry VI, then only a few months old.

More wealth would come their way when Henry moved on to Paris. Although they had been away for 18 months, much of the time bored almost to death under the walls of Rouen, Sirs Richard and John headed for home, having accomplished their mission. Of their army, they had lost seven archers to illness and two from wounds suffered from canon fire at Rouen.

Visits to the men's families to impart the bad news, pay their respects and to give them monies due, were carried out immediately by both men when they arrived back in Kent.

Another bloodbath for the Fusiliers

Thomas Holland set off towards the first line of German trenches on the outskirts of Ovillers with Lieutenant Walton hard on his heels, keeping as close to the creeping barrage as possible. His leg was troubling him following the wound he had received on July 1st and he could see through his trousers that it had started to bleed again. He passed one shell hole with five Fusiliers in it, all wounded. He shouted at them to follow, but there was no response. The Company Sergeant Major, Joe Collins, was standing fully exposed to the withering machine gun fire and urging the men forward. 'Come on, you lot. We're nearly there! Get stuck in!' he was shouting.

There had been some success in quelling the incoming fire, but men were still dropping like flies. Thomas saw Captain Childs go down, hit in the head and the chest, and he began to realise that there were very few officers still moving forward. He leapt into the German trench not knowing what to expect, except that he instantly realised he was out of the terrible fire that was raking No Man's Land. He held his pistol ready to shoot anyone he came across in the trench, but there was no one other than fellow Fusiliers who were pouring in.

'Where the hell have the Huns gone?' he shouted to the man next to him. Then he realised that apart from the machine gunners, the Germans had retreated down into the dugouts when the artillery and mortar barrage had started and because it had only just lifted as it crept forward, they were still down there.

'Here, give me a couple of Mills bombs,' he yelled. Lobbing them down the entrance, he shouted, 'Take cover!'

Shielding himself from the explosion by pressing himself against the parapet, he waited for the 'crump' from deep inside. 'Corporal, pour fire down into there in case any have survived, and then follow me,' he called.

Thomas could hear the Germans further along the trench and stick bombs started to be hurled in their direction. 'Corporal, get your men to have two Mills bombs ready each, and as soon as we round this corner, let 'em have it!'

He set off round the slight bend in the trench, stooping low, only to be hit hard in the shoulder by a bullet. He fell backwards, groaning in pain as waves of nausea swept over him. He could feel the blood pouring over his chest as the Sergeant Major propped him up on the side of the trench. 'Don't worry sir, we'll get some help for you' said the Sergeant Major. Just stay put.' With that Thomas passed out.

The next thing Thomas remembered was being carried on a stretcher at the run across No Man's Land back the way he had come earlier. His first thought was of relief that someone had found him and that he wasn't going to be left out in the open, in some cases for days, as so many others had been on July 1st. The pain was indescribable and he hadn't a clue whether anyone had given him anything to relieve the agony he was feeling. He asked the stretcher-bearer if they had taken the first line. He replied that they had and that they were moving on towards Ovillers itself.

Thomas knew his war was over for the time being and he suddenly had an immense feeling of loneliness. He wanted to know that Richard was OK, but suddenly everything glazed over and he passed out again.

Then someone was shaking him gently by his good arm. He was lying out in the open in a field with a long line of other wounded. A brown paper label, getting bloody from his wound and blowing in the breeze, had been attached to his tunic.

'We'll have you in the tent shortly, sir. You've been given something for the pain and we've just about managed to stop the bleeding. Just lie as still as you can.'

Richard was exhausted. If he thought July 1st was bad, then this was worse. The casualties had been awful. Those damned machine guns had ripped them apart. Why oh why hadn't the artillery knocked them out?

When orders came through for them to be relieved, the men had to walk some way to find the transport that was waiting for them. After negotiating the long line of trenches heading back, the first thing Richard saw was the Regimental Sergeant Major standing in the middle of the road, waiting for the Fusiliers to return. A Corporal was the first to appear.

'Fall out the 8th Battalion!' the RSM shouted.

'I'm the only one left,' the Corporal replied.

'You can't be. You can't be!' said the RSM.

Richard walked past and the RSM saluted and said, 'That was bad, sir.'

'Yes, Sergeant, about as bad as it gets.' They came in slowly in ones and twos.

After a couple of hours, once the trickle of the returning men had stopped, they moved back to Albert. Sergeant Lewis had been hit in both legs as he reached the trench and had fallen in headfirst. He was in a bad way. The Company would miss him. It seemed 'A' Company had taken the first line trench, but casualties had been heavy. Someone had said they thought Captain Holland was injured, but they knew no more than that. As soon as Richard got back to HQ, he would go and find out what had happened to his friend.

He considered how lucky he had been. In two major engagements, where the rate of dead and wounded had been as high as 80%, he had come through. He looked up to the sky and thanked the Almighty, praying that Thomas would be OK.

Finding an individual among the wounded was a challenge in itself. He found the registration area and was told that Thomas was in tent 2B. That part was easy. Finding tent 2B was the problem. The military brain had not yet thought to put 2B before 2C and after 2A. He eventually found it next to 4L. Thomas was lying flat on his back with his eyes shut. When Richard approached he turned his head and smiled.

'Hello, I won't ask you how are you because everyone

probably says that. Just that it's good to see you again and I'm very relieved that you are still with us, even though you took a nasty one.'

Thomas slowly raised his good arm to shake him by the hand, and suddenly became very emotional. Once he had recovered his equilibrium, but with his voice still choked, he said, 'Christ, that was awful. Do you know there wasn't one officer left unwounded in either of our companies except for you. And Captain Skye, the adjutant, completely disappeared. There is no trace of him whatsoever. I still find that so hard to come to terms with.'

Not wishing to trouble his friend any further, Richard tried to change the subject by asking what the damage to the shoulder was.

'It was a rifle bullet, which I suppose was better than a machine gun round. I was crouching forward at the time, so the bullet went in almost on the top of the shoulder and out the back and hit the shoulder blade as it went. They are sending me to a hospital on the coast, but they think I may have to go back to England for recovery and physiotherapy. Oddly enough, you know that scratch I got on the leg on July 1st? That's become more painful than the shoulder. It's infected. So that's got to be sorted out as well.'

'You heard Lewis got hit?' Richard asked. 'Well, he took machine gun bullets in both legs. He has already had one taken off and it looks as though he'll lose the other. He was such an inspiration to the men that I've put him in for a Distinguished Conduct Medal. Can you believe that the Colonel has put me in for a Military Cross?'

'Well done Richard, you thoroughly deserve it.'

Out of 800 men of the 8th Battalion that went into action attacking Ovillers, 180 came out. And the village was still not taken.

Thomas was due to be seen by the doctor the next day and had been told that they could do nothing more for him at this time. He would be sent to Le Tréport and then probably back to a hospital in southern England before undergoing further treatment and physiotherapy. They were desperate for his bed at the dressing station, so he knew he would probably be moved within hours. He needed to see Richard before he went. He knew he was still in Albert, where the 8th Battalion was being brought up to strength, and he asked the orderly if a message could be urgently got to him before he left. The orderly promised to do what he could.

As the day wore on, Thomas was getting fretful that Richard had not been to see him. An orderly came by late in the afternoon, to tell him that he was leaving early the following morning. There was an ambulance train departing from Albert station heading for the coast and he would be on it.

'Can you do me another favour please?' Thomas asked.

'I'll try,' said the orderly, 'but we are a bit busy at the moment.'

'Yes, I know, but that letter you took was to my best pal and it looks as if he won't be able to make it here before I leave. If I write a note for him, can you please see that it gets to his Battalion for me? I would be very grateful. We have been through an awful lot together.'

'Sure I will, sir.'

With that, Thomas felt a bit easier in his mind. He set about writing Richard a note.

My dear friend. It looks as though I am going to be away for a while, so I just wanted to say a few things before I set off. The past few weeks have been a real baptism of fire for both of us. I really don't think I could have handled it without your friendship. I know that moving battalions was something we both chose to do, but if I am honest, I did so because I wanted us to stay together, rather than the possibility of us leaving this earth at different times and from different places. Please take care of yourself while I am away and should I convalesce anywhere close to where your mother and father live, I will try and say hello. I have just got to make sure when I come back that I get posted to your battalion! God bless. Your best pal, Thomas.

In his reports to the Ministers back home on the first few days of the battle of the Somme, Sir Douglas Haig, after consulting with General Sir Henry Rawlinson, gave the view that there had been some successes and a few reversals. There was no mention of casualties in his report, but the Adjutant General said that 'with casualties from the first day at around 40,000, this cannot be considered severe in view of the numbers engaged and the length of front attacked.'

'To sum up the first five days,' Haig said, 'on a front of over six miles from the Briqueterie to La Boiselle, our troops had swept over the whole of the enemy's first and strongest system of defence, which he had done his utmost to render impregnable. They had driven him back over a distance of more than a mile, and had carried four elaborately fortified villages.'

Reading the report, if you were a soldier who had been engaged in the grim fighting, particularly at Ovillers, where the report stated that 'the enemy had for the time being resisted our attack,' you might have taken exception to this comment when the casualties had been so appalling.

Excerpt from Haig's diary, letter to Lady Haig, July 8: 'The troops are fighting well and the battle is developing slowly but steadily in our favour. In another fortnight, with Divine Help, I hope that some decisive results may be obtained.

Excerpt from Haig's diary, July 11: ' I am not quite satisfied with Rawlinson's plan of attack… his proposal to attack at dawn over an open plateau, for a distance of 1000 yards, after forming up two divisions in mass, in the dark, appears to be a manoeuvre which one cannot do successfully…so I gave him my opinion that it was unsound, and that he would change it, as I had suggested, making the main attack against the line Contalmaison Villa-Bazentin le Grand Wood from Mametz Wood, while threatening from the rest of our front, namely from Ovillers to Trones Wood. At around 3pm Rawlinson still considered his plan the best. I considered that the experience of war, as well as the teachings of peace, are against the use of large masses in night operations.

Montreuil – July 1916

Ever since Gilles had left to return to the front, Cécile had been in an awful state. She was full of remorse for the way she had treated her husband. She kept telling herself that she did not know why she had acted as she did, but in her heart of hearts she knew very well. Her daughter was pregnant by the one man she had wanted while Gilles had been away, and she was jealous. She was also jealous of the way Gilles take taken the news of the baby, almost in a state of happiness. It was as if he had become closer to his daughter than to his wife. She had not really understood his inability to perform in bed, assuming that as soon as he came home, it would be the first thing he would want. So Cécile had taken it personally when it appeared to be the last thing on his mind.

A doctor she had spoken to after Gilles had returned to the front had told her that it was not uncommon for this to happen during times of great stress, such as Gilles was experiencing on his return from Verdun. He also said that it was very distressing for the man, so much so that occasionally men had been known to take their own lives as a result. The pressure to perform had made the whole situation a hundred times worse.

When Simone arrived home, her mother was sitting on the floor in floods of tears.

'Mother! What is the matter?'

'Oh, Simone, I have treated your father so badly. When he came home, I wanted him so much, you know what I mean, and because he was so ill, he couldn't make love to me. As I have since found out from talking to a doctor, it was probably what he needed as badly as I did. I turned against him for it, and he left here an unhappy man. And I love and miss him so much. I don't know what to do.'

Simone and her mother had not been particularly close in recent weeks, since Gilles' latest visit, but now Simone felt a wave of sympathy for her mother. At first, she didn't realise what her mother was talking about, but then it dawned on her. But she knew that her father adored Cécile and that it could only be something in his mind that was preventing him from expressing his love for his wife. It was also perfectly natural that her mother needed fulfilment, just as she did. Throughout France, millions of women were experiencing the same problem. How they dealt with it was entirely up to their individual conscience. Having the man she loved at home for a period of time had re-awakened Cécile's desires and passions. After all, Simone had always wanted to take Richard to bed, so why should her mother not have the same feelings about Gilles?

'What you must do straight away is to write to him telling him all of your feelings, how much you love and miss him and that you are so sorry for being selfish and not understanding the problems he was having,' said Simone. 'Do that now and we will go to the post together.'

'Yes, you are right. I will do it now, I will tell him everything.'

At the same time as Cécile was composing her letter to Gilles, Richard had some free time at the end of the day in Albert, and had decided he must write to Simone. Apart from the letter he had written on the eve of the battle, he had not corresponded with her since receiving the letter about the baby, and now that the Battalion had been relieved and Thomas had left for England, he was able to think a lot more clearly about things. He must also write to his parents. There had been a message from GHQ raising the possibility of compassionate leave because of his mother's illness, but they had said that it was a decision that he had to make, and given the nature of what was happening at the front at the present time, there would be no pressure put on him to leave his comrades at this difficult time. The message was quite clear.

Back to the front

Richard was billeted with seven other officers in an old four-storey house close to the market square. Albert was constantly on the receiving end of artillery shells from the German guns, which were stationed only a couple of miles away, so this could not be described as a safe place of rest, but nonetheless the town was pleasant and there were a few places to eat and drink.

He found a quiet corner in the sitting room of the house; the only other person there was a Major from the Royal Artillery, who was sitting on a settee smoking his pipe and reading an old newspaper. He sat down at a desk to compose a letter to Simone.

My darling Simone

Firstly I must say that I am sorry not to have written earlier, but as you may have gathered, we have been heavily involved in the fighting. I have come through it unscathed and we are now out of the front line for a short while. My best friend, Thomas, however, took a bullet in the shoulder and has been sent home to England to recover. At least he is safe.

And now to your wonderful news! I was in a state of some shock when I read your letter and had to read it again and again to take it all in. What was really wonderful was that it was conceived at Le Touquet on that very special day we spent together, where I felt that we found true happiness. Are you sure it happened there? It has given me so much to think about and so much to look forward to. Whilst I now worry more about my responsibilities, I am pleased that I joined my regiment in the front line. They have had such a terrible time that had I not been a part of it, I would have regretted it for the rest of my days. So thank you for not making a big issue of it. I am sorry that your mother is not pleased about the pregnancy, but hopefully she will feel better about it as time goes on.

Do you know when the baby is due? What do you think it will be, a boy or a girl? Please write and tell me. You must take care of yourself and not let that matron give you too much to do. Does she know yet? You will have to tell her soon presumably as there will be a little (or not so little!) bump under your uniform!

I adore you too my darling and consider myself to be the luckiest chap in the world to have fallen in love with you. I will write as often as I can. I send you every ounce of my love.

Yours for ever, Richard.

He put his pen down and wondered for a moment where they would live when the baby was born - France or England? A lot would depend on the outcome of the war.

The time had come for Richard to move back up to the front. It was early August and they were heading towards Pozières.

When he had been with the 8th Battalion attacking Ovillers, he could see the church on the skyline at Pozières and suddenly the memories of that terrible day came flooding back to him. The village of Ovillers had only finally been taken after a week of constant battering against a determined and well dug-in enemy. The 10th Battalion had been sent up to support the 13th Rifle Brigade, but they had been badly held up and mauled by the machine guns again. At one point, they had lain out in the open in an advanced position for two days under heavy shell-fire, waiting for further orders. There was nothing worse than just lying there taking casualties. They would much rather have been racing forward doing something. Still orders were orders.

When Richard arrived back with the 8th, he was warmly greeted by the new Commanding Officer, Lieutenant Colonel Justin Parker, who had replaced William Ashurst.

'I am very pleased to see you, Waller' he said. 'We are desperately short of experienced officers. I understand you have been in action close to here recently?'

'Yes, sir, I was with this Battalion at Hawthorn Ridge and at the attack on Ovillers.' He thought he better not mention what he thought of the carnage on both those occasions.

'Terrible days for the regiment, Waller. Just terrible. I lost some good friends there. Still, we've got a job to do here. You'll be leading 'B' Company. Lieutenants Ward and Palmer will be with you and there are some good platoon leaders there. Our first objective is Fourth Avenue, a trench north-west of Pozières on the Ridge. Good luck Waller. As an old hand with the Fusiliers, I knew your father. Is he well?'

'I believe so, sir, but my mother has been ill for a while and he has had to curtail his duties as a Recruitment Officer in Sussex to look after her.'

'I am sorry to hear that. Please pass on my best wishes to them both when you are next in contact.'

'Thank you, sir, I will.' He seemed a good sort, Richard thought.

A very tough looking RSM came up to him and standing smartly to attention, introduced himself.

'Good morning, sir, I am RSM Williams and will be with you in 'B' Company. I know you had a rough time recently with the 8th, but I thought you would like to know that Ron Lewis passed away at the hospital a couple of weeks ago. I don't know whether you were aware that he had one leg amputated, but then the other had to come off and he got a serious infection and that was it. He was a good mate of mine you see, and he spoke very highly of the way you looked after your men, sir. I just thought you would like to know that.'

Richard looked him straight in the eyes and could see the pain he felt inside. His eyes were moist with grief and understandably so. He knew only too well how he felt, because the bond that forms when you are in situations like this was like no other. You would do anything for your friends without giving it a second thought. It was how he felt about Thomas.

'You don't know how much I appreciate you telling me that, Sergeant Major. Lewis was a giant of a man and a huge inspiration to his men. They would have followed him anywhere, such was the trust they had in him. The regiment will miss him greatly.'

'And so will I, sir. I know you have recommended him for a DCM and if it comes off, he would have been tickled pink about that. And for that I thank you.'

'No thanks are needed Sergeant. It was the least he deserved.'

With that, the RSM did an immaculate parade ground about turn and went back to his Company.

The following morning, they moved forward to link up with the 6th Buffs. It was to be a night attack commencing at 11 pm. The Australians, who had been repulsed several times and suffered great losses at Pozières, were on their left. They had taken some stick, quite unfairly, from Haig over their failures. He accused them of being over-confident – their typical Aussie brashness was obviously grating with him.

The preliminary barrage started two hours before the off and at 11.15 pm when the barrage had lifted, 'A' and 'B' Companies of the 8th Battalion walked slowly for the first 200 yards and then lay out in the cover of darkness about halfway towards the German trench. Richard thought how different this was to Hawthorn and Ovillers. There was no wire to negotiate and after a five-minute mortar barrage, they moved forward until they were 50 yards from the German trench and then charged. RSM Williams was up first with Richard and Lieutenant Ward alongside him. Ward went down just short of the trench and when Richard and Williams leapt in they found it full of Germans. They had been sheltering from the barrage and had been taken completely by surprise.

'Watch out, Sergeant Major, these guys are ready for a fight!' shouted Richard.

They both ducked low and opened fire at the first group, three of whom fell instantly. Williams then shouted at the troops that had come in behind him to throw their Mills bombs further along the trench. There were four or five 'crumps' and the Germans started raising their hands in surrender. Some were seen running away and they received a heavy volley of fire before they disappeared into the dark. Richard went forward with his pistol at the ready, followed by Williams and about 20 troops from his Company to round up the prisoners. They took 92 in all, including two officers, one wearing the Iron Cross.

'Well done, men! A good night's work,' said Richard.

The Buffs, who had attacked with them, had also managed to secure a foothold in the next trench, Fifth Avenue. Although the enemy had counter-attacked twice, they were beaten off. A little later, while 'B' Company were consolidating their position, another company was seen charging the captured trench on the right flank. Richard suddenly realised that these were the Royal Sussex who had lost their way in the dark. Only by good fortune was a disaster averted.

When Richard starting walking back with the RSM for roll call, he realised that his foot was causing him pain.

'Just a second, Sergeant, I think I have got something in my boot' he said. He undid his laces and tried to get the boot off but it was too painful, and there was blood pouring out.

'I think I have been hit in the foot, Sergeant. I didn't know anything about it until just now. It must have happened as we charged the trench.'

'Here, sir, lean on me. We'll get you back to the assembly point and you can get off to the dressing station.'

'I want to stay until the roll has been called, Sergeant,' replied Richard.

Compared to previous operations, this attack hadn't been anywhere near as costly as the others, but they still lost two Lieutenants killed, one of them Ward, one wounded and about 150 other casualties - one of which was now Richard.

When they cut his boot off, they found that a bullet had gone straight through the foot and out the other side, fortunately without causing too much damage. They cleaned the wound and dressed it, and having almost stopped the bleeding by keeping his leg up in the air, moved him out to a recovery tent. 'Most people would give a lot of money for a wound like that,' the doctor said with a smile. 'I would be a happy man if all I had to deal with were wounds such as yours. You should be fine, but it will be painful to walk on for a while. You must keep the leg and foot still for a week or so and make sure it doesn't get infected. Then you can start walking gently, but you must give the wound time to heal properly.'

'Thanks, Doc, I will.'

Later that day his CO, Colonel Parker came to see him.

'Glad to see you're OK, Waller' he said. 'Not too painful I hope?'

'Not too bad, sir, I didn't even know that it had happened at the time, but it's been a bit more painful since.'

'Well, the important thing is to let it mend properly and come back when you think you're OK. If I know you from your records, you won't want to be away for too long!'

'It might be a good opportunity to take a bit of leave once I am mobile if that's all right, sir? When I was at GHQ, I met a lovely girl and would like to spend a few days with her and her family if that is OK.'

'I'll organise the pass when I get back for when you're ready. I'll make it a ten-day pass and that will give you a week there to relax a bit. You've been hard pushed since just before July 1ˢᵗ and a bit of R&R would do you good. Your contribution to the success of the attack on Fourth Avenue has been duly noted in the records by the way and you may get a 'Mentioned in Despatches'. Also, your Military Cross has come through. You should be very proud. Congratulations!'

Shortly after, RSM John Williams walked in with an orange in his hand. Richard still had a smile on his face.

'Like gold dust these are, sir, but I thought you could probably use it' he said.

'That's very kind of you, Williams. I won't ask where you got it from!' he said grinning.

'No, don't sir! Glad to see you're OK. The attack went well and I was very pleased to hear about your MC. I am also pleased to tell you that Lewis got his DCM, albeit posthumously. The CO wanted me to tell you, which I thought was very nice of him.'

'Yes, that was. And I am very pleased. I didn't know if he was married or not, but whilst the pain of losing a husband must be a terrible thing to bear, the fact that he won a medal for something that was so dear to him, his regiment, I hope will mean a lot to his family in the difficult years ahead.'

'That's a nice thought, sir, and yes he was married. I shall go and see his widow when I am next home on leave. I have already written to her.'

'That was good of you, Sergeant.' He could see the Sergeant struggling to control his emotions. Time to change the subject. 'Do you know what is happening to the 8th, Sergeant?'

'No news yet, sir. The 9th, who were with us on the attack at Fourth Avenue, stayed to fight on with the Royal Sussex and the Aussies at Fifth Avenue. And I suppose we must wait for the outcome there before they decide where to send us next,'

'The CO has given me a ten-day pass for a bit of leave when this foot has healed up,' said Richard. 'I've got a girlfriend in Montreuil who I met when I was at GHQ. I haven't seen her for a while, so it will be good for us to spend some time together.'

'I didn't know you were at GHQ, sir. Why on earth did you leave there for this hell-hole?'

'Ah well, Sergeant, that's a long story.'

The front line revisited,
over ninety years on

On a gloriously sunny spring day, a group of English schoolchildren left their hotel in Albert to head towards the battlefields. As part of their history studies, this group of year elevens had already visited Arras and were now heading towards Beaumont Hamel, which had been in the front line on July 1st, 1916.

'Listen up all of you,' said Tim Hurt, the history teacher. 'We shall be arriving at the Newfoundland Memorial Park at Beaumont Hamel shortly. This is a huge site, and not just a cemetery. It contains segments of the original trenches – both British and German - as well as monuments of historical importance, landmarks where vicious fighting took place, a visitor centre and three cemeteries. You are strongly advised not to wander away from the designated paths, as there is still undiscovered ordnance here. That means bombs!'

'Why is it called Newfoundland Park, sir, that's in Canada isn't it?' asked one of the pupils.

'Good question, Stuart. The eighty acres of land which makes up the Memorial Park, was purchased after the war from the French Government by the regimental chaplain of the 1st Battalion of the Royal Newfoundland Regiment, which was almost annihilated on July 1st. Of the 780 men who went over the top, 684 became casualties - that's almost 90% - and one third of those were fatal. This was the second highest fatality rate of any battalion on the first day of the Somme offensive. So this land will stay, in perpetuity, as a memorial to these brave men forever. If you consider for a moment the size of a country like Newfoundland, which had at that time a population of 200,000, casualties of this level, on just one day, were absolutely horrendous. Every year, children just like you come over from Canada as part of their studies, to work in the visitor centre. That's how much this place means to these people from thousands of miles away.

'When we've finished our tour here, we'll visit the Thiepval Memorial to the Missing on the Somme, which you will be able to see on the skyline from the Newfoundland Park. That memorial commemorates almost 73,000 men from the Somme battles who simply disappeared in 1916 and 1917. Then we will come back to the Memorial Park to visit Hawthorn Ridge, where an enormous mine was set off under the German lines early in the morning of July 1st – too early in fact. Still, more on that later. Right, don't forget to take your bags with you when you leave the bus. You've got lots of notes to make!'

After a long day, during which the numerous headstones and memorials all started to fade into one another and young minds started to drift into other things, Tim Hurt stood up on the coach and said, 'Right, and now for something very different before we go back to the hotel. Remember when we were in the visitor centre this morning, you saw that famous photograph of the explosion at Hawthorn Ridge? Well, we shall be there shortly. This site is famous, or perhaps I should say infamous, for two reasons. Firstly, the mine went off at 7.20 in the morning, ten minutes before the troops went over the top. This was a major tactical mistake, as it gave the Germans time to get out of their trenches and get ready for the first wave of attacks. This one error was responsible for thousands of deaths and casualties. Had it not been made, it could have shortened the Somme offensive by months. Secondly, this was the place where there was some success on July 1st. After the mine had exploded, a Company of Fusiliers were ready and as soon as the debris and dust cleared, they rushed the crater and managed to secure the near side of the crater, but not the far side.'

Alighting from the bus, one student said 'I thought you said that this was a huge crater, sir. All I can see is a small hole in the ground.'

'Well, over the years, the farmers, and nature have filled it up. Immediately after the 40,000 tons of ammonal explosive had gone off, the crater was 150 metres long, 100 metres wide and 30 metres deep. The British also exploded a second one a few months later alongside, almost as big as the first.'

'What happened once the Fusiliers had got this far, sir?'

'Sadly, their casualties were so serious that they had to retreat,' said the teacher.

'Well, that was a waste of time then. Sounds like a giant cock-up to me sir.'

'Yes my boy, in many ways it was the biggest 'cock-up', as you say, of the entire First World War.'

STARK WHITE STONE

By Maisie Barlow, aged 13, schoolgirl from Cambridgeshire,
written following a school trip to the Flanders battlefields.

Graves by the thousand we went and saw,
All that's left from years of war

Crosses and headstones, row upon row
White and stark in winter's glow

Fathers, brothers, sons – all dead
Lying forever in a cold foreign bed

Thousands of young men killed every day.
Why was that the price they had to pay?

What happened here? I wonder why?
Why were so many allowed to die?

Those poor young soldiers once flesh and bone
Now all to recall them is stark white stone

We must never forget that loss and pain.
If we do, that war was fought in vain.

Southern England – August 1916

It was a typically English summer's day, warm, not hot, with a bright blue sky and white fluffy clouds being blown by light winds slowly towards the horizon. Everything seemed so peaceful. Broomlands was a recovery hospital just outside Tunbridge Wells, on a south-facing slope with stunning views towards Broadwater Forest. For the soldiers who had been sent there, sitting in the grounds was a real tonic.

Thomas had been there for about ten days and was already feeling well and truly rested. Unlike most of the soldiers there, he had been keeping as up to date as he could with the progress of the war, particularly on the Somme. They thought he was crazy; the last thing they wanted to hear was anything at all to do with the war. The real reason for Thomas' interest was to keep an eye on what was happening with the Royal Fusiliers. The list of casualties was in no way reassuring. The hospital doctors did not encourage patients reading stories in the press, for fear of undoing their recuperation work, but Thomas made sure that one of the kitchen cooks, who had taken a shine to him, kept him supplied with daily national newspapers from the local shop.

The view from the terrace of the hospital was simply breathtaking. Formerly the dower house for the manor house in the village, Broomlands had been requisitioned in 1915. It had been kept well supplied with patients coming directly there after the Channel crossing from France or Belgium, or from hospitals in London and the South of England. All the patients required therapy of some kind, physical or mental, before being fed back into the wartime mincing machine.

Thomas' parents, who lived close to nearby Sevenoaks, had been to see him twice since he had been admitted. For them, it was a relatively easy journey as they had their own car and it only took about three quarters of an hour to drive to Broomlands. Thomas' father owned a farm at Seal just outside of Sevenoaks and was very busy with the harvest, which was early this year due to the wet weather in June and July and the subsequent long periods of sun which followed it. The country would be grateful for that, he thought. With all the shipping being sunk, the home harvest was crucial.

'You're looking well, Thomas,' his mother said. 'How's the shoulder getting on?'

'Much better, thank you. I can almost raise my arm level with the shoulder. They are making me do exercises with it every day, so it won't be long before they discharge me.'

The look on his mother's face said it all. The prospect of her son going back to the trenches filled her with horror. She was rather hoping he might get offered a desk job, but she knew her son wanted to get back to his regiment.

'That's a shame. You could have helped me bring the bales in!' said his father, half-jokingly.

'Stop it, John,' she said, turning away and pretending to admire the view.

'By the time it has healed completely, I should be back at the Battalion at about the same time as Richard,' Thomas said.

'I don't know whether you realise it, Thomas,' said his father, changing the subject, 'but your ancestors came from a substantial house just down the lane from here called The Hollands. It is an amazing coincidence that you are recuperating so close by. Sir Thomas Holland - same name as you - lived there in the 1300s I believe and he married a lady called Joanne, who was the granddaughter of King Edward I. Yes, a real King of England! She later went on to marry The Black Prince. One of his descendants, Sir John Holland, fought at Agincourt with great honour and was knighted by Henry V.'

'Really? My goodness, I've heard you talk about it in the past, but never really paid much attention to it,' exclaimed Thomas. 'I don't know whether I told you in my letters but Richard also has family connections around here. The Waller family lived at Groombridge Place, which is very close by I believe. We spent some time talking about it just before we went over the top on July 1st. I must try and visit the house before I leave. So we really do have aristocracy in our blood then?'

'Yes we do. Not sure what good it will do you though! I'm sure that it is not the original house any more, but I know there's still a house of some description there.'

As they stood up to leave, the doctor came past. 'He has made very good progress,' he said to Thomas' parents. 'The arm is almost back to normal, so we shall be discharging him in the next couple of days. I expect he can spend a little while with you before he is due back to join his regiment.'

'Thank you for all you have done, Doctor,' said Thomas. 'I shall be sorry to leave such a lovely spot. Mind you, in some respects the Somme can look very similar to southern England if you can just forget the war, which is, of course quite difficult.'

Richard on leave in Montreuil

It was almost two weeks after the Fourth Avenue attack before Richard felt that he was somewhere near able to undertake, without too much difficulty, the journey to Montreuil. He had written to Simone to tell her that he had been wounded in the foot and that he had been given a ten-day pass. He hoped to be able to come and see her in the third week of August, but he couldn't say for certain exactly when. He also told her how desperate he was to see her – and her 'bump'.

Thomas had written to Richard at his battalion to say that his operation had gone well and he was shortly being moved to a rest hospital in Kent for therapy to get his shoulder working properly again. All being well, he said, he hoped to be back with the regiment some time in September.

Richard was pleased to receive the letter, not only with the news that his friend's shoulder was OK but from a purely selfish point of view, he wanted to be back with the Fusiliers when

Thomas returned. In the circumstances, it had worked out for the best. His foot was healing well, but was still painful to walk on. They had given him crutches, which helped, but he felt a little reluctant to use them because he had been told that walking gently on the foot would help the recovery process. He did have a feeling of guilt over his parents for not applying for compassionate leave, but he had written to say that he was in hospital with a not-too-serious wound and he would be in touch again in the next couple of weeks. He said he prayed every day for his mother's recovery, which he did. He had always been much closer to his mother than his father, mainly because his father had been away with the regiment a lot. He had sent her a photo taken just before July 1st of the CO and officers of the 8th Battalion outside of their HQ. He had hoped it would cheer her up, but if she had known how few of the men in the photograph were left, it most certainly would have had the opposite effect.

Richard's batman had arranged a lift in a staff car to get him to Albert Station. He was nervous about seeing Simone again, or was it excitement? He couldn't decide. Maybe a bit of both. What he did know was that he had made the right decision to go to the front line when he did. He had been fortunate enough to get through the first weeks of the battle, during which the British Army had suffered the worst casualties it had ever endured. To make getting around easier, he had just one small suitcase with him and he would try to get Simone a present somewhere, as he knew there were bound to be delays en route.

Normally, he would have taken the train to Arras and

across country to Montreuil, via St Pol sur Turnoise. But the line, when it left Albert, followed the Ancre river and went right through the front line as it was on July 1st. He had been advised to go to Amiens, then change to pick up the connection for Abbeville and then on to Montreuil. He had prepared himself for a long journey and had borrowed a couple of books from fellow officers. One was Charles Dickens' *Nicholas Nickleby*, which he had started at school but had only read the first few chapters. The other was *The Portrait of a Lady* by Henry James, which he knew nothing about. They were both substantial reads, so they should be more than enough for the journey, there and back.

The train to Amiens left pretty well on time and followed the Ancre river to Corbie before running west alongside the Somme. Everywhere along the route there were signs of an army on the move. He saw hundreds, if not thousands, of vehicles and wagons of every shape and size, transporting everything a modern army needed to fight with. There were even double-decker London buses taking reinforcements up to the line. It was an incredible sight and reminded him of his staff job earlier in the year when he, along with Frank, Colonel Scott and the others were putting this whole show on the road. A peculiar way of putting it.

They pulled in to Amiens, which he could see was a substantial place. He knew he was going to have a wait of at least three hours here, which would give him the opportunity to look round. He checked at the ticket office and they confirmed that the train to Abbeville would not be leaving until 2 pm.

As the capital of Picardy, Amiens had had a long association with the English. Various peace treaties had been signed here with Kings of England over the centuries and in the first month of the war, Amiens was the first base for troops arriving from the UK.

For a short period at the end of August 1914, the Germans occupied Amiens and after demanding money, supplies and taking hostages, they withdrew after the French army drove them back to Fricourt, some 20 miles inland on the Somme. The British then took over the city, and it had since become a major centre for depots, hospitals and recreation centres for the army.

Richard could see as he walked round that a lot of 'recreation' was going on. The military police were very busy, even at this time of the day. There were bars everywhere, along with brothels, restaurants and some good quality shops. Amiens was an industrial town and it was obvious that there was wealth here, probably a lot more now because of the war. There were still some places that were benefiting from the conflict, and this was obviously one of them.

Richard stopped to look in the window of a smart ladies' dress shop and admired a leather handbag which he thought would make a beautiful present for Simone. He also thought he should buy something for Cécile. He wasn't yet sure whether he was staying at their house or at the officers' mess, but in any case he would almost certainly be enjoying some of their hospitality. He went in and received a genuinely warm welcome from the proprietress, who immediately rushed forward with a chair for him to sit on when she saw that he was using crutches.

'How can I help you, monsieur?' she asked politely.

'There is a handbag in the window that I would like to buy for my girlfriend. Can you tell me how much it is please?' asked Richard.

'Yes, of course Captain. It is twenty francs.' After a short pause, she said 'I see that you have the Military Cross. You must be very brave.'

'Oh no,' said Richard, embarrassed. 'I have just been lucky.'

'Is your young lady French or English, monsieur?' she asked.

'She is French, very pretty and I am a very lucky man,' he said smiling.

'As you are here in our country, helping to rid us of those terrible Germans, the price to you is just fifteen francs.'

'That is very kind of you,' said Richard, realising that this was the first time in his entire life that he had ever been into a ladies' shop to buy anything. Then he realised he could not buy a present for Simone without also buying one for her mother, irrespective of the circumstance.

He said, 'I would also like to buy a scarf for her mother, as she is being very kind and is looking after me for a few days. Could you suggest something?'

'Can you tell me how old the lady is without being indiscreet?'

'She is about forty I think, but like her daughter, she is very attractive and certainly doesn't look her age.'

'I think I have just the perfect present for Madame.'

She went to a separate part of the shop and came back with an exquisite silk scarf with an ornamental pin. The pattern was quite modern, almost art nouveau in design and he liked it instantly.

'That is lovely. I will take them both please.'

'Would you like me to wrap them for you?' she asked.

'That would be very kind,' he said.

She went away for about ten minutes and came back with the two presents, beautifully wrapped.

'It was a pleasure to serve you, monsieur,' she said and with a twinkle in her eye. 'If you and your girlfriend ever part company, come back and see me!'

'I bet you say that to all the boys!' he said smiling at her. He walked away from the shop feeling very pleased with his purchases and headed for the station as it was getting on for two o'clock.

The train from Amiens to Abbeville ran alongside the Somme river for the whole distance. From there to the sea it became the Somme Canal, emerging into the English Channel at St Valery sur Somme. Richard did not have to change trains at Abbeville, but carried on to Etaples and Le Touquet. This next-to-last leg of the journey was very pleasant, following the coast in a northward direction. He thought of the day he had gone to the cliffs on the other side of the Channel with his father. It seemed so long ago, but in reality it was only four months.

Getting off the train at Le Touquet reminded him of the very special day he had spent there with Simone. Perhaps, he thought, they could pay a return visit before he went back. No, he mustn't think about going back, he hadn't even got to Montreuil yet.

Waiting for the last connection was a nervous time for him. He wondered whether he had changed, whether she would notice anything different in him. And, apart from the pregnancy, would she be as he remembered her that last time?

He was brought to his senses by the hooting of the train. The last ten miles were about to be covered by the slowest train in the world. He was sure that they were doing it on purpose, just to prolong the anticipation.

With a huge sigh of relief, the train pulled in. He had arrived at Montreuil-sur-Mer. It was just after five o'clock, and he wondered if Simone was still at work. It was a 15-minute walk up through the ramparts to the town and, with luck, she would still be at the hospital. The crutches would be difficult on the cobbles, so he decided to take a pony and trap which was available outside the station. Surely only the fittest could walk up the long hill. He was sure she wouldn't mind if he went first to the hospital, although Matron might!

Slightly nervous of meeting up with Cécile, and feeling the need for a little Dutch courage, he went into the bar opposite the hospital where he and Frank used to go. He wasn't a great fan of brandy, but there was no whisky to be had. He could have gone to the officers' mess, but that would be better another day.

After the drink, he was feeling a little more relaxed. When he went through the hospital entrance on his crutches, the receptionist thought he was a patient come for treatment.

'No,' he said, 'I have just come to see if Simone Deberney is still at work and whether I could see her for a moment.'

'It is very difficult monsieur. Matron is very strict about visitors during working hours.'

'I realise that and I am happy to wait. All I want to know is if she is still in the hospital. Is it possible to find that out?'

She thought for a moment and said, 'Just wait here a moment. I am not supposed to do this but I will leave the desk for a moment and get someone to find out for you. I know which ward she is on. If anyone comes, just ask them to wait a moment. Say I had to go to the toilet!'

Fortunately it was quiet in reception and there were no other visitors. The woman came back breathless, saying that Simone was in the ward, but he would have to wait until she finished at 6.30 pm. It was more than her life was worth to try and get a message to her, she explained, because Matron was bound to find out. Richard said that was fine and as long as she didn't mind him sitting there reading his book, he would stay and wait.

After what seemed like an eternity, he heard footsteps coming along the marble corridor. He couldn't tell why he knew they belonged to Simone, he just did. He stood up and waited, putting his crutches on one side. She stopped dead in her tracks and dropped her bag to the floor. Putting her hands to her face, she cried out,

'Richard. Oh, my Richard!' and threw herself into his arms. She wept and wept but it did not matter. 'I can't believe you are here. I had forgotten how handsome you are. Give me a big hug, but not too tight, there are two of us now,' she said quietly.

He gently stroked her lump and she purred with delight. The receptionist was watching all this going on with a big smile on her face and she too had tears in her eyes.

'Come on, let me help you with your case, so you can use your crutches. Has the foot been all right?' she asked.

'Not too bad. I had a little while to wait in Amiens, so went for a walk around. It hurt a bit after that,' he said.

'Oh, I am so pleased to see you. And what is that on your chest?'

'That is the Military Cross. Are you proud of me?'

Filled with pride, she could not resist kissing him deeply on the mouth, heedless of anyone watching. She held his arm as he used the crutches, and they walked slowly towards her house. They didn't stop talking all the way, about something and nothing. It didn't matter. They were together and that was all that was important.

They approached the house, with its pretty front garden adding a touch of colour to an otherwise dull row of architecture. Simone opened the door and walked in, shouting, 'Mother, guess who has come to visit us?'

Cécile came slowly towards Richard, greeting him with a combination of warmth and reserve, like a friend whom she had not seen for quite some time.

'Richard, how glad I am to see you!' She kissed him on both cheeks. 'You are looking well, apart from your crutches,' she said with a smile. 'I hope your foot is not too painful?'

'No, thank you, it is healing well. How have you been?'

'Oh, you know, the war is not easy for anyone and I miss my husband so. Come and sit down. Would you like something to drink? As soon as Simone told me you were coming to stay, I made sure we had some coffee. It is very difficult to get hold of these days.'

'Yes, that would be nice. You really shouldn't have bothered on my account. I do not want to put you to any trouble.'

Cécile went into the kitchen to put on the kettle. While she was out of the room, Simone whispered to Richard that she would talk to her mother about the sleeping arrangements. A little embarrassed and concerned, he said, 'Oh, perhaps I should stay at GHQ, they have visitor's accommodation there. I do not want to cause any difficulty with your mother.'

Thinking about it for a second or two, she said, 'Nonsense. You must stay here, but we'll talk about that later. But I need you Richard,' she said. 'It has been too long.'

Cécile came back into the room with the coffee. 'You don't know how good that smells,' said Richard. 'While I was in Amiens this morning, I had time to do a little shopping. Simone, here is something for you.' He passed her a beautifully wrapped parcel tied with a pretty bow.

'Oh, Richard, what a surprise! I wasn't expecting anything. What is it?' she asked.

'Open it and see.'

Gently taking off the ribbon so that she could keep it for another day, she removed the wrapping. When she saw what is was she gasped with delight.

'Richard! It is so beautiful. It must have cost a fortune. Oh, it is truly lovely. Thank you so very much.'

She kissed him on the lips, slightly embarrassed in front of her mother.

'Cécile, there is a little something for you as well' he said. 'I wasn't sure what to get you, but I hope you like it.'

She opened her present and promptly burst into tears, rushing from the room.

'What is wrong?' asked Richard. 'Doesn't she like it?'

'No, Richard. It is lovely. Since Gilles left to go back to the front, she has been a little sad. She will be fine. Just give her a moment or two.'

Simone and Richard sat on the settee, desperate to be as close as possible to one another. A few minutes later Cécile came back, holding a handkerchief to her face. 'I am so sorry, Richard,' she said. 'That is such a beautiful present. I cannot thank you enough. Let me kiss you too.' She put her arms around him.

'Tonight, I want you two to sleep in my room and I will sleep in yours,' she said. 'Simone has been missing you so, and, after all, you can only make one baby at a time!' She left the room with a cheeky smile on her face, putting the scarf round her neck. Richard decided to make sure that the door was firmly closed.

They lay together in each other's arms, slightly tense because of Cécile next door, but enjoying just being together. Richard had fallen in love with their 'lump' and the more he stroked it, the closer he felt to her. The baby suddenly moved and she took Richard's hand and put it there, so he could feel it too. It was a moment of such excitement that he laid his head on her stomach, hoping to hear or feel more movements. The warmth, the smell of her skin, made him want her.

'We must be careful, Richard' she whispered. I don't want anything to happen to our baby. The doctor said it would be fine as long as we were sensible. Here, come into me gently,' she said as she made herself ready for him. 'Oh Richard, that's beautiful. It feels better than ever. Just be quiet when you get there or mother will hear us!'

Afterwards they lay there quietly, both feeling totally fulfilled, before falling asleep. This was the first time they had stayed together all night and he thought it couldn't get any better. He wondered what Cécile was thinking.

The next morning Simone woke first. She thought she would let Richard sleep on, as he had been very tired when he had arrived yesterday, although it didn't seem to have affected him last night, she thought, with a big smile on her face. Now he was here, she could talk to Matron about having some time off to spend with him. She had worked almost every day for months, except when her father came home, and she had already mentioned the possibility of leave to Matron when she received Richard's letter.

She said goodbye to her mother, saying that Richard was sleeping and asking her to let him sleep for as long as he wanted, as he had been very tired when he arrived the day before. She said she would try to get home a bit earlier and hoped that Matron would be understanding about her taking some time off.

Realising that this was probably the only opportunity she might get with Richard, Cécile was determined to make the most of it, although she was not sure how he would react. She waited a while in the hope that he would wake, but by eleven o'clock she decided that she had waited long enough.

She crept quietly into the bedroom and saw that he was lying on his back fast asleep. She couldn't help but notice that he had an erection, a very strange thing to happen while he was asleep, she thought. Maybe he was thinking about her.

She slipped into bed alongside him, gently stroking his

head. Richard stirred slightly, still dead to the world. Moving very gently, Cécile took his hand and placed it on her breast, moving it around until her nipple started to ache.

Suddenly Richard realised that something was not right. He opened his eyes to find himself looking straight into Cécile's. At first he was not sure who he was looking at.

'Richard, do this for me just this once and I promise that I will not ask again' she said. 'I promise I shall never tell Simone that it happened. Please, Richard. Please. I have not had a man for so long and I am desperate to feel something deep inside me.' She took hold of his flesh and began to caress him.

'Stop it, Cécile!' he gasped. 'How can you ask me to do this? Your daughter is five months pregnant with our child, your grandchild. This is very wrong.'

'Don't say that word, it makes me feel old,' Cécile said sulkily. 'Just do it to me this once and I won't ask again. If you don't, I will tell Simone that you wanted to make love to me. I mean it.'

After a slight pause, she said 'Richard, you know that scarf that you bought for me? Well, I am wearing it. Look!' She threw back the bed cover. The scarf was all she had on.

Seeing this beautiful woman virtually naked beside him, he found his resistance ebbing away. She lay on her side, gently caressing his erection. Then she moved her hand down, took his hand and placed it between her parted legs. At the same time she pulled his head down onto her breast.

'Suck me gently Richard, they are very sensitive. I will tell you when I am ready.'

After what seemed like an eternity, she whispered, 'Now,

Richard, come to me!' She moved on top of him and guided him into her. 'Make it last, Richard. I want this to be long!' He moved gently and almost immediately, she was moaning with pleasure.

'Oh, that is so good,' she said. 'Let it go on and on.'

Gasping, they both subsided onto the bed. She raised herself on one elbow and looked at him.

'I told you that I wanted you. Now do you believe me?' she asked.

Richard was dismayed, realising how weak he had been in not resisting her advances. 'That should never have happened,' he said. 'I feel thoroughly ashamed.'

'Don't say that' she murmured. 'What we did was wonderful and very private. I have waited so long for that. No one will ever know except you and me, and I promise you I won't ask again. I know you and Simone were made for each other and I won't do anything again to come between you. You two love one another, all I wanted was a man to satisfy me. You did what I asked and I know you enjoyed it too.'

Richard was so nervous as he waited for Simone to come home that he decided to walk towards the hospital, hoping she would leave at her normal time. As he left the house, Cécile said to him, 'Thank you, Richard, and stop worrying. It's our secret.'

He had almost reached the hospital when Simone came walking towards him. He needn't have worried, as she was her usual happy smiling self. She kissed him full on the lips.

'This is a much nicer way of kissing than on the cheeks' she said. 'I can see the curtains twitching!'

'Did you manage to get any time off?'

'Yes, it is OK. Matron was nice for once and said that I can take a week off, starting tomorrow.'

'That's really good,' he said, thinking this would prevent a recurrence of Cécile's advances. 'Why don't we take the train to Le Touquet tomorrow?'

'Oh, Richard, that would be so nice. Do you think we should ask mother? She has been so kind to us.'

'Let's keep tomorrow for us,' said Richard. 'We'll ask her if she would like to come somewhere with us later in the week.'

'Yes, OK then,' she said skipping along beside him while he limped along on his crutches.

The next few days were blissful, and the worry that Cécile might say something seemed to disappear. She too seemed very content, so much so that Simone said to Richard that his appearance seemed to have cheered her up no end.

While they were walking along the bank of the River Canche one day, Richard decided to raise an important subject with Simone.

'I have been thinking about something ever since I got your letter about the baby' he said. 'Do you think we should get married? I know that doesn't sound very romantic, and I apologise, but we are not living in normal times and I don't really know what you think about it. You would make me the happiest man alive if you were to say yes. I will be off again in a few days and won't be back on leave almost until the baby is born.'

She looked him straight in the eyes and said, 'I have long since decided that you are the only man I ever want to spend my days with, so the answer is most emphatically YES! I want our baby to have a proper father when it is born and it would please my parents as well. You are the love of my life, Richard, and eventually I want more than one baby.'

He swung her round, trying to pretend his foot wasn't hurting, and kissed her passionately on the lips.

'We had better get moving then. Where can we buy our rings?'

They had a small civil ceremony in the Place Gambetta. Richard had wanted to ask Thomas to be his best man, but the fact that he was still in England made this impossible. His best friend at GHQ had been Frank Skinner, who was delighted to be asked to officiate. He suggested that they should have a small buffet and drinks in the officers' mess after the ceremony, which both Simone and Richard thought was a lovely idea. Jeremy Scott came, as well as John, Arthur and Cecil from GHQ and several of Simone's best friends from the hospital. She was delighted to see Dr Froget turn up. He got a very special hug.

'Doctor, let me introduce you to my lovely man, Richard Waller – even if he is English!' she said with a wide smile on her face.

'Enchanté, Monsieur. You are a very lucky man, but I expect you realise that already. I have volunteered to look after your wife during her pregnancy, with your permission of course.' He bowed slightly. 'The way she dealt with a problem her father had when he was on leave was exceptional, and he went back a lot better than when he arrived.'

He looked at Richard's uniform. 'I see that you have been

awarded the Military Cross' he said. 'My congratulations. They do not give those out to everyone. I won't embarrass you by asking how you won it.'

'I am very grateful for that, sir, and the fact that our child will be in good hands while I am away.'

Creeping up behind Richard, Frank said discreetly, 'I say, Simone's mother is an absolute cracker. I can see where she gets her good looks from. Shame she's married. I am on the look-out for someone just like her to look after me on the long lonely nights. Keep me posted! By the way, how are things at the front? Was it what you were looking for? It didn't take you long to get made up to Captain and win the MC.'

'These things happen so fast, mainly because of the chaps we have lost' replied Richard 'But yes, Frank, I'm glad I went. It was ghastly, but it will stay with me forever. And the comradeship when you are all in the same boat is quite extraordinary.'

One of Cécile's friends got quite merry and began to take a strong interest in Frank Skinner. They were last seen disappearing out of the mess arm in arm.

Richard was aware that they had to clear the room in the mess by 3 pm, so he thanked everyone for coming and made sure the photographer would get the prints run out quickly, because he wanted to get a letter and photo to his parents before he went back.

'Well, Madame Waller, do you feel any different?' he asked her.

'Only closer to you than ever. And apart from making it

official, it is lovely to be wearing your ring. I will always wear it with great pride. The only shame was that my father wasn't here but, like you with your parents, I will send some photos of the wedding to him. It will cheer him up no end.'

The week passed far too quickly and before they knew it they were saying their goodbyes. Cécile gave Richard a very voluptuous kiss when Simone wasn't looking and whispered to him, 'You see, I kept my promise. What you gave me I shall remember always. Take great care of yourself and I shall look forward to the day when you come back to our house as my son-in-law.'

Richard and Simone had made slow gentle love the night before and he gave the 'lump' a long kiss. 'I shall see you in three months' time,' he murmured to it. 'If you are a girl, you will be as beautiful as your mother and if you are a boy, you must be strong and true and whatever you do, be something other than a soldier!'

She walked part of the way to the station with him, carrying the bag Richard had bought for her, which was now her pride and joy. She was also playing with the ring on her finger, trying to get used to it being there. He had asked her not to come the whole way, because he didn't want the long, tortuous goodbye standing on the platform. They reached La Grande Place and he kissed her long on her beautiful soft lips and caressed her stomach.

'Take good care of this little one, as well as yourself,' he said. 'I shall apply for leave a few days before the date Dr Froget has given you as soon as I get back to HQ. But I will write as often as I can. I love you, Simone, more than I can ever truly tell you.' With that he turned and walked away, limping slightly. She realised he had left his crutches behind.

The journey back was not unpleasant, but he felt completely empty inside. It was as though he left part of himself behind in Montreuil; perhaps he was not just missing Simone and their baby but Cécile as well. Because of the honourable way she had behaved, he felt that she had been sincere with her promise and for that he felt very grateful. There were times when he still felt hugely guilty about what had happened and he worried that she might have come back and demanded more, making life very difficult. But she hadn't. And he knew that it could never happen again.

He had to change trains at Amiens, and he wanted to go back to the shop to tell the lady how well the presents had been received, particularly the scarf. However, the thought of it brought him out in a hot flush of embarrassment, and in the end, he decided against it.

He went into the café at the station and had a glass of beer and some Picardy pancakes, which were delicious. Then he found somewhere comfortable to sit in the gardens of the cathedral while he waited for his connection. He got his book out, though it had attracted little of his attention since he had left HQ, and found that he could not concentrate here either. Maybe when he got on the train, it would be easier. All he could think of was Simone and the baby.

He walked slowly back to the station, where the train for Albert was waiting. As he stepped into the carriage, he could hear the guns quite distinctly and was instantly aware of what he was going back to. When he had first left GHQ in Montreuil for the front, he had a feeling of excitement, of anticipation, of the great unknown. This time it was completely different. He knew what he was returning to, and now there was fear mixed with the anticipation. But at least Thomas would be there.

She kissed me when we came to part,
A generous kiss, passionate and from the heart.

It made the leaving full of sadness
And back to a world full of madness.

Author unknown

Renewing a friendship; September 1916

The air was thick with dust as Richard came out of the station. Albert was heaving with troops from every imaginable regiment, and with vehicles of every size and description on the move in all directions, it gave the appearance of organised chaos. It was not helped by the fact that shells were still landing intermittently, causing casualties and much structural damage to the town. Still, at least the Military Police were directing the men and machines to all roads leading out of the town centre. Richard went up to one.

'Excuse me, Corporal, you don't know of any vehicles going to the 8th Battalion, Royal Fusiliers?'

'Afraid not sir, but that guy over there, the CSM, is a Fusilier. He might be able to help.'

Richard walked over and tapped the sergeant on the shoulder. Taking a step back, he said 'Good afternoon, Captain. What can I do for you?'

'You're not going anywhere near the 8th Battalion by any chance?' Richard asked.

'Yes, I am as a matter of fact, sir. I'm with the 9th and the 8th are our neighbours. Can I offer you a lift?'

'That would be very good of you.'

Richard got into the front seat of the Bristol truck alongside the CSM.

'Been away on leave, sir?' asked the CSM.

'Yes, Sergeant. And I got married at the same time.'

'Well, blow me down. Was that back in England?' he asked.

'No, Sergeant. When I was with GHQ at Montreuil, I met a lovely French girl who lived in the town and we decided to tie the knot.'

'May I offer you my congratulations sir,' and he shook him by the hand.

'Thank you very much.' After a short pause he asked the CSM, 'Has there been much going on during the past few weeks?'

'The fighting around Guillemont has been going on for a while now and the 1st, 4th and the 12th Fusiliers have been in action there,' said the CSM. 'The 20th have had a rough time at Delville Wood and have just been joined by the 12th. Your Battalion, like ours, have been in reserve.'

Richard wondered whether Thomas had returned yet. They had so much to catch up on that he hoped that there would be plenty of time for a chat before they were called back into the line.

'Here you are, sir. The 8th HQ is just over there, behind that farm building.'

'Thank you, Sergeant.' On stepping out of the lorry, Richard hurried over towards HQ, still limping slightly. There was a large tented area in the courtyard of what had been a fairly substantial farm. He saw a sign saying '8th Battalion, The Royal Fusiliers', attached to an old stable block.

He was directed to part of a barn where the adjutant was based. The stench as he walked across the yard was rather overpowering and he was not sure whether it was from the farm or human debris. Knocking on the door, Richard stepped in, to be greeted by Captain William Campbell, who seemed very pleased to see him. There were half a dozen desks in the building, most laden with company orders.

'Hello Richard, I am delighted you're back. First, I hear from someone at GHQ that you're a married man now. Congratulations are well and truly in order. My warmest wishes to you both. We'll organise a knees up in the mess in the next day or so. Secondly, I have to tell you that your promotion to Major has come through. This will make you second in command of the Battalion and I/C HQ Company. More congratulations are in order, well done Richard.'

'Thank you, William, I am obviously very pleased, but does this mean that I shall not be commanding a rifle company?' asked Richard. 'I should not like that. I would much prefer to be up at the front with my men.'

'We'll have to talk to the CO. I'm sure he will want you where the action is, but lines of succession are so important with the rates of casualties as they are these days. Battalion Commanders are dropping like flies and GHQ needs to be convinced that capable officers are ready to step into their

CO's shoes when anything happens. I'll talk to the old man later.'

'Is Thomas Holland back yet?' Richard asked.

'Yes, he got back the day before yesterday. His arm has healed very well.'

At that moment, Richard heard his name being called from across the other side of the barn. He turned to see a familiar face walking towards him. It was Thomas, beaming from ear to ear.

'It's great to see you again!' said Thomas.

They embraced each other, at first rather embarrassed in the presence of brother officers, but then they burst out laughing, which made everyone in the room smile.

'I hear you've tied the knot, you lucky chap,' said Thomas.

'Yes, it was all very sudden. There I was on a ten-day pass, walking on a pair of crutches and suddenly deciding that I should do the honourable thing… and she said yes! You weren't around to be my best man, which was a shame, but one of my old colleagues from GHQ stood in in your place. So the Simone you have heard so much about, is now Madame, or Mrs, Waller.'

Sitting down in the corner of the room on two easy chairs, they relaxed for a minute or two.

'Tell me about your time in England. What did you get up to?' Richard asked.

'Well, I wrote to you from the hospital in South London where the surgeon carried out the op. That went very well and the nurses were pretty nice I can tell you. But, of course, you're not interested in that any more are you?' said Thomas jokingly.

'I'll always look at a pretty girl. It's one of life's great pleasures, even if I am an old married man,' Richard said.

'I was there for ten days. Then I was sent to this hospital just outside of Tunbridge Wells, where they put me through some intensive therapy to get the shoulder working again. It was a wonderful place. You felt as though you were miles from anywhere, which I suppose was part of the idea. And how's the foot? You look at though it's still giving you some trouble.'

'Mine was nothing compared to yours. I didn't even know I'd done it at the time. I was walking back after the attack on the German trench outside of Pozières when I felt the blood in my boot. The CSM got me to the Walking Wounded Station, where they cut off the boot. That's when it really started to hurt for the first time. So it was foot up for a while until I was ready to take some leave. The Colonel gave me a ten-day pass. One really strange thing that happened while I was there was that just after I left the marquee where they were dressing the wounded, a German shell landed right on the tent and killed three men, all German prisoners. How's that for justice?'

Feeling incredibly thirsty, Thomas said, 'Let's get a drink, then I can toast the bridegroom. What will you have?'

'Oh, I think I'll have a beer if there is one. Thanks.'

When the drinks arrived at what had been hastily pressed into service as a bar, Thomas raised his glass and said, so that all the other officers could join in,

'I wish you both every happiness and trust that the marriage has been well and truly consummated!'

There were wild cheers from all round the mess at that comment.

'I can assure you that all is well in that department, thank you!'

After a pause to lubricate his throat, Richard asked Thomas if he had managed to see his family.

'Yes, they came down from Sevenoaks a couple of times. Being at that hospital was really handy, because they were only about 45 minutes away. It couldn't have been better arranged if they had tried. Mother was fussing over me as usual. One fascinating thing I learned while I was there was that our old family ancestral home, The Hollands, was literally just down the lane from the hospital. An English knight by the name of Sir John Holland, who fought at Agincourt with Henry V, lived there and it stayed as the family home for quite a long time. I told my parents about your family association with Agincourt and the capture of the Duke of Orleans. I don't think my father could quite believe it.'

'I'll tell you something else as well,' said Richard. 'When I arrived in France with the Fusiliers as a mere Corporal in 1914, we embarked at Le Havre and camped the first night at a place called Harfleur. And that's where Henry V landed with his forces in 1415. Do you realise the significance of that? Five hundred years after Agincourt, which is of course on the Somme, both of us are, it seems, related to men who fought there. This time though France is on our side!'

'That is really extraordinary,' said Thomas, 'I remember my father mentioning it years ago, about the family history, but it held no great interest for me at the time. We must sit and have a chat about all this before we go back to the front.'

'Good idea,' said Richard, 'It's Sunday tomorrow. Maybe we'll have time then.'

At that moment, the adjutant came in. 'Attention please,

gentlemen' he said. 'There is a church parade in Albert tomorrow and there will be communion for those who feel the need. John, you are representing Lance Corporal Brown at a Court Martial at 11 am for going AWOL, so you are excused duties. Frank, you are to take 'A' Company to the baths in Méaulte at 2 pm. Your men are getting a bit smelly! The rest of you are requested to attend a conference with the CO at 2.30 pm in the mess, which should last for about an hour. It has to be over by 4 pm, as there is a visit from General Rawlinson planned. Also, the CO has requested the pleasure of your company this evening, as the Divisional band is playing a concert starting at 6.30 pm and they apparently have a guest making a surprise appearance. Please don't ask me who it is, I haven't a clue. The only way you'll find out is by going, which I suppose is the general idea.

'That's all for now. I'm sure you are all as pleased as I am to see Richard and Thomas back. That almost takes us up to full strength. No doubt that will mean that the General will have some more work for us soon!'

CHAPTER FORTY TWO

Families at war, September 1916

Back in Montreuil, Simone and Cécile had resumed their daily routine as mother and daughter. They had both missed Richard terribly when he had returned to his battalion, but Simone was pleased that her mother seemed to have got over the remorse she had felt when Gilles went back. She did write to him immediately after he had left to apologise and assure him that her love for him was as strong as ever and that she couldn't wait for him to come home again. She hadn't had a response yet, but it was early days. She did know that the regiment of which he was Commanding Officer had been sent to the Somme, which made her feel closer to him, both geographically and emotionally.

Dr Froget had taken a keen interest in Simone's pregnancy and was obviously very impressed with her new husband. He wanted to do all he could to make sure the birth of the baby went well.

'Richard is a fine young man,' he said at her first examination after their wedding. 'I think I have always been a good judge of character and he will make a wonderful father. Have you written to your father about the wedding?'

'Yes, Doctor. As soon as the photos were developed, I sent several copies to him with a description of the day. You know, when I told him about the baby, he seemed to be really pleased. He said that in this awful world we are living in at the moment, it was a wonderful piece of news. Unlike my mother, there were no lectures from him, just happiness.'

'Well, you appear to be very well. Your blood pressure is fine, which is a relief as it was a bit high the last time I saw you. Just take everything in your stride. Gentle exercise is fine. You presumably have told Matron about the baby?'

'Yes, I told her several weeks ago,' said Simone.

A smile flickered across his face. 'How was she?'

'Surprisingly, she was fine about it. She has put me on less heavy duties, no lifting of patients. She has been very sweet actually.'

'She possibly feels a bit like your father. Her fiancée was killed very early in the war and it made her very bitter. He had been her childhood sweetheart and she took it very badly. She needed her job to get her through the pain, but as you know she was inclined to take out her bitterness on others, including you! Maybe she sees your pregnancy as something she would have hoped for, a sign of something good to come out of all the evil.'

He helped her up out of the chair. 'If you have any worries at all, come and see me' he said.

'Thank you, Doctor, you have been very kind - to all of my family.'

News from France

'Mother! A package has arrived from Richard,' Hubert Waller shouted to his wife, who was resting in her favourite chair in the lounge. He couldn't say why he still called her mother after all this time - habit presumably - but she didn't seem to mind.

'Look, the postman has just delivered this. Would you like to open it?' he asked her.

'No, you do it, I haven't much strength in my hands these days,' she said.

'The military postmark says Montreuil. That's a bit odd, I wonder if Richard has gone back to GHQ? I shall be so pleased if he has.'

His excitement at that possibility soon disappeared when he started reading the letter that was enclosed, along with some photographs.

'What are those pictures?' she asked, looking at him going through the contents. 'They look like a wedding group.'

Hubert decided to read the whole letter before saying anything to his wife.

'What is it, what does the letter say?' she asked impatiently.

'Wait just a moment dear.' He finished reading the letter and passed it to his wife. 'There you are. Richard has got married.'

Dear Mother and Father, I realise that this may come as a huge shock to you both, but I have married the most beautiful girl in the world. I would have wanted you both to be there more than anything, but circumstances would unfortunately not allow it. I met Simone when I was at GHQ in Montreuil in February and she discovered in June that she was pregnant. Initially, we were both shocked, but were very happy about. It didn't change my desire at the time to be at the front, but when I was injured last month, I had a ten day pass to help the recovery process. So I decided to go back to Montreuil to see Simone and ask her to be my wife. I have met her mother, who is very nice and her father is a Colonel in the French army. He was very pleased with the news of the baby, but he is away with his regiment so he missed the wedding.

Please do not be too upset. We are very happy together and we hope this awful war will end soon, so that we can come to England and all get to know one another. I know that you will love her every bit as much as I do. Mother, you must fight your illness with all your strength, so that you can spend some time with your grandchild. And Father, do all you can for Mum, which I know you will, so that, please God, we can all meet in the new year. I include some photos of the wedding. It is obvious who the married couple are! Simone's mother Cécile is standing next to me, with Frank Skinner from GHQ, who was my best man, next to Simone. By the way Dad, we had the reception in the officers' mess and, please note the MC on my chest, and that I have a crown on my shoulder, rather than three pips. My promotion to Major came through a short while ago. I am about to go back to the battalion now, so will write to you again soonest. I enclose in this envelope Simone's address should you wish to make contact. Her married name is obviously Madame S. Waller! Love you both very much and God bless, your son, Richard.

They both said nothing for a moment. Richard's mother had tears in her eyes, whilst Hubert Waller stood erect with pride at the thought of his son firstly winning the MC, but also being a married man with a child on the way, irrespective of the circumstances. He thought this news might be just the boost his wife needed.

'We must be very happy about this news and write and tell him so. It would mean so much to him,' he said. 'It is such a shame that we cannot get to meet our daughter-in-law with the war going on.'

Richard's mother was very quiet; she simply stared into space.

The French Army on the Somme – September 1916

The French 6th Army under Fayolle was moving slowly towards Combles with the British 56th Division on its left. This joint thrust was taking place at the eastern side of the September 1916 fighting, having begun with a major offensive on September 12. It had quickly run out of steam, due to the high casualty rate and the acute absence of fresh reserves. A new offensive was planned for the 15th with both the British and the French totally committed. Twelve divisions were involved on a ten-mile front stretching from Combles to the Ancre valley. There was some immediate success for the British with the villages of Guillemont, Longueval and Bazentin being captured. However, the French had found it hard going, taking Rancourt and the village of Frégicourt, but again with heavy casualties. A further advance was planned for the 25th, to be preceded by a 24-hour bombardment, but the autumn rains had come early and the battlefield quickly became a quagmire.

A bombardment started on the 24th and by the 25th a general attack was launched against Morval, Les Boeufs, Gueudecourt and heading towards Martinpuich. In this operation 32 armoured fighting vehicles, later to be called 'tanks', were supporting the attack. The French were noticeably worn down by this ever-increasing war of attrition. This engagement was probably going to be the last of the year for them in Picardy before the weather made any forward movement impossible. Snow had already fallen as well as sleet, and it was still only September.

Colonel Gilles Deberney of the 8th Infantry Regiment was in his third year of the war and miraculously had only suffered minor injuries. Since the offensive had started on September 12, the French gains had been meagre. Rancourt had fallen, but at a heavy price. The tanks had come unstuck in the mud and the attack had all the signs of grinding to a halt. But the British still had many divisions going forward and were determined to reach and take Combles, supported by the French on their right.

Gilles had been ordered by his General to ensure that the advance on Combles kept up with the British and that it was ultimately successful. The artillery barrage, which had started on the morning of the 24th, continued on into the following day, when the barrage started to creep forward at 7.30 in the morning, the time set for the attack.

Gilles never ceased to be amazed at the incredible loyalty his men had shown him, even though there were rumours of massive dissent throughout the French Army. They just wanted the opportunity to give the enemy a taste of French steel after the terrible casualties they had suffered at Verdun.

The first wave of Gilles' Battalion stepped up onto the scaling ladders in the trenches and, when the whistles blew, started walking towards the German lines. The pace of advance was determined by the artillery barrage, which crept forward at the rate of a hundred yards every five minutes. It wasn't long before the machine guns opened up. Gilles shouted above the horrendous noise to his support officer, Michel, who was standing alongside him, to get the mortar section to zero in on the machine guns that were positioned on a rise about 100 yards behind the German trenches. They were taking heavy casualties from the shelling as well as from the machine gun bullets, and Gilles could see that the advance on the left flank was faltering badly. The mortar shells were just starting to come over, but had not yet hit their target.

'Capitaine, get the Hotchkiss guns to fire over the heads of our forward infantry and drop it into the trenches,' said Gilles. 'The first wave is still some way off. We must silence those machine guns, they are murdering us.'

The left flank appeared to be making no progress.

'We must give the left some more support,' Gilles said. 'Move the covering fire over and send the second wave in to help them out. NOW!' he shouted.

There was smoke blanketing the sky and shells bursting everywhere. On the right and in the centre, things seemed to be going better. On the right, the first of the French infantrymen were in the German trench and prisoners were starting to appear with their hands held above their heads. A few riflemen couldn't resist shooting them, while others were throwing phosphorous bombs into the dugouts and bayoneting the Germans as they came out. After so many months at war, honourable behaviour had long since been forgotten. Those that got past the first wave of troops found themselves being shot at by the second wave as they came forward.

The left was still under considerable pressure, and Gilles shouted to Michel that he was going over there to find out what the problem was. All contact with the officers leading the advance had been lost. Running forward with his number two and his batman, he found many men lying out in the open, terrified of going on because of the machine guns that were still pouring devastating fire down on them. Gilles shouted across to his support officer, 'Tell the mortar sections from me that if they don't knock those machine guns out instantly, I will personally go back and shoot them. Make sure that they understand the message.'

He saw a Corporal lying on his side about ten yards away to his left with his uniform covered in blood. 'Corporal, can you hear me?' he shouted.

'Yes sir. Who is that?' he asked.

'This is Colonel Deberney. What has happened to your officers?'

'They're all dead or wounded, sir. There's not one left.'

'Right, are you able to move?' he asked.

'No, sir, I've been hit in the ankle and the right knee.'

'Stay there. I'll get stretcher-bearers to you as soon as I can. Michel, can you see on your right whether there are any senior NCOs over there?'

Crawling on his belly, he moved over to the next bunch of

men lying in the open. Above the noise, he shouted, 'Are there any NCOs here?'

One man raised his arm and shouted back, 'Me sir, Sergeant Foulis.'

'Are you injured, Sergeant?' Michel asked.

'Just a slight wound in my left arm, sir. What do you want me to do?'

'Stay there. The Colonel will be over in a moment.'

Reporting back to Gilles, he told him that there was a Sergeant able to help about 15 yards away.

'Right, Michel' said Gilles. 'When I shout 'go', I want you and the Sergeant, with me, to get as many men on their feet as quickly as they can and we'll run like hell for the trench. Leave everything other than your weapons behind. Get that message to him and we'll go in about three minutes. Got it?'

'Right, sir,' Michel shouted back. The mortars were at last having some effect on the machine guns - two of the three were now out of action.

'Right, Michel, are you ready?'

'Yes, sir.' With that, Gilles stood up with pistol in his hand and shouted across to the men lying out in the open,

'Allez, mes braves. Let's give the Hun a taste of his own medicine. Go, go, go!'

About 50 men arose from the ground and charged forward, screaming at the tops of their voices. The Senegalese troops, who were not good under weak leadership but were a fearful sight once they got fire in their bellies, leapt up. That's all they needed, Gilles thought, someone to take them forward. Weaving left and right, they got to within ten yards of the trench when he went down. He had been shot clean through the head. The last thing he saw was the black soldiers jumping down into the trench before all went dark.

Once the trench had been secured, his batman came back to find his body. He looked at the man who had given his life for France in the most courageous way possible. He was lying on his back with his eyes open looking up at the heavens. The batman crossed himself, closed the Colonel's eyes and took his dog tag, ring and watch and emptied his pockets. One of the items was a small teddy bear with a label round its neck saying, 'Tedi says be safe, from your ever-loving daughter'.

It was too much to bear. He saluted his hero and walked away.

The French took the town that day with the London Scottish regiment. The following day, General Joffre decided that enough was enough and that they were to consolidate their position ahead of the severe winter weather coming in. Gilles was immediately recommended for France's highest honour for bravery in the field, the Chevalier de la Legion d'Honneur. The 8th Regiment, of which he was a proud Colonel, was twice cited for merit and carried the fourragère of the Croix de Guerre on its colour. Just one more day and Gilles would have made it, thought Michel.

At the end of hostilities, President Poincaré conferred the Legion of Honour on the whole Regiment with the following citation:

'A magnificent Regiment whose soldiers converted into heroism their anguish at knowing that their families were enslaved and their homes destroyed. Particularly in all the major actions of the war, on no occasion did the Regiment withdraw in the face of an enemy attack, and on no occasion were the enemy able to resist the impetus of their attacks.'

CHAMPS D'HONNEUR

Soldiers never do die well;
Crosses mark the places,
Wooden crosses where they fell;
Stuck above their faces.
Soldiers pitch and cough and twitch;
All the world roars red and black,
Soldiers smother in a ditch;
Choking through the whole attack.

Ernest Hemingway

Getting ready for the next challenge

The meeting was chaired by the CO, Lieutenant Colonel Justin Parker, who advised them that they would be going back into action within the next two to three weeks. The 2nd London Fusiliers were fighting as he spoke at Ginchy, the 26th and the 32nd Battalions were about to move up to attack Flers and the 11th was being held at readiness for an assault on Thiepval. So the emphasis was on preparing the Battalion the best possible way before the off. RSM Williams had been instructed to put the men through their paces on the temporary parade ground, with additional training with the bayonet and on bomb throwing. They had seen in the recent fighting, the bayonet and the bomb had become extremely important elements of the attack.

The Colonel walked up to Richard. 'I took up the issue you raised about the poor state of communications,' he said. 'In order to try and improve the situation, representatives of all the platoons with the Signals support section have been away on courses with the Royal Corps of Signals. You were right to raise it as a problem.'

Turning to the other officers, he said, 'Right, we currently have four rifle companies which will be commanded by Major Waller, congratulations to you on your promotion by the way. And congratulations also go to Thomas Holland, Freddie Howe and Jonathan Fuller on their respective promotions. The strength of the companies is about right with around 160 men and five officers in each. The platoon strengths are also OK but we are short of experienced NCOs. We are also short of mules to carry the Vickers. Smithie, can you see what can be done about that? It must be remembered that many of these men have only had very limited training back in England, with the training times getting shorter and shorter. It's up to us to do the best we can with the resources we have. That's why men like RSM Williams will be crucial.

'Right, any questions? We have the General here this afternoon, so he will be interested in talking to some of you. So be on standby please. That's all for now.'

Richard and Thomas retired to a quiet corner. They hadn't had much chance to catch up on things since they had both returned.

'How were things in Montreuil?' asked Thomas

'Pretty good really. It was great to see Simone again and the wedding, all things considered, went very well. We had the reception in the officers' mess at GHQ, which was Frank Skinner's idea. Considering we only had three days to arrange everything, it all went remarkably smoothly. It was a shame that you couldn't have been there, and Simone's father and my parents as well. But war makes things rather difficult.' He smiled. 'And with the baby being due around Christmas and the chances of me getting any more leave before then being remote, getting married when we did was all the more important. I'm not saying I wouldn't have asked Simone to marry me under normal circumstances, she is the most wonderful girl in the world, but maybe I might have waited to ask her until after this war is over. Still, we are both very excited about the baby. Hopefully there is something good to come out of all this.'

'And is the foot really OK now?' asked Thomas.

'It's fine. I went away on crutches and came back jumping for joy!'

'This ancestor's thing is interesting, isn't it?'

'Well, apart from the coincidence with our families, it's pretty amazing that this little Somme adventure is happening around 500 years to the year after the last one. What do you know about your ancestor?' asked Richard.

'All I know about Sir John Holland of Agincourt fame was that his father was the first Duke of Exeter, who was executed for treason by Henry IV. John obviously redeemed himself in the eyes of the King and he apparently fought well at the battle. Funnily enough, he was captured by the French of all people at another engagement, the Battle of Bauge, and wasn't released until ten years later. What about the Wallers?'

'I don't know much at all really. Sir Richard came back from Agincourt having captured the Duke of Orleans and held him at Groombridge until the French government paid the ransom.

It must have been a huge sum for them to have waited over twenty years to settle it. The Waller family were originally the de Valers from Normandy, but the name has changed over the years. The ransoms were so important, apparently, because they had to pay for the individual knights' armies. Many had to mortgage their estates before setting off under the King's flag, in order to put an army together.'

'I'm glad we still don't have to do that! It's all extremely interesting, I must say. Whether Sir Thomas Holland and Sir Richard Waller were living next to one another at the time of Agincourt, I know not. When this is all over, we really must find out more about it.'

Their conversation was interrupted by the arrival of the General. 'Good afternoon, gentlemen' said Rawlinson. 'I wanted to pay you a visit to thank you personally for the considerable efforts your Battalion has made since the start of July. You have taken terrible casualties, but you've stuck to the task in hand with tremendous spirit, and for that the nation is very grateful. We shall be calling upon you again in the near future, when your determination to rid us of the enemy in this part of France will be crucial. Do not fade in your endeavours, gentlemen. Your King and Country are depending on you. That's all, and thank you.'

He walked over to a group of the officers, including Richard and Thomas.

'Waller, it's good to see you again and congratulations on your MC. I bet your father is a very proud man, although I am not sure whether he is pleased that you are at the front.'

'Thank you, sir. I'm sure he is. I did pass on your best wishes.

He was very pleased to hear you were here looking after his son!'

Rawlinson laughed and said 'Tell him I'm doing my utmost.' He then turned on his heels, and with his staff entourage, headed back to the column of vehicles waiting outside.

When they had gone, Thomas turned to Richard. 'You didn't tell me you and the general were on speaking terms' he said. 'How come?'

'My father was an adjutant at the time when the General and he were in the Fusiliers together in India, and I was introduced to him when I was at GHQ. I was very impressed that he remembered my father.'

Richard had a spare hour or two after the Divisional band concert that Sunday evening and he had promised himself that he would write to Simone as soon as he got back.

My dearest Simone, I have been back a few days now and I have been so busy that this is the first real opportunity I have had to sit down somewhere quiet and private to write to you. All the way back from Montreuil, I reflected on what a lovely day our wedding had been and how peaceful and enjoyable the whole week was. Our walks by the river, the visit to the cinema and yet another wonderful day in Le Touquet - if the rest of our life is going to be as happy as that, then we are in for a real treat. Your mother was so kind to us, letting us sleep together. That must have been very strange for her. There were no problems on the journey back and I managed to get a lift back to the Battalion from Albert Station. It was good to meet up with Thomas again. You must meet him - you will like him a lot. General Rawlinson, you remember I met him when he was in

Montreuil? He was here today and we talked again. He served with my father in India and seems a nice man.

There was a letter waiting for me from my parents when I got back. My mother's illness has stabilised a bit and they seemed a little happier. I wonder what they will say when they get the envelope with the wedding photos! I hope it's not too big a shock for them. They will love you to bits! I hope you are well and that our 'lump' is going from strength to strength. I miss you more than I can say. The only comforts I have are the photographs of the wedding and my wedding ring, which I kiss every morning. It brings me closer to you for a second or two. I must get some sleep now - I am taking my Company out for a route march early in the morning to keep them fit. You are never far away from my thoughts and I feel so privileged to have you for my wife. Yours for always, Richard.

Excerpt from Haig's diary, September 17: 'After church, I presented French decorations to two officers in the General Staff here; saw General Swinton and congratulated him on the success of the 'Tanks'. In the afternoon General Foch came to see me. He explained the failure of the French attacks on the 15th against Frégicourt and Rancourt. Then he asked me to leave the others and go into the garden. It was here that Foch told me about a meeting which Lloyd George had with him very recently where Lloyd George asked why it was that the British had suffered much greater casualties than the French, and had not gained any more ground. Foch replied that the French infantry had learnt their lesson in 1914 and were now careful with their advances. He didn't mention the mutinies in the French Army.

Sadness in Montreuil

Simone had woken feeling quite sick. It was the first time this had happened to her and she was in two minds as to whether to go to work or not.

After an hour or so she felt a little better and said to Cécile that she would go in and if she got any worse during the morning, she would come home. Cécile always had a herbal drink first thing - someone had once told her that it was good for her complexion, of which she was very protective. Her skin still had the touch of her youth and she would do anything to protect and preserve it. She asked Simone if she would like a cup to help her sickness, but the thought and the smell of it just made her feel worse.

About ten minutes after Simone had left, there was a knock on the door and Cécile thought Simone had come back, but on opening it, she saw a telegram boy standing there. At first she wondered what he was doing there, and then she went pale and felt slightly faint.

'Telegram for Madame Deberney. Will there be any reply?' said the boy.

Cécile shook her head, gripping the door for support. She did not know whether there would be a reply or not, but, at that moment she just wanted to be on her own.

She closed the door gently and walked through to the kitchen, the one room in the house that was her domain, somewhere she felt comfortable and secure. Odd really, as it was here where she had spent the whole day when Gilles first went away. Oh, Gilles, she thought, this telegram is about my lovely husband. If only Simone was there. Should she wait until she came home? No - if the news was bad, she must break it to her gently, for the baby's sake. She must be strong. Simone would need her. This was the moment she had so often dreaded. She had seen the telegram boy going to other houses and, as he did so, the net curtains started to move as though everyone in the street felt the entrance of this intruder into their lives.

With shaking hands, she opened the telegram.

Dear Madame Deberney

It is with the utmost regret that I have to inform you that your husband, Colonel Gilles Deberney, has been killed in action whilst leading his men in an attack on the German trenches at Rancourt on the Somme. He died without pain, fighting for his beloved France in the most gallant manner and without his inspirational leadership, it is almost certain that the attack would have seriously faltered.

From the first days of the war, he gave his all for the Regiment, fighting in some of the most difficult campaigns from The Marne to Verdun and to the Somme. I believe that you would be proud to know that your husband has been recommended posthumously for France's highest honour for bravery in the field.

I personally knew Gilles for over two years and he was, as I am sure you know yourself, a remarkable man. He often spoke about his family with enormous affection and he will be greatly missed by everyone in his Regiment.

Please accept my deepest condolences at this time of extreme sadness.

Yours sincerely

General Fayolle, 6th Army.

Cécile began shaking uncontrollably. Then she heard a knock at the door. She chose to ignore it, for she wanted to be on her own. It would be the other ladies in the street wanting to know the news, or maybe they were just being nosy. No, that was being unkind. They were, she was sure, ready to offer comfort and support having seen the telegram boy arrive. The tears wouldn't stop.

Her next thought was that Gilles hadn't written to say that he understood what she had said in her letter, and that made it even worse. She felt totally distraught and alone. The man she had loved since she was 17 years of age, her only love, the perfect husband and father, had been taken from her. Another widow of France. How many more? What to do now?

Another spasm of crying hit her. Simone would leave her soon to live with Richard. She would be on her own. She thought about the child. Gilles would not see his grandchild.

More tears. More sadness. Oh, life can be so hard. Should she call the hospital? No. She must be careful with Simone. She loved her father so very much. He was so pleased about the baby. And me? I behaved so badly and was full of secret jealousy. I must make it up to her. For the baby's sake.

It was rare for Cécile to meet Simone after work. She decided that this would be best, but then she changed her mind and walked back home to avoid meeting anyone in the street.

Simone left the hospital on time after her shift and walked slowly down her road, noticing that it was very quiet. All the doors were shut and there were no children out playing. Very unusual, she thought. Suddenly she felt a shiver come over her. She opened the door, and immediately knew from her mother's expression that something had happened.

'It's not news about Richard is it?' she asked, going very pale.

'No, Simone, it's not. I'm afraid it's about your father. I received a telegram this morning and I keep telling myself to be very brave for yours and the baby's sake. But it's no good.'

She burst into tears and took her daughter in her arms. She didn't need to say the words 'he is dead'. Simone just knew.

'Oh, mother! I just thought somehow that he would make it. He had gone through so much without being too badly hurt.'

Cécile collapsed onto the floor. 'What are we going to do?' she sobbed. 'Our man won't be home any more. The man I have loved for so long has been taken away from us.'

She was inconsolable, and Simone knew that she was going to have to be the strong one. She loved her father deeply and knew that it was going to hit her some time soon, but at that moment it was her mother who needed all the help she could get. Cécile reached up and put her hand on Simone's stomach.

'Grow well and strong. We need you' she whispered.

The house in Montreuil was in mourning. Black drapes filled the windows and Cécile had not been out, other than to go to the church to see what she should do for Gilles. There was no body to bury. She had been notified that a temporary grave had been dug just outside Rancourt, but he would be moved to a permanent place of rest later on. There were many Frenchmen from Montreuil who had died for their country and regularly there were requiem services held at the Abbey in the Place Gambetta. She decided that this is what she would like for Gilles and arranged for a service to take place in a few weeks' time. Gilles had become something of a hero in the town, not only because he was a Colonel, but because confirmation of his decoration had come through. The Military wanted to attend the service and present Cécile with his medal at the same time. From thinking initially that this was not what she wanted, she decided in her own mind that it would be a fitting tribute to her husband and was pleased to agree.

The day after her visit to the Abbey, an envelope dropped onto her doormat. She recognised the handwriting immediately. It was from Gilles. She came over all hot and cold and just stood there looking at the letter. It can't be, she thought. He is dead. Then she realised that this was the letter she had hoped would come. Even so she opened it with some trepidation, for it could say what she didn't want to hear.

My Dearest Wife,

It took two full days to meet up with the Regiment, which gave me time to think things over after my leave. I know how disappointed you were with me and for that I am sorry. It is not unnatural for you to want your husband when he has been away for so long, but during this period something happened to me that I can't explain. It was nothing to do with my love for you, which remains as strong as ever, and always will. When this dreadful war is over, we will have plenty of time to get to know one another again and, who knows, it could be quite exciting for us both.

We have much to look forward to with our beautiful daughter and her English officer and their baby, our first grandchild.

Nobody means more to me in the whole wide world than you and I can't wait for us to be together again.

I will love you for ever.

Your Gilles.

After all her worries, he had loved her all along. Tears once again filled her eyes. She had been so wrong to behave as she had, but he had not held it against her. He understood. What a wonderful man. Oh, how she would miss him.

She ran upstairs and fell onto the bed, crying uncontrollably.

The Fusiliers go forward – October 1916

The 8th and 9th Battalions of Fusiliers moved forward on October 6 at about 10 am. They had been billeted in several leaking old barns between Warloy and Albert and had got very cold and wet, so in some respects they were pleased to be on the move. They were transported as far as Contalmaison, where they disembarked to commence the rest of the journey on foot.

'Come on you lot, look lively!' shouted RSM Williams. 'We've got a nice little walk lined up for you! But because I like you, you can leave your packs here and carry light. Aren't I good to you?'

'You're an angel, Sergeant,' shouted a voice from the back.

'Is that you, Wilkens? I thought you were dead!'

'No, Sergeant. You can't get rid of me that easily,' he replied.

'Well, I'll just have to try harder then, won't I?'

Richard walked up to RSM Williams and said quietly, 'Take it easy with the men today Sergeant, we've got a fair way to go and they'll need all their energy in the next few days.'

'Right, sir, just an occasional prod and bellow to keep them on their toes,' he said with a grin on his face.

Richard thought what a wonderful man Williams was to have at his side - just like Lewis. The men might give him the old backchat, but deep down they thought the world of him - as he did of them.

The rain had been falling steadily as they went forward, passing innumerable trenches, artillery positions, stores and camps. The great chess game of moving troops and transport from one position to another, trying to gain the maximum advantage over the enemy, would have been fascinating to an observer watching from afar.

When they had reached the outskirts of Bazentin, Williams shouted at the men to rest at the roadside. 'Lunch will be served, you 'orrible lot! But keep your heads down. That nasty German has a habit of throwing some heavy objects in our direction.'

Richard caught up with Thomas and over the sound of heavy gunfire, said to him, 'We'll rest here for an hour before setting off again. That shelling is starting to get a bit too close for comfort.' He consulted his map. 'There's a sunken section of the road a little further on' he said. 'We'd do better to rest the men there.'

'I'll just ask the RSM to move them on a bit,' said Thomas. 'Catch up with you later.'

The rain just kept coming down and it was fairly unpleasant

for the men sitting there with water pouring down their necks. Still the RSM walked among the men, trying to keep them as cheerful as possible given the conditions.

'Right, that's your three course lunch over!' he bellowed. 'We've got to pay a visit to some nasty little men who are making life a misery for a lot of people. On your feet, and get fell in, NOW!' he shouted.

As they started to move off, a couple of shells landed close by and sent some of the men slithering down a small gulley at the side of the sunken lane, sliding on their bottoms in the mud.

'Get back up 'ere, you miserable little sods!' roared the Sergeant.

'That's a good one, Sergeant. Sods, mud, get it?' said Wilkens.

'Thank you, Wilkens. If you don't shift your arse, I'll do it for you!'

Shortly they passed some huge craters and old German trenches, which made them feel better, as at least someone had advanced in this appalling weather. One section of the trenches was still immaculate, with incredibly deep dugouts and well-built solid firesteps. It looked as though the Germans had left in a hurry.

The craters brought back memories to Richard of that awful first day attacking Hawthorn Ridge and the subsequent fighting at the crater. He shuddered at the thought of it. There was a pungent smell of decaying flesh around, which suggested there had been some recent fighting here. It always made everyone feel very uncomfortable. The shelling wasn't letting up at all, which gave all the indications that they were getting close to the front.

A halt was called for the day, close to what was left of the village of Gueudecourt. Richard called across to the RSM to tell him that they would camp there for the night and that the CO would be talking to the assembled Battalion at 18.30.

Promptly at the appointed hour, with the Battalion in front of him, he told them that they would be going into the attack at 1.45 pm the following day. The 8th and 9th Battalions would be advancing together and the 26th and the 32nd would be alongside. The fact that four battalions of Fusiliers would be engaged in one attack was a proud moment for Richard and he expressed the hope that, as usual with the Fusiliers, they would fight well for the honour of the King and the Regiment. On that thought, he dismissed the men.

The night was pretty terrible. They were out in the open in a series of trenches, making shelters where they could in order to get at least a few hours' sleep. Richard's batman had constructed a tent which could just about sleep two men, so he asked Thomas if he wanted to share. The rain was still belting down and it had become noticeably colder. The noise of the artillery was also relentless. When they had retired for the night, after making sure that the men were as comfortable as they could be, Richard and Thomas exchanged letters for their respective families, just in case. They also gave letters to the Chaplain, should anything happen to either of them. Thomas had with him a hip flask with some excellent whisky which he had bought back from England. With a generous swig each, they settled down for the night, feeling a little warmer than they had at the start of the evening.

'Let's hope we can get a bit of shut-eye,' said Thomas. 'You don't snore, do you?'

There was a briefing at 7.30 am, during which the CO outlined in detail their objective.

'We will set off towards Gueudecourt in a westerly direction. Our objective is Bayonet Trench and it's held, if our intelligence is right, by the 4th Division of the Prussian Guards. This is a highly rated unit with a splendid reputation as first class assault troops, so we shall have our work cut out. But they haven't come across the Fusiliers yet! We shall move forward at 10.00 hours to Cobham Trench, which is where we will stay until the off at 13.45. Richard, you will lead 'A' Company, Thomas 'B' Company, Freddie 'C' Company and Jonathan 'D'. 'A' will take part in the attack on the centre, 'B' will take the right, 'C' the left with 'D' in reserve. You can see from the map that we are part of a nine kilometre front attack by the Fourth Army and we have an Australian Brigade some way off on our left at Le Sars who will be attacking the trenches to their front simultaneously to us. Any questions?'

'What about artillery cover, sir?' Richard asked.

'A bombardment will commence at 8.30 am, that's in less than an hour, concentrating on the Bayonet Trench. Although our objective is to take the ground 500 yards beyond the trench as well as Bayonet itself, HQ felt that to blitz the front line up until immediately before the advance was the right thing to do and then creeping the barrage forward as we advance. As you will be aware, the ground is exceptionally waterlogged, so any movement whether by foot or by vehicle will be difficult. The carrying of rations and ammunition will be a hard job. So be warned. If anything happens to me, Major Waller will assume command. Any further questions? Right Smithie, over to you.'

What the CO didn't realise was that the Germans knew full well the tactics being adopted and had pulled their machine guns back out of reach of the artillery barrage. As soon as the barrage was lifted, they would rush the guns forward.

The men were fatigued, for the night had been noisy, wet and cold with precious little sleep. A hot breakfast of porridge, bacon and bread and butter with a mug of sweet tea had cheered them up a little, but they needed to dry out their clothes. And it was still raining. The weather over the past few weeks had been appalling, and although some had managed to rig up tarpaulins over the trenches during the night, shelter was in short supply.

'Get yourselves ready to move out,' said RSM Williams. 'We shall be going up the line at 10.00 hours into another trench system, so I recommend any of you who found some waterproofing last night to carry it with you. You may need it!'

They marched forward for half an hour and arrived at Cobham Trench, which was knee deep in water and mud.

'Got any water wings, Sergeant?' asked Wilkens.

'Just shut your trap, Wilkens. I've heard enough from you. Any more and you'll be on a charge.'

After about half an hour, the rain stopped. It was still cold, but it gave some of the men the opportunity to try and dry out a bit.

'RSM,' shouted Richard, 'can you make sure that a fatigue

detail brings up plenty of spare ammunition for the Vickers and the Lewis? I have a feeling we will need all the covering fire we can get.'

RAIN! RAIN! RAIN!

Ever since I landed here,
Things have looked so dull and drear,
Wonder if this war's in vain,
We know not, only the rain

Author unknown

The bombardment was gaining momentum and there were only 30 minutes until the off. The butterflies were starting to take hold and with pulses racing, the RSM told the men to get to the latrine now or it would be too late. The enemy was aware they were coming, for you could see the activity in the trench. Richard had wished Thomas good luck and they had a wager as to who would be the first to reach the enemy trench. Richard was pleased to stand on the firestep, if only to get out of the water in the bottom of his trench. With his whistle in his mouth and his pistol in his hand, he looked at his watch and blew.

'Come on men, let's show the Hun what a Fusilier looks like!'

As soon as they were out of the trench, the machine guns opened up. Bobbing and weaving, Richard could see men falling all around him, and he quickly realised that most of the machine gun fire was concentrated on the centre.

Then he had another problem. Because of the heavy going on the ground and the weight the men were carrying, they were having trouble keeping up with the barrage, leaving them exposed and right out in the open. The RSM recognised the same problem and stopped to urge them on. He was immediately hit by machine gun fire and was dead before he hit the ground. Richard saw him fall and immediately realised he had lost the best right hand man that he could have wished for.

They were never going to reach the trench with this level of casualties, so he gave the order to dig in. He could see that the other two companies were suffering a similar fate. As the radio operator was still with him, he told him to get a message to 'B' and 'C' Companies to do the same, although from what he could see of 'C' Company, it seemed that it had almost ceased to exist. A message came back that they were to hold the ground at all costs until the next day and that 'D' Company would be sent up to support them.

Terribly exposed, they dug in as fast as they could while the Vickers and Lewis guns pumped a hail of bullets in the direction of the German lines. Because the ground was so wet, it was easier than normal to dig for cover and they managed to dig to a decent depth and stand to in case of a counter attack. But it wasn't long before water started seeping into the hastily dug shell holes and they found themselves lying in a foot of liquid mud, which was very, very cold.

Richard shouted across to the radio operator. 'Get onto HQ and tell them that we have had to dig in. Tell them to stop the barrage from creeping forward and get them to hit the forward trench and those machine gun nests. Give them the map reference.'

He crawled over to where Sergeant Longley was last seen and told him to get the men prepared for a counter attack. They would need more ammo for the machine guns and plenty of Mills bombs, so he sent a message to get 'D' Company to bring both of these things when they came up. *Christ, I miss Williams*, he thought. *I didn't have to ask him to do things, it was second nature to him.*

The artillery seemed to have quietened the enemy for a while, or at least the machine guns had stopped their terrible rattle. Maybe they were just lying low.

'Get 'B' Company on the phone, quick as you can,' Richard ordered. The sergeant handed him the handset once they were connected,

'Thomas, how goes it? Over.'

'Pretty bad. We've lost three officers and a lot of NCOs and the shelling has been particularly bad. Until we can get those machine guns sorted, we can't move. Over.'

'We are under orders to stay put until tomorrow, so get ready in case of a counter attack. Take care of yourself. Over.'

'You too, over and out.'

It all went quiet for the rest of the day and into the evening, when thankfully the rain held off, but it was still damn cold. 'D' Company came up in support and brought with them additional ammunition for the machine guns and some food and water. Extra grenades were distributed because Richard was certain that an attack would happen, if not during the night then the next morning. Star shells soared into the sky for most of the night, turning the churned-up countryside into a surreal landscape of black and white. He remembered from the Infantry Training Manual what it said about the predicament they were in: 'Entrenchments are only used when, owing to further advances being impossible, the efforts of the attacking forces must be limited temporarily to holding ground already won. The advance must be resumed at the first possible moment.' Food for thought.

Nobody got much sleep and Richard stayed awake to make sure the sentries did as well. If Williams were here it would have been a different story, he thought.

Dawn rose, and before they knew it the enemy came at them in force, with a platoon managing to get into their hastily-dug positions on Richard's right. Fortunately, the Lewis gun was well positioned to sweep the ground and for once it was the Germans who were on the receiving end. They had got close enough to throw some stick grenades and, as a result, there were casualties on the British side, but they were able to drive the Germans back.

Richard saw an opportunity to take the initiative and he told the radio operator to get a message to 'B' and 'C' Companies that he was going to charge the trench while they were still running back to their lines. The communication cable had been cut, so the signallers had to send messages by flags.

Leading from the front, Richard got his men to their feet and they rushed forward. The Hun in the trenches couldn't fire on them for fear of killing their own, and with 'B' and 'C' following, they managed to enter Bayonet trench. It was chaos.

Bombs were being thrown, rifles were being discharged and bayonets were being driven home, but there were far more enemy soldiers than at first appeared. They had come out of the dugouts in large numbers and the attackers couldn't hold them. Retreat was the only option.

They got back exhausted and greatly reduced in numbers, but of Richard there was no sign. Sergeant Longley got a message to HQ that the attack on the Bayonet Trench had been beaten back and they had followed it up with a charge, but they too had been beaten back. He reported that Major Waller had gone missing, although he might still show up. Nobody had seen what had happened to him. Knowing the friendship between the two officers, Longley then got a message to Thomas in 'B' Company. He looked across at the part of the German trench where Richard's Company had gone in and prayed and prayed that he was all right.

Excerpt from Haig's diary, October 7th. 'The enemies fighting qualities continue to deteriorate. The fighting at Le Sars had failed and the Canadian 3rd Division had been driven back from the trenches they had captured the day before. The French had done well - General Fayolle had copied our system of the creeping barrage and made good advances.

Montreuil honours its hero

The memorial service for Gilles was held at the Abbey, and the huge church was almost full. Representatives from his Regiment lined the entrance to the church and a Staff General from the 6th Army was there to present the medal won by Gilles for his bravery in the face of the enemy. Many of the family's friends were present, as were several officers from the British GHQ in the town. Cécile wanted the service to be a celebration of his life and not to be a morbid affair. Simone had been a tower of strength since they had first heard the news, and although Dr Froget was at first concerned for her in her current state, he realised that she was made of strong stuff. She had received a letter from Richard a couple of days before which had cheered her up no end.

After an opening prayer, the congregation sang one of Gilles' favourite hymns, which lifted the spirits of those in attendance. One of the leading figures from the bank where Gilles had worked for ten years before the war went to the pulpit to say a few words. The General from the élite Third

Bureaux of GHG, the equivalent of the British GHQ, then went forward to the front of the church, where he waited for Cécile to walk towards him. He cleared his throat.

'I give this honour, the highest that France can give a soldier in the field, to the wife of Colonel Gilles Deberney in recognition of his outstanding gallantry at Rancourt on September 25th' he said. 'Colonel Deberney sacrificed his life leading his men into the attack and, as result, the day was won. For that, France owes him and his family an eternal debt of gratitude.'

He stepped forward and pinned the medal onto Cécile. He then took a pace back, bowed his head, turned and walked back to his seat. With Cécile still standing there, Simone came and stood by her side while the congregation sang a final hymn. They then walked out of the church together. Six riflemen from his Regiment fired two volleys into the air to mark the end of the service.

For the second time in less than three weeks, the dreaded letter was delivered to their door. This time it was addressed to Mrs R. Waller. Simone was at work, although she was by now almost seven months pregnant. It was a military envelope, and Cécile did not know what to do. It might not be bad news of course…

Then she had a thought. She would go round to the old Ecole Militaire, now the British GHQ, and ask if Frank Skinner was there. He would be able to tell from looking at the envelope what was inside, or maybe without opening the envelope, call the Battalion to find out what the contents were. At least then she would be able to prepare herself for how to deal with the situation, if there was one. She put on her coat and scarf, for it was a bitter autumn day with a biting wind, and headed into the town centre.

When she arrived at the reception area, a young corporal asked her who she wanted to see. When she told him, he asked if she had an appointment. No, she said but it was a matter concerning her son-in-law, a British major serving in the front line. He understood the significance of that response and asked her to take a seat for a moment. He went away and said that Major Skinner would be with her shortly. He took her along to a small private meeting room, the same one Simone had come to when she saw Frank Skinner before.

Time was ticking on and Cécile was very anxious. Some twenty minutes passed before Skinner put in an appearance.

'Hello, Madam Deberney. I am very sorry to have kept you waiting. When the corporal told me you were here, I thought for a moment about the likely reason for your visit and I took the liberty of putting a call through to Richard's Battalion. Is that why you are here?' he asked.

'Yes, this letter was delivered to our house this morning and I obviously feared the worst. I wondered whether from the envelope you could tell what the contents might be so I could prepare myself for dealing with it with Simone.'

'I thought it may have been something like that. I spoke to the adjutant of Richard's Battalion. I do have some news for you I'm afraid, which may or may not be bad. Richard has been posted as missing. There was a major assault on the front line and Richard was leading an attack on a trench where the fighting was so severe they had to withdraw. When they got back to their lines, Richard hadn't returned. Please sit down, you look a little pale. Can I get you some water?'

He went to the door and shouted down the corridor for a glass. When he closed the door, Cécile said,

'That is how my husband died you know, leading his men into an enemy trench. Oh, my poor Simone. First her father and now her husband. I am concerned that the shock of the news may harm the baby.'

'It may not be the worst news, Madam. He may have been taken prisoner or have been wounded. If that is the case, we should know soon. All we can do is wait. Richard was a good friend of mine when he was at GHQ and I feel I have become a friend to both you and Simone. I know it sounds like a cliché, but if there is anything I can do, both personally and through the military channels that will help, all you have to do is ask. And I genuinely mean that.'

'Thank you, you have been very kind,' she said. 'So, is that what the letter will say? That he is missing?'

'Yes. I don't want to appear presumptuous, but if you would like me to be there when you tell Simone, I will happily do that. I could answer any questions she may have to try and help put her mind at rest.'

'That may be a way to soften the news a bit. You just don't know what to do for the best. I could invite you round for dinner. No, that will sound very contrived.'

She put her hand on his and said, 'You have been very good to all of us and I could tell at the wedding how pleased you were to be Richard's best man. Let me just think about it for a while and I will let you know.'

Full of sympathy for her predicament, he said, 'I will keep the next couple of days free, just in case you should call or leave a message. They are very efficient at reception. I am very sorry to hear the news, we can only hope for the best. The adjutant did tell me that he had written to Richard's parents as well. They will take it badly. The mother is not well and his father, who used to be in the Regiment, wanted him to work at GHQ to keep him away from the front line.'

They sat there together not saying anything for a moment or two, each with their own thoughts.

'Thank you for sparing the time to talk to me about this,' said Cécile. 'Whatever we do, Simone and the baby must be foremost in our minds. I may take you up on your offer. I just need to think of the best way of dealing with it. I will be in touch.'

They both stood up and he took her hand and kissed it. How very gallant, she thought.

· She went and sat in La Grande Place in the winter sun and realised she was stroking the scarf that Richard had given her. Let him come home safe, she thought. Her mind took her one way and then the other. Eventually she decided that she would tell Simone when she got home from work that night that she had bumped into Frank Skinner while walking past the Ecole Militaire that morning, and had invited him round for dinner the following day. That way, it would not seem strange. The only problem was delaying the delivery of the news, but there was no way that Simone would hear it from elsewhere and hopefully Frank being there would help ease the pain a little.

She went to the stationery shop and bought some writing

paper on which to write a note to Frank advising him of her decision and asking him if he could join them for dinner. She also asked him to keep the news confidential until then. She walked back to GHQ to deliver the note and then set off back home.

Home, she thought, a lonely place now. Even though Gilles had not been there during the day when he was at work and rarely when at war, his presence had always been there. Now as he had passed away, so had his spirit. Even with Simone there, there was still something missing. Hopefully the baby would restore some warmth back into the house, and that soon Richard would be there as well. Or would they move away, to England perhaps?

Simone hadn't thought it strange that Frank should come to dinner. In fact, she appeared quite excited by the prospect.

'I promise I won't bore him to death by showing him all the wedding photographs,' she said. 'Just a few of them!'

Frank arrived promptly for dinner in uniform, which surprised Cécile at first, but then she realised that in the circumstances, it might be for the best.

'I can offer you a glass of wine or brandy' she said. 'I'm afraid I do not have any whisky. Gilles could never get to like it and…' she was about to say something about Richard and thought better of it, 'so we never kept any in the house.'

'A glass of wine would be nice, thank you,' said Frank. 'I see you have Gilles' medal in a frame on the wall. How proud you must be. The Chevalier is, I understand a very rare honour.'

'I believe so,' said Cécile. 'Anyone who has mentioned it

has been very impressed. But I would rather have Gilles than a piece of metal in a frame.'

'Of course,' said Frank, thinking that he should change the subject. Discussion started to get a little difficult as they tried to avoid talking about anything that would involve Richard being mentioned. So much so that it wasn't long before Simone said,

'It's very nice to have you to dinner in our house Frank, but I get the feeling that there is another reason for you being here. Is there? Does it concern Richard? Because for the last half an hour, the one person who is common to us all has not been mentioned.'

Frank looked across at Cécile and saw her face fall in dismay.

'That was very perceptive of you, Simone,' said Frank. 'Yes, a letter has arrived for you and your mother asked me as a friend of the family if I would be here when the time came to open it.'

Simone clasped her hands tightly together. Her face was ashen.

'Do you know what it says?' she asked him.

Frank looked her straight in the eyes and said very gently, 'Yes, I do. I had a call from Richard's Battalion.'

'Then I would rather you told me than read it from someone I do not know. But be gentle with me please.'

After he had told her all he knew, there were no tears, just pain and shock. Her first reaction was to ask what could she do to help try and find him. He must be here, she thought, when the baby is born.

'Who deals with the prisoners of war and the wounded?' she asked. 'Is it the Red Cross? I am a nurse. Perhaps I can pull some strings?'

Frank gently put his hand on her arm and said quietly, 'You must let things take their course. I will do all I can from this end. I will put in for some leave and visit the Battalion in the field to find out what I can.'

'Can I come with you?' she asked imploringly.

'It's absolutely out of the question,' he said with compassion. 'It's far too dangerous and you must look after yourself and the baby, for Richard's sake. I will take my leave now, but you can rest assured that I will do everything in my power to help.'

Cécile saw him to the door and said quietly, 'Thank you for that. I think she found it much easier to take from a friend. You didn't have any dinner!'

'No, in the circumstance it is probably better for me to go now.'

'Well, perhaps another time then,' she said. 'I would like that a lot.'

Simone opened the envelope and started to read:

In The Field

15-10-1916

Dear Mrs S. Waller

I regret very much to have to inform you that your husband, Major Richard Waller, has been missing since the recent fighting on the Somme near Gueudecourt.

He was involved in a particularly difficult engagement and the casualties on both sides were very heavy. The trench that the 8th Battalion were given to attack changed hands twice during the fighting and therefore it is possible that he was taken prisoner. If this is the case, then you should hear from him soon via the Army or the Red Cross and I would be grateful if you would let me know if this occurs. However, I must say that the chances of him being alive are not particularly good. The trench was so heavily under fire for most of the day that I am very anxious about him.

Whatever his fate, his loss to the Battalion will be great. He was such a dedicated and brave officer and was greatly admired by his men. His rise through the ranks was testament to the high regard in which he was held by those above him. When he arrived at the Somme, it was the most difficult time in the Regiment's history, including Gallipoli, but Richard performed his duties with the utmost courage, winning the Military Cross for his actions.

In spite of his young years, leadership of his Company was outstanding and whether he was killed in action or has been taken prisoner, I personally will miss him more than I can say.

My thoughts are with you and the child you are expecting, which I understand is due at Christmas time.

Yours sincerely

J.S. Parker, Lt Colonel, 8th Battalion, Royal Regiment of Fusiliers

It was then that all the tears she had held back when Frank was there came flooding out. She couldn't come to terms with the news. If only Richard had not gone to the front but had stayed behind at GHQ, all would be well. But he had made the decision before she knew she was pregnant, and would it have made any difference anyway? She thought not. He had felt that it was all wrong to have his father 'protecting' when so many were dying in the field. It was a courageous decision and she loved him for that.

They had to find him. The baby was the most precious thing in the world and she had to protect its life.

She put her hand on her stomach as if to offer comfort to the baby inside, saying that everything would be done to find Richard and that she would remain strong, for all of their sakes. Before, she had been quite indifferent about the sex of the child so as long as it was healthy, but now she felt it was so important to have a boy.

She suddenly thought of Richard's parents. Frank said that someone had written to them. They must be distraught.

> *I dream that you are here, and not gone from me*
> *That you will return so that I can see*
> *Your smiling face and all that can be*
> *Forever which I hold dear.*

> *Author unknown*

CHAPTER FORTY NINE

The news reaches Richard's parents

The house in Crawley Down was deathly quiet. The letter had come, the one that every parent dreaded. In some respects, receiving a letter to say someone is missing is worse than the absolute finality of death. There was always a chance that he could be a prisoner, and that was what Richard's father kept saying to his wife. She was, however, taking a very negative view of the letter, focusing on the fact that his Colonel had said that the chances of finding him alive were very slim, rather than the thought that he could possibly have survived.

Fighting the cancer had taken a lot out of her, physically and mentally, and he was worried about what effect this news would have on her. He went to the chest of drawers in the lounge and took out the wedding photos. He remembered that Richard had given them the address of Simone and her mother. He decided that he would write to offer some comfort to her in her pregnancy. It was the least he could do. Richard had sounded so in love with this French girl that she must be in an awful state with the baby due in a couple of months. As a prospective grandparent, he felt he needed to do what he could to help. If it weren't for the war, they could go by train if his wife were strong enough to meet Simone and her mother in Montreuil. It would be good for all of them. He wanted to know what Simone was able to do in the search for Richard. Maybe there was something he could do from this end? He sat down straight away and composed the letter, wanting to get it in the post that day.

The search for a fallen hero

Following the attack on Bayonet Trench, the 8th Battalion was taken out of the line. It suffered serious casualties and failed to reach its objective. The 8th alone lost nine officers killed or missing and 244 other ranks, among them Richard. The 9th, 26th and the 32nd all suffered as badly and fared no better in terms of success. But it wasn't without a gallant fight. General Boyd Moss sent a message to the four Fusilier Battalions saying: 'Will you please thank all ranks of your Battalion for the magnificent gallantry they displayed yesterday. They advanced under heavy fire, which only the finest troops in the world could have faced. Though unfortunately unsuccessful, their gallant conduct has added to the fine reputation of the regiment, which you have already earned for yourselves.' This message was read out by the CO to the assembled survivors before they staggered back exhausted for a well-earned breakfast.

One person who felt in no mood to eat was Thomas Holland. His best friend was missing, and he was determined to do all he could to try and find him. The trench was still in enemy hands with No Man's Land piled high with hundreds of bodies, so it was impossible to get anywhere near it for the moment. He needed to find out from the Colonel when the next attack was to take place. Then, hopefully, if successful, they could arrange a truce to allow them to get in and bring out the dead and wounded. In the meantime, he had to go to check for himself the registrations at the dressing stations and field hospitals to see if Richard had been brought in. Lists can be wrong, as had so often been proved, so he had to see for himself.

As the days went by, there was no news, although there had been no notification yet of any men being taken prisoner that day. There had also been no resumption of the attack on the trench, which was still being held by the Prussians. The British had tried raising a white flag to initiate a truce to allow them to bring out the dead and wounded from the field, but it had been met by a burst of machine gun fire. Considering that there were German dead out there as well, it was a pretty callous act. But the Germans had a reputation for spending time looking after their lightly wounded, because they could get them back into action quickly, and not worrying too much about those who were dead or badly injured. Presumably they rated those lying out in No Man's Land in the latter category.

A week had gone by since Frank had been to their house and Cécile felt that she would like to invite him back to dinner, particularly as he had missed out last time. She tentatively broached the subject with Simone, worried that it might bring back bad memories, but she was very keen on the idea. She wanted to know if Frank had made any progress with his searches, although she knew deep down that if that had been the case, he would have been in touch.

This time he arrived in 'civvies' and he looked so different. The whole evening was much more relaxed, and Frank now had something to report. He said he was going with a GHQ party to Albert the following week and had asked his senior officer if it was OK to pay a visit to the 8th Fusiliers, who were camped just outside the town. He had been in touch with a representative of the International Red Cross, who had reported back that the Germans had stated that prisoners from the Fusiliers had been taken in that area on the days October 7th and 8th, but as yet there were no details of battalions or names. Still, it was a start.

Frank advised Simone to write to the Red Cross as Richard's next of kin. They had offices in Paris and Boulogne as well as in the UK, and it was important to register him as missing quickly because of what was happening on the battlefield.

'In order that they can help you, you have to tell them where he was in action, his name, number, rank, Regiment, Battalion, Company and the date,' Frank explained. 'I can help you with that if you like. Apparently they print out lists every month of prisoners known to be captive, including those who are wounded, and send them to GHQ to distribute to the adjutants' departments of relevant Regiments.' He looked at her. 'I'm sorry about all this uncertainty. How are you coping?'

'Every day is different,' she replied. 'One day I am excited by the prospect of some reassuring news, the next I think there is not much hope. But then, the little one inside me gives me a kick and I realise my responsibility to this new life and know that I must carry on regardless.'

Cécile walked over to fill his glass.

'I think you are both remarkable women,' said Frank. 'You have gone through so much in the past few months and yet you have managed to carry on and deal with your grief and sadness in a most dignified way.'

'But we are also fortunate to have friends like you who are such a comfort to us,' said Cécile.

'By the way,' said Simone, 'you must ask for Thomas Holland when you go to Richard's Battalion. He was his best friend there.'

Thomas makes contact with Simone

Thomas sat down one evening to write what would probably be the most difficult letter he had ever had to write. He was used to writing to loved ones of those killed or missing from his Battalion, most of whom he knew by name, but had no personal attachment to. This was different. Richard had been such a good friend in the five months that they had known one another, almost like brothers, and he knew that all the confidences they had shared could only have been shared between two people who trusted each other implicitly. Richard had come back from leave so full of love for his wife and baby to be that he couldn't imagine what she was going through at the moment.

Dear Mrs Waller

We have never met and yet somehow, particularly at this time, I feel very close to you. My very best friend, your husband, and I shared so many experiences together that I doubt whether I shall ever have such a friend again. I live in hope that our friendship can grow as strong as mine was with Richard. In the many moments of danger that we shared, the comradeship built up between us was like no other and I always felt that as long as Richard was alongside me somewhere, I was safe. Hopefully only temporarily that friendship, trust, companionship and mutual respect has been taken away. I am doing all I can to find out what has happened to Richard and will not rest until I have found an answer. I have applied for some overdue leave and, as the Battalion is not scheduled to be in action again for a while, it has been granted. I would like to take the opportunity to come and see you if that is all right? I shall have to take my leave soon, so you will probably not get the opportunity to reply before I have to set off. But, if for any reason at all, you decide that it would be too upsetting or for any other reason, I shall completely understand. I cannot guarantee what date I should arrive in Montreuil, but it should be approximately seven days from the date of this letter. Hopefully this reaches you before I do!

Yours sincerely

Major Thomas Holland, 8ᵗʰ Battalion, Royal Regiment of Fusiliers

Simone received the letter from Thomas a couple of days before he was due to arrive, and was delighted. She had heard so much from Richard about his friend that it was impossible not to like him before they had even met.

On the same day, she received another letter. This time it was from her father's adjutant, Michel Geraint. He had written to say that he had been with her father when they had advanced towards the enemy and had gone back to where her father had fallen afterwards to make sure he was laid to rest properly. He had also collected the valuables which his batman had recovered from his body, including his watch and wedding ring, all of which would be returned in due course.

But the real reason for writing was to say that his batman had found in her father's trouser pocket a teddy bear with a message tied around its neck from his daughter. He wanted her to know that her father had carried it with him wherever he went, and that it would come back to her with the other items. He finished by saying that he was a wonderful man and a good friend.

Simone was deeply touched by the fact that he had bothered to write, and she showed the letter to her mother. It made Cécile cry to think that Gilles' wedding ring would be returned to her. That meant far more to her than the medal on the wall.

Thomas knocked on the door of the Deberney house in Montreuil. On the advice of Dr Froget, Simone had now given up work. Mentally, she had been through so much recently that he felt that there was a danger of her collapsing through exhaustion. He said he wanted to see her regularly to check her heart rate and blood pressure, but also felt it was important that she had someone outside the house to talk to if she needed to, to act as a release for her worries.

As she opened the door, Simone saw his uniform and smiled.

'You must be Thomas,' she said.

'And you must be Simone' replied Thomas Holland.

Feeling awkward and stupid, they both burst out laughing.

He put out his hand to shake hers, but she stepped forward and with difficulty because of her pregnancy, gave him a hug.

'Please come in. I have been so looking forward to your visit. You must come and meet my mother,' she said.

Hearing the sound of voices, Cécile came out of the kitchen.

'Mother, this is Richard's friend, Thomas Holland.'

'I am very pleased to be able to welcome you to our house, monsieur. Please take off your coat, for I think you will find it warmer in here than outside. The weather has been awful lately.'

Looking at her, Thomas could well understand why Richard had fallen head over heels in love with this woman. And the similarity between mother and daughter was startling. He had seen the wedding photographs, but they did not do either woman justice.

'What are you staring at, Thomas?' Simone asked.

'Oh, I'm sorry,' he said, a little embarrassed. 'I can see why Richard thought you were the most beautiful person in the world.'

She blushed profusely, with tears welling up in her eyes and turned her head slightly sideways, as if to hide her pleasure at this comment.

'I can also see where you get your good looks from,' he said, looking towards Cécile.

'You are going to be most welcome in this house,' said Cécile with a cheeky grin. This was the first time for some while that either woman had had something to smile about.

'Come and sit down, you must be tired after your journey,'

Simone said, realising that she had used the same words to Richard the last time he had been there.

'Oh, it's nothing. It is just such a pleasure to be away from the Battalion for a while,' he said, choosing his words carefully. 'I see, madame, that there is a medal on the wall. Excuse me for being nosy, but I have always been interested in such things.'

Simone quickly realised that Thomas would have known nothing about the death of her father. 'You should know so that we are all not embarrassed to talk about it that my father, Cécile's husband, was killed less than a month ago leading his Regiment on the Somme,' she explained. 'He won the Chevalier de la Legion d'Honneur posthumously.'

'Oh, I am so dreadfully sorry. I had no idea. Richard told me that he was in the French Infantry, but… madame, please accept my deepest condolences, and to you Simone, of course. What a dreadful time for you both. I now feel that I am intruding on your home at a time when you should be left to mourn for him. I did wonder why there were black curtains in the window when there is still hope that Richard will be found. And, of course, you also have Richard to worry about. I feel I should take my leave and come back another time.'

'Oh no, please,' said Simone, 'we need people like you, particularly someone who was so close to Richard, to be here with us. It will do us both good and I promise we will not be mournful all the time, just occasionally!' she said with a gentle smile.

It was that smile, Thomas thought, that was so beguiling. Her mother had almost exactly the same smile.

They sat together after Cécile had gone off to make some coffee. Simone wanted time to get to know him, but was slightly worried that just as they were getting to know one another, the time would come for him to go back. But you can't go through life thinking like that, she thought. You have to grab every moment and enjoy it while it's there, as she had with Richard.

'You know that Richard worked at GHQ in the town for a while?' she asked.

'Yes, he told me all about it and how you two first met,' Thomas said. There was that lovely coy smile again.

'Well, his friend Frank Skinner, who stood in for you as best man, has been doing all he can for us from this end to try and find out what happened to Richard. He was here a few days ago and has taken some leave to go to your Battalion to find out what he could. What we didn't know then was that you were on your way here. The two of you have probably passed en route. We asked him to ask for you when he got there.'

'That's a great shame,' said Thomas, 'but we must all collate what information we can find at the end of the day. He must be a good friend to have around.'

Coffee arrived and Thomas asked when the baby was due.

'The doctor has given me a date of December 22, so we have got six weeks to find Richard. I do so want him here for the birth,' she said.

'At the moment, Simone, the best we can hope for is that he is a prisoner of war and if that is the case, I'm afraid he will not be here for the birth.'

'Oh, I know, it's just a dream I have had for so long. One I don't really want to let go of.'

After a pause, she asked, 'Tell me a little about what you and Richard used to do when you weren't in action. I used to try and think about what Richard might be doing at certain times of the day, but I really had no idea.'

'Of course I can, but if it wouldn't upset you too much, I have brought some photos taken by the Battalion photographer - Richard and I are in some of them. It gives quite a good idea of all the daily routines of army life. When Richard is home, and I have to believe that he will come back, you will be an army wife and this will help paint a picture of the kind of things you will be subjected to.'

'I would love to see them. If it gets me upset, I shall soon tell you,' said Simone.

Thomas' time with them passed quickly, and it wasn't long before he was getting ready to go back. It had felt to Simone that he had become a surrogate husband and at the same time a very good friend. She believed before he arrived that she would like him, and she was not mistaken. He had taken some of the pain away and had promised to do all he could to help them both.

'I am very sorry to ask this question, but are you all right financially?' he asked, 'Because I have more than I need and if I can help in any way, you must not be embarrassed to ask. I must do this for Richard, and the baby you see?'

Simone went up to him and kissed him on the cheek and said, 'You are very kind and I promise you that I shall ask if I need to. I have heard from Richard's adjutant that a gratuity is paid plus a pension of £140 a year. With what Cécile receives from the French Government, I think we shall be OK. We both intend to go on living here after the baby is born.'

'I will come and see you in the New Year and it may seem presumptive, but I would like very much to be involved with the baby in some way. You see, Richard meant the world to me as a friend and I feel it is the least I can do for him until he comes home. He would do it for me, of that I am absolutely sure.'

With tears welling up in his eyes, he kissed her on both cheeks to say goodbye and thanked Cécile for her generous hospitality. He walked away from the house and waited for a few minutes until they had gone back indoors before returning to put an envelope quietly through the door with some money and a note in it. He knew that if he offered it in person they would say no. This way, they had little choice but to accept.

Sad news back in England

Not long after receiving the news about Richard, his mother took a serious turn for the worse. Hubert could tell she was in great pain, but she never complained. He wondered if it had something to do with being the wife of a military husband. Having travelled with him and his regiment around the world, the wives became hardened to the conditions and learnt to expect bad news. There was a time in India when there had been a serious mutiny among the sepoys and there were deaths in the Regiment. But she was always there for him, a tough old cookie he thought. Now it was different. The doctor had visited the day before and quietly said to Hubert that there was nothing more they could do. He would increase the morphine to help the pain, but it was now just a question of time. Once they had a son to live for, one who would carry on the family name, but she was convinced that he was not coming back. And that thought had dimmed her eyes, knocked the stuffing out of her. Not even the thought of a first grandchild due imminently could help. The fight was gone. Her life was coming to a close.

IN MEMORIAM (from the *Crawley Observer*)

WALLER, Margaret, Louise. Beloved wife of Hubert. Passed away in her sleep from an illness carried with tremendous fortitude and from a broken heart after hearing that her only son, Richard, was posted as missing, believed killed on the Somme, October 1916. Private service to be held at St Mary's Church, Crawley on Thursday November 7 at 11 am. All donations please to the Benevolent Fund, Royal Regiment of Fusiliers.

The funeral was a small but dignified affair. Hubert couldn't help but think as he stood looking at her coffin that if his wife could have held out for just a little longer, the new-born child might have given her something good to think about in her passing. But there was nothing but sadness.

The days passed and there was still no news. Thomas had written to thank Simone and Cécile for their hospitality and to say that he had heard nothing other than that a Fusilier from the 9th Battalion who had fought alongside the 8th on the day Richard had gone missing had contacted the Battalion, via The Red Cross, to say that he had been wounded and was being held by the Germans in a military hospital. But there was no news of the other 62 members of the Battalion who remained unaccounted for.

Because of the appalling weather around Gueudecourt where the advance had taken place, all attacks had been put on hold after the last failure in early to mid- November. The ground Richard had crossed and the trench he had entered were still under enemy control, so any further investigation in the area was impossible. Frank had also called round, after visiting the 8th Battalion whilst on leave, to say that nothing had come up. It was as though Richard had vanished into thin air. Frank spoke to some of the troops who had attacked the trench that day, but they could add nothing. Richard had last been seen in the trench moving forward before the decision was taken to retreat. After that, nothing. They were now solely reliant on information coming back via the Red Cross or from sources within Germany.

A son for Simone

Simone's mood seemed to change daily. Dr Froget told her it was partly to do with her pregnancy, which may or may not have been true, but she knew it was mainly to do with the uncertainty over Richard. As she got nearer to the due date, she found herself missing him more and more. Both Thomas and Frank had been wonderful, but she realised quickly that they were getting as frustrated as she was with the lack of feedback from anywhere. Even at Richard's Battalion, the adjutant's department had kept in regular touch with her by post, but with nothing more than holding letters. So, as was to be expected, she had good days and not-so-good days.

Cécile seemed to have been depressed lately, and Simone was encouraging her to get out and about. 'Why not ask Frank round again?' she suggested. 'Perhaps he will feel more comfortable about asking you out somewhere. He's probably not sure about whether he should be asking a lady who has been recently bereaved. He was very good company, the last time he came.'

'Maybe I will. I just want to be here for you for the moment. The rest can come later.'

They were much closer now as mother and daughter than they had ever been, and Simone knew how much she was going to need her mother and how emotional the delivery was going to be. Dr Froget had promised to be there for her when the time came and he had even cancelled a family Christmas holiday to their house by the sea in Normandy. He must be a godfather, she thought, along with Thomas. They both loved Richard in their own way, but not in the same way as me.

The labour pains started two days early and Dr Froget called at the house.

'It is well advanced, young lady,' he said. 'I might even be able to get away to Normandy for Christmas after all. I see no reason why you cannot have the baby here, as you wanted. So we had better get you upstairs. Can you manage?'

He and Cécile helped her up to her bedroom, and he asked Cécile to get towels and hot water ready.

'I shall come back as soon as the contractions start in earnest' he said. 'Cécile, you have a neighbour who can get to the hospital quickly?'

'Yes, doctor, it is no problem,' said Cécile. 'And in any case, I am quite looking forward to acting as midwife. This baby is so important to us.'

After a reasonably short if painful labour, the baby was safely delivered, and Dr Froget had great pleasure in telling Simone that she was the mother of a beautiful healthy boy weighing in at a healthy seven and a half pounds. There were floods of tears from all parties, even the doctor. They were tears of relief, joy and sadness, all rolled into one.

Simone had to have stitches, so she was in a little discomfort, but it mattered not. Her greatest regret was that Richard was not there to see his son, but she still hoped he would be soon. The child would be called Richard Gilles Waller. with Richard being pronounced the English way. Cécile could barely control her emotions and Simone was radiant, considering what she had just been through.

'I hope this boy will see a better world than the one we are experiencing at the moment,' said Dr Froget, 'and may he live a long and fruitful life in the knowledge that he had a wonderful father and grandfather. It is now time for me to leave you to enjoy this moment. I shall see you when I return, Simone, but just take it easy for the next few days.'

'I shall, doctor, and thank you for everything. Have a lovely Christmas with your family.'

'We will, as best we can, with ours.'

Richard's father had written to Simone in November after he had been told that his son was missing. It was a short letter, because he found it difficult to write to someone he did not know. He knew she would still be full of hope, mingled with despair, at what had happened. He expressed sadness at the news, but would not give up hope that one day soon his son would be found, hopefully as a prisoner. He told her that their thoughts were with her and asked her to let them know when the baby was born, saying that one day soon they hoped to visit Simone. He had not mentioned that his wife had passed away. She had enough to worry about for the moment.

Christmas in the Deberney household was a strange affair. Simone was only just on her feet and still feeling very tired.

She was breast-feeding young Richard, so the nights were disturbed as well. Frank had been round at the first opportunity to see the baby and had used the visit to invite Cécile to the theatre in Montreuil between Christmas and the New Year. Cécile asked Simone if she minded, which of course she did not; she was pleased for her mother to be doing something else. She had been so supportive during the birth and immediately afterwards that she deserved a night out. It would also give Simone some time on her own with young Richard. Whilst he was asleep, she wrote a letter to Thomas telling him the good news. It made her think about Richard's relationship with him, how strong it was and whether it had anything to do with their families' historical background. Perhaps it was important that young Richard should have the opportunity to carry on the family tradition.

Simone and Cécile spent Christmas Day together, each consumed by their own thoughts. Baby Richard took their minds off things, but the uncertainty over his father continued. Frank had heard nothing and Thomas had written to say that he too had drawn a blank. Simone had sent Thomas and Richard's parents Christmas cards telling them about the arrival of young Richard and hoping to see them in the New Year. She had received a Christmas card from the Battalion with a message inside saying 'thinking of you at this time'.

Early in January, Frank received a copy of the Red Cross list of those missing that were being held by the Germans as prisoners of War. The name of Richard Walter of the Royal Fusiliers was on it, and Frank immediately began to wonder if this might be a spelling mistake. Before he did anything else, he checked to see if there were any Richard Walters reported as missing on the Somme and found that there were none. He was not sure whether to tell Simone or not, but decided against it until he had spoken to Thomas and put an enquiry through to the Red Cross to double check the information. Thomas said that he would make all the necessary enquiries with the adjutant's department if Frank could deal with the Red Cross. They agreed not to say anything to Simone until they had fully explored the situation.

Frank asked them to confirm the spelling, the date of capture and the prisoner's state of health and number. He knew this would take some while as there were almost 80,000 missing on the Somme alone from July 1st to the end of the year. Some of those had been held prisoner. Three days later, the Red Cross confirmed that the name should have been Weller, and apologised for the error. Thank goodness, thought Frank, that they had not said anything to Simone.

Richard's father had been pleased to hear from Simone about the baby and decided that he must make every effort to get over there, although he realised that the trip would not be without difficulties. He telephoned his old Regiment and explained the situation and a Major Cummings promised to call back.

Three days later, he received a letter. As an Honorary Colonel in the Regiment, they suggested that they could arrange travel documentation for him on the basis that he was visiting GHQ in Montreuil on an important military matter. That sounded perfect to him and he wrote back straight away to agree and say that he could go as soon as it could be arranged. He must write to Simone to tell her to expect him shortly, but he couldn't tell her exactly when.

When the letter arrived in Montreuil, Simone was delighted. She told Frank of the impending visit and Frank said that it would be no problem putting him up at the mess. They had accommodation there for visiting dignitaries. Richard's father made up his mind to buy his grandson a gift - something very English.

When the day came for him to leave for France, he went to his wife's grave before catching the train. It was a bitterly cold January day with snow in the air. He put a small posy by her headstone and told her that he was going to see their grandson.

He left Crawley wearing the uniform of a Colonel in the Royal Fusiliers. After spending over 40 years with some attachment to the Regiment, the uniform made him walk more upright with a spring in his step. In recent weeks, his shoulders had been slouched forward, without a purpose.

At Victoria, he caught an omnibus to Charing Cross. He felt a bit of a fraud being saluted by the many soldiers he passed. After all, it was years since he had held a full commission. His Regiment had arranged for him to travel first class, for which he was grateful, as the train was heaving with troops heading back to the front after leave. He shared a compartment with other officers, one of whom asked him where he was heading. On being told that he was going to France, the Captain commented that he seemed a little old to be going back to the battlefield. Hubert turned to him and said, 'There's no counting the value of experience you know!' Feeling pleased with his response, he buried his head in his newspaper, so as to avoid any further questions.

It was late afternoon when he arrived in Folkestone, where he had booked a hotel for the night. This was the first time he had been away from home without his wife, and he suddenly felt desperately lonely. A few whiskies helped him get through the hours before settling down for the night. He was awoken at just after six by a ship's hooter in the harbour and realised that he was on his way to see his daughter-in-law and grandson for the first time. As his son had fallen so deeply in love with this Simone, he too felt that she must be rather special. He felt suddenly excited by the prospect of meeting her.

He arrived in Boulogne after a rough crossing - it was the middle of winter, after all. The port was heaving with troops coming and going. So many different regiments and nationalities. He saw the kilts of the Highland regiments and the turbans and fine beards of the Indian Army, which took him back momentarily to his time there with the Fusiliers. He had arranged to get a train to Montreuil-sur-Mer, where a driver from British GHQ would be waiting to take him from the station up the hill into the town.

Hubert was not disappointed when he arrived at the house at last and Simone opened the door. She truly was a beautiful girl. For her part, Simone could immediately see the likeness between father and son.

'Welcome to our home, Monsieur Waller' she began. 'We are very pleased that you could make it here. Travelling in time of war can't be easy.'

'I am delighted to meet you. Please call me Hubert. The

reason I am in uniform is that the easiest way to arrange this visit was through my old Regiment. As I am still active, albeit in a temporary capacity, they were able to say I was visiting GHQ on official business.'

'I understand. Now you must come and meet your grandson. I am sure you will be very proud of him.' She lifted the little boy out of his cot, and Hubert's eyes filled with tears.

'He is just beautiful' he said. 'Just like you, my dear. How are you coping with all of this?'

'With the little man, very well. With his father, that's not so easy. It is not knowing that's so difficult. But it must be very hard for you and your wife as well,' she said.

'I'm afraid my wife passed away last November,' he said. 'She had been ill for some while, but the news of Richard was just too much for her to bear.'

'Oh, I am so, so sorry, I didn't know.'

'I didn't want to tell you at the time. You had enough to worry about,' he said.

That is exactly the sort of consideration that Richard would have shown, she thought. She kissed him on the cheek. 'It was very kind of you to think of me, when you had enough troubles of your own' she said.

'I do miss her so, particularly at a time like this. She would have loved the little man.'

Taking him by the arm, she took him into the lounge.

'My mother will be home in a minute or two. She will be very pleased to meet you and I have arranged with a good friend of the family, who was Richard's best man at the wedding, for you the stay at the officers' mess at GHQ. It's only just up the road.'

'I'm sorry to put you to any trouble. I just felt it was so important to see him and I'm so pleased that you decided to call him Richard. It suits him well! I have bought him a small gift, which he will have more use for when he is older.'

Simone opened the box and inside was a pewter mug. 'Oh, it's lovely,' she said

'They are very popular with English men for drinking beer' he said. 'But he's got a few years yet before he will be able to use it!'

'I see that you have had it engraved,' she said. 'Let me read it – 'To Richard II, The son of a Lionheart who fought bravely for his country in France. 1916.'

from the Crawley Observer, February 1917

Colonel Hubert Waller (retd), who had been missing from his home in Crawley Down for several days, has been found by a fishing boat in the English Channel floating in the direction of the French coast. Neighbours said that he had been distraught recently over the death of his wife and that his only son had been posted as missing in action on the Somme in Northern France. His car had been found abandoned on the top of the cliffs at Seaford Head, somewhere, according to friends of the family that he liked to visit with his son.

The George & Dragon Inn, Speldhurst, Kent, 1440

There was a huge amount of noise coming from the snug, mainly because the drinks were being paid for by the most important man in this part of the county. Sir Richard Waller of Speldhurst, High Sheriff of Kent, the hero of Agincourt who had captured the Duke of Orleans during the battle, had received the news that the King of France had finally agreed, after 25 years, to pay the ransom for the Duke's release. And it was a mighty ransom. Only right and proper, thought Sir Richard. After all, he had put together, and paid for, an army of archers to fight in King Henry V's army in 1415, many of whom were celebrating with him today, and it was a just return on his investment. Many had also fought with him at Rouen some three years later.

The Duke had been held 'in honourable restraint' at Groombridge Place for all that time and there were those among the drinkers, and elsewhere in Speldhurst, who were sad he was going back to France. While in England, he had been a very generous benefactor to the church, where he had prayed every day, and while in captivity, had made a name for himself as a poet of considerable renown. Still, not a day to be maudlin, thought Sir Richard, who was feeling rather benevolent.

'There is a gold sovereign for all my brave archers who fought alongside me at Agincourt' he called out. A huge cheer went up.

'And also to the families of those archers who have since passed this life. May God be with their souls.' This brought another cheer, with tankards being banged on the counter.

Sir Richard had sent word to his neighbour, John Holland, the 2nd Duke of Exeter, who had also fought with him at Agincourt and at Rouen, to join them in celebrating the good news. Holland had become a very senior military commander and in 1435 he had been made an Admiral of England, Ireland and Aquitaine. He was the King's appointee in Aquitaine, where he spent most of his time these days. It was from there that he sent his apologies and congratulations on a 'long overdue' reward. Sir Richard was very pleased with the way his friend and neighbour's life had turned out, considering his father had been executed for conspiring with others to assassinate Henry IV.

Thomas on leave, spring 1917

After the long winter of 1916/17, Thomas Holland was asked by his CO if he wanted to take some leave. The 8th Battalion were 'at rest' near to Albert and he had not been away from the front line for four months – far too long. The week before, whilst there was still snow on the ground, a party of Germans had infiltrated the battalion's front line and it had been a particularly unpleasant engagement, with bayonets being used and only the cool head of a private manning a machine gun keeping them at bay. The private had been recommended for a Distinguished Conduct Medal and Thomas a Military Cross for his courage in bringing back wounded Fusiliers under fire. The Battalion had lost four officers, two of whom were mortally wounded, and 41 other ranks killed or wounded. It was a bad day.

'Thank you, sir. I could use a break. I will get home to see my family in Sevenoaks and also visit Major Waller's wife and baby in Montreuil.'

'There's been no further news then about Richard?'

'Fraid not, sir. It's six months now and I imagine his wife will have given up hope. Although knowing her as I do, that may not be the case,' he said with a wry smile on his face.

'Well, you have certainly earned a rest. Go down and organise your passes and hopefully your MC will have been confirmed by the time you get back.'

Thomas caught the train from Albert to Amiens and then followed the coast up to Montreuil. He wasn't sure whether to go to England first, but as far as he knew, his parents were well, and Simone might need his presence more.

He felt quite at home in Montreuil, not because he had been there often, just that it had been the topic of conversation between him and Richard so many times that the intimacy of the town permeated his soul. He had written to Simone to say that he had been granted leave and hoped to get to see her and 'little Richard'.

The station lay at the bottom of the hill by the River Canche and it was quite a climb up through the walled ramparts to the town itself. Little did he know that Richard's father had covered this route by car a couple of months earlier.

He remembered Simone's house from his last visit, but this time there were no black curtains in the window and there were spring flowers in the front garden. She was very pleased to see him. The sight of an officer of the Royal Fusiliers standing on the doorstep had several of the neighbours' net curtains twitching.

'Oh, Thomas, you don't know how happy I am to see you,' said Simone, kissing him on both cheeks. 'It has been months, and you look as though you need feeding up! Please come in and let me take your coat.'

'The food on the front line leaves something to be desired, to be honest,' he said. 'And it has been so cold. The feet get it really bad, no matter how many pairs of socks you wear. I did get frostbite, but at least I didn't lose any toes. Mind you, that might have got me a ticket home if I had.'

'Please stay here with us. There is room and it will be nice to have a man about the house again. I will introduce you to Richard junior when he wakes. I think you will be impressed. I assume you have heard no further news?'

'No, sadly not. At this stage, it will only be from the Red Cross if he has turned up as a prisoner. I am really sorry, Simone.'

'In my heart, I have in a way come to terms with it. There are so many wives and mothers here in Montreuil who are suffering from this terrible war. And it must be the same in England. Richard's father was saying when he visited here that there are no towns or villages that have escaped the bad news. The streets are full of women walking around dressed in black from head to toe and men with no arms or legs, begging in the streets for help. Richard would not want to see that.'

'Is there anything I can do to help?' he asked.

'No, just to have you here is a real tonic. I would like to hear you talk about the Regiment, but in some respects I would rather not. And I am sure that you would like to enjoy the little time you have away from the trenches without being reminded about it.'

'Before Cécile comes home, there is something I would like to ask you,' he said.

Simone took his hands in hers and looked down at the

floor. 'Thomas. I think I know what you are about to say and the answer must be no. Richard to me will always be the most precious thing ever in my life and I will love him always. Our son will be a constant reminder, as if I ever needed one, of that great blessing we enjoyed for such a short time. It was a lovely thought and I thank you dearly for it, but it would mean so much to me for us to be really good friends and nothing would give me greater pleasure than for you to be Richard's godfather.'

With a mistiness in his eyes, he said, 'Was it as obvious as that? And of course, I understand. My motives were entirely honourable. When Richard was around, we looked out for one another. It was a partnership of trust and now he is no more, I felt it was the right thing to do. It wasn't a question of love, more to offer protection and comfort to the family of my best friend. I suppose I thought that maybe love might grow out of it one day.'

'Thank you for that, Thomas. Now don't let us get too sad and emotional. I can hear the young man stirring. Come and meet your godson.'

Thomas stayed for a couple of days before setting off to see his parents in Kent. He had decided that after almost two years of continuous exposure to munitions of every shape and size coming at him from all directions and the appalling conditions in the trenches, he would apply for a posting to the Royal Flying Corps. If Richard were still around, it would be different, but flying seemed to be the vanguard of modern warfare and being a pilot had always excited him. Watching aerial combat over the trenches was, to Thomas, about as exhilarating as it could get.

The train from Charing Cross pulled into Sevenoaks station. Thomas had asked the hotel in London to ring his parents and tell them he would be there about midday and could they meet him. He walked out of the station, asking himself what they would say when they saw him. His mother would comment that he had lost weight and looked tired and drawn. His father would just say that it was good to see him. The last time they had seen one another was at the hospital just outside Tunbridge Wells when Thomas had been recovering from his shoulder wound. That was only about nine months ago, but it seemed a lifetime.

He would talk to his father about transferring to the RFC, but not to his mother. She would not understand why he wanted to do it, especially since the papers talked continuously about the life expectancy of pilots being much shorter than that of an officer in the trenches. He was still pondering his future when his parents arrived in the motor car, which was coughing and spluttering, producing enormous clouds of smoke from the exhaust.

'Hello, son, it's good to see you,' said his father, leaping down from the running board with his arm outstretched. His mother was looking tearful, with her hand up to her face.

'Oh Thomas, what have they done to you! You look awful, so thin and pale,' she said. As expected.

'Thank you mother, for that warm welcome. It has made me feel so much better,' he said, smiling.

'Come here and give me a hug. It's just, well you know… mothers like to think that their boys are looking after themselves, even in this dreadful war. We'll make sure you put on a few pounds before you go back.'

'Don't start talking about going back yet, mother. We have not even got home!'

They had a very pleasant dinner, and Thomas told them about Richard. They knew he had been posted missing, but had heard nothing more.

'How are the mother and baby coping? Have they given up all hope?' asked his mother.

'Oh, I think so, but they are pretty well considering the circumstances. I went to see Simone on the way here and she asked me to be godson to Richard junior. I was very touched.' He did not mention the proposal.

'Why don't you men go into the study and have a brandy and a cigar, while I clear away?' suggested Mrs Holland.

'Good idea – a bit of man talk is good for the soul!' said Thomas' father.

'Nothing has changed since I was last here, except your chair has got tattier than ever and there are still papers all over the floor,' said Thomas.

'I love that chair, it fits my shape. I've got a farm to run and, that means enormous amounts of paperwork. And I know where everything is, that's the key. What about you? Are you coping?'

'Only just. There have been times when I could have happily walked away from the horror of it all. But last year, I had Richard as my constant companion and strength. We built a bond of friendship I didn't think was possible. Maybe it is only possible in times of acute stress and danger. And now there is no one to replace him. I still find myself looking to my right or left for his support when times are tough. And it is this that has made me think I need a change. I want to join the Royal Flying Corps as a pilot. Whatever you do, please don't mention it to mother until after I have returned. They might not want me anyway. But it excites me and I desperately need to get away from the claustrophobia of the trenches.' He paused. 'Did I mention that I have been recommended for a Military Cross?'

'No you didn't. Congratulations. I won't ask what you did, but I'm sure it is well deserved. I won't try and talk you out of joining the RFC, because only you know why you feel you must do this. I won't even tell you to take care of yourself because I know you will, but there is a farm waiting for you when this is all over, and remember, you are our only son.'

'Thanks Dad, for being so understanding. Remember, mum's the word!'

An aerodrome just outside Albert, autumn 1917

A heavy smell of petroleum spirit pervaded the air. Refuelling was carrying on at a swift pace in order to get the planes back in the air as quickly as possible. From the morning's flight of eight, one had failed to return and one had been badly damaged but had made it back, just.

'Put that bloody fag out!' shouted the sergeant in charge. 'You'll blow up the bloody lot of them.' Captain Thomas Holland MC was leading the flight which was about to take to the air. He had had to give up his army rank to become a pilot, as all squadron leaders in the Royal Flying Corps were Captain by rank. No. 70 Squadron was based at Becordel, flying Sopwith Camel single-seater biplanes, which were fairly new to the RFC but were proving themselves to be superior planes in many respects, once you had got used to them.

The pilots in his flight were gathered around him.

'As you know, we are acting as guardian angels for three reconnaissance planes today,' Thomas began. 'They are taking some photographs of the German trenches in the area around Bullecourt, south east of Arras. They will be at 12–15,000 feet and our job is to give them cover. We can't afford to lose any more aircraft, so watch those take-offs. I know the Camel is not the easiest plane to fly, but once you are up there and haven't stalled on take-off, you should be able to outmanoeuvre any German plane that comes at you. It's a great machine and our squadron is lucky to have them. The more experienced flyers should please keep an eye on the novices. They will spend a lot of time keeping control of their machines rather than watching for Jerry.

'Right, let's go. We rendezvous with the recons in fifteen minutes and we only have two hours keeping them company before we have to return to base. Good luck!'

They took off in line into the wind, with the sun on their right. It was a typical October day on the Somme, a bit of sun, a bit of rain and a lot of wind. They quickly rose to 12,000 feet on a compass bearing which would bring them over Bapaume in around ten to fifteen minutes, depending on wind speed.

Thomas gesticulated to his number two on his right that he could see British artillery firing from their positions close to the Ancre river towards Croisilles, the direction in which they were heading.

His number two pointed to his right, where Thomas could see a number of dots approaching them from the east. Thomas fired a brief burst from his twin .303 machine guns to alert the others, signalling that half the flight should carry on while he, his number two and two others turned to deal with the threat. The German planes were about 3,000 feet above the Camels, so Thomas indicated that they should turn towards them and climb to 18,000 feet to get above them with the sun behind.

The unmatched manoeuvrability of their machines enabled them to complete the climb at over 100 miles per hour and come at them from height and from a south easterly direction. Thomas' number 2 fired first at the perfect range, and the enemy Fokker flipped over to its right and plunged down with smoke pouring from its engine. Thomas took on two in line with a five-second burst, which resulted in one of the pilots - obviously hit - slumping over his controls and the other turning tail with bits of his left wing in tatters. The other two then turned away with the other members of Thomas' flight in pursuit. As this engagement had taken less than five minutes, Thomas signalled the others to regroup and head for their original destination.

It was not long before they rejoined the flight, which was in line astern 'mothering' the reconnaissance planes as they carried out their duties. There were no more German planes to be seen and when their time had run out, Thomas signalled for his flight to return to base. He flew down, waggling his wings to the recons to tell them they were departing.

As he dropped his nose, his Clerget engine started to cough and splutter and then it cut out.

'Shit!' said Thomas. He tried to restart the engine, but to

no avail. He would have to glide down, keeping the aircraft level, and try to belly-land in an open space. The problem was that he wasn't sure whether he was in British or German territory and the fields were covered in trenches and shell holes. There was nothing for it to but to keep the nose up, which wasn't difficult because the tail on these planes was heavy, and hope for the best.

A gust of wind hit him in the side and he felt the plane veer towards a copse of trees. Just my luck, he thought, the only trees still standing and I am about to hit them. All I can do is cross my arms across my face and hope that the impact doesn't set the plane on fire. There isn't much petrol left in the tank, but even so….

Suddenly the leading tree in the group grew awfully big. The Camel hit it head on.

'Fire!' The next salvo left the barrels of the 15-pounders, sending a massive dose of high explosive towards the German lines. Lieutenant Oliver Watkins of the Royal Field Artillery was in command of the battery, and like his fellow gunners, he was wearing plugs to protect his ear drums. How many times had he seen these chaps with blood coming out of their ears because they couldn't be bothered to put them in? Either that or they wanted to get signed off and sent back to Blighty. Thanks to his cocooned environment, he did not hear the approaching Sopwith Camel until it flashed past just above where he was standing, causing him to duck. He followed the trail, wishing it a safe landing, and saw it veer to the right and plunge into the copse.

Watkins was the proud owner of an Enfield motor cycle with a sidecar. He shouted to Corporal Murray, 'Start her up Murray. Let's see if we can help.'

They set off towards the wood, which was about a mile away, taking a track which led to an old farm building, long since destroyed by the shelling. From there, they had to ride across a rutted field, not good for the springs, he thought.

The plane was completely broken up, with just one of the wings still intact, pointing up to the sky. The pilot was hanging from his harness, bleeding heavily from a head wound. He was very pale. Lieutenant Watkins jumped off the bike and sprinted towards the wreck, which was smoking and in danger of exploding.

'Can you hear me?' he shouted to Thomas. There was no response.

'Murray, can you give me a hand here? We must get him out double quick, before this thing goes up.'

They managed to release the harness and pull Thomas out of what was left of the cockpit. They laid him gently on the ground, at which point he opened his eyes.

'Where are you hurt?' Watkins asked.

'I'm not sure but I don't think I can feel my legs' muttered Thomas in a weak voice.

'I'll go back and get a stretcher. Murray, you stay with him.'

Just before Christmas, Thomas found himself back at Broomlands Hospital. He had been told that he would never walk again. His back had been broken and one leg had such a serious compound fracture that they had to amputate it just above the knee.

When his father heard the news, he said, 'Well, at least Thomas is alive. He'll be able to run the farm.'

'Is that all you can think about, your bloody farm?' said his mother angrily.

CHAPTER FIFTY SEVEN

The history lesson continues

The day after they had visited the front line from July 1ˢᵗ, 1916, the English schoolchildren returned to the giant monument to the missing at Thiepval to spend some more time there as part of their project. The monument stood proudly on the skyline and could be seen from miles around. Designed by Sir Edwin Lutyens, it had been unveiled in 1932. It sat above a labyrinth of trenches which formed the vital arteries of the impregnable Thiepval fortress.

Tim Hurt gathered them in front of the massive central arch which made up the memorial. 'Right, when we were here yesterday, you could fully understand, I hope, why this memorial is so important. Inscribed on these walls are the names of 72,104 men who simply vanished off the face of the earth here on the Somme in 1916 and 1917. Just think about that for a moment. These are not the names of those killed, just those who were never found. Why do you think that is?'

Joanna raised her hand.

'Yes, Jo?'

'One thing we learnt yesterday sir, was that this small area was fought over time and time again, backwards and forwards, and completely destroyed by the artillery. So presumably, those who were killed or wounded just got blown to pieces.'

'In a nutshell, that's about it. And sadly, of course, this is not the only memorial to the missing. At the Menin Gate in Ypres in Belgium there are over 50,000 names of the missing recorded there.'

The group were very quiet. The only sounds pervading the air were the birds chattering away in the nearby trees. 'Can you hear the birds?' asked their teacher. 'There are still places on the Somme today, like Delville Wood, where the birds have never returned. They say it is because of the death that still hangs in the air, almost a hundred years after the slaughter.'

After letting them take that fact in for a moment, he said, 'Right, there are two things I want you to do. And to be honest, this is an exercise to get you to understand the enormity of what went on here. I want you to find people with your own surname listed on here and then select one of them - because there is every chance that you will find many more than one - to find out more about that person. Then I want you to write up what effect it might have had on the family back home when this person was posted as missing. There is an excellent bookshop in the visitor centre, if you feel like spending some of your pocket money on some background information, and the internet will also be of great help in your mission. We'll be leaving in an hour, so use the time wisely, and that doesn't mean hiding behind the monument having a smoke, Murphy!'

Found at last

In 1928, the year the world powers signed a peace pact in Paris, Simone was getting her eleven-year-old son ready for school when she received a letter from the British War Office. She thought it was something to do with Richard's pension, but on opening it she went deathly pale, her hand shaking. The letter was to inform her that they believed his body had been located, alongside three other members of his Regiment. They had been identified from dog tags, cap badges and Regimental shoulder badges. Richard still had his wedding ring on and they would be pleased if she could identify it to confirm that the body was that of her husband. There was also a silver cigarette case inscribed 'Hubert Waller'. Having checked on the records, they believed the fallen soldier to be Hubert Waller's son.

Simone collapsed into a chair, and her son asked her what was wrong.

With tears in her eyes and her voice completely choked up, she said, 'I have always told you everything about your father, about how he was recorded as missing in action during the war on the Somme. Well, it seems that all that uncertainty is over. They believe that they have found his body, along with three others, after all these years. A farmer working the fields uncovered them. He called the police, who then called the British Military.'

This news was a huge shock to the boy, who could not understand what his mother was saying.

'What do you mean, found by a farmer?' he asked.

Simone had read about bodies from the First World War coming to the surface when farmers ploughed the fields. She thought this would upset him, but she wasn't sure she could avoid the question.

'Just like your father, there were many, many soldiers who were never found during and after the war and one of the reasons was that their bodies got buried by earth from exploding artillery shells. When the farmers drive their tractors over the fields, they sometimes come across bodies, as well as munitions, barbed wire, rifles and all sorts of things.'

'What happens now?' asked young Richard, somewhat shaken.

'The letter says that all four men are to be buried with full military honours at Longueval Cemetery in a few months' time. This will give them time to notify all the relatives concerned. I'm not sure that I can cope with that, nor with meeting the families of the other men who died with him,' she said.

'But you must, we must! He died for his country in our country and I know how much he meant to you. I never knew him and this will be my one chance to say thank you for what he did. We owe it to his memory. And we'll have somewhere where we can visit him.' She could see him thinking for a moment, and then he asked, 'Do you think I will be allowed to wear his medals?'

Simone thought how grown up he was, and how proud she was of him. Richard would have been just as proud.

She never did marry again. Thomas came back in the summer of 1917 for the christening and it was a happy occasion. He met Frank for the first time and they got on famously. After his crash, he started writing to Simone, a habit he maintained for many years. His injury prevented him from attending his old friend's burial.

Thomas did manage to visit Montreuil a couple of times, but each trip was fraught with difficulties. On his last visit, Simone suggested that when Richard was old enough, perhaps he could go to England and stay with him to learn about his father's home country. Thomas said that nothing would give him greater pleasure.

Cécile did remarry. Her need for a man was greater that her daughter's and she and Frank married quietly, much to the disgust of some of her neighbours, although Simone was very happy at the union. They moved to a different house in the town, Frank having taken a job with the Empire War Graves Commission on leaving the army. Because he had been a staff officer throughout the war, he felt he should stay with those who had not returned home.

One of his jobs was to instruct the removal of Richard's name from the Thiepval Memorial to the Missing, which was now under construction.

In 1939, the war clouds grew over France again and on September 3rd, when Richard Waller junior was 23 years of age, Britain and France declared war on Germany. Simone wondered how she was going to go through it all again.

IN FLANDERS FIELDS

In Flanders fields the poppies blow
Between the crosses, row on row,
That mark our place; and in the sky
The larks, still bravely singing, fly
Scarce heard amid the guns below.

We are the Dead. Short days ago
We lived, felt dawn, saw sunset glow,
Loved and were loved, and now we lie
In Flanders fields.

Take up our quarrel with the foe:
To you from failing hands we throw
The torch; be yours to hold it high.
If ye break faith with us who die
We shall not sleep, though poppies grow
In Flanders fields.

John McCrae, 1915